FOR

EVER

FOR EVER

The Instant Always
book two

a novel by
ari wright

Blue-Eyed Books

This book is a work of fiction. The names, characters and events in this book are the products of the author's imagination or are used fictitiously. Any similarity to real persons living or dead is coincidental and not intended by the author.

For Ever: The Instant Always Book Two

Library of Congress Control Number: 2023935209

ISBN (Paperback): 9781662938436
eISBN: 9781662938085

Author's Note

To all returning readers, my sincerest thanks and welcome back!

To all new readers, I'd like to note that For Ever is the *second* installment of The Instant Always series.

While each novel in the series focuses on different characters and entirely new plots, readers will definitely see familiar faces and hear details from previous novels in each stand-alone work.

To avoid spoilers, I recommend starting with the first title in the series, For Always, and reading in order!

xoxo,

Ari

TO MY GRANDMOTHERS

YOUR WIT, WISDOM, AND WORRY
HAVE MADE ME.

THANK YOU FOR EVERYTHING…

…INCLUDING ALL THE PRAYERS FOR MY SOUL
AFTER YOU READ THIS BOOK.

PLAYLIST

THING OF BEAUTY—DANGER TWINS
(WHO DISCOVERED) AMERICA?—OZOMATLI
POISON—BELL BIV DEVOE
SHOWIN' OFF—DANGER TWINS
TRAMPOLINE (JAUZ REMIX)—SHAED, JAUZ
SLACKS—ST. SOUTH
UN REFLEJO BREVE—UNA MARIA
SOUL—ROMEO
BEJEWELED—TAYLOR SWIFT
WOMAN—DOJA CAT
GOOEY—GLASS ANIMALS
COFFEE—SYLVAN ESSO
HEY MAMI—SYLVAN ESSO
DOLCE N GABBANA—KEVGEE
MIDAS—MARIBOU STATE, HOLLY WALKER
THE END—JPOLND
HEARTBURN—WAFIA
CAFÉ MOCHA—JESSE COOK
NDA x DADDY ISSUES (REMIX)—NVBR
HONEY—TRACE
ECSTACY—$QUEEBS
I HATE U—SZA
LOVE YOURSELF (SHORT REPRISE)—SUFJAN STEVENS
GET GOOD (INFINITEFREEFALL REMIX)—ST. SOUTH
LOUDER—KATÉA

EXTENDED PLAYLIST IS AVAILABLE ON **SPOTIFY**

❖❖❖

PROLOGUE

Juliet

Cinderella was an idiot.

I remember the first time I saw the movie. I was seven, new to America, and just fluent enough to understand the English version of the classic film.

I watched it on the floor of my abuela's tiny apartment, over the tailor shop, while she worked below. It was only a few weeks after she took me from her son, my father, so maybe I was bit more jaded than the average seven-year-old girl.

But, honestly. Who wrote that *mierda*?

A man, of course.

But I digress.

I was seven, watching the animated movie alone in our small, cramped home. As I watched the story unfold, I just could not understand. Was I misinterpreting the language? Or perhaps missing some sort of cultural cue?

Or was Cinderella truly just a *weak ass bitch*?

There were no imaginable circumstances under which I would suffer through years and years of abuse at the hands of my own family in order to…*what*? Have some dusty attic room full of *mice*? How, pray tell, was that an improvement upon being alone but being *free*? Why would anyone trade their *dignity* just to be able to say they weren't lonely? What was so wrong with independence?

I watched on, thinking I must be missing *something*. Surely, the heroine of one of the world's most classic love stories wouldn't just lie back and take this crap. Certainly, she would *do* something to save herself.

Pero no. She slaved away without a peep until a random fairy godmother gave her a makeover—a *temporary* makeover… as if someone with magical powers couldn't have given the girl some setting spray—and then she crashed a party and met a guy and *didn't even tell him her name*… but somehow *fell in love* with him?!

What kind of utter *lunacy*? I mean, truly.

As I kept on watching, I began steeling myself for the tragic ending—the big life lesson I knew must come at the end of this sordid tale.

Well, we all know how it ends. In fireworks and true love and forever-afters.

The credits rolled. I sat open-mouthed on abuela's floor, completely dismayed.

Because I may have been seven years old, but I had seen enough to know the truth. That women who take abuse, get more abuse. That men don't show up to save you in your darkest hour. That *no one*—not one single person—can rescue you from your own choices.

Cinderella wasn't a heroine. She was pathetic.

And I would do better.

Chapter One

January 20, 2017

Juliet

It's amazing how often I wake up to an argument.

This morning, Abuelita went in on Marco before I even opened my eyes. Because our small two-bedroom apartment above the tailor shop had paper-thin walls, I heard every word of their disagreement. Marco showed up to drive me into the city and, from what I gathered, my poor *primo* decided not to eat breakfast.

Abuelita wasn't having it. She shoved some eggs and a plate of empanadas at him. He kept telling her he wasn't hungry. But, by the time I put my robe on, chewing garbled my cousin's deep voice.

I emerged from my room, stepping right into the small kitchen at the center of our home. Marco was, in fact, eating; begrudgingly ripping bites out of a beef empanada as he watched Abuelita fuss over the stove. The look on his face felt all-too familiar—some blend of exasperation and undying affection. Only Abuelita could force my 6'5", ox-like, body-guard cousin to sit down and eat his eggs.

She muttered to herself as she stirred a pot of soup. "*Se parece un pollito flaco, pero no quieres tu desayuno? Ay Dios mío...*"

Snickering, I kissed her weathered cheek and patted her stooped shoulders. "*Buenos días*, Abuelita." I shot Marco a look as he glowered at me. "I would *love* some breakfast."

Abuelita grumbled something about how I always tried to make her use English, but passed me a plate of empanadas nonetheless. I reached for the French press beside Marco's plate, plucking the last of the coffee up before he managed to snatch it.

"Morning, primo," I chuckled, dropping into a chair at our tiny breakfast table. I poured the dark-roast into the mug waiting at my place and nodded at our grandmother. "She needs to practice," I told him. "Junior is quite insistent."

"*Hombrecillo mucoso. Quiere inglés? Tengo una palabra en ingles*—asshole."

Marco smirked at Abuelita's mutterings, but turned his keen eyes on me. While I scarfed down half of my empanada, he asked, "Still giving her grief, huh?"

The owners of the tailor shop below our apartment—a Colombian family like ours—recently handed the reins over to their third-generation grandson. "Junior", as he was less-than-fondly known in our house, now insisted that Abuelita only converse with customers in English. It wouldn't have bothered me if he'd also held the young, single girls working there to the same standard.

Marco's face said it all—he would gut Junior like a fish. As a newly-minted lawyer, though, I had other ideas. Legal ones.

"I'm monitoring it," I murmured, sighing as Abuelita continued her diatribe… completely in Spanish, of course. I swallowed the last of my food and talked with my mouth full of coffee. "*Que hora es*?"

Marco shoved the rest of his empanada into his mouth and spoke around it, too. "Ten of eight."

I downed my remaining coffee in one gulp. "*Carajo*."

"*Julieta Isabelle Rivera*," Abuelita barked at my use the curse word. "*Deberias avergonzarte*."

My full name was a reprimand unto itself. She didn't need to add the "be ashamed" part. Wincing, I rushed to my feet and hurried past her.

"Sorry, Abuelita. I'm late and I haven't chosen a dress yet."

Her thickly-accented voice chased me into my room. "At the back of your door, *muñeca*. I put the dresses."

"*On*," Marco corrected gently. "On the back of the door."

"Is what I said," Abuelita tossed back, already returning to her stove.

Smiling to myself, I shut the hollow slab and found Abuelita's latest offering—four hand-made dresses, in an array of bright colors. My heart gave a pang at the various hues. It would never occur to her that orange or hot pink would not be appropriate for my new job. She simply chose shades she knew I ordinarily loved.

Not wanting to hurt her feelings, I selected the most acceptable of the bunch—a dark, berry red. Long-sleeved, with a square neckline and a slit up the back, it toed the line between professional and provocative... maybe a little too closely.

I stepped into it anyway. As I clasped the button at the nape of neck, it occurred to me that a woman with a straighter figure could easily get away with any of the dresses Abuelita made. They wouldn't be considered too sexy for a thin, white woman.

And that pissed me off.

Out of spite, I eschewed my usual nude sling-backs for a matching pair of dark-red platform heels and clasped an eye-catching gold chain around my throat. One look in the mirror told me I was probably a smidge *over* the line… but I figured, *what the hell?* I'd never been one to do things in half-measures.

When I stepped back into the kitchen, Abuelita had gone to her room, but Marco examined my outfit with wary eyes. He whistled lowly before asking, "That? For work?"

His disapproval only spurred me on. I'd long ago learned to use spite as an effective motivator. "So women with certain body types have to dress differently than other women?" I shot back. "For what possible purpose? In order to avoid breaking men's fragile grasp on basic human decency? Anyone who doesn't approve of me wearing this dress because I have an ass can fight me."

Marco poured a fresh round of coffee into two paper cups he snagged off the top of the yellowed refrigerator. He smirked as he offered me one while he held up his other hand in surrender. "Alright, *prima*. Consider my question withdrawn."

With a shrug of his massive shoulders, he slipped a black jacket over his equally dark button-down. "I just wondered if there was some sort of dress code inside the office. All Grayson asks of me is basic suits in dark colors."

Sometimes, it nettled me that Marco got so much face-time with our boss. They were on a first-name basis, after a few years.

I should have been too grateful for annoyance—Marco *was* the one who secretly slipped my resume to the ultra-young CEO of Stryker & Sons—but my temper wasn't so easily satisfied. It didn't help that my older cousin treated me like a student who didn't know the school dress code.

"Their policy simply states dresses, suits, or slacks for all employees," I informed him. "They don't even have gender-specific rules anymore. If they did, they'd be *asking* for a law suit."

Marco flashed his bright white smile. "Well, you would know."

Abuelita shuffled back down the hall, carrying a ball of gold fabric under her arm. "Wear with this," she told me. "Matchings."

"Match*es*," Marco and I both amended.

Abuelita placed the flashy coat in my arms and pinched both of our cheeks as she hobbled between us. "Is what I said."

Marco chuckled at me the whole way to the car. Turned out the bundle of shimmery fabric Abuelita insisted on was the world's glitziest coat, much more suited to a night of clubbing than a boardroom. I'd have to remove it before I even walked into the building, and planned to stash it in my desk during the day.

"Looks like I'll be ordering *in* for lunch," I sighed, pinching the shiny fabric and shaking my head. "The sad part is: I *like* it. I wish I could wear it without looking like I charge by the hour."

Marco shrugged. "Most lawyers do."

I slapped the back of his neck as we rounded the final corner. The private garage housing Stryker & Sons fleet of vehicles required two key-cards and a thumb-print to gain entry. Marco went through the security measures on auto-pilot, swiping us through all three doors to the control room. He nodded at the guard on duty, took a few sets of keys, and led me to the pristine row of Mercedes gracing the underground lot.

Today called for the largest of the luxury SUV's, apparently. I followed Marco to the matte white car, stepping up into the passenger seat as he took the driver's. The decadent scent of leather mingled with the pungent aroma of our coffees. I sat back against the plush interior, sighing. "What's on your agenda today?"

Marco shook his head, gazing impassively out the front windshield as he merged us into traffic. "Nice try."

The Strykers' schedule was a closely-guarded secret, even for employees. In my two weeks at the company, I'd learned that meetings with the company's CEO often didn't appear on our calendars until the day-of—and, usually, they didn't mention him by name.

"Whose side are you on?" I demanded, only half-kidding.

He shot me a stern *primo mayor* look. "The side of both of us keeping our jobs."

I folded my arms and sighed, unable to argue with that logic. As much as his company loyalty niggled at me, I had to admit I admired his devotion. I knew it was a rare trait… especially for men.

My cousin truly made an ideal security director. Steadfast as could be, he combined muscled strength, sharp eyes, and a quick mind into one neat package.

When he started working for Mr. Stryker, the position wasn't all that prestigious. But as his father edged into retirement, Mr. Stryker took over the role of CEO for their family's illustrious development firm. Marco's job altered accordingly, and he went from acting as a chauffeur for a trust-fund-baby/college student, to directing security and transportation for an entire company.

The scope of his influence still stunned me. When he suggested giving my information to Mr. Stryker after I passed the bar exam the previous fall, I only agreed because I figured it couldn't hurt. I never expected Mr. Stryker to personally call me in for an interview and give me the last in-house junior counsel position in his legal department.

According to Marco, such personal attention to detail was typical for our boss. He often remarked on the young CEO's noble character, and convinced me to take the position by detailing how good Mr. Stryker was to all of his employees.

So far, I had to admit, I was impressed. The staff seemed happy, the pay was highly competitive, and vacation/personal time was strictly enforced. The office was always spotless, calm, and humming with industrious energy. On the handful of occasions when I'd met with Mr. Stryker, he more-than returned the respect others afforded him.

I nudged Marco's elbow with mine. "Thanks again for hooking me up."

He smiled broadly, reminding me why all of the girls in our *barrio* constantly crushed on him growing up. "You deserved the job," he told me. "Top of your class at NYU Law? And he wanted someone bilingual. Frankly, I think they're lucky to have you. Though I did wonder why you suddenly changed your mind about corporate law."

The answer was simple, but the word felt bitter in my mouth.

Money.

"Immigration reform is still my passion," I murmured instead, watching Queens disappear in our side-view mirrors as we descended into the Queens-Midtown tunnel. Darkness engulfed the car, so I got away with a half-truth. "It's prudent to cultivate a diverse resume. Five years with Stryker should give me enough experience in corporate law to lend some credibility when I turn to non-profit work."

And it will give me enough cash to save Mami.

Marco's fingers drummed on the steering wheel. "I guess that makes sense." He gestured to my new dress. "Abuelita's coming along, then?"

Our grandmother hated that I sold out and took a corporate job after focusing on immigration law for three years. We fought about it constantly over the holidays, right up until the morning of my first day at Stryker & Sons… when I found a brand-new, hand-stitched navy suit hanging on our fridge. Abuelita simply shrugged, like she had no clue where the outfit came from, and muttered, "Eh, something to wear," in Spanish. We hadn't spoken about it since.

I wondered if she changed her tune because of my first paycheck. The signing bonus alone was almost five figures—enough to pay our rent, all our bills, a few debts, and leave plenty for me to sock away in my new savings account. I knew it would only take a handful of months for that account to hold enough to hire an expert immigration attorney who could get my mother her long-awaited Green Card.

As much as Abuelita hated the *codiciosos* ("greedy bastards") who ran Manhattan, she'd always been a pragmatic woman. She seemed to forgive me, now that she saw why I chose to compromise my morals. As an immigrant and a single woman, she'd done the same, once upon a time. I knew she understood me.

"She saw our bank account and bought steak to make this weekend," I told Marco, chuckling. "I think that's about as close as I'm going to get to her admitting I was right."

Marco's face turned to me as we cleared the tunnel and cold winter light filled the car. "Abuelita's making steak?"

I had to laugh at his expression. "And ceviche. Sunday after church."

He groaned. "So we have to go to church to get the food? Diabolical."

He was right. Abuelita was a woman with a plan.

I came by it honestly.

Graham

It was hard to tell exactly how fucked I was.

But the fact remained, I definitely should not have been there.

That didn't stop me from lying about having an appointment with a dentist. It didn't stop me from hailing a cab and taking it up to midtown instead of over to Wall Street. It didn't stop me from throwing a $50 at the driver and striding up to the building like I owned the place.

I figured—Grayson was my best friend and *he* owned the place, so close enough.

The lobby of Stryker & Sons brought elegant minimalism into this century. The base of the twisting cylindrical building sprawled for fifty yards in any direction. Snowy marble covered the expanse, gleaming in the weak January sunshine.

The pure white stone reflected enough light to burn my eyes. Instead, I focused on the one focal point of the monochromatic scape—a wide, obsidian vein that started in the center of the room and stretched toward the elevators, into a gaping yawn of onyx.

And there, amidst all the black, I saw her.

A bolt of heat snaked down my spine, stopping me mid-stride. My hands fisted in my pockets while my eyes followed the blatantly sensual sway of her hips.

Hot damn.

Had I ever seen such a dirty girl before? My cock told me no—but he was a notoriously fickle bastard. *Surely*, she wasn't the sexiest thing I'd ever seen. I dated famous super models. Visited brothels in Thailand, Amsterdam's famed Red-Light District.

Why, then, did this random woman stop me in my tracks?

Was it the red dress? I had to admit, no matter how pedestrian the proclivity, the color appealed to me. Like a bull reacting to the crimson flash of a matador's cape.

But I refused to believe I was that easy.

No, it must have been the way the cut followed every line of her dangerous curves. *Lethal* curves. At least from the back…

Deep red fabric skimmed over her thighs and covered an absolutely stunning ass. Up higher, it nipped into a tight, thick waist before flaring a bit up top to accommodate two ripe, round breasts. The slit in the back offered a tantalizing glimpse of her thighs. Bare—which was curious, considering the 20-degree weather outside. Almost as intriguing as the gold coat draped over her arm, a shimmering "notice-me" signal.

All signs pointing to girl who wanted it. Bad.

My body moved of its own volition, clipping across the marble floor with too much haste to maintain my usual air of detachment. I couldn't stop, though.

The elevator opened and I guess I stepped on. All I knew was, I was there and so was she. The matte black doors slid closed at my back. My gaze rolled over the front of her. My mouth watered.

Jesus.

The square neckline of that godforsaken dress might as well have been a frame for the perfect caramel swells of her cleavage—outlined by the dark crimson fabric on three sides and the thick gold chain clasped around the base of her throat.

And what a picture they made. Art, plain and simple.

I stared. Gaped, really.

And she noticed. Of course. Because I was the only other person on the damn elevator and I hadn't even bothered to pick a floor.

"Excuse me?"

Ah shit.

Without a word, I turned and hit the top button—Stryker & Sons executive floor—before shoving my hand back into my pocket, fisting it around my phone again.

The air grew awkward, but I decided not to address her indignant remark. It was one elevator ride. A minute at most. A stranger I'd never have to see again. I slipped my phone out of my pocket and moved to swipe it open.

"*Excuse me.*"

That time, the sharp edge of her voice instantly turned my head. Her breasts leapt out at me again, drawing my focus before I even had a chance to glance at her face.

They really were exceptional.

It was rare to get to ogle a random woman so completely, too. Most of them spun away or covered themselves up on instinct. But this woman did neither. Instead, she stood taller, sticking her tits out even more.

Fuck me.

A husky, humorless laugh sliced through the confined space. "You *wish*, asshole."

Christ. I said that out loud?

Irritated with myself for my exaggerated attraction—and her for picking such an insanely hot dress—I scoffed. "Baby, if you don't want to be fucked, maybe you shouldn't dress like you do."

WHAP

Her palm connected with the side of my face, backed by stinging force. The shock of it finally jolted me from my gawking. Automatically, my eyes flew to her flushed, furious face.

That *gorgeous*, flushed, furious face.

Arresting gold eyes snapped with fire, lending her lush frown true ferocity. A dark blush stained her high, wide cheekbones, highlighting the diamond shape of her face and the way it tapered to a pointed, defiant chin.

Her gaze bored into mine, unrelenting. So fiercely revolted, I felt it scrape at my insides. If I ever wondered what true hatred looked like, now I knew.

It was a fearsome, beautiful sight to behold.

While I stared, the heat blazing in her golden depths cooled into disdain. She reached up as if to deliver another blow.

And—*goddamn it*—I flinched.

Victory lit her gaze and played at the corners of her full, wide lips. Instead of striking me, she merely reached for the control panel and hit a button somewhere in the forties. It didn't even occur to me to look at the directory and check which business she visited. I was too busy fuming.

"Are you aware," I hissed, "that you just assaulted me?"

But she simply tossed her dark, glossy hair back as the elevator glided to a halt. Cocking a single brow, she shot me a derisive look over her shoulder. "Sue me."

Juliet

There is a Colombian phrase Abuelita mutters from time to time.

Que gonorrea.

It basically means: "Look at this fucking guy."

I mumbled it to myself as I stepped off the elevator eight floors early and made a beeline for the service stairs.

Normally, such blatant attention from a man like the one on the elevator would stir my interest. But there was something about him that instantly pissed me off. I tried to put my finger on what as I climbed the remaining eight floors.

Was it the way he didn't even have the courtesy to *pretend* not to stare at my boobs? The small, sardonic smirk tugging at his lips as he ignored me? The obvious wealth evidenced by his outfit?

The eye-catching ensemble—a cerulean-blue three-piece suit, lined with fine gray pinstripes, offset by his silky red tie and pocket square—irked me for some reason. I hated the way he took such obvious care with his clothing, yet sported dark-chocolate hair long enough to curl against his bright white collar, and days' worth of stubble over the expanse of his solid, slashing jaw.

By the time I reached the fiftieth floor, I decided: it was his eyes. I'd never seen a pair so dark. Colorless. Feral, almost.

The sound of the front desk buzzing me through derailed my train of thought. I blew out a big breath and pushed the door open.

Game face, I coached internally. *You've got this.* Setting my features into an impassive mask, I strode onto the executive floor and made a left, into the legal department.

The building's cylindrical layout didn't lend itself to a traditional office set-up. Instead of grids of cubicles or long hallways with closed office doors, a wide, open space occupied the center of the floor. To capitalize on the stunning views of midtown Manhattan, smoked glass separated our departments into individual pods instead of walls. Each pod started in a single archway and then flared out; cone-shaped, with one point of entrance, like slices of pie.

I walked through the wide arch that fed into our department and subtly ran my gaze across the row of executive suites at the back of the space. Mercifully, my boss, Dominic's, light was on—meaning he'd already arrived and wouldn't walk past my desk anytime soon.

Relieved, I dropped into my chair and turned on my lamp. I shoved the flashy gold coat into the drawer where I also stashed my purse, grateful there were no witnesses.

As demonstrated by the three vacant desks around mine, the other junior associates weren't in yet. I always made a point to beat them to work. I was also the youngest attorney in the division by at least five years. And the only woman. And the only Latina.

My colleagues were all Ivy League graduates. And white men. And late.

Fancy that.

In an effort to present myself as professionally as possible, I eschewed anything personal on my desk. I had the standard-issue MacBook port, Bluetooth phone system, and chargers. Otherwise, a small silver espresso machine and one porcelain espresso cup were my sole possessions. I kept everything else—espresso pods, sugar, cosmetics, hair clips, and my one framed photo—locked in a drawer.

I managed to make myself two more shots while my MacBook booted up. Sipping my espresso, I pulled the day's agenda from our department's shared drive and perused it. I nearly choked when I saw a new item slotted in for nine A.M.

A boardroom meeting.

Those only meant one thing.

I had to figure out a way in.

Before I could plot, Dominic appeared, leaning against the side of my desk and staring down my dress. "Juliet," he purred, the corners of his eyes creasing as he grinned at my breasts. "That dress is sensational."

I suppose if Dominic Carter wasn't a colossal sleaze, he might be sort of handsome. Somewhere in his forties, he sported a fit build and a head of salt-and-pepper hair cropped short. An average decent-looking man who clearly thought the world of himself.

Ordinarily, I played along. But after the elevator incident, I had reached my daily threshold for male nonsense. I ignored his compliment in favor of a question. "Heading to the meeting with Mr. Stryker?" I asked casually, as if I hadn't been blindsided by the news seconds earlier.

Dominic sighed at me. "Only here two weeks and you're already better-prepared than any of these other guys." He waved his arm at the empty desks. His gaze flickered back to my neckline. "I guess that means you get to sit in," he said to my boobs.

I almost asked if *I* was welcome as well, or if he only intended to invite my breasts. But instead, I forced a smile. "Let's hit it."

Graham

"Graham Everett."

Grayson's personal assistant greeted me with a deep frown. Her sharp grey eyes matched the tight silver bun at the back of her head. And her dour expression went perfectly with her joyless black suit—one of a hundred, I was convinced.

In addition to a never-ending stream of ugly office wear, Beth also seemed to possess an infinite supply of maternal disapproval. Shaking her head at me, she rounded her desk for our stand-off and drew herself into a formidable stance—quite the feat, for someone a foot shorter and three times my age.

"You know you're supposed to wait down in the lobby and let me buzz you up," she chided. "There are security protocols in place for a *reason*, young man."

"I—"

Her gaze cut into mine, silencing me. "And I won't have you derailing his schedule today," she continued, reaching out to smooth her wrinkled hand over my red Brioni tie. "No more of your three-hour lunches. He has a someone special waiting for him at home, now; and, besides that, he is a CEO. He must act like one."

Grayson exited his office and appeared behind her, smirking at me. "She gives me the same lecture at least once a week," he chuckled, laying a hand on Beth's shoulder. The woman gave a long suffering-sigh and turned to adjust his tie as well.

"Did you get that suit off of a corpse?" I asked my best friend, eyeing the dark grey material and matching tie. "Or are you working for the Secret Service now?"

Grayson inspected his sleeves, unbothered by my critique. "Ella's favorite. It's Armani."

"It's boring as fuck," I corrected, only to have Beth shoot me a glare. That was another one of her rules: no profanity in the office. "I mean boring as *frick*. Do excuse me."

Excuse me.

The words reminded me of my elevator encounter. I shifted on my feet, wondering if the semi I'd been sporting since the lobby would abate any time soon. *Probably not, as long as you keep picturing her tits. And ass.*

"You're excused," Beth snapped, still eyeing me like a fox in her hen house. "Now both of you run along to the conference room. It's five after nine and the first group is waiting. The next set will be in at ten."

Grayson's green eyes lit up. "Including—"

Beth's mouth almost flitted up at the corners. "Including the future Mrs. Stryker, yes. I will bring her in myself after I have you all settled."

Beth dismissed us and we turned toward the archway that led out to the main floor. "Two sets?" I said, looking at him askance.

Grayson nodded at someone as we walked past. "Professional and personal."

"Which set am I? You told me block out nine to eleven."

His smile turned ominous. "You're both."

Gradually, his meaning sank in. "Oh God. You had me haul my balls all the way up here for *wedding planning*?"

He laughed, steering us toward the single largest room on the rounded floor, opposite the elevators. "Not entirely. The first hour will focus on my personal holdings, finances… and investments." He shot me a pointed look. "That's where you come in."

I did my best to keep a straight face. But, inside, my stomach clenched. *You shouldn't be here*, my conscious rasped, its voice hoarse from lack-of use. *You made a promise.*

But it wasn't a promise in writing. And it wasn't a promise that benefited me. So why should I care?

Because he's your father, the voice argued, hissing. *Because you gave him your word.*

Yes, I did. Unfortunately for dear old Dad, though, he and I were cut from the same flimsy cloth.

My father's father was a famous investment banker, known for his ability to triple even the most obscenely-wealthy's bottom-line. He started our firm, Everett Alexander, after the Great Depression. When my father, Hugh, came of age, Grandfather brought him onboard. The elder Everett passed away some years ago, but, before that, they steadily produced amazing returns for their clients. And made themselves very wealthy in the process.

Now, it was my turn.

At least, I thought so.

Dad, however, believed that I needed to earn my place by doing grunt work. My father gave me the CFO title, but stuck me in an old storage room to molder with filing cabinets full of tax returns instead of assigning me clients of my own. I wound up spending my days with all of our archived account books, entering records into our computer system line-by-line so we could eventually go paperless.

That was my life—data entry. And boredom so dire I swore one day I'd just drop dead at my desk.

But I was a licensed trader. A Columbia finance graduate. And Graham Fucking Everett. If he wouldn't give me real clients from the firm… I would find my own clients.

Clients like Grayson Stryker, the youngest billionaire CEO in Manhattan.

Well, not personally a *billionaire*. Yet. But by the time I got through with his portfolio, I vowed to myself, he would be.

"So I'm your broker for the next fifty-three minutes and then I'm your bitch boy?" I quipped, yanking the conference room door open.

Grayson strode past me, his air as unruffled as ever. "I think they call it 'best man.' Although, 'bitch boy' has a nice ring to it."

The boardroom was just as colorless and modern as the rest of the office. White walls to the left and right that matched the marble floor, a massive black table lined with clear acrylic rolling chairs.

I thought the room could use some serious color. A few art pieces. Something by Basquiat would've worked nicely. Maybe a sculptural piece in a corner. Or even an abstract by whomever passed their derivative Pollock-esque pieces off as originals that week.

At least the curved wall of windows at the back offered a staggering view of midtown—specifically, St. Patrick's Cathedral and the urban sprawl beyond. I kept my eyes trained on it as I dropped into the seat nearest to the door.

Grayson made his way to the head of the table, throwing out introductions as he went. "Good morning, everyone. This is my friend, and fellow Columbia grad, Graham Everett. For the purposes of this meeting, he'll be acting as my broker. Graham, this is my accountant, Milton Boyle. My head of real estate acquisitions, Beatrice Dunn. My director of legal, Dominic Carter; and our newest junior counsel, Juliet Rivera."

My eyes followed his words, sliding from one new face to the next until they finally landed on the person next to me. On her.

The woman in the red dress.

Jesus.

At least now I knew just how fucked I really was.

Chapter Two

January 20, 2017

Juliet

The look on that smug bastard's face when he finally turned to look at me was priceless.

Because I watched him file into the room, I had a moment to collect myself before we found ourselves face-to-face. It gave me an advantage. Part of me longed to call him out and humiliate him. Part of me wanted to slap his right cheek so it matched the left.

You're a professional, I reminded myself, gritting my teeth. *Even if he isn't.*

In the end, I settled on complete and total indifference. By the time his wild eyes touched mine, I might as well have been made of ice. He stared at me, horrified, until Dominic reached across my chest to offer his hand… effectively brushing my cleavage as he did so.

The two men shook hands. I knew I had to extend mine as well, but the thought of touching him again made my stomach flip. I ruthlessly tamped down my nerves.

"Mr. Everett, was it?" I asked, reaching out.

His hand gripped mine with more strength than I expected, given his pretty-boy outfit. A charge skirted up my arm, raising goosebumps on my skin.

"Miss Rivera." Those fathomless black eyes ran over my features and flitted down to my boobs one last time before snapping back to mine. Molten heat shifted in his dark depths. Irritation filled space around his full mouth, making a lie of the words, "A pleasure to make your acquaintance."

I couldn't help the small smirk twisting my lips. "Oh, *likewise*."

Around us, the others settled in. Someone asked Mr. Stryker about his upcoming weekend plans; while they chatted, Graham casually leaned into the charged space between our seats.

"'*Sue me,*'" he quoted, muttering as he trained his gaze on the view across from us. "And you're an attorney. Cute."

The memory of my own private joke nearly broke my concentration. I swallowed a mocking laugh and shuttered my features. "If you think that was cute," I murmured, "then the sexual harassment suit I'm considering will be downright *adorable*."

His head turned toward me. I resisted the urge to respond in kind—despite his repugnant personality, I found his appearance fascinating. The gentility of his clothing, those wild, impassioned eyes, the indolent way he spoke and carried himself. So many contradictions. Inconsistencies that the lawyer in me longed to resolve.

He opened his mouth to speak, but Mr. Stryker chose that moment to begin the meeting in earnest. "As this gathering is a little different than the usual business around here, I want to personally thank everyone for being here this morning. I know it's Friday and we all want to clear our desks for the weekend so we'll keep this brief."

Mr. Stryker blew out a breath and rubbed his hand over the back of his neck, a gesture that instantly made him seem more approachable. His chiseled lips quirked into a rueful smile. "I'll just be real with all of you and say: I feel uncomfortable commandeering your work time to discuss my personal finances and holdings. So I'd like to offer you all an out. If you'd prefer to return to your company business and leave me to fend for myself, I have nothing but respect for that. Frankly, I don't want to spend an hour talking about me, either."

His accountant and Everett chuckled. They clearly knew the intent of the meeting before they agreed to attend. Dominic joined them, though I could tell he knew nothing more about our agenda than I did. The real estate acquisitions manager and I exchanged a brief glance—as the only women in a room with the CEO, we didn't care what the meeting was about. We weren't leaving.

"Alright," Mr. Stryker said, nodding. "Don't say I didn't warn you all."

He waved his hand and his omnipresent PA began passing out tablets. Mr. Stryker winced slightly as he spoke. "For security purposes, we're not able to distribute this information on paper. The iPads are encrypted and password protected. You'll each have access to a set of data as it pertains to your specialty. We'll share plans and collaborate throughout this meeting by using a program to project your information on that wall."

He gestured to the blank white space behind me and then tapped a few swipes on his own iPad. The wall flickered to life as a projection of an MLS listing popped up. It was a townhome… a twenty-three-million-dollar townhome on the Upper West Side.

"Miss Dunn," Mr. Stryker clipped, taking his seat. "You're up."

The real estate acquisition woman looked about my age. She clearly knew what she was doing—her fingers flew over her iPad screen as she pulled up information she needed and rose to her feet.

With a shoulder-length head of shimmery auburn waves and a wide, white smile, she commanded our attention easily. Her navy jumpsuit and short, matching blazer gave her a trendy air of professionalism I admired. It also highlighted her lithe, willowy figure. I found myself fighting the urge to glance at Everett and see if he was ogling her the same way he gawked at me.

Beatrice Dunn reviewed the property with us. It seemed like a huge place for a bachelor—and on the "wrong" side of the island for a midtown executive. But it was a gorgeous pre-war building, completely renovated throughout, and full of charming architectural quirks.

Beatrice gave a brief description to accompany the photos before jumping to the business-side of things. "The property is overpriced at twenty-three-point-two," she said, tapping to bring up a chart projecting property values. "Classic over-rehab. So I've submitted an as-is cash offer for twenty-one-seven, which I've been assured will be accepted before the day is out."

Twenty-one-point-seven million dollars in cash*?* My stomach flipped.

She tapped again. "At that price point, projected returns within five years fall somewhere in the neighborhood of three million dollars."

Everett's voice came as a surprise from the place beside me. "And Stryker's condo on the East Side?" he interjected, drawing my eyes. Instead of his iPad, he had a legal pad in his lap. His right hand scratched notes as he waited for Beatrice's reply.

Numbers, I realized. He did math while he listened.

"I have an offer going under contract next week for fourteen million," she answered coolly.

Everett flashed a quick smile, turning on his charm to soothe the sting of his interruption. "Great, thanks."

Beatrice gave a dismissive bob of her chin and turned to address me and Dominic. "The contracts for both of these properties should be there on your tablet. They need to be reviewed and approved as soon as possible."

I looked down at the application on my screen, wishing I'd had time to familiarize myself with the program in advance. It seemed simple enough, though—a few taps led me to the main menu, then a section clearly titled "contracts." There were several documents stored within, but only two with addresses in their titles.

"I'm with you," I told her, pulling up the condo contract. "I assume the West Side property will be top priority?"

Beatrice smiled warmly at me. "Naturally."

"And the East Side sale; standard conveyances?" I confirmed, scanning the relevant section of the document.

Mr. Stryker cut in. "Yes. It all goes."

I nodded and turned to Dominic for his answering directives… only to find my boss fumbling with his tablet, frowning at the screen. "I don't have either document."

Without much thought, I reached over and navigated his way to the same list I had. "There," I told him, pointing. "Third from the top."

Dominic stared at the screen without touching anything, clearly not paying attention to me. Mr. Stryker checked his watch. I sensed that the motion indicated he was losing his patience.

"Don't sweat it, Carter," he tossed out. "Miss Dunn will confer with Miss Rivera. I'm sure she's more than capable of two contract reviews." A frown marred his brow. He gave me a sincere look. "Unless you have other plans this weekend, Miss Rivera."

Aside from church and steak, I didn't. But I appreciated his consideration either way. "Not a problem," I demurred. "Real estate moves at warp speed in this city. We have to be quick to stay competitive."

Mr. Stryker nodded. "Well put. Miss Dunn? Get with Miss Rivera after we conclude? I'll rest easy this weekend knowing you two are on it."

Beatrice nodded again, shooting me a friendly smile while she slid back into her acrylic seat. "I look forward to it."

"Great," Mr. Stryker said, turning to the accountant. "Milton, talk to me about property taxes. How screwed am I?"

Mr. Boyle started his portion of the presentation. Thrilled, I bit back a smile and flagged the two contracts in question. They were the first I'd been trusted with independently—and they were Mr. Stryker's *personal* properties. It seemed like a huge vote of confidence.

Dominic managed to redeem himself somewhat as the meeting progressed. A bona fide tax law expert, he had so many ideas for legally evading taxes, I actually started to get a little nauseous. I could tell Mr. Stryker didn't feel completely comfortable with it either.

"I can't believe capital gains have a cut-off," he muttered, rubbing the back of his neck again. "I'll have to consider my options and get back to you all. Look for an email detailing my decisions on Monday."

Finally, it was Graham's turn. Unlike the others, he remained seated, pivoting his chair to address the room at large. His expression looked casual, but a mysterious spark gleamed in his eyes. His opening remark seemed to surprise everyone.

"Let me ask you all something," he started. "When's the last time you went to a mall?"

The room remained silent. Graham's mouth drew up at the corners, lending his handsome features a boyish quality I tried not to like. "Anyone?" he prompted, looking at each person in turn before his eyes fell on me. "Miss Rivera?"

I didn't appreciate being put on the spot, but I refused to quail under his bright black stare. "A true shopping mall?" I hadn't gone to one in *ages*. As much as it pained me to help him prove his point, I had to admit, "It's been years."

Graham gave a decisive nod. "And when's the last time anyone in this room sent a contract in the mail?"

Beatrice actually snorted. "As in the *mail*-mail?" Her hazel eyes widened. "I don't think I've ever done that. And I've been licensed for years."

Graham's cocky smile widened. "Has anyone *called* a restaurant to make a reservation lately?"

No one replied. With a sardonic smirk, Mr. Stryker shot his friend a look. "We get it, Everett."

Graham clapped once. "Of course you do. Because it's common knowledge. Old media, old commerce, old communication. It's all *old.* And while we may not be willing to admit it yet, we're done with it. We're not going back. So why should we allow our investments to ascribe false value to the 'old'? Why not take our money and put it where it belongs?"

"Which is…?"

The words popped out before I could stop them. I curled my fingers around the arm of my chair, resisting the urge to press them to my errant mouth.

Graham's answering grin renewed my goosebumps. It was somehow smooth as silk and razor-sharp all at once. "The future, Miss Rivera."

I didn't have a retort for that. No one did.

Graham took advantage of the silence, swiping through his iPad program to pull up a graph of market projections. "This is what Wall Street is telling you," he said, waving a blasé hand at the chart. "They want you to invest in AT&T. Walmart. FedEx. They give projected returns on these investments that look tempting, even to me. But let me ask you a question; if we know that the way of the world is changing—or, arguably, *has changed*—why are these companies still among the most highly recommended for diverse portfolios?"

Again, no one had a response. Graham's grin returned. "Because of entrenched powers and complicit brokers," he told us. "These companies pay brokerages to inflate their value, keeping their stocks higher than they have any right to be. But it's false growth. Slow, too."

He tapped his screen. The projections on the wall morphed, tripling instantly. "This is what I propose instead," he concluded. "I'll let you read for yourselves."

I did. My eyes scanned the projections, noting that none of the stocks were businesses I recognized but they all sounded familiar. My mind reeled back to a *Wall Street Journal* article I read the previous summer.

"Crypto currency," I murmured, narrowing my eyes at the names. "It's *all* crypto?"

"Yes, it is," Graham replied, not looking at me. "Entirely."

At my other side, Dominic scoffed. "No one deals in crypto-currency *exclusively*. The risk is enormous. And with the rates as low as they are now…won't it take years to get anything back out?"

Mr. Stryker's green eyes looped over the projections as he spoke. "I have *time*. The wait for returns doesn't disturb me, as long as we're certain there *will be* returns." He pinned Graham with a searching look. "How sure are you?"

Graham didn't so much a blink. "Completely."

A smile flirted with Mr. Stryker's features. "Where have I heard that before?" he mumbled to himself, shaking his head good-naturedly. "Say I go for this—how much?"

Again, Graham replied instantly. "Give me five. I'll give you back one-fifty in three years when it's time to sell."

Million, my mind squeaked again. *One-hundred-and-fifty* million*?!*

Mr. Stryker stroked his forefinger over his jaw while he stared his friend down, considering. Dominic swiveled back and forth between the two, his expression aghast. "Surely," he sneered, "you're not considering taking your *entire* portfolio in such a volatile direction. Your father always adhered to market projections and—"

Mr. Stryker held up a staying hand. "I'm aware," he cut in, his voice flat. His gaze finally flickered from Graham to Dominic. "But I'm not my father. And this is the future. My future."

He turned back to Graham with a single nod. "Do it. Five million of my personal funds. We'll see where we're at in six months and, if your strategy proves successful, discuss the possibility of transitioning Stryker & Son's vested interests over to you."

I wanted to be a shark. Truly. But I was *sick* at the thought of being responsible for so much of someone else's money. Two high-stakes real estate contracts already felt incredibly intimidating and all I had to do was *review* them.

Thank God I'm not writing this investment contract, I thought, running my gaze over the projections again. *Too rich for my blood.*

"Miss Rivera?"

I looked up at the sound of Mr. Stryker's voice. "Yes, sir?"

He tapped at his iPad a few times. My own screen flickered as a deluge of documents appeared on top of the two I'd flagged.

"Since Mr. Carter objects to this change of strategy, I'll assign my personal Everett Alexander contracts to you. Graham will tell you what he needs from you and from me in order to initiate the trades. I'd like to start the process immediately, but I know it's a lot to read through; and the two of you will likely need to hammer out some details in person. I'll sign as soon as you've come to agreeable terms. Shall we shoot for a week from today?"

Carajo. Shock obliterated all other thought. If someone dropped a pin in my mind, they could have heard it fall.

I must have nodded, because a second later Mr. Stryker motioned to his PA, who made a note on her own legal pad. Satisfied, Mr. Stryker offered me a brief-but-encouraging smile before turning to the rest of the room.

"I think you've all suffered enough," he announced. "Thanks for being here. There's a catered lunch coming in at noon. Beth will send an email out when it arrives."

Just like that? It felt as if one meeting launched my career into a different orbit. And I was floating in a new plane of space, untethered.

I blinked down at the list of contracts, still in disbelief. *Game face, Jules. Don't let them see you sweat,* I told myself. *Especially Everett. Not to mention…*

A terrible thought finally sank down through the awe.

Dios mío.

Dominic.

One glimpse confirmed my fears. For once, my boss's eyes weren't glued to my boobs. Instead, they burned the side of my face with ill-disguised animosity. Scowling at me, he opened his mouth, only to be cut off by both Graham and Beatrice.

"Miss Rivera—" Graham started first, but Beatrice gripped my elbow and yanked me to my feet, rotating us toward the door.

"Sorry, Mr. Everett," she said over her shoulder, "These contracts simply *must* be reviewed today. I'm sure Mr. Carter can give you Miss Rivera's contact information and you can email her to align your schedules for next week."

Beatrice leaned closer to me, muttering while she fixed her eyes on the exit. "Keep walking. Don't turn around. I swear to God, smoke is coming out of Dominic's ears. And that Everett guy looked like he was about to *eat* you." She huffed an agitated breath. "These men, I swear."

Gratitude flooded me. "*Thank you,*" I murmured back, injecting appreciation into each syllable.

"No sweat," she whispered. "I'm thrilled they hired you. We need more women around here and you're clearly twice as smart as balls-for-brains back there."

I liked her more and more by the second.

We made it halfway across the main floor before she turned to me and grinned, offering her hand. "Beatrice, by the way," she introduced herself. "But call me Tris. 'Beatrice' is soooo crusty."

Giggling, I shook her hand. "Juliet," I replied, "But my friends call me Jules. And if today is any indication, we should definitely be friends."

Tris widened her hazel eyes. "*Please.* I know Mr. Stryker is doing his best to change things up, but this place is such a boys' club. I swear his father never interviewed a woman for any role apart from administrative—"

She swallowed the rest of her sentence on the spot, then pinned a bright smile to her lips and spoke through her teeth. "Oh. Here comes Mr. Stryker's fiancée. I'll introduce you."

His fiancée? That explained the big townhome purchase. And why I never saw him check out any of the women in our office. Not that a fiancée would stop *some* men from behaving like animals… I shook the thought of Graham Everett out of my mind and pivoted to find Beth approaching with a gorgeous blonde beside her.

Dressed casually in a slouchy ivory sweater that revealed one freckled shoulder and dark, high-waisted jeans, the girl clearly didn't work in the office. But she also didn't look like the fiancée of a mega-mogul. Her basic dove booties and understated pearl earrings certainly didn't scream *hundred millions*. And she carried, of all things, a plastic container full of brownies.

The girl beamed at Tris and I found I liked her immediately—she exuded irresistible, genuine warmth. "Tris!" she exclaimed, throwing her arms around the realtor, affording me a flash of the flawless oval diamond gracing her ring finger. "I'm so glad I caught you!"

"Me too!" Tris replied, stepping back to present me. "Jules, this is Ella, Mr. Stryker's fiancée. Ella, this is Juliet Rivera. She's a new junior attorney here. We're just about to go over your townhome contracts."

Ella blushed brightly, looking chagrinned. "Oh Lord, the townhome. Obscene isn't it?"

Tris' smile sharpened. "Not for Manhattan's hottest CEO and his gorgeous bride."

Ella rolled her deep blue eyes at Tris before looking at me. "I can't tell if she's an expert saleswoman or I'm an easy mark," she quipped, grinning.

Recognition suddenly lit her gaze. "Wait—Juliet? As in Marco's cousin? Oh, he told me so much about you! I just adore Marco. Gray would be lost without him, seriously. He's just downstairs parking the car, but I think he's coming up for our *meeting*." She chuckled at the term. "So silly. Only Gray would call wedding planning a *meeting*."

Gray... It took me a moment to realize she was talking about Mr. Stryker—*Gray*son Stryker.

Tris touched my arm, her expression sly. "Ella hired my roommate Alice as her wedding planner. They used the meeting this morning to lure Graham here and trick him into discussing his best man duties."

"It was totally Ali's idea. She's a *genius*!" Ella giggled. "Anyway. How do you like it here, Jules? Are they treating you well or do I need to kick Gray's behind?"

A startled laugh escaped me. "No, Mr. Stryker is great! I'm so grateful he decided to give me a shot here. I know he usually hires people with more experience."

Tris waved her hand dismissively. "*Psh*. You crushed that meeting. We're lucky to have you aboard."

"You're obviously brilliant," Ella said kindly, smiling at me and Tris in turn. "Look how you've already fallen in with the right people."

Ella glanced around us. Her face turned coy. "So am I late? Is Gray in there, checking his watch compulsively?"

I swallowed a smile when I realized I was right about Mr. Stryker's watch-checking earlier. Of course he was impatient—he wanted to see his fiancée. And I didn't blame him. She was a delight.

"We better let you go before he comes looking for you," I teased. "Because if he comes out here, he may give me more contracts to review."

We all laughed. "Okay then," Ella said, "For your sake. But come by the break room later and grab a brownie! Assuming the boys don't eat them all."

With another eye-roll, Ella waved and walked away. Tris and I watched her go. "She's awesome," I decided aloud.

"Totally," Tris agreed. She checked her phone. "Come on. Let's knock this contract out and then grab some lunch. We can go to my department so Dominic won't bust your balls."

I laughed, relieved and appreciative. "You're on."

Graham

"Graham."

The sound of my name interrupted the lascivious bent of my thoughts as I watched Miss Rivera's hot ass sway out of the conference room. I faced my friend, quirking my brow.

His stern glower immobilized me. "No."

"Pardon?" I asked, pretending not to understand.

He eyed me shrewdly, not backing down. "No," he said again.

No fucking the hot new lawyer. No matter how achingly sexy I found her. No matter how hard it made me when she interrupted me to ask her bright, cutting questions. No matter how badly I wanted to take her back to that goddamn elevator and flatten her up against the black metal doors.

And I had to meet with her again. Multiple times. How in God's name was I supposed to avoid fucking her?

Discipline, I told myself. *Get a grip, Graham.* I had a multi-million-dollar deal on the table. I needed to get my head out of my ass. Or out from between Miss Rivera's thighs, as it were.

I gave a single nod, sweeping my notes into a tidy pile. "Understood."

The starch leeched out of Grayson's posture, transforming him from a CEO back into my best friend. He offered me a half-smile. "That was fun, huh?"

Truly? I was about twenty seconds away from hurling my guts all over Rivera's lap the entire time—starting with her unexpected appearance at the meeting and ending with the elder attorney disparaging my bold investment strategy. If the layer of sweat drying under my vest was any indication, I wasn't nearly as self-assured as I forced myself to act. I wondered if anyone could tell.

I made my way to the head of the long table, willing my posture to stay loose. "A twenty-million-dollar townhouse. A five-million-dollar crypto investment." I shrugged. "Typical Friday."

The accountant scurried off, but Grayson's attorney lingered until my friend reluctantly turned to him. "Need something, Carter?"

I'd noticed that Grayson tended to use men's last names when he didn't like them very much. But that Carter guy didn't seem to take the hint. He crossed his arms and stared Grayson down. "Will you need me for the next portion of your meeting? I overheard Beth saying your fiancée will be in attendance."

Grayson eyed him warily. "Yes. Why would that necessitate your input?"

"We should begin drafting your pre-nuptial agreement," Carter stated, his voice smooth. "Immediately."

The air around us evaporated, leaving a vacuum of tension.

Oh fuck.

Grayson snarled, biting out his words individually, "There will be no pre-nup."

I did my best to hide the frisson of shock that ran through me. *No pre-nup?* Grayson was worth hundreds of millions; his family and their company, billions. Even if he secured the Stryker wealth by other means, without a pre-nup, the returns on the investments I brokered for Grayson would make his fiancée independently wealthy overnight.

I opened my mouth to say as much, but Carter jumped on the grenade before I could. "Mr. Stryker," he chuckled, the picture of amused arrogance. "I'm sure you're still learning how all of this works, but if you'd allow me to explain the implications of entering into a marriage without proper protections—"

"Enough, Carter." Grayson's voice cracked like a whip. "I suggest you drop this. Permanently. And perhaps, going forward, your time would be better spent learning the basic technology this company utilizes instead of making assumptions about my personal life. If I require your presence for a meeting, I will inform you. Currently, you're dismissed."

Sufficiently chastened, Carter turned and fled. I started to comment, but Grayson was no longer paying a speck of attention. Because Ella walked in.

Ugh. These days, nothing made me quite as nauseous as being around Grayson and Ella.

I suppose, if I were being generous, it wasn't really his fault he turned into such a major pussy whenever she walked into a room. After years of longing for The One Who Got Away, he recently recovered the love of his life. And they were… *happy.*

All the time.

No matter what.

Happy.

It was pitiful, really. The second she appeared, his entire world visibly shifted on its axis, reorienting to focus only on her. He brushed past me, pre-nup rage forgotten, and closed in on the small blonde standing beside the doorway.

Grayson wasted no time tucking his fiancée under his arm and kissing her forehead. Mooning down at her, he murmured something too quiet for me to hear as he skimmed his fingertips up her cheek. Ella blushed, smiling at him like he personally put the Sun in the sky every morning.

I tried to fend off an instinctual wave of bitterness with humor. "Should I retch here or in the hallway?"

"Hallway," Grayson replied, not looking at me.

Ella, on the other hand, bent around his body to toss me a beatific smile. "Good morning, shithead."

Her loving nickname always made me chuckle, even if I didn't want to. Truly, Ella was just so… warm. Impossible to hate. Believe me—I had tried.

Closing the space between us, I lifted her hand to my lips for a gentlemanly kiss. "At your service."

Predictably, Grayson scowled and tugged his fiancée's fingers out of mine. Ever since I tried to hit on her the first time he introduced us, he'd been so *touchy*. I personally thought it was unfair—how could he fault me for flirting with a girl like Ella?

Frowning at me, she smoothed her hands over my shoulders in a motherly gesture. "Graham, have you been eating? I swear these suits get more ostentatious and looser-fitting every time I see you."

Damn the woman and her sweet, insightful nature. I hadn't been eating most days until well after dinnertime. In an effort to earn some clients of my own, I spent the past few months trying to finish years' worth of record digitalization in record time by going in early and staying there late. I often got so focused that I forgot about meals until I got home.

She held up a plastic Tupperware box. "Here. Have a brownie."

I started to roll my eyes and turn her down, but then Grayson pouted. "Those are *my* brownies."

"I made these for everyone," Ella corrected breezily, offering me one. "You get plenty of brownies at home."

Just to goad Grayson, I snagged two and winked at his fiancée. Making her blush was just so deliciously *easy*. I couldn't resist. "Thank you, gorgeous. Grayson's always going on and on about your… *brownies*."

Grayson opened his mouth to bite my head off, but Ella flattened her hand against his chest. Cheeks glowing, she fixed me with a narrow-eyed look. "Pretty soon I'm going to make you call me Mrs. Stryker, shithead."

My friend smiled at his fiancée. "Just three more months."

Christ. Three?

It finally occurred to me that there might be a pressing reason why we were meeting about their wedding less than a month after Stryker put a ring on it.

I glanced down at her stomach. "Oh shit. Is there a reason we're rushing?"

It was Grayson's turn to flush. While his ears burned, Ella giggled, smacking my arm. "Graham, I know you've never had a single romantic impulse but try to keep up: we *want* to get married. That's why we're 'rushing.' Although, really, a four-month engagement isn't *that* rushed."

Grayson tightened the arm around Ella's middle. "We wasted enough time," he murmured, staring down into her eyes. "If it were up to me, we wouldn't even wait until April. I'd marry her tomorrow."

Ella grinned at him. Her eyes flashed with mischief. "But then we wouldn't be able to torture Graham for the next twelve weeks," she pointed out. "And I wouldn't get my dress."

Ugh. Dresses and vows and flowers and cake. My Stryker-specific nausea surged.

Grayson cupped Ella's face in his hand, crooning to her as if they were alone. "I want you to get anything you want, Ellie. And I can't wait to see you in your dress."

Beaming, Ella batted her lashes at him. "Speaking of me getting my way," she hummed. "I want to ask your new lawyer to drinks next Thursday with Tris and Alice. We had plans to meet up and I think Juliet would have fun if she came, too! Is that alright with you?"

Lord God, say no.

"Sure." Grayson shrugged. "I don't see why not."

A sound somewhere between a snort and scoff burst out of my mouth. "You can't be serious," I argued. "She's an *employee*."

Ella tightened her dark blue gaze. "She's a *person*. And I was thinking that she probably hasn't had a chance to make many friends here yet."

Grayson crossed his arms at me. "We're about to sign a contract making you my broker and we hang out all the time—how is that any worse than Ella spending time with one of our lawyers?"

I couldn't explain why I hated the idea so much. "Yeah, but we've been friends for years. This chick is a stranger. What if she witnesses something embarrassing? Or if she hears details about the wedding? Isn't it some sort of big secret affair because of security and shit?"

Ella threw her hair back with an irritated flick of her wrist. "She's Marco's cousin. And she's bound by attorney-client privilege. I would argue she's one of the *safest* people to go drinking with. If she told the press anything she overhead, she could be disbarred."

Grayson's shit-eating grin made my fists clench. "The future Mrs. Stryker is correct," he told me. "As per usual, shithead."

CHAPTER THREE

January 20, 2017

Graham

"You gonna order or what?"

I pressed my palms into my bleary, burning eyes and sighed. "More coffee."

My new waitress was not impressed. "That's it? Deanne says you've been sitting here for hours."

Deanne was not wrong. After a torturous pow-wow with Grayson's wedding planner, I hiked back downtown just in time to watch my father blow out of our office at noon. I tried to settle myself in my usual windowless room and rectify accounts, but the stagnant air made me claustrophobic after a couple hours. I wound up collecting my weekend's work and abandoning ship.

The idea of working at my apartment didn't appeal. Instead, I wandered into Katz's—an old-school Jewish deli in the Lower East Side, one block up from my place. After sitting there for the better part of the afternoon and all of the dinner shift, I still couldn't get the numbers in front of me to make sense. And I couldn't put them into our system until they made sense.

What the fuck is wrong with me? I knew the books were correct. The deals went through years before. I was only reviewing them to be conscientious. And I had an effing finance degree from an Ivy League University. I knew what I was doing.

So why couldn't I understand them?

Maybe I'm dyslexic. Or attention-deficit. Or just… dumb. Maybe I shouldn't have even graduated.

The steady stream of weak coffee and angry servers hadn't helped my imposter syndrome at all. But I refused to admit defeat. And I refused to allow myself reprieve until the goddamn math made sense.

My mood darkened by the hour. It was already shit, thanks to Miss Rivera's elevator assault, not to mention my nagging conscience and the pressure of closing my first major deal…for my best friend. But the longer I sat at the metal table, staring down into a soup of accounting gibberish, the worse it got. Guilt and frustration seethed in my gut. Worry crowded in.

"Is that it?" the waitress demanded again. "It's after dinner and you didn't even order food."

Unbidden, Ella's concerned expression popped into my mind. She had a point about my suits fitting looser… Having them all re-tailored would be a bitch. And maybe a meal would restore my ability to do basic math.

"Fine," I grunted, still glaring at my ledgers. "Pastrami and latkes."

"Sour cream or applesauce?"

"Both. Obviously."

She harrumphed and stalked off, but it didn't cheer me up. Normally, arguing with strangers amused me. I enjoyed fighting in general. Something about ruffling other peoples' feathers while remaining completely calm pleased me. I considered myself unflappable.

Except when beautiful Latina women slap you.

Growling, I flipped back a few pages and re-read the ledger notes for the millionth time, then flipped forward again.

Nope. I don't get it.

Had I lost my mind? First I chased down a random woman and basically sexually harassed her on an elevator in the middle of Midtown, during a work day. Then I brokered a deal I didn't have permission to make. Now I couldn't read a basic accounting ledger.

Disgusted with myself, I slammed the books shut, only to realize they weren't even the right ones. I'd pulled them from my usual stack, but the binders were green instead of the typical blue. Who knew *what* I was even looking at? And I'd wasted *hours*.

"Fuck me."

It was Friday night and I was in a *deli*. Easting Pastrami. Alone.

How the mighty had fallen. Four months ago I would have been out with Grayson at whatever club no one else could get into, drinking too much in some VIP section we charged to our companies and meeting women we had no intention of remembering.

Now I was working late and clogging my arteries while he wrote love poems to his fiancée's pussy. Or whatever engaged dudes did to convince themselves they wouldn't get bored sleeping with the same girl for… ever.

My phone chimed and I snatched it, tamping down the thrill that surged through me. Ever since I got Juliet's email address from Beth and shot her a few terse lines about arranging our contract meeting, I leapt every time I got a notification.

Because you want the contracts signed so you can make a shitload of money, I told myself. *Obviously*.

But it wasn't an email from the sexy-ass lawyer. It was an all-too-familiar text.

My stomach sank, taking my appetite along with it. Even so, I flagged down my server and tore my wallet out of my pocket.

"My order?" I muttered. "Double it. And wrap it up to go."

My dark mood was a black hole by the time I got the food and took a cab to Greenwich Village.

If I didn't feel like shit, I might have found an entertaining sort of irony in my surroundings. Five years before, the dorms at the university were a familiar hook-up spot for me. I went home with a lot of NYU girls back in my college days.

Now, wearing my three-piece suit, holding a briefcase full of account ledgers, the damp dorm hallway felt... wrong. The girls seemed uncomfortably young. The music was way too loud.

And—*God*—had it always been so *grimy*?

Losing what little patience I possessed, I slammed my palm against the door with more force. "Chris!" I yelled, pounding again. "Let me in, damn it."

The handle turned and the slab fell away, revealing a cramped rectangular room. Two twin beds occupied the back corners. The desks shoved against the ends of the mattresses were both overflowing—one with laundry, the other with pages and pages of shit. Pieces ripped out of magazines, printed sheets, loose-leaf covered in scribbles.

And there, hunched over the notes, was my half-brother, Christian.

Before I even stepped over the threshold, he started babbling. "—going to be huge, Graham. I swear. I know I'm right about this. You have to look at the markets in Asia to see the trend but—"

Cocaine, tonight.

Some nights, I found him falling in the other direction, down an opioid-induced rabbit hole of depression. I had a hard time deciding which I hated more.

I couldn't focus on his words. I was too preoccupied with the way he twitched and scratched at his wrists. His eyes were normally blue, but they looked black in the dim glow from his desk lamp. I stepped closer and saw it wasn't a trick of light—his pupils were blown out.

An instinctual rush of fear trickled through me. The urge to act rose up, as strong and noble as ever. *You've tried*, I reminded myself. *He doesn't want help.*

Still, I started to try to calm him down. "Christian—"

He bounced his leg, continuing his rambles. "—gonna be huge. You have to tell him. He won't listen to me but he'll listen to you. You have to tell your dad."

"Our dad," I corrected automatically, fighting the heavy sensation spreading through my chest. Dread, I realized.

"Our dad," Christian muttered, then gave a humorless smirk. "Right."

He couldn't stop moving. Jiggling his legs, itching his forearms, tugging the sleeves of his sweatshirt, tipping his head back and forth. I recognized the usual symptoms.

Even so, I asked, "What did you take, Chris?"

Christian didn't look up from his pages of nonsense. "Bunch of stuff. Here." He handed me a list covered in a barely-visible layer of white powder.

"Chris. Jesus Christ," I mumbled, feeling sick. "Do you need to go to the hospital?"

He shook his head but then couldn't stop. He twisted it back and forth for a full minute. "I'm fine," he lied. "Did you bring me food? I smell pastrami."

It was incredible that he could smell anything apart from the sharp stench of B.O. pervading the air. Then again, he knew to expect a meal when I showed up.

It was our uncomfortable arrangement. Christian used all of his meager allowance on drugs, forgot to grocery shop, and then texted me for help. I always brought him food. I used to bring him cash, too, but I'd long since learned that just led to more drugs and more texts.

"Katz. I got latkes, too." I offered him the bag, figuring he could eat both sandwiches. My appetite wasn't going to come back. "Listen, Chris…"

He grabbed the bag and started ripping into it. I watched, at a loss for words, wondering when he last ate. I guessed it had been a couple days, because he downed half of a sandwich before I managed to finish my thought.

"Listen, Chris," I tried again. "You need to come with me. If Dad saw you, he would…" *Help?* I didn't want to say it because I wasn't sure I believed it.

Guilt swamped me. If I were the one with a drug problem, my parents would spare no expense to make me well again. But life was always different for Christian. He was born four years after me, seven years into my parents' ill-fated marriage… to a woman who was not my mother.

My father conducted many affairs throughout the years. I guess Mother usually ignored them. But she couldn't ignore a baby born out of wedlock, especially when Christian's mom sued Dad for child support and shared custody.

The lawsuit splashed our family's drama all over town. Mother never recovered from the humiliation of the whole sordid ordeal. She filed for divorce—to save face, I always suspected. Shortly after, my parents separated and I got a part-time brother.

Luckily, I was too young to really understand what all the fuss was about. After four years of solitude, Christian was a delightful addition, as far as I was concerned.

We stayed fairly close all our lives, though he never attended the schools Dad selected for me. It took a while for me to realize: I was sent to top-tier establishments while Christian went to B-list private schools.

When I turned sixteen, I got a car and driver. Christian got a cab allowance and a subway card. When I graduated from prep school, I went backpacking in Europe for two months. Christian got a weekend trip to the Hamptons. When I got into Columbia, my father gave me a limitless credit card for all my expenses. Christian had to go to NYU, take out loans, and live on a stipend.

I always, stupidly, assumed that Christian would come work with us at Everett Alexander. He was better with numbers than I was—

and, normally, I was pretty damn good. He also had unparalleled instincts that put mine to shame.

Now I knew better. Though no one ever *said* as much, Christian wouldn't get a job offer from our father. He wouldn't get anything from him ever again, I'd wager.

It had taken me twenty-some years to understand, but, lately, I finally got it: my father only had enough love for one of us. And he picked me.

So there I sat, with a bag full of accounts I couldn't understand, holding a list of investment strategies Christian made while high as a kite.

And they were *brilliant.*

Inspired, really.

I swallowed the uncomfortable lump in my throat and held the paper back out to him. "I can't take these."

Food seemed to temper Christian's manic high. He finished the first sandwich and moved on to the next with much better manners. "I want you to have them," he murmured, subdued. "I made them for you."

The knot in my gut swelled, pressing into my lungs. "Chris, if you'd show these to Dad, maybe he would—"

Christian's dilated gaze met mine, unwavering. His mouth curved into a bleak smile. "He would use them and take all the credit and keep all the money."

The truth sent a burning bolt of hatred through me. "He's a fucking dick."

Grim acceptance filled the features so similar to mine. "At least, this way, you get the glory. Not him. He's… limited. I've accepted it."

I gestured at the general squalor around us. "Is that what all this is about? Trying to be okay with things the way they are? Because it doesn't have to be like this, Chris. You know you can come stay at my place anytime. For as long as you want."

I didn't have a second bedroom in my current apartment… but, hell, I could move.

Christian's next smile almost looked believable. "Wouldn't help. Because you'd still be you and I'd still be… me."

A drug addict.

That's what he meant—it didn't matter where he lived, because he would still be sick.

He looked down at the remaining half of the second sandwich, licking his cracked lips. I knew he wanted it. In the end, though, he handed the pastrami and rye bread to me. "Here. Eat. You look almost as shitty as I do."

I held the Katz wrapper in my hand, not wanting to turn him down. What if it was the last time he ever handed me something? What if this was the last meal we ever got to eat? Would he pull himself back from oblivion again next time? Or finally slip over the edge?

I didn't have any answers. So I folded his notes into my jacket pocket and took a bite of the sandwich, accepting what he offered. "Thanks."

Juliet

On Sunday—after Abuelita's church friends spent forty minutes trying to convince me I needed to quit working and get married before I turned thirty… *and then* proceeded to cook and eat food my job helped purchase for the rest of the afternoon—Marco came over.

He let himself into the apartment, barreled down the hall, and barely said hello to Abuelita before locking his hand around my arm in an iron grip and hustling me into my room. After hours speaking Spanish to all the abuelas, my exclamation came out in my first language. "*Que carajo, primo?*"

Marco dwarfed my tiny bedroom with this wide, muscled frame. In a dark sweater and black jeans, he looked like a stunt double from an action movie. His frown was intimidating—even to me.

"I think I should be asking you the same thing, Jules," he gritted, shoving his phone under my nose. "What the fuck was *that*?"

My blood chilled as I watched the video clip on his screen. Crystal-clear and completely, undeniably me… slapping Graham Everett.

In the elevator. At the office.

I gasped, gripping the iPhone and hitting the replay button. "No," I breathed. "There are *cameras*?"

Marco yanked his phone back. "*Of course* there are cameras, Jules. This is 2017."

He crossed his thick arms over his chest, glaring at me. "If I had known you were going to go around acting like *la puta loca*, I never would have put my ass on the line and asked Mr. Stryker to give you a shot."

His words stung... like a slap to the face. *Ironic.*

"I'm not a crazy bitch!" I spat, my temper rising. "That *asshole* practically harassed me. He *ran* to get onto *my* elevator, crowded me in, and then stood there staring down my dress. I asked him to stop and he told me that I should—that if I—" Too angry to repeat Graham's callous taunt, I shook my head. "He was a *dick*. He deserved that slap."

Marco's expression remained impassive. "Of course he did. He's a notorious asshole who's gotten everything he ever wanted his whole life. All of them are, Jules. Even the nice guys like Grayson. They're spoiled and entitled—and too spoiled and entitled to realize it."

He blew out a breath, jamming both hands through his hair. Tension tightened his features. "But you can't let them get to you like this, Jules. People like us have to be better than all of them, to get just a little of what they have."

His lecture aggravated me, regardless of how much I deserved it. "I *know* that," I grunted.

Marco's thick brows knit together in consternation. "I know you know that," he mumbled, glancing down as he kicked his booted toe against my rug. "So why did you let this guy get to you?"

Because he makes me crazy.

I still couldn't explain it. Not even to myself. Why did I slap a complete stranger? Why did I avoid him—a well-connected, valuable networking asset—while he was in the office after our meeting? Why had I allowed his email to go unanswered in my inbox all weekend?

To piss him off.

That much I understood. I also knew that I wouldn't invest my time to make any other random guy angry after one brief negative encounter. Especially if my work and reputation were on the line.

No. There was something about Graham specifically that brought out the absolute worst in me. I lost my temper when he was rude to me. Then, I interrupted his presentation multiple times. Now, I was passive-aggressively ignoring a *work* email.

Petty, juvenile, impetuous behavior… but the thought of irritating him absolutely *thrilled* me.

"He just…" I couldn't justify it, so I hedged. "He caught me on a bad day."

I twisted my fingers in the hem of my tee shirt. "Do you think Mr. Stryker will fire me when he sees the video? I was worried Everett would tell him what happened, but then I realized it makes him look bad, too, so I thought I was off the hook. But now this…" I waved at the phone clutched in his brawny hand and bit my lip.

Marco watched me steadily, suspicion shifting in his gaze. "It's my job to review the elevator footage at the end of the week and bring anything concerning to Mr. Stryker," he told me and held up the video on his screen. "I haven't shown this to him yet. And

I guess, as long as you're both okay and I'm *certain* nothing like this will happen again, I don't need to show him at all."

I opened my mouth to thank him and he cut me off. "But I'm serious, Jules. If I delete this clip and some shit goes down later, we're both fired."

The group of ladies assembled in Abuelita's kitchen laughed on the other side of my door. "If we both lose our jobs," Marco added, "How will Abuelita buy her steak?"

"I'm sorry," I told him. "Really. And thank you." I tried for a smile. "Don't worry. I got my shot in; it won't happen again."

He bleated a laugh, still shooting me a warning look. "If it does, and you get caught, I am *so* throwing you under the bus."

"You can tell Mr. Stryker I snuck into the building in a cat suit and deleted the file before you could watch it," I offered.

Marco shook his head at me. "Always such a drama queen." His wary eyes slid over to my door. "Speaking of, how screwed am I if I go out there? I'm starving, but last week Señora Reyes spent an hour trying to convince me to commit to an arranged marriage with her niece from Bogota."

I snorted. "I've already gotten two vicarious proposals and a lecture on how to bag a husband. They've only been here since two." When he grimaced, I suggested, "Go get some food and then tell them I'm waiting for you to FaceTime Mami with me. She would love to see you, anyway."

Marco's frown grew. "You know you two go too fast for me. I'm only *half* Colombian, remember?"

The bitterness in his voice was not lost on me. Marco grew up among friends and family who spoke Spanish as their first language. But his father was not Colombian like his mother—he was from Syria, where they spoke Arabic. Because English was the only language his parents had in common, Marco wasn't raised with fluency in either of this parents' native tongues. He only learned bits and pieces of each—though more Spanish than Arabic, thanks to Abuelita.

"We can dumb it down for you, *primo*," I teased, patting his shoulder.

Marco's glower returned. "I'd rather take my chances with Señora Reyes," he grumbled, "But tell Tía Louisa I said hello. Or *hola*. And tell her that her daughter has the pugnacity of a prize fighter."

He made his exit, inciting a chorus of old bitty chatter as he emerged into the kitchen. I shut the door before they got any ideas about calling me out.

I'd had the same tiny bedroom for eighteen years. I outgrew it ages ago, but it recently began to feel even smaller than usual. After three weeks at my new job, surrounded by all the elegance and wealth at Stryker & Sons, the space so small it barely fit a double bed just wasn't enough for me anymore.

I wanted more.

Not *too much* more. But something better than eight-hundred square-feet above a dress shop. I wanted it for myself, sure, but I also wanted it for Abuelita.

And Mami.

But first I had to finish the job my father abandoned—I had to get her out of Colombia and into America.

I always knew it wouldn't be easy. That was common knowledge in Jackson Heights and every other immigrant community in New York. After all, if she could just hop on a flight and be here the next day, she would have done it once it became clear that my father wasn't going back for her…

I'm not sure, though, if I ever truly understood just how difficult the process would be… until we studied immigration in law school. I would never forget that week of classes; how I sat there, swallowing lumps of unshed tears, listening to apathetic professors list all the reasons I would possibly never see my mother on American soil.

Each lesson made my heart heavier. I spent every night poring over my notes, full of impotent fury. Why wasn't there a path for people like her? She didn't have any education, any extra money, or anyone to vouch for her. As far as our immigration system was concerned, all the reasons she urgently needed to escape only made her "unfit" to be a potential citizen. The entire scheme seemed rigged against those who needed help the most.

For weeks, hopelessness circled over my head like a vulture. I avoided Mami's calls and emails, ashamed to face her when I'd all but given up. I even started looking into other types of law and considered changing my focus to something that wasn't so mired in futility.

Until one day, in the law library, I overheard a conversation that changed my mind.

A group of third-years chortled amongst themselves at the table behind mine, discussing the upcoming election. It didn't seem like a particularly funny topic to me—if anything, the subject filled me with dread. The wrong president…the wrong balance in Congress… it all had a direct impact on people like my mother. People like me.

"I say we build the wall," one guy said, smirking. "It probably won't stop their dumb asses from trying to get in but it would be funny to watch them try to climb it."

Another one snickered. "We can just line the fence with Border Patrol agents to *take them out*." He snapped his fingers. "One shot per group and they'd scatter like cock roaches."

I felt physically ill. Bile flooded my mouth. Heat rushed to the surface of my skin, slicking my back and chest in a fine mist of sweat.

"We'd be doing those other countries a favor, honestly," the last guy chimed. "They don't want those criminals any more than we do. Isn't it better for everyone if they just die?"

"Ugh," the first one grunted. "And all these bleeding-heart libs trying to defend them like they somehow *deserve* to be here. If they really deserve to be in this country, there are *legal* ways to do it."

But not really.

Hadn't we just learned that in class? The "legal" way was expensive—bordering on extortionate—and arduous—if not *impossible*. Designed to keep people *out*, never to let them in. Didn't they *get* that?

Another sniggered while they gathered their books. "Yeah. Tens of thousands. Legal fees. Translators. Simple." They started to shuffle off, leaving one chilling, sarcastic remark in their wake. "When I'm a senator, I'll make sure it gets *even simpler*."

I'm embarrassed it took that long for it to hit me, but it did.

The system wasn't an accident.

It wasn't a mistake.

It wasn't a runaway steam engine or a tangled lump too complicated to fix. It existed exactly as it was for the sole purpose of maintaining the status quo. So that assholes like those guys could continue oppressing others.

So they could continue to oppress *me*.

And there, in that moment of horrible clarity, something amazing happened.

I got *mad as hell*.

Fuming, I crumpled up my list of alternative specialties and chucked it across the library floor. I'd be damned if I was going to leave politics in the hands of those assholes. Men like them would not determine my future or my mother's. I wouldn't stand for it. And if the system was meant to keep those dicks in power, then I would simply have to change it.

Easier said than done, but I wouldn't give up. I had a plan, and it started with making a decent living at Stryker & Sons and helping Mami. The rest would come in time.

I just had to survive Graham Everett for one week.

Chapter Four

January 23, 2017

Graham

Jesus Christ.

Juliet Rivera was going to kill me.

How was it *physically possible* for her to look even better this week than she did last?

It violated the laws of physics or chemistry or *something*, surely. There had to be some point when her sensual appeal would finally peak, right? Though the law of diminishing returns dictated it, I was no longer convinced.

I figured her charm *had* to lessen over time—and, therefore, assumed there was no way she'd be as hot Monday as she had been Friday. For one thing, I expected she would wear a different outfit; and I'd spent the better part of two days persuading myself that the evil red dress was the problem. Not the woman in it.

False.

Monday's ensemble proved *worse*. The baby-blue suit should have been a perfectly professional choice. *Would* have been, on anyone else. But her luscious curves over-filled the tight pencil skirt hugging her ass and nipping at her waist. The visible outline of her breasts swelled under the ivory shell beneath her cropped blazer.

And the color—much like the berry red of Friday's cursed dress—complemented the smooth honey hue of her skin.

Maybe it wasn't the clothes, I decided, still staring. Maybe it was the way she had her hair twisted back. It looped into a low bun, showing off the elegant arch of her throat, her sweet little ears, the stubborn slant of her jaw.

I wanted to wrap my hand around that jaw, pull it up out of the way, and bite her neck. I wasn't normally one for hickeys, but something about her maddening air of defiance stirred a savage longing to mark her. I felt like a wild animal, desperate to sink my teeth into her, desperate for her to tear her claws into me.

All this while standing in the middle of Stryker & Son's executive floor. At noon, on a Monday. With Beth clucking beside me.

She frowned ferociously as I snapped to. "Young man, are you listening to me?"

No. I was imagining ripping the slit up the back of Juliet's skirt, bunching it around her thick hips, shoving her onto her desk, pulling her legs apart…

"Graham Everett!"

Beth's murderous expression quelled my rising erection. Her knowing grey eyes swept from my face over to Juliet—who sat at her desk, dark brows knit together, typing with admirable speed and concentration.

"Don't you even *think* about it, young man," Beth chided. "That woman is out of your league."

I scoffed, equally amused and offended. "Excuse me?"

Beth straightened her posture. Her gaze sharpened. "You heard me. You leave that girl be. She has enough to deal with around here as it is."

I followed the woman's subtle nod back toward the legal department, where I found Miss Rivera was no longer alone. Her boss loomed over her desk, leaning down so his chest pressed into her right shoulder blade. He turned his head, inches from the side of her face, and murmured something to her.

An instinctual rush of jealousy raised my hackles. His proximity made their relationship clear—either they were fucking or…

Wait.

She leaned as far to the left as she could manage in her rolling chair. He set his hand on her other shoulder and she hunched forward, slipping out from underneath his touch.

I recognized the stiff set of her spine from our elevator incident—she didn't enjoy his overtures. She suffered them. Most likely because she couldn't slap her boss the way she decked random assholes.

And that made me… *furious.*

Without another thought for Beth, I stalked toward the legal department, right through their arched glass entrance. My feet carried me straight to Juliet's desk, not stopping until I stood directly beside it.

"Miss Rivera."

Dominic immediately snapped up and stepped back. His eyes widened, then immediately narrowed when he recognized me. "Graham Everett. To what do we owe the pleasure?"

I searched Juliet's face for signs of distress, driven by some foreign protective instinct I didn't fully understand. All I knew was, if he'd somehow scared or harmed her, I would be the one doing the hitting.

But if I expected even a modicum of vulnerability or gratitude, I was doomed to disappointment. Miss Rivera's fiery golden gaze burned as hot as ever, regarding me with the same ill-disguised distaste she had for her boss.

Something about her disapproval pleased me, perversely. I longed to get under her skin—in *every* way, it seemed. A slow smile pulled at my lips. I inclined my head at her as I replied, "I'm here for Miss Rivera. We have a meeting."

The middle-aged dick had forehead wrinkles when he frowned. "During lunch?"

I shoved my hands into my pockets, hiding my clenched fists. "It's all my schedule allowed, unfortunately." *And the only time I could get away from Everett Alexander undetected.*

He opened his mouth to comment, but I was already bored with him. Instead, I turned back to Juliet. For a moment, her beauty stunned me all over again.

Irritated with myself, I barked, "Are you ready yet? I had Beth reserve one of the vacant office pods for us."

Juliet angled her chin defiantly. "If you'd allowed the front desk to buzz me, I would have been waiting for you when you walked in."

Why did she look so goddamn beautiful when she got angry? I felt my eyes drift over her features as I forced a taunting smile. "I'm a big fan of the element of surprise."

Images of the many ways I could surprise Miss Rivera flickered through my mind. *On her desk. In the conference room. In that fucking elevator.*

She gathered a neat pile of files from the corner of her desk along with her MacBook. Then she reached for her bottom right-hand drawer and pulled out a soft, purple square with ropey black handles.

A lunchbox.

Something about it—Juliet, with her intimidatingly quick mind and scorching temper, packing herself a sack lunch—amused me. For the first time in Miss Rivera's presence, I actually felt like smiling for real.

I knew watching her walk in front of me would be too great a temptation, so I paced myself half a step in front of her as we exited the legal department. I should have guessed she wouldn't be meek enough to follow me in silence. Halfway across the center of the floor, she gave a derisive little snort. "Do you even know where we're going?"

I ground my teeth against the all-consuming desire to look at her again. Another wave of aggravation assaulted me. Not allowing myself so much as glimpse in her tantalizing direction, I kept my eyes forward.

"I was here when this place was an empty shell without walls," I muttered. "I helped Stryker decide where to *put* the damn meeting rooms. So, yes."

It took a moment for her to issue her airy reply. "Fine. My schedule said Room C."

I knew the one. And—hell—I knew it was the smallest...and the most private. A portion of the room wrapped around a structural pillar, into a fire wall, rendering it partially obstructed. The other pods were completely open or visible through their front walls of glass.

I could take her to the hidden corner and— My fingers ached from gripping the insides of my pockets. If I ripped a seam, I would be fucking pissed.

I'd chosen one of my favorite suits for my second run-in with Miss Rivera. Another three-piece set, with a rich navy jacket and pants. A bright white vest with matching blue pinstripes covered most of my white shirt and equally blank silk tie. I ordinarily put a gold pocket square in the jacket pocket, but, that morning, I chose red again.

It seemed fitting, I supposed, for impending bloodshed.

Years of ingrained etiquette forced me to pull the door open for her and step aside. The teasing scent of jasmine sent a prick down my back as she swept past me. As predicted, the sight of her from behind nearly undid me. All lush, gorgeous curves, covered in soft blue fabric that fit her like a second skin. And that godforsaken slit. *Fuck me.*

Watching her full hips sway took me from semi-erect to fully hard in an instant. I let the glass door fall closed behind us and took a moment to discreetly adjust myself inside my pants.

Manners also dictated that I remain standing until the lady present seated herself. This meant another two minutes of torture while she arranged her work area—stretching, bending. She opened her laptop, shuffled her folders, and laid out her lunchbox while I stared unabashedly at the split up the back of her skirt.

Finally, she lowered herself into her chair and glanced down at my empty hands. "No lunch?"

"I never eat lunch," I lied smoothly. "Too busy."

Her gorgeous face pinched in disbelief. "You *never* eat lunch?" She glowered. "Not once—ever?"

Rolling my eyes, I dropped back into my own chair and folded my hands behind my head. "You are *such* a lawyer. Jesus. Yes, counselor, I have indeed eaten lunch at one point in my life. I just don't eat lunch *now*."

Her tawny gaze regarded me impassively. "Don't you get hungry between breakfast and dinner?"

A bitter laugh scraped out of my throat. "Breakfast. Ha. You're cute."

Her eyes narrowed. "So you're telling me you haven't eaten since dinner?" Without waiting for my answer, she sighed and unzipped her lunchbox. "Here. You'll be useless to me if you're starving."

I started to tell her that there was no way on God's green Earth that anything she had packed in that sad little lunch pail would ever appeal to me. But then she placed half of a the most delicious-looking sandwich I'd ever seen in front of me. Wrapped in brown parchment, two pieces of crusted bread held a thick layer of thin-sliced steak, an herb salad, some sort of sautéed vegetable combo. My mouth watered.

"*Bistec encebollado*," she said, her musical accent caressing the words. "Colombian steak. I had it for dinner last night and turned the leftovers into a sandwich." She pulled a baggie of chips out of the bag and place them between us, then tossed me a haughty look. "You're welcome."

Her attitude was almost as attractive as her luscious ass. I refused to show gratitude, but smiled despite myself. "Are you Colombian?"

I asked, sliding the surrendered sandwich portion to my part of the table.

Juliet took a healthy bite out of her half and used her free hand to unlock her laptop. When she spoke with her mouth full, I had to swallow another smirk. "Yes."

"Have you ever been there?"

I didn't know why I wanted to ask her questions. We had shit to do. I needed to get back to Everett Alexander within a reasonable time-frame. But some part of me longed to un-riddle her.

If I understand her, it will be easier to control our interactions. That's what I told myself as I watched her click around on her MacBook, anyhow.

Her guarded expression stayed firmly in place. "I was born there. I moved here when I was six." Her burning gold eyes snapped to mine, pinning me in place. "Eat. We need to work."

I hated doing what she told me to do, but her bossy tone heated my blood. If I fucked her thoroughly enough, could I soften her, get her to submit to me? That would give me untold satisfaction. Though, not being able to conquer her would also leave me buzzing with admiration. I figured I would enjoy trying, either way.

With a grunt, I picked up the sandwich and inspected it up close. It looked incredible. Some sort of avocado spread peeked out from under the perfectly rare steak. The fresh salad and sautéed medley were embarrassingly appealing—*God, when was the last time I had a vegetable?*

I took a bite.

It was a mistake.

Because I knew instantly I would never eat another sandwich that delicious again.

My awe must have registered on my face, because Juliet snickered. "Yeah," she drawled. "Abuelita doesn't miss when it comes to food."

I wanted to ask her who "Abuelita" was and what other foods she could cook, but that fucking sandwich was magic. I couldn't stop eating it, even when Juliet's smirk turned unbearably smug. "I knew you were hungry, *pinchao*."

"*Pinchao*?" I managed to mumble between bites. Fuck, it was *good.*

Her smile took on a secretive edge while humor brightened her eyes. The enigmatic amusement made her even sexier. More beautiful. Staring at her, I had the same sinking sensation I got when I bit into the damn sandwich— a brief moment of fleeting of perfection, the feeling of the best slipping through my fingers.

Will I ever meet anyone else as drop-dead gorgeous as her?

I swallowed the last of the life-changing sandwich. I missed it already.

"Don't worry about it," she replied, still smirking to herself.

She took another graceful bite of her half of the lunch, then slid a small stack of documents over to me. "I took the liberty of printing copies of everything you sent me. I only had time to read one of the sample contracts you provided; but I have to tell you, based on my research, it needs a lot of work."

Back to battle so soon.

I leaned forward slowly and dragged the papers over to my place with the tips of my fingers. Everett Alexander's standard client contract sat on top, slashed to ribbons with red ink and rude orange highlighter.

"So your two days of research revealed problems with the contracts my company has used for decades?" I retorted, pitching my voice between amusement and condescension. "Do tell."

Juliet finished her food and set her lunchbox aside, then straightened into a regal pose.

"Perhaps, *because* they've been in use for decades, they're outdated," she suggested, her voice too-sweet. "Legal standards evolve over time due to the establishment of new precedents. The banking crisis ten years ago created a lot of new guidance for contracts such as these. Would you like me to speak with your in-house counsel directly to discuss? It may be over your head."

Her features pulled into an insincere smile that didn't touch her hard, topaz eyes. So far, it was the only expression of hers I didn't like.

Besides, I knew her game—the old kill-them-with-kindness trick. With an added pinch of dismissal. If she thought she'd get rid of me that easily, the woman clearly had no idea who she was dealing with.

I gave a sharp laugh just rile her. "Listen, cupcake, I know more about that banking crisis than you ever will, okay? My family lived it, along with every other banking crisis in the last *seventy years*."

An answering spark of fury lit her gaze, vindicating me. Miss Rivera stared, curling her lip into a sneer. "I thought you might say as much."

She picked up another portion of the files stacked beside her and unceremoniously dropped them onto my copy of the marked-up contract. "Here."

There had to be hundreds of pages, laden with notes, tabs, and Post-Its. The first sheet alone made my vision swim. "What is this?"

Juliet preened, clearly pleased with herself. "Precedent for every single change I recommend. You'll find that my suggestions on the contract are numbered; those numbers correspond to the numerated tabs in the case notes."

I thumbed the edge of the stack, quickly counting up the documents. It was days—nay, *weeks'*—worth of work. "You did all of this in one weekend?" I asked, incredulous.

Heat crept up my neck at the image of her bent over books, writing her notes, with a highlighter between her teeth. Miss Rivera's intelligence turned me on in a novel way I'd never experienced. Her mind was as sharp as her tongue… and both struck me as hard as her initial slap.

"On Saturday," she returned. "Then I spent Sunday morning drafting this." Another sheaf of papers fluttered onto my growing pile. "It's *my* proposed contract for Everett Alexander and Mr. Stryker."

My throat tightened around a twinge of guilt. I hated that I couldn't tell her or Grayson the truth about my position at the company. The truth was, I wasn't authorized to make any deals on behalf of Everett Alexander. I would have to change the contract covertly to reflect the proper titles if I wanted it to be binding.

To hide my eyes, I glanced down at my vintage Rolex. "Mind waiting while I read it?"

Juliet gave a careless shrug, momentarily mesmerizing me with the bounce of her breasts. "That's what I get paid for."

She slid a second copy out from her files and held it up. "I'll read along with you." Another smug smirk teased her full lips. "In case you have any questions."

I flopped back in my chair and began to scan the document. Her prose was as impressive as I expected—clipped, concise, and yet punishingly detailed. A few pages in, the door swung open behind me.

Grayson leaned into the office pod, his expression somewhere between suspicious and surprised as he met my gaze. "Beth told me you were taking a working lunch in here and I didn't believe her," he admitted before flashing a smile at Juliet. "Hello, Miss Rivera. Thank you for sacrificing your break to deal with this leech."

Juliet chuckled quietly, but kept her eyes on her lap. "I tend to eat at my desk anyway, so it's no trouble, sir. I think we're making good progress here."

I noticed she was only at the top of page two while I had nearly cleared page three. "Or we *would* make good progress," I put in, shooting her a taunting look, "if *some* of us read faster."

Loathing flashed in Juliet's eyes. Her grip on the contract visibly tightened. Her lips parted but nothing came out.

Grayson filled the silence by clearing his throat. I looked up to find him frowning at me. "English is Miss Rivera's *second* language, Everett. Last time I checked, that's one more language than you speak, is it not?"

Ah shit. I was a complete asshole. She told me she moved here from Colombia as a small girl… *Of course* she had to mentally translate everything she read.

With an awkward cough, I picked an imaginary speck of lint off of my lapel and mumbled, "My apologies, Miss Rivera."

Her answer dripped insincerity. "No offense taken, *pinchao*."

I still didn't understand the name she kept calling me, but Grayson snorted before laughing loudly. I always forgot he spoke a smattering of Spanish because of his mother. The thought of him sharing jokes with Miss Rivera at my expense rattled me.

I won't let her win, I reminded myself.

But Grayson started excusing himself. "I see you have him well in hand, Miss Rivera, so I'll leave you to it." With one last warning look directed at me, he disappeared.

Juliet was already hard at work as I swiveled back to her, but I interrupted. "You know, if you insist on giving me a nickname I don't understand, I'll have to come up with one for you, too."

A cool laugh floated out of Juliet's open lips. She turned her gaze back to the contract, pointedly not looking at me. "You heard the boss; you don't know any other languages with which to insult me, *pinchao*."

So it is *an insult.*

I'd sort of figured as much.

"I learned enough French to get me through a three-month study abroad program in Paris," I retorted. "Surely I could come up with *something*."

Unbothered, Juliet continued her contract review. "Do your worst."

She kept reading and I kept staring at her profile, wishing for the hundredth time that she wasn't so damn striking. I found it impossible to maintain a proper level of antagonism when constantly assailed by her beauty.

"*Bijou.*"

The word popped out before I really considered it. It wasn't an insult at all, really. More a term of endearment, albeit a mildly patronizing one. It meant "jewel"; fitting, since I heard Ella call her Jules on Friday.

Besides… she reminded me of a jewel. Full of fire and facets. Brilliant. Rare. Sharp edges that cut and caught light and made her more interesting than any smooth, rounded pebble could ever be.

Juliet lowered her papers and faced me head-on, startled. "*Bijou*? Doesn't that mean 'kiss'?"

The thought of kisses and Juliet sent a bolt of lust to my prick. What would those full lips feel like if I crushed them into mine?

"Nope. That's *bisou.* Close, though. Try again, *bijou.*"

A steely glint lit her eyes as she raised her stubborn little chin. She looked so glorious—her prim posture, the flames snapping in her gold gaze.

I felt insane. Had I ever wanted a woman so much? Without even the slightest provocation from her? Yet, even though she hadn't done or said anything suggestive, it seemed impossible that the current cracking between us was one-sided.

Did she feel it?

I got my answer. Our gazes melded together, but I from the corner of my eye, I saw her chest rise and fall on one quick breath. Her torso twisted slightly, giving away the moment she pressed her thighs together under the table. Her tongue swept over her lower lip, followed by the scrape of her teeth.

She wanted me, too.

And then she said the one thing that obliterated every last shred of my control.

"Make me."

Juliet

Graham Everett suddenly shoved away from the table in Meeting Pod C and stalked to the concealed corner of the room.

With glittering black eyes, he backed up against the wall. His hands went to his pockets, his stance one of easy confidence as he watched me. Waiting. Thinking I'd follow.

And—*ayúdame Dios*—I wanted to.

His fine, flashy clothes fit his lean strength to a T. There was something sexy about the way he pulled off outfits no other man would dare attempt. From his spotless white tie to his navy wing-tipped shoes, the man had style and elegance all his own.

It didn't hurt that he continued to be one of the single most gorgeous males I'd ever laid eyes on. With his dark, overly-long hair slicked straight back and his face clean-shaven, I could admire every line of his arresting features—the straight nose, the bulging muscles in his jaw, the divot gracing his chin.

I stared at him, raising my brows primly, feigning bemusement as to his location change. But, inside, I knew why he moved to the corner where no one would see us. And I wanted to join him there.

Pulsing energy pooled in my core. The thrill of it tightened my nipples into hard points and gripped my gullet, squeezing the breath from my throat. Even though I knew I wasn't, I told myself I had to be mistaken. Surely, Graham Everett wouldn't come on to me in the middle of our very official meeting, inside of Stryker & Sons.

Right?

Dark heat smoldered in his eyes, contradicting his casual posture. The velvet depths shifted restlessly as he jerked his chin up.

"Get over here."

I clamped my legs closed to stave off the ache his raspy command created. A firestorm raged inside of me, burning all of my logic and defenses to heaps of ash.

I couldn't give in to him. I knew I had to tell him no. Yet, when I tilted my head to the side and opened my mouth, I didn't issue a denial.

"I said, *make me*."

And then I was against the wall, with his long, strong fingers wrapped around my wrist, holding it up next to my shoulder. His other hand pressed into the space beside my head, his arms forming a cage around my much-shorter body.

A breathless quiver escaped while I looked up at him. His gaze traced each part of my face before settling on my lips. His eyes snapped shut and his nostrils flared on a sharp inhale, like he was attempting to gather his self-control… and failing.

I pressed my free hand flat against his chest, telling myself I would find purchase and move away from him gracefully. But as my palm spread over the spotless, proper vest, I felt his heartbeat pound against my fingertips, strong and sure and real.

That pulse tempted me. I wanted to slip my touch under all of his civility and feel his warm skin. The vital strength of flesh and blood reminded me he wasn't some grand ideal or caricature. Graham Everett was just a man, after all.

It ruined my restraint. Yearning burst through my body. Before I knew it, instead of shoving back, I found myself fisting the fine fabric to hold myself closer to him.

"Damn it, Juliet," he muttered, staring at my lips. "Tell me this is all in my head. Tell me to stop. Slap me again. Anything. Just—"

He wanted me to reject him. Instead, the small sliver of humanity betrayed by his indecision left me weaker than ever.

Graham's wary midnight eyes considered my face for one long moment. His body drew nearer, until his hips skimmed my torso and his rigid length prodded my belly. I shut my eyes, expecting him to steal his kiss, but instead I felt his forehead press into mine.

"Tell me stop," he murmured again, his voice rough. "Stryker's like a brother to me and you work here and we—"

My fingers found their way to his lips, silencing him with a gentler touch than I intended. I didn't need to hear all of his reasons; I already knew them all.

So I said, "Don't speak."

And I kissed him.

My hand moved to cup his clenched jaw as my mouth crushed his. Even in heels, I had to arch my back to reach; but the second I did, Graham snatched me up against him.

A low, feral sound tore from his throat while one hand clutched the back of my neck and other curved around my ass, tugging me tighter against his lean hardness. When I felt the size of his cock, a startled inhale escaped me, parting my lips to the sweep of his tongue.

He ground his erection into me and rumbled against my mouth. "All for you, *bijou*."

My traitorous body had a mortifying response to the notion of his big cock being all mine. A liquid rush of desire filtered through me. My core tightened to the point of pain. The twinge between my thighs throbbed, begging for the thick slide of him inside.

His tongue mimicked the thrusts I desperately wanted elsewhere, claiming my mouth with possessive plunges before retreating in slow, tantalizing strokes. I moaned into his kisses, bowing backward to press my heavy, tingling breasts into his chest.

Graham liked that. His fingers speared the low chignon at the nape of my neck, holding me just so and slanting his lips over mine from a new angle. The hand cupping my backside swept lower to find the slit in my skirt. He caressed the sensitive skin there before leisurely gliding upward, to the place where my thighs met my ass.

Belatedly, I recalled that my tight pencil skirt didn't allowed for underwear without causing obvious panty lines. Graham made the discovery the same second I remembered. He pulled back with a grunt, stabbing me with his molten black gaze.

"Where *the fuck* are your panties?" he growled, low and thick.

I wanted to give him a cheeky reply, but couldn't stop panting. His fingertips curled into the cleft of my center, teasing the wet heat he inspired. His jaw ground as his eyes fell closed.

"Jesus," he whispered. "Juliet."

My name on his lips sent a new thrill coursing through me. I slipped my hand between our bodies and grasped his steely length through his pants. Unable to curb the impulse, I stroked him in one long tug. A broken snarl tore from his chest. On the second stroke, he dropped his face into the crook of my neck and spoke through labored breaths.

"What are you doing to me? I can't *stop*."

I knew the feeling. I'd never been so turned on in my life. Lust thundered in my blood, obliterating my awareness of anything but him.

Squeezing his erection in both hands, I bit into his neck, just above his collar. A lung-full of air sloughed out of him, along with a groan. "Juliet, please."

I didn't know if he was begging me to stop or keep going, but it didn't matter; I couldn't resist the way he reacted to me. By the fourth pass of my palm over his rigid cock, Graham started to grind into my touch. His fingers responded in kind, finding my opening and teasing me with soft, circular caresses until I clenched against him.

"Goddamn you," he cursed, taking my mouth in another punishing kiss.

All of my muddled passions bled together as he pushed one long finger inside of me. Tightening around him, I gasped against his lips, "I *hate* you."

Graham's member swelled under my hand. "I have never hated anyone this much," he agreed, resuming our kiss.

A second finger joined the first inside of me, curving to reach a spot that made me hiss. I fumbled with the fall of his trousers, not able to stand another second of the barrier between us, dying to feel the heat and hardness of him in my palm.

But Graham suddenly froze. His fingers slipped out of me in a wet rush while his other hand tightened around my nape.

"Fuck," he muttered.

Another sound sank past the hum of my pulse. My heart nearly stopped until I turned and saw that it was—thank the Lord—just an alarm, clanging out of his abandoned iPhone. Our hour was up.

Just as abruptly as the tryst began, I found myself alone against the wall. My body pulsed with pent-up need as a shiver of loss chilled my spine. Everything between my legs throbbed.

Like a feral jungle cat, Graham stalked back to the table. He bent over it, spreading his arms wide to brace himself while he stared down. To an onlooker, it would seem like he was reading one of the many pages scattered over the surface. But his eyes were closed. His chest heaved subtly as his hands gripped the edge of the metal tabletop with white-knuckle force.

"Fix your hair," he directed, his tone as black as his expression.

For the first time, I did as he told me. He'd only managed to loosen a few pins. It took me a second to right them.

Without opening his eyes, he continued, "Now I'm going to leave and you're going to stay here for five minutes to gather up your shit. You're flushed right now. You need to settle before you walk out there."

He blew out a long breath and stared straight at the window opposite him, not glancing in my direction. "I'll read all this shit and come back tomorrow at the same time. Do *not* reserve this room again. Put us in Pod A, where everyone can look in."

His head snapped to the side. His black eyes pierced me. "This never happened, Juliet. Agreed?"

I swallowed back the irrational swell of hurt that welled in my throat. He was, after all, completely correct in every way. It couldn't happen again… and it would be best to pretend it hadn't happened at all.

"Agreed."

Graham swept his portion of our work into an untidy pile and adjusted the visible bulge in his pants. "Motherfucking hell," he muttered. With one last shake of his head, he turned away from me and made for the door.

CHAPTER FIVE

January 23, 2017

Graham

Juliet Rivera kissed me. And I was starting to believe I'd have to undergo some sort of shock therapy to get rid of my hard-on.

My cock throbbed through two endless meetings back at Everett Alexander. Three trips in traffic. And spending an hour in the weight room at my gym did nothing but encourage it.

Back at my place, after my workout, I jacked off twice to the memory of her wet, glorious heat—once in the shower, then again, an hour later when the scent of jasmine clinging to the files I brought home got me hard all over again.

Disgusted with myself, I poured a glass of nice wine and chugged it before refilling the crystal with a second serving. I needed to mellow myself out enough to get through the damn work. I couldn't show up for our meeting unprepared. I wouldn't give her the satisfaction.

I wandered over to my record table and put on my favorite bossa nova album, hoping the combination of Barolo and Gilberto would take the edge off. The quiet strains of the acoustic bass echoed off the exposed brick walls, up into the high ceiling.

When I purchased the place using my trust fund, I expected that the fashionable Lower East Side loft would feel homier over time. I carefully selected pieces from my favorite artists to grace the walls, invested tons into a surround-sound system that catered to my record collection and cache of digital music.

When none of that helped, I employed a decorator to furnish the living room, bedroom, and dining area. She did a decent job of capturing my eclectic tastes and penchant for color. Gave decent head, too. But, alas, the furniture and rugs and blow jobs didn't fill the emptiness, either.

My kitchen served as a monument to the idea of cooking. I'd gotten a wild yen one month and convinced myself I would learn how to prepare gourmet meals. On impulse, I ordered thousands-of-dollars-worth of five-star equipment. The rack of untouched stainless steel cookware hanging over my island now mocked me on a daily basis.

It didn't seem to matter what I did to the place. The fact remained—I didn't like being there.

Maybe I'll talk to that Beatrice chick, I told myself, carrying my work over to the sitting area in the living room. *She's a realtor. She's hot. I could ask her about putting this place on the market and take her out...*

I knew I was only fooling myself. Moving to another over-priced apartment wouldn't squelch the cool solitude of my existence any more than fucking Beatrice What's-Her-Face would slake my insatiable lust for Miss Rivera.

Who I hated.

Passionately.

Too damn passionately.

Flopping back onto my sofa with my wine, I let out a sigh and willed myself to focus. I originally planned to spend the evening going through her objections to the Everett Alexander document so I could combat them one-by-one. But I found myself reaching for *her* proposed contract instead.

By the time I finished reading it, I was half-hard all over again. *Goddamn that woman.*

Her contract was good. It was *great*, actually. And I found that possessing such deep (albeit begrudging) respect for the woman I lusted after did strange things to me.

I briefly entertained the thought of hiring her away from Stryker. I would need the help of someone like her to form my contracts for future clients. Obviously Everett Alexander's were out of date. Never mind the fact that I was technically operating on my own at moment.

I felt more and more guilty about my deceit every time I thought of it. Shame was an unfamiliar feeling. I didn't tolerate it well. It made my stomach twist…and the nausea reminded me that I hadn't eaten anything since Juliet's delicious sandwich.

My cock twitched in my sweats.

Graham Everett. Hard over a fucking sandwich.

One kiss—and the woman had utterly ruined me.

Juliet

I got home two hours later than usual after staying late at the office and enduring a particularly grueling commute on the subway.

The journey into and back-from the city never felt so arduous before taking my job at Stryker. Now, the trip seemed ludicrous. An hour in the morning and evening if I took the subway, or forty minutes each direction on the days Mr. Stryker didn't need Marco early in the morning and he could drive me.

My feet and back ached as I climbed the stairs to Abuelita's walk-up. My spine slumped after twelve hours in heels, not to mention the veritable mountain of work I carted home with me.

Tris planned to close on Mr. Stryker's new townhome the following week. She sheepishly dropped off a file of documents for my review at 4 P.M., wincing when she informed me they needed to be finished by lunch the next day. She promised to buy me a round at Thursday's happy hour to make amends for the quick turnaround and I somehow managed to smile and wave her off like I wasn't already drowning in work.

It didn't help that Dominic had determined a strategy to get even with me for taking over so many of Mr. Stryker's personal legal matters. He, too, piled on the paperwork—dropping folders on my desk every hour all day long and throwing out murky deadlines to accompany them. "As soon as possible," he said sometimes. And, "This is time-sensitive," at others.

A quick review of the files confirmed my suspicions of revenge—he purposefully gave me multiple projects in different areas of the company, ensuring I wouldn't be able to use my research from one case to apply to any of the others. It also did not escape my notice that none of the work went to the other junior attorneys, even as my inbox overflowed.

But the worst part of the whole shitty day was still Graham Everett.

Who I hated.

So much that I cursed his name every time I thought of it. *Carajo con ese cabron...*

The smell of dinner greeted me at the top of the steps and I froze. The unmistakable scent of *ajiaco* filled my nose. Abuelita's Colombian chicken soup could only mean one thing—

"Who died?" I asked, bursting through the door.

Abuelita stood at the stove with her back to me. She waved one wrinkled hand over her shoulder. "*Nadie*," she muttered, stirring the large simmering pot with a long wooden spoon.

"In English, Abuelita," I chided gently. "You need practice—*hay que practicar, bien?*"

I expected her usual scowl and some more Spanish muttering. Instead, she wiped her hands on her apron and turned to face me with a regretful sigh. "*Bien, muñeca.*" Sadness filled her dark eyes. "Was work?"

How *was work*. "I was very busy today."

Fighting with Graham Everett. Loathing him. Wanting him. Hooking up with him in a conference room.

I set my tote bag full of files on one of the empty kitchen chairs. Everything suddenly seemed too heavy for me to carry. "You made *ajiaco*?"

She nodded. The dim light from the hood over the range steeped half of her face in shadows. "*Necessito*," she said simply.

I watched her ladle the soup into two bowls. She shuffled toward me and set them at the breakfast table while I pulled off my heels and my blazer. "Why do you need it?" I asked, rubbing an ache in my left foot. "Do you feel sick?"

Abuelita scoffed. "I never sick."

"*I'm*," I corrected automatically.

She slowly gathered soup onto her spoon. "Is what I said." Her grey brows knit together as her gaze roamed over the bag of folders beside me. "You working hard, *muñeca*."

She meant *too* hard, but I purposefully misunderstood. "It's good to work hard. You taught me that."

Her lips tightened. "Stubborn."

"I wonder where I learned such a trait," I returned, shooting her a pointed look. "Now tell me why you made *ajiaco*."

Abuelita considered me for a long moment. "Is no's thing, *muñeca*. Only cold, so I makes *ajiaco*. Now, eat."

I crossed my arms over my chest, not buying her deflections. "Abuelita."

My grandmother rolled her eyes to the heavens and threw up her hands. "Fine. I tell. Your *papi* come today."

Dread turned my stomach to lead. My father only made appearances every six months or so. After years of listening to me berate him every chance I got, he stopping coming over when he thought I'd be home.

I was fine with that arrangement. After what he did to my mother, I preferred not to see him at all. His visits always upset Abuelita, though. She never forgave her son for his callous treatment of his wife… or for abandoning me after bringing me to America. His visits normally infuriated her. Tonight, though, she seemed subdued.

"What did he want?" I demanded.

"No's thing," she lied into her soup. "I handles him. Not you worry."

But he *was* my worry. He always would be, no matter how hard she tried to protect me from his sorry ass. After all, he was technically still married to my mother. As soon as I got her here, I would have to deal with him to get her a divorce.

The thought was yet another reminder of why I couldn't let Graham get to me. Men ruined women, the way my father ruined my mother. And I would never let a guy past the walls I spent years carefully constructing.

"Tell me," I ordered, out of patience for horrible men. "I'll deal with it."

Abuelita pinned me with a glare. "Eat. *No hables.*"

Don't talk. Her decree reminded me of my shameful lapse in judgement. I gritted my teeth and tried to gather scraps of resolve. My abuela qualified as a formidable opponent on a *good* day, and I was running on fumes.

"Abuelita—"

Her ferocious expression stopped me in my tracks. "Julieta Isabelle Rivera—*basta*! Eat. *Now.*"

I truly didn't have it in me to argue with her any more. I had to save my strength for work… and building up new defenses for tomorrow's meeting. Yet, as I took my first bite of the delicious comfort food, I found myself wondering if Graham would like it for lunch the next day.

The next morning dawned, chilly and wet. I dressed myself in the most boring, conservative work clothes I owned—partly because of the cold, but mostly to fend off Graham.

The rich brown turtleneck covered every inch of skin from my chin to my hips. I wore it tucked into a fawn-colored skirt with absolutely no slit to speak of, and sported matching sheer tights over my ugliest granny panties.

So far, Graham had equally passionate reactions to my hair being up and down, so I figured something in the middle might be my best bet. Using a tortoiseshell barrette, I clipped half of it back into a matronly style. Simple black pumps rounded out the dull look.

There, I thought, satisfied by my reflection. *No color. No skin. No jewelry*. I was as far from sexy as a girl could get. Just in case, though, I borrowed one of Abuelita's frumpier coats to wear over the whole outfit.

By the end of my commute, I was freezing, hungry, and my eyes burned. Exhausted from working well into the wee hours of the morning, I slogged up Madison at half-speed. For the first time in my month at Stryker & Sons, I barely arrived on time.

Dominic awaited me at my desk. His gaze flickered down over my uninspiring ensemble. I watched the exact moment he decided that I wasn't currently hot enough to merit any niceties.

His lip curled back. "All bundled up today," he sneered. "Like a nun in a blizzard."

I did my best to paste a good-sport smile on my face. "Just guarding against the cold!" *And your pervy ass. And my own lack of self-control whenever a certain broker sniffs around.*

When I slipped my coat off and bent to put it in my desk drawer along with my other bags, he changed his tune. "Still lovely, as always," he hummed, somewhat warmer. "Did you make much progress on the items I gave you yesterday? I was hoping to review them with you over lunch."

Over lunch?

It made sense for Graham to come meet me during my lunch hour, because he came from outside the office and we were dealing with Mr. Stryker's personal holdings, as opposed to company business. But Dominic asking to meet with me during my break seemed decidedly odd. I could think of no reason why he would require such a thing, aside from some sort of misplaced jealousy. Perhaps he didn't like Graham occupying my "free" time.

"I have another lunch meeting with Mr. Everett," I replied brightly, doing my best not to appear suspicious. "I've reserved Pod A for us."

My thighs clenched at the memory of Graham's voice, growling instructions at me. I mashed my lips together and turned away to hide my expression, busying myself by arranging my work for the day.

Dominic rounded the desk, coming to stand in front of me with his hands on his hips and a peeved expression on his face. "I don't want you scheduling any more lunch meetings. It's against company policy."

I wanted to glower at him, but forced a bewildered face instead. "Oh dear, is it? I just assumed it was acceptable since Mr. Stryker dropped in on my meeting yesterday and didn't mention any issues with the timing. In fact, he *thanked* me for working during lunchtime. But if you think it's an issue then *of course* I'll adjust accordingly."

Carajo. That last part started to veer dangerously close to sarcasm. Between Dominic's blatant sexism, Graham's inexplicable appeal, and my father's bullshit, I simply did not have my usual finesse.

"I don't think I like your tone, Miss Rivera," Dominic snapped.

My jaw clenched against the urge to point out that he ordinarily never used my last name. When my tits were out, I was *Juliet.* He'd even dared to call me Jules on a few occasions.

Exhaling through my nose, I raised my face to look him in the eye. "My apologies," I demurred. "I was up very late and haven't caffeinated sufficiently." I threw in a coy smile, hoping to get to him by stoking his endless ego. "Forgive me?"

He gave a curt nod. "Just don't get into the habit of scheduling lunch meetings," he repeated. Walking away, he issued one last demand over his shoulder. "I expect notes on all of the cases I dropped off yesterday by tomorrow morning."

The reality of another sleepless night settled over me. The thought hunched my shoulders. "Yes, sir."

The same second Dominic's door slammed, Beth appeared in the archway of the legal department behind me. I turned just in time to catch her glaring at my boss's office. Her sharp grey gaze snapped to mine. "Miss Rivera?"

I swiveled in my seat. Somehow, it was easy to find a smile for the older woman who managed Mr. Stryker's life—and, really, Mr. Stryker himself. "Good morning, Beth. I wish you'd call me Juliet. Or Jules, even."

Beth's tight lips spread into a rare smile. "Juliet, then." Her eyes flitted over my shoulder for another second before settling back on me. "Is Mr. Carter giving you grief?"

I tried for a bright, breezy tone. "Nothing I can't handle. Did you need something?"

She eyed me intently. "Mr. Stryker would like to speak with you privately this afternoon. His schedule allows for a three o' clock. Would that do?"

Panic gripped my gut. Why would Mr. Stryker want a one-on-one with *me*? Anything work related could be discussed in front of my colleagues. And it certainly wouldn't be anything untoward; Mr. Stryker clearly adored his fiancée beyond all measure. Marco deleted the elevator footage, so he didn't have any reason to reprimand or terminate me, unless—

Dios mío. He saw us yesterday.

For the first time in as long as I could remember, I felt like crying. All of my hard work and determination was spiraling down the drain—all because of a man I didn't even like and should not want. Because I let myself lose control for a single moment.

I knew I deserved whatever I had coming, though. What happened during our "meeting" was indecent, bordering on profane. I cringed just thinking of what Mr. Stryker might have witnessed. The fact that he was one of the few men I actually respected made the whole thing all the more devastating.

"Three?" I croaked back. "Yes, ma'am."

Beth's somber gaze felt heavy on my face. "Alright," she replied slowly, her lips pursed as she considered me. "I will let him know. Thank you, Juliet."

I forced a smile, just in case it was my last chance to give her one. "No problem."

Could my day get any worse? I wondered.

Little did I know.

Graham

"Graham?"

I blinked a few times, remembering myself. *You're at work, you idiot. Look alive.*

"Sorry, what was that?" I asked, turning my bleary eyes toward my father.

He sat at his ornate, polished desk, looking exactly like me if I went through a thirty-year time warp and gained sixty pounds. The way he stared when I met his eyes put a fine mist of sweat over my brow.

The large room felt stifling to me. Despite its size, his office always seemed stuffy. The sumptuous antique furnishings were priceless collector's items, but that didn't make them attractive. Or comfortable.

I shifted in my usual chair, looking for a position that didn't make my lower back hurt. *Jesus, I'm old. And completely checked out.*

His dark eyes seemed to pierce directly into my thoughts. "You've been distracted this week," he noted, disapproval cooling his voice. "I saw you had accounts with you when you came in from the weekend. The green binders? I expected them on my desk yesterday."

Ah yes. Yet another of my recent failures. I took another stab at the account ledgers Sunday evening before once again throwing in the towel. In truth, I'd been so preoccupied by my Stryker deal and Miss Rivera, I forgot all about the math I couldn't seem to focus on.

Still, he didn't need to be a dick about it. They were just old account ledgers I studied as a learning exercise and digitized for the sake of convenience. No one needed them back right away. And I did have actual, current accounting work to manage for the company, all of which I completed on time or months ahead of schedule. Why was he busting my balls?

"I'll get them back to you as soon as possible," I replied, steepling my fingers. "Is there some reason you need them right away?"

His frown deepened and I wondered if I, too, would eventually wind up with grooves bracketing my mouth.

"No," he admitted. "The only urgency is the value of your time. There are a lot more accounts for you to review and enter data from before I can give you clients."

Little did he know I already had a huge deal in my pocket. I swallowed the smug urge to flash him a grin. "Naturally, I agree that my time is valuable," I drawled. "So if you'll excuse me?"

I started to rise, but froze in place when I felt his eyes travel down my frame. "What?" I demanded.

My father shook his head. "Nothing."

But the crease between his brows made a liar of him. "What is it?" I asked again, glancing down at myself.

"You're dressed differently," he pointed out, shuffling his papers and avoiding my gaze. "More professional. I like it."

The dark brown pants, camel-colored jacket, and plain white shirt pained me. My muddy green tie and tweed vest were equally uninspired. They formed as dull an ensemble as my wardrobe allowed, but I'd chosen them with a mind to keep a low profile. I made one single allowance for flair—the damned red pocket square, folded into my breast pocket.

"Christ," I muttered. "I'll have to burn this suit now."

Dad flashed one quick smirk and I paused. Whenever he smiled, it gave me a renewed perspective on the man. Ordinarily, I thought of him as a sheep in lion's clothing—a man whose great wealth and influence hid a weak heart full of cowardice. A man who couldn't be faithful to his partners or his second son. A man who couldn't stand up to his own father and take control of Everett Alexander before the old man passed away.

Sometimes, I secretly saw those failings in myself. After all, I'd never committed to anyone, helped Christian in any meaningful way, or demanded that my father give me a real job. All of the things I hated about myself were directly from him. My illustrious inheritance, it seemed.

But when my father smiled, he became someone else. Charming and likeable and almost… magnetic.

Another commonality we shared: charisma. It enabled him to bag a whole host of wealthy clients. People responded positively to him… and to me.

Unbidden, the image of Juliet's furious face and stinging slap slipped into my mind. The memory brought a rueful curve to my lips as I turned for the door.

Well, most people.

At twelve-to-noon, my cab pulled up in front of Stryker's. I debated running up the block to grab something to eat during our lunch meeting, but thought better of it once I checked the time. I refused to give Miss Rivera ammunition by arriving late.

The stark splendor of Stryker & Sons always felt like another planet after a morning entrenched in Everett Alexander's pomposity. The wide, white lobby provided a bracing burst of freshness—like opening a window for cold winter air after leaving the furnace on all night. Invigorated, I clipped my way across the lobby. Until, halfway to the cursed elevators, I saw her.

A sense of déjà vu skittered up my spine as I jerked to halt in the middle of the marble floor, once again standing in the chasm of the black vein bisecting the gleaming expanse. This time, though, instead of standing in front of the row of elevators, Juliet stood all the way off to the side of the oval lobby, looking strangely small.

I'd come to view her as a formidable force of nature. Now, with her head bent and her arms wrapped around her torso, she seemed less like a storm and more like a speck. A bit of warm earth, engulfed by a snow-white blizzard.

The urge to go to her hit me head-on, but I reined it in, telling myself there were any number of practical reasons why Juliet might be in the lobby so close to lunchtime. Maybe she was waiting for a food delivery… or a quick visit from a boyfriend.

The errant thought chilled my blood. *Jesus.* I never even *considered* a boyfriend. And I certainly never *asked* her if she had one before helping myself to everything up her skirt.

I watched, appalled, as Juliet's head turned, tracking the movement of a man crossing the floor from the check-in desk. At first glance, he seemed too old for her, but the distance between us didn't do me any favors. I couldn't tell if his face was truly as worn as it appeared. From my vantage point, he also looked short, with a sunken chest he puffed out in front of him as he marched in her direction.

My hands fisted in my pockets. I realized I couldn't look away, even when the man barreled right into Miss Rivera and hugged her. Juliet froze with her arms wrapped around herself, pinned between them.

I drifted toward her slightly, trying to catch a glimpse of her expression. The man pulled back and grabbed her shoulders, shaking her while he spoke animatedly. Juliet grimaced.

She slipped free from his embrace and stared while he spoke. The more he went on, the smaller she looked. Her shoulders hunched gradually, pressed forward by some invisible weight.

You shouldn't care, I told myself. *You hate her.*

But her stricken expression reminded me of the moment I tore away from her the day before, the way she looked when I left her panting against the wall. The recollection winded me.

And, in that moment, I didn't care who the man was or how much I supposedly disliked Miss Rivera. My steps ate up the floor to bring me to her.

The closer I got, the clearer the scene became. The man wasn't her boyfriend—I would have put money on that. He looked too old, for one, with weathered russet skin and dull, yellow teeth. His slick black hair hung limply around his face, cut in a choppy, shapeless style.

In her plain black pumps, Miss Rivera stood almost as tall as he did. Her clothing matched her somber expression—all earth tones with nary a hint of her usual flash. Even covered in brown from chin to ankle, she was striking. I particularly liked her hair. She wore it pinned halfway back, so I could take in her beautiful features and still enjoy the way her long, shiny tresses fell to the swell of her breasts.

The fierce urge to kiss her again—right there, in the very public lobby, in front of the anonymous asshole—clawed up my insides. I tamped it down and jerked to a halt at her side, finally drawing her attention.

"Graham."

My first name fell from her lips for the very first time as breathy gasp. Concern welled in my middle when panic flared in her golden eyes. "What are you doing here?"

"I'm early," I put curtly, pivoting to pin the man in place with an assessing look. "Graham Everett," I told him, extending my hand. "I'm a colleague of Miss Rivera's."

The scent of liquor assailed my nose as he swayed close enough to take my hand in his flaccid grip. "Julio Rivera," he returned, his accent a much thicker version of Juliet's. Which made sense a second later when he added, "Julieta is my daughter."

Julieta. I hadn't realized her full name wasn't Juliet. Another stupid oversight on my part. Of course she had a Latin name.

Jules shifted on her feet, obviously uneasy. "*Papi*, Mr. Everett and I have a meeting. You'll have to come back another day."

Julio scowled, narrowing his cloudy brown eyes at his daughter. "I came all the way from the Heights to have lunch with you, *mija*. The least you can do is tell this *pinchao* to wait."

I really needed to look that word up.

But instead of siding with her dad, Juliet edged closer to me. "I can't, *papi*. I'm at work and Graham and I are in the middle of a project."

"I tried to do this the nice way," he grumbled, "But you're not listening, just like your *abuela*. If you're going to be *la mucosa,* I suppose I'll have to make you come with me."

He reached for her arm and grabbed her wrist. She hissed, trying to pull back. My instincts took over. The next thing I knew, I had pushed a hand into Julio's chest and stepped between them. My other arm guided Juliet behind my body, tearing her from his grasp.

"I'm afraid Juliet's time is spoken for," I told him, glaring down. "As she said, you'll have to come back."

I felt her posture tauten behind me. "Although," I added, guessing at the reason for her stiffness, "perhaps it would be better not to discuss private matters at all while she's at work."

Then I felt her touch, feather-light, brushing from the back of my elbow to my wrist. Somehow, the small gesture of gratitude warmed me. I automatically reached back to gather her cool fingers in mine.

Julio watched the exchange with a disgusted snarl. "Ah. I see. Is this how you got your fancy job, *mija*? Everyone in *el barrio* talking about how you hustled to get here, but really you're just a whore like your mother, eh?"

My fist cocked before he even finished his insult. But Juliet's fingers desperately squeezed my other hand, holding me back.

When I turned my head, I found her eyes shining and wet. "Please don't," she whispered. "He's just drunk."

Hatred—true, flaming abhorrence, directed at her asshole father—burned down my throat. It reminded me what real loathing felt like. A sensation I'd never actually experienced for Jules. What I felt for her may have burned just as brightly, but it was a different sort of fire altogether.

I snapped back to Julio. "Leave," I told him. "Now."

The man looked ready to argue, but as he took a step in my direction he swayed again. His lack-of balance sapped his confidence. Gritting his jaw, he leaned back and spat, "Fine. I'll see you later, *mija*. We have many things to talk about."

He lumbered away, leaving me to face Juliet. I rotated toward her, keeping our hands entwined between us.

"What the fuck was that about?" I asked, noting the way her eyes followed her father to the door warily, as if he might change his mind and come back for her at any minute.

Her complexion blanched from warm caramel to wan beige. "He wants money," she said woodenly. "He heard about my job here. He wants 'his piece'. Says he needs it for medical bills."

I tried my best not to act completely repulsed by his entitlement. "Is he sick?"

Her head shook robotically. "His girlfriend is having a baby boy. Apparently."

Inside my grip, her hand started to tremble. I held it up between our bodies, wrapping my other palm over her chilled knuckles to warm them. "You're shaking."

"Yes." The defiant chin slant that drove me mad made its appearance. Even quivering, with tears in her eyes and no color in her cheeks, she had her self-respect. And I admired her for it.

We were alike in a lot of ways, I realized. Proud, stubborn, passionate. She clearly wanted to cry, but she refused to do it in public. How many times had I done the same, swallowing the lumps lodged in my throat whenever someone asked about Christian?

"Come on," I murmured, already moving, pulling her along with me. "I know a place."

Juliet

Graham drug me past the elevators, over to the service stairs in the back of the oblong lobby. Once we made it through the black metal door, he released my hand and turned away, facing the closed slab, holding it shut.

I understood right away; he knew I was about to break down. He was trying to allow me to do so without losing my dignity.

"I'm fine," I growled, but my throat constricted on the words, turning them into a squeak. I had to sniffle before continuing. "You don't need to wait here with me. It was just a—" My voice cracked. "Shock."

Graham's tense figure spun suddenly. He unwound, reaching for me, but I stepped back to put more space between our bodies. His jaw clenched at my movement. Taking in my tears, his dark eyes flashed.

"*Bijou.*"

I'd looked up the word on my subway ride home the night before. It meant "jewel." At the time, the revelation confused me. But now that I heard him say it again, a curious warmth licked low in my belly. The sensation made me weak—and, just for a second, I softened.

Graham didn't miss his opportunity. He closed the gap between us and cupped my cheek with his large, long-fingered hand.

"You're tired," he whispered, skimming his thumb over the dark circle underneath my eye, collecting the tears gathered there.

It wasn't a question, but I nodded.

"And now your dad turned up with bad news..." Graham's dark, slashing brows knit. "But there's something else. What is it?"

Was this truly only our third meeting? He already seemed to know me.

While I debated how much to tell him, he extracted the red handkerchief from his breast pocket and dried the tears off of his fingers and my chin. The tender gesture took me by surprise, and I blurted out my response without polishing it.

"Mr. Stryker asked to see me at three today. Alone. I can't think of why he would want that unless he saw us yesterday and wants to fire me."

Every part of Graham went eerily still. Seconds passed. His eyes didn't so much as flicker, but I saw the wheels of his mind spinning. Finally, he blew a slow breath out through his nose and folded the red cloth back into his pocket without meeting my eyes. "I'll handle it."

A bitter laugh scraped up my throat. "If you think I'm some sort of damsel in distress who's just going to sit on my hands while you charge off to fight my battles for me, then you're deluded." I squared my shoulders. "My father had me at a disadvantage, showing up unannounced at the place I work, when I already think I'm about to be fired, then telling me I'm going to have a sibling because he took another mistress. Just because I lost my grip for moment doesn't mean I need you to swing into my boss's office and defend my honor."

Graham's exasperated expression was distinctly at odds with the way he held my face. His features said he was at his wits end, but his touch was gentle, almost reverent.

"Stubborn woman," he ground out, smoldering those midnight eyes into mine. "Why do I want to fuck you every time you argue with me?"

"So all the time?" I quipped, sniffing back the rest of my tears.

His crooked, boyish grin heated the air between us. "Yes."

A shadow suddenly crossed his visage as some thought occurred to him. He raised his other arm and glanced at his wrist, frowning. "Damn. We only have fifty minutes. Less, by the time we make it upstairs."

The thought of returning to the executive floor with tear-stained cheeks mortified me. It would also seem suspicious for us to arrive together, late, without some sort of take out.

Wincing at the thought, I asked, "Can we go sit somewhere? This already looks weird to everyone... if we go up there now..."

Graham's hand fell from my face. He gave a single nod, brusque. "Understood." He indicated the leather messenger bag slung over his shoulder. "I have all the stuff you gave me yesterday in here. We can work off of my copies."

A small smile played at my lips as we made for the exit. "Amazing," I muttered. "I think we just agreed on something."

The small dim sum restaurant tucked around the corner happened to be one of my favorites. I was pleasantly surprised when Graham led me into the cramped bistro and waved at the hostess like he knew her.

The short walk over passed in silence, giving me a chance to fortify myself. I wanted to believe I was ready to resume our usual animosity, fully girded against his charms. But then he flashed his rogue's grin as he pulled out my chair for me. And something in my middle *flipped.*

"Best dumplings in midtown," he told me, folding himself into the seat opposite mine. "For those of us with taste."

Graham could not have looked more out of place. It never ceased to irritate me that he could pull off such eccentric styles. And, yet, his appeal was undeniable. His tweed-and-camel outfit reminded me of *Downton Abbey* and British country fashions. He looked like a debonair lord about to mount a horse and ride off for a hunt.

Annoyed by his general handsomeness, I narrowed my eyes at him. "I thought you didn't even *eat* lunch."

He shrugged with his trademark indolence. "You do."

My stomach gurgled as if to agree with him. *Maldición.* Straightening my posture, I scanned the familiar menu items even though I already knew what to order.

"So," he said conversationally. "Still hate me?"

The question caught me off guard. My eyes flew to his, finding one dark brow arched in a gorgeous mask of mild curiosity. I opened my mouth to issue a sound jab, but my stupid brain chose that moment to recall the feel of his hands holding my face. My gaze drifted to the red handkerchief in his pocket.

With a sigh, I had to admit, "No. I don't."

He gave a single nod, his face carefully impassive while he looked back at his menu. After a moment, he considered me with a new, wicked gleam in his dark eyes. The look turned his next question into a challenge. "What type of dumplings do you get?"

"Shrimp and pork, of course." As if there were other worthwhile dumplings.

His grin widened. "Fried or steamed?"

"Fried for the shrimp, steamed for the pork. Obviously."

Graham's gaze never left my face, even when the waitress appeared at his elbow. "Two orders of fried shrimp and two orders of steamed pork," he said, then cocked his head at me. "Obviously."

His humorous regard had me biting back my own smile and issuing myself a stern reminder. *You may not despise him, but this is still not a man you can afford to like, Jules. Get back to business.*

I gestured to his bag. "So lay it on me."

Graham's heated smile curved his sensual mouth. "You're going to want to rephrase that."

I glowered. "Graham."

"*Bijou*," he returned.

His grin faded, leaving his expression intense while he stared me down. "I was wrong yesterday, about acting like nothing happened. We can get back to work and do our jobs. I'll sit here and eat lunch with you and act like a civilized adult. But I can't pretend yesterday didn't happen. I won't. It happened. I had my fingers inside of you, your hands on me. I'm not going back to the way we were before."

Carajo. What could I say to *that*?

My pique felt childish in the face of Graham's unflappable calm. *Maybe he's right*, I thought. Much to my horror, he *did* have a point. It *had* happened. As a lawyer, I knew how silly it was to quibble about a fact.

And the fact was: Graham and I made out. After I kissed him, he kissed me back and put his hand up my skirt while I stroked his cock through his pants. Because we were both attractive adults who found each other physically appealing in a forceful—almost *chemical*—way.

Perhaps acknowledging our magnetism would make it easier to move past it. If anything, it was certainly more mature than denial.

"Alright," I acquiesced. "That's fair."

Satisfied, Graham extracted my files from his bag. He set them on the table between us, then flattened his palm on top. "The contract you wrote is very good," he praised, solemn and unwavering with his intent stare. "*You* are very good."

I was used to be people being surprised whenever I turned out not to be an airhead. Shooting him a smug look over my glass of water, I asked, "Thought I had boobs-for-brains?"

He glanced at my breasts, then back into my eyes. "It's unusual to meet *anyone* so smart and so sexy." A sardonic smile played at his full, soft lips. "Yet another thing we have in common."

Another?

Just days ago it felt like we had *nothing* in common. How could we? He was a wealthy white guy who grew up in penthouses with hired cars and an Ivy League education. And I was an immigrant who lived in a shoebox with her grandmother and took the subway for an hour just to get to the city. He had everything gift-wrapped and waiting for him while I continued to scrap and work for all the things I wanted.

It made sense that we would be opposites, at first.

Now? I wasn't so sure.

I pried the contract out from under his hand, surprised to see my draft annotated with slanting cursive in the margins. Some of the notes were terse, but most just offered simple explanations. There were even some questions and—*shocking*—a couple brief compliments.

"I take it this means that—assuming I still have a job at the end of the day—we can work from my version instead of yours?" I inquired, doing my best not to sound too haughty.

Graham leaned back in his chair and pretended to pick lint off of his jacket. I recognized the sheepish gesture from the day before. "I suppose that would be acceptable."

"Alright then, *pinchao*," I replied, smiling despite myself. "Let's get to it."

He smirked. "Again, *bijou*. Poor choice of words."

Graham

I turned out to be even more fucked than I originally realized.

Pacing outside Stryker's building, I repeatedly pushed my hands through my hair. I'd already blown my lunch hour to hell and texted my father some made-up bullshit about a migraine. Though, ironically, the tension in my neck had started to stir the beginnings of a real one.

After ten minutes, I figured Jules would be safely installed back in the legal department. I wanted to slip into Grayson's office without her noticing. Despite her rejection of my chivalry, I couldn't let her get fired over something I started.

But it was more than that.

Fuck me. Damn it all to hell. Motherfucking....

A litany of expletives filled my mind while I rode the elevator up all fifty stories and cut across the main floor as quickly as I could. Beth startled when I burst through the archway leading to Stryker's office.

"Mr. Everett," she snapped, hawk-eyed as per usual. "We weren't expecting you."

My foot tapped against the marble floor, expelling the nervous energy that built every time I stood still. "Is he in?" I demanded, unable to summon any sort of charm. "It's time-sensitive."

With a clear air of disapproval, Beth leaned forward to press the intercom button and spoke into her headset. "Mr. Everett for you, Mr. Stryker."

A second later, I stepped into his office. Similar to the conference room, the wide curved space had white walls, a glass front, and a floor-to-ceiling panoramic view behind a smoked charcoal desk.

My best friend sat behind it, smiling until he saw the look on my face. We'd been friends a long time—he knew me.

His expression clouded over. "Graham?"

"I'm fine," I huffed, flopping into one of the leather Eames chairs opposite his. "Sorry to barge in. Finish whatever you're doing. I'll wait."

Grayson clicked around on his computer for a few seconds and then shoved the work on his desk off to the side. "Alright," he said, focusing on me. "Go."

I meant to ask about Miss Rivera's job. I planned to admit to whatever he might have seen and spin a story to reduce her culpability. And then—depending how pissed he was—I decided I needed to broach the topic of running his investments through me instead of my father's company.

That last part gradually sank in over lunch with Juliet. Her contract was air-tight. Even if I managed to get away with switching out the names at the last second… I didn't want to tarnish her hard work like that.

Her starkly earnest face drifted into my mind. *"No,"* she'd said when I asked if she still hated me. *"I don't."*

I didn't want her to change her mind. And I didn't want to lie to Grayson.

Because I… *cared.*

Revolting. Bordering on intolerable.

But there it was.

I opened my mouth to say all of it… and then something completely different came out. "I want to leave Everett Alexander."

What. The. Ever-loving. Fuck.

Stryker leaned forward like he couldn't have heard me properly. "I'm sorry, *what*?"

Clearly, I'd lost my mind. From the moment I all-but assaulted Juliet in that elevator last week to that very second—I didn't recognize myself.

It was her. She was like some sort of parasitic worm, wriggling her way into my brain, eating away the pieces that always served me so well. Entitlement, self-protection, apathy, impudence.

But as I sat there, with the most ludicrous statement I ever uttered hanging in the air, I didn't feel sick or regretful. A sudden rush of calm rolled over me. For the first time in years, I felt… *right*.

The possibilities quickly came together in my head. I could walk away from my father's business. The "legacy" that had always been touted as some holy grail. Because, lately, it felt less like a gold medal around my neck and more like a noose.

In one brilliant moment of clarity, I realized: I didn't want to prove myself to the likes of Hugh Everett. I wanted to rise so far above his level in every category that I would never find myself beholden to him again.

I could do it. I already had the education and countless cutting-edge investment strategies. I would have to find a client base more quickly than I originally planned… But I already owned my apartment outright and I had my trust fund to cover other expenses in the meantime. Plus, Stryker's account would be *huge*, if my projected returns proved accurate.

If I could sell him on my sudden insanity.

I took a page out of Juliet's book and rolled my shoulders back, facing him with all the confidence I could muster. "I want to leave Everett Alexander and start my own firm," I said, relishing the rightness of the statement as it reverberated through my bones. "And I want you to be my first client."

Grayson watched me for a long moment. I knew from years of friendship that he was scrutinizing my demeanor, trying to figure out how serious I was.

Finally, he spread his hands. "This is your proposal?"

I wanted to wince. He had a point; most start-ups would never approach the CEO of a company like his without a detailed business plan. And I had nothing to offer him other than my word. Which, up until that moment, had been flimsy, at best.

"It's a new plan," I replied. "Very new. But it's the right move for me." I blew out a deep breath. "I can do this, Grayson."

I expected caution. Indecision. Maybe even a few loaded jokes about my less-than reputable past. After all, the guy witnessed all of my most disgraceful moments. Every time I carelessly skipped class, ruthlessly blew off a woman, somehow cheated on an exam; he was there. He'd seen me blacked-out, coked-up, and everything in between.

But still he looked me dead in the eye and said, "I know you can do it."

The simple statement hit me like a gut punch. He trusted me. He… believed in me.

Had anyone else ever done that?

"Thank you," I replied, clearing the thickness from my throat. "I want to do this the right way. Let me write up a proper business proposal for you to peruse and, if you like what you see, we can talk about drafting new contracts."

Grayson inclined his head. "No."

I blinked at him. "No?"

He cracked a sideways smile. "Like I said: I know you can do this. I don't need a proposal. And I guess it could be fun to play the big-shot and make you sweat, but I'm not dick so I won't do that. You're my best friend, Graham. Our best man. You have my business."

Triumphant, I leapt up to shake his hand, but Grayson rounded his desk and clapped me on the shoulder instead. "So we're good?" he asked. "We can get a drink to celebrate Thursday night if you're up for it."

I stepped back, dazed, buzzing with the thrill of what I'd just done. *Holy shit.* I still didn't know what had come over me, but I was glad for it.

"Thursday's great," I chipped. My mind spun, forming to-do lists and contingency plans. "Though I think I could use a drink right now."

Stryker laughed. "I would offer you some of the gin I keep in my desk, but I have a three o' clock."

A three o' clock. The thought sunk through my jittery stupor. *Fuck. Juliet.*

I watched Grayson saunter back to his seat, considering. Obviously, he didn't know about the incident in Pod C, or he would have been pissed at me. And, if that were the case, he wouldn't happily hand me five-million dollars to invest through my fledgling company.

As long as he was clueless, I wanted to keep him that way. Mentioning Juliet now would only make him suspicious.

"I suppose I'll need a good lawyer," I muttered, half to myself. "I don't have a non-compete contract with my father, but he's going to try to throw the book at me, I'm sure."

Grayson's eyes widened. "Shit. That's going to suck." He rubbed the back of neck. "You'll also probably need someone to work on your contracts for clients who don't have their own attorneys. And someone to review vendor arrangements, insurance agreements."

My throat went dry just thinking about all of the logistics of being a CEO. I knew there were hundreds more he hadn't even touched on.

"We can talk shop Thursday night," I agreed. "Do any of your attorneys here do freelance or would that be a violation of their non-competes?"

Stryker shook his head. "Non-competes only apply to our competitors and clients. If it were anyone else, I'd be put-out by one of my people doing work for another company on the side; but since it's you, I'm fine with it. Talk to Dominic. I think he used to work for some hedge fund downtown. Maybe he can do some start-up work to get you going and point you in the right direction for someone more permanent. His hourly rate is probably pretty handsome, though."

Dominic was the asshole head of legal I saw leaning all over Juliet. *Fuck that.* I'd have to find someone else.

"I'll let you know if I borrow anybody," I hedged, half-kidding. "After hours only, of course."

Grayson started to turn back to his computer while I made for the exit. Though, he did toss out, "Yeah, don't fuck with any of my people during business hours or I'll be fucking pissed."

The memory of taking Juliet up against the wall three offices over made me smirk. *Too late.*

Chapter Six

January 25, 2017

Juliet

Marco drove me into the city Wednesday morning.

Even with a cup of coffee in my hand, I felt every bit of the previous night's sleep deprivation. After having a huge fight with Abuelita about hiding my father's request for money from me, I proceeded to eat a bagel for dinner and work until two A.M. to finish Dominic's assignments.

My cousin looked at me askance as we barreled into the darkness of the Queens tunnel. "You okay?"

Great, I look as shitty as I feel.

I threw myself together after snoozing my alarm three times. My hair hung in a limp ponytail. My emerald blouse and black skirt were as basic as my hairstyle. At least I remembered to put some earrings and makeup on.

"I'm fine," I grunted, taking two big gulps from my coffee. "Just a shitty week."

Marco kept his expression blank. "Saw you on Mr. Stryker's schedule yesterday. How did that go?"

Ironically, my dreaded meeting with the CEO turned out to the one boon in my otherwise-bleak day. He'd asked me to draft a prenuptial document for Ella—one that would guarantee, under any or all circumstances, that she stood to inherit every penny of the Stryker estate upon his demise…

He also wanted the arrangement to dictate entirely equal terms in the event of an unlikely divorce, virtually handing over half of his net-worth to his fiancée upon their marriage. Irrevocably.

It was a trial to endure the meeting without gawking at him. What he requested was highly unusual. Normally, spouses who separated only split whatever they acquired *during* the marriage. But he wanted her to have half of *everything* he owned if she ever left him.

He even used those exact words: "if she ever leaves me." Implying that he could not fathom any scenario in which he would nullify their union.

It was about as romantic as a contract meeting could get.

The thought of Graham's mouth on mine drifted through my brain. *Well,* almost *as romantic as a contract meeting can get.*

"Attorney-client privilege," I mumbled.

Marco shot me an answering grin. "So he's putting you to work, then? I'm glad. That Dominic guy is a prick."

I bit my lower lip to stifle a giggle. I hadn't had the balls to ask my boss why he wanted me to do his pre-nup instead of the head of my department, but I got the sense he didn't like Dominic any more than I did. After all, the marriage contract would be the third major personal project he put me on in a week.

"Maybe that's his problem," I mused, "Maybe Dominic has a micro penis and it's given him a dick complex."

Marco grimaced. "A dick complex?"

"Yeah." I pinched my fingers together an inch apart. "He doesn't have one, so he *acts* like one."

We both chortled. The car sped out of the tunnel and I squinted against the sudden flare of bright light. The weather was cold, but sunny. I wished I wasn't bound to spend the whole day indoors.

Marco's phone rang. "Damn it," he muttered, answering immediately with his last name, "Amir."

Mr. Stryker.

"Yes, sir," Marco said a moment later, casting a nervous look at me. "The only thing is—Grayson, I have Juliet in the car with me.... Yes.... Are you certain? ...Yes, okay. Twenty-five minutes."

He hung up with an apologetic look. "Looks like you'll be late. Grayson needs me to swing up to the East Side and get him right away. A last-minute breakfast meeting came up. I told him you're with me and he doesn't mind. He told me to tell you to text Dominic and let him know you'll be in by nine-thirty, per his orders."

My stomach knotted at the thought of texting my superior with news of my tardiness... especially after the way he reacted when he found out I had a one-on-one meeting with Mr. Stryker the day before.

When I told him Mr. Stryker asked that I keep all contents of our meeting strictly between us and refused to give a summary, Dominic stormed out of the legal department and marched over to the CEO's office before Beth intercepted him. I couldn't hear their argument, but there were *a lot* of hand gestures...

"Just drop me off at the next cross-street," I requested. "I'll take a cab the rest of the way."

Marco rolled his eyes. "And have it look like you're avoiding Grayson? Not brilliant, *prima*."

Maldición. He was right.

I sent the requisite text and hid my phone in my bag where I wouldn't have to read Dominic's reply right away. I knew he would hit the roof. I'd be lucky if there wasn't a huge stack of folders on my desk when I got in.

We sped up the FDR, along the edge of the island, then finally cut inland around Lenox Hill. I recognized the address for Stryker's building from the closing contracts I reviewed for him. The place was, of course, even grander in person. I only had a moment to take in the ultra-modern architecture before a small blonde bounced toward the car.

Ella.

She appeared at my window and I rolled it down, already smiling at the glee on her face. "Jules!" she chirped. "Gray told me you were in the car, so I popped down with him."

Behind her, Ella's fiancé offered her an indulgent smile. "She's *supposed* to be getting dressed," he told me, then turned back to her. "You know Marco is just dropping me off and coming right back for you?"

Ella pulled a face. "I know, I know," she grumbled. Then, to me, "Grayson is basically *forcing* me to go shopping. I suspect Marco is coming to make sure I actually meet with the personal shopper and not for security purposes."

Mr. Stryker glowered at her, but spoke to me, the same way she did. "It's her birthday in February and I'm taking her to Aruba for a week. She needs swimsuits and resort wear; but every time I try to take her to a store, you'd think I was marching her to the gulag." He shook his head, exasperated. "So I'm bringing in professionals."

Ella cast me a knowing look. "He has trouble being firm with me," she translated, "so he's making Marco do it."

Mr. Stryker seemed like a different man around her. His posture loosened, his smiles came easier. I was surprised when he wrapped his arm around Ella's waist and pulled her into his side, bending to drop a kiss on her neck without even a twinge of hesitation. He whispered something in her ear and then stepped away, flashing her a smile that made *me* blush.

The poor girl didn't have a chance. While he slid into the back of the Mercedes, she blazed pink and then spun back to me, dazed.

"Anyway," she said, blinking to clear her thoughts. "I wanted to make sure you're coming out for drinks with us tomorrow!"

In my current state, all I wanted was sleep. But I couldn't turn her down in front of my boss… and, moreover, I didn't want to disappoint her.

"Sure," I replied brightly. "I'll have Tris text me the details."

"Perfect!" Ella beamed and gestured at the rear of the car with a wink. "You'll keep him in line for me?"

I was still laughing as Marco pulled us into traffic. Mr. Stryker settled into the backseat with a chuckle. "Marco, if she *really* doesn't want to go to Bergdorf's, just take her to Sarabeth's, okay? She likes their popovers and she didn't eat breakfast yet. I'm sure I'll figure out some way to get her in a swimsuit."

Marco pinched his lips to hide a smile. I sensed that Mr. Stryker giving in to Ella's whims was an on-going theme in their daily interactions. "Yes, sir."

Dominic decided on the silent-treatment as my punishment.

He never stormed out of his office to berate my tardiness. He didn't come hover over my shoulder and not-so subtly stare down my shirt. I dropped my finished research and notes off in his inbox and left his office without so much as a look or a glance from him.

Fine, I thought crisply. *He wants to ignore me? Sounds like a vacation.*

And it was. I worked diligently all morning, plodding my way through the revisions Graham and I agreed on over the previous day's lunch and beginning my final review of Mr. Stryker's new townhome purchase.

Mr. Stryker asked for the pre-nup before the end of the month; now, I suspected he wanted it behind them before Ella's birthday and their vacation. That thought brought a small smile on my lips as I saved the finalized real estate agreement to our portal, careful to share it with Mr. Stryker and Tris.

"Huh," a deep, rich voice intoned behind me. "That might be the first time I've ever seen you smile without it being at my expense."

Graham.

I didn't know when I'd stopped thinking of him as Mr. Everett and started to refer to him by his first name in my thoughts. As if I conjured him, he appeared beside my desk, wearing his boyish grin and the most ludicrous suit ever conceived.

"*Dios mío, pinchao,*" I startled, aghast. "Is that *velvet*?"

Graham's smile heated. He leaned closer. "You shouldn't speak Spanish to me here, *Miss Rivera.*" The rumble in his tone raised goosebumps on my skin. "It *distracts* me."

I refused to give him the satisfaction of sounding as breathless as I felt. "A velvet suit," I continued, acting appalled. "In red, of all things."

Graham inspected his arms, tugging at the black shirtsleeves underneath. The slim-fit jacket had wide, slanted lapels trimmed with matching onyx piping. His silk vest mixed the black and claret colors into a swirling paisley pattern that blended seamlessly with his tie.

"It's more of a burgundy, actually," he commented, then pointed to the square in his jacket pocket. "Aside from this, that is."

The red handkerchief.

I saw his point. The bright crimson didn't really match his outfit at all; but, then, it hadn't matched any of the other ensembles he wore it with, either. Clearly Graham Everett was a man who made his own rules.

As evidenced by the coordinating black-velvet footwear I glimpsed seconds later.

I laughed before I could help it. "Oh no, the *shoes*!"

Graham's eyes flit over my features while I giggled. Finally, he dropped his gaze to his feet and gave one of his signature shrugs. "How else is a guy supposed to get away with slippers at work?"

He truly was a handsome man, especially when he smiled. The fine layer of stubble around his sculpted mouth emphasized the bright white flash of his teeth. I wondered, idly, if he only shaved on Mondays. His facial hair seemed to accumulate gradually from day-to-day, but his face was smooth the day we made out.

I shook my head and gathered my meeting materials. "Honestly, what possesses a person to go to their closet and decide on a *burgundy* velvet suit?"

Graham stepped back as I stood up. A slight wince marred his brow. "Sometimes you choose a confident outfit because you feel confident; sometimes you choose one because you *need* to feel confident."

I might have smirked at him if he didn't sound so sincere. Part of me longed to ask him why he needed extra confidence, but I couldn't admit that I cared. Instead, I held up my lunchbox and waved it like a taunt as we exited the legal department.

"You'll be *begging* me for lunch today, *pinchao*," I crowed. "Abuelita made it."

Graham slipped his hands into his pockets while we crossed the floor to the meeting pods. "Your grandmother again?"

I nodded, holding my head high. "I live with her in Queens. She's a fantastic cook on a good day, but even better when she's angry. We had a fight last night and this lunch is her passive-aggressive way of making me feel bad for being mad at her. So it's bound to be *amazing*."

He smirked, amusement lighting his midnight eyes. "Your grandmother revenge-cooks?"

I didn't like the intent, teasing way he regarded me. It made my stomach do a silly somersault. "That amuses you?" I asked tarty.

Graham held the door to Pod A open for me. "Only because it seems like something *you* would do."

"Me?" I demanded, narrowing my gaze at him as I rounded the table and took the seat facing the glass wall and door. There, I would be reminded that we weren't alone every time I looked across the table.

"Yes," he clipped, gracefully slouching into his seat. "Convincing someone they were wrong by blowing them away with your talents seems *exactly* like something you would do, *bijou*." He held up the final draft of our contract—the one I wrote that eventually won him over. "Exhibit A."

I sniffed as regally as I could. "Well thank God for me, then. At least now we can finalize the arrangement and we won't have to keep meeting like this."

Graham didn't buy my ice-queen act for a second. "That bad, am I?" he drawled. "Weird. I could've sworn you were pressing those gorgeous thighs together under the table just now."

His dark gaze took in my quiet gasp, sharpening while they watched me. "No reason to pretend, remember, *bijou*? Just like I won't pretend I haven't been hard since you demonstrated your talent with tongues a few minutes ago."

How could he turn me on so *quickly*? Just a few words, a slight curve of his lips. I had to force myself not to shift in my seat. I glared at him instead.

"Focus, *pinchao*. We have to finish this today. I have a whole other document to draft from scratch before the weekend."

He straightened his shoulders, snapping back to business. His eyes drifted over my shoulder, to the spectacular view of midtown. "Agreed. I've suddenly found myself with a lot more on my plate than I previously had. I can't keep running up here every afternoon."

He didn't mean it as an insult, but the statement stung me. I huffed back, "Fine then. Let's get this over with."

Graham's dark eyes pinned mine. "Fine. Go."

Very deliberately, I folded my hands over the papers and made no move to read them. When I opened my mouth, black fire crackled in his eyes.

"*Do not* say 'make me'," he warned. "Or I will fuck you on this table in full view of the entire office and *actually* get both of us fired."

The breath hissed out of my lungs. I couldn't say the words without throwing down the gauntlet. I also couldn't let him win. So I fixed him with my sharpest smile. "You know what? Don't speak."

Graham

There was no help for it.

I had to have her.

Not there. Not *now*, but soon. Any noble notions I'd entertained about leaving her alone after our business concluded were shot to hell the moment she laughed at my shoes.

Such a sweet, lusty sound. She laughed with *abandon*. It reminded me of the unrestrained way she melted in my arms.

The effect of her amusement took me by surprise. I made some stupid joke about my slippers and then proceeded to say too much by admitting I needed a confidence boost that morning. It was all too true, though.

I felt… unmoored. Everett Alexander had been my future for as long as I could remember. Imagining my life as my own was invigorating… and shit-my-pants terrifying.

I spent the night writing out all of the lists I started to compile in my head the moment I told Grayson my wild plan. I vacillated between feeling brilliant and feeling like a lunatic. But I knew one thing for certain: none of it would work if I didn't find some faith.

With her sexy command issued, Juliet continued, "Pick up your copy. We'll go through it line-by-line out loud. Then I'll get your verbal approval and finalize the draft to be signed in person Friday morning."

I willed away the erection pressing at my zipper. "Fine," I gritted. "But right off we should strike out the names as written and revise.

The contract will no longer be between Stryker and Everett Alexander. It will be Stryker and myself." I withdrew the documents folded into the inside pocket of my jacket. "Or, rather, my new company."

Juliet's shapely brows lowered over her eyes, blending with the coal fringe of thick lashes to shroud her skeptical golden gaze in shadows. Her voice dropped. "*Your* company?"

I did my best to stay stone-faced while I slid the articles of incorporation over to her. "Yes."

Ever a true professional, she reviewed them thoroughly before regarding me with a dispassionate air. "G&C Capital?"

"Yes."

Juliet inclined her head, her long, lush ponytail cascading over her shoulder. "Who is 'C'?"

Of course she caught that. The name was one of a thousand ultra-important business decisions I remained utterly unsure of. In my rush to incorporate as quickly as possible, I only had a day to come up with a title. I knew I wanted something with my name and Christian's, but I couldn't use our surname. "Everett" was too well known around town… and inextricably tied to our father's firm. After some brainstorming, I settled on mine and my brother's initials.

But I couldn't very well *tell* people that.

Investments were all about trust and respect. If everyone in the city knew I saved a place at my company for a drug abuser, I'd never build a client base.

Grayson was the only exception to that rule—but he'd known Chris since he was in high school and he knew *me.* If I told him my intention to get Christian cleaned up and help him build a future, he would trust me to know how much responsibility to give to my brother, and when to give it to him. Society acquaintances and strangers would not.

Which was a bunch of hypocritical bullshit, since half of the wealthy people I knew were drug addicts in their own right. Fancy, expensive drugs procured through "proper" channels. But still.

I truly didn't even know if Christian would ever be fit to work with other peoples' money. I just knew he was brilliant. And my little brother. If he wanted a real shot at a better life, I would do anything to encourage that.

I picked a speck of thread off of my sleeve. "No one."

Her lips quirked to the side. "You're lying."

Christ.

Did she have to be so goddamned *smart*? All. The. Time. It made me want to fuck her and argue with her in equal measure. Which was really something, because before meeting Juliet I'd never wanted anything as much as I now wanted to fuck her.

Refusing to concede, I stared her down. "G-and-C. Just good alliteration."

"Mm hmm," she hummed flatly. "And this company of yours is a new development, I take it?"

"New," I confirmed. "Yes."

I didn't like the assessing way her topaz eyes flicked over me. "Well I know you didn't get *fired*, because then you wouldn't be so nervous."

Narrowing my gaze, I glowered at her. "How do you figure?"

Her beautiful breasts bounced when she lifted and dropped her shoulders. "If you got fired, started a revenge-company the next day, and planned to sign Mr. Stryker the same week, your bid for retaliation would be a resounding and immediate success. No need for anxiety, as you'd really have nothing to lose and everything to gain."

She folded her hands, searching my features and seeing way too much. "But you *are* anxious. So that means you stand to lose a lot by this move. And what could a guy like *you* lose? Your inheritance, of course: Everett Alexander. Which means, I'm guessing, you're starting G&C Capital for another reason. Without telling your family. And I bet it all hangs on Mr. Stryker's deal."

Fuck. Me.

"Got it all figured out, huh?" My voice came softer than I intended, but Juliet's cheeks colored under my intense regard.

"You're not as mysterious as you like to think you are," she sniffed.

Well, what could I say to *that*? It was true.

"Neither are you," I shot back, pissed at her and myself and everything all at once. "In fact, after what I saw yesterday, I thought you would be a little less judgmental. It's not like you have it all figured out, Miss Rivera. *I'm* not the one with a deadbeat alcoholic father who stalks me at work."

Ah, shit.

That was below the belt. I wanted to recant the words as soon as they flew out of my mouth. Her dad's failings had nothing to do with her. In fact, I suspected that she succeeded *in spite* of them.

Across the table, Juliet had gone from my usual hot-tempered, warm-blooded opponent to a statue. Still and ashen, her jaw ground while she met my gaze unflinchingly, taking the undue criticism without so much as dropping her defiant little chin.

Shoving both hands through my hair, I started backpedaling. "I mean, obviously, your family issues aren't *your* fault… I only meant to say that all families have their shit and maybe there's a *reason* that I'm leaving Everett that isn't anyone else's goddamn business… Even exceedingly sexy, young lawyeresses."

Juliet's expression did not move, but fire flashed in her eyes again. I swore it warmed the whole room. "Lawyeress isn't a word," she scolded evenly. "And certainly not 'lawyeresses.'"

I shrugged, hoping she would melt for me. "We could always agree to disagree, Miss Rivera."

"Us?" she snorted, smirking. "Dream on, *pinchao*."

She never gave an inch. Stubborn and brilliant and furious and *right* to the very last. Her passion called me to an elemental level. When our gazes locked, I *felt* it—beaming out from her center, echoing through mine. So much raw energy arched between us… I wondered if she could feel it, too.

"*Bijou—*" I had no clue what to say. An apology, maybe. Or something outrageously inappropriate. Maybe a combination of the two.

It didn't matter, because she cut me off. "Let's just get back to work."

Sensible. She was that, too.

Practical and erotic. Primly professional and still disarmingly real. A wild animal who tamed *me.* A puzzling combination of all sorts of contradictory qualities that should not have fit together and yet, somehow, made… Juliet.

"Alright," I agreed, picking up my copy. "Aside from the aforementioned name change, my next correction is on line 32. Find clause six-B…"

We went on to review the whole contract before Juliet began collecting her things. I glanced at my watch to find that we'd exhausted her whole lunch hour and she hadn't even eaten. Idly, I wondered what her grandmother made her. The thought gave me a sharp pinch of guilt.

"You didn't eat," I pointed out, busying myself with my own files.

"I'll live. Besides, I won't be working through any more lunches after today. I think you'll agree our hands-on work is done, so I'll finalize our draft this afternoon, then send it over to you and Mr. Stryker through our encrypted portal. The three of us will reconvene Friday morning, as planned, to sign everything. Is that agreeable?"

No, damn it. Because if I didn't see her every day at lunch, when would I see her? Never? That thought seemed obvious and impossible simultaneously.

"I'll let you know if I need anything else from you," I hedged coolly, stepping out from around the table. My eyes automatically roamed down over her body, tracing all of the small features I'd come to appreciate.

I realized I would *miss* her. And the thought was…

Unacceptable.

I straightened my posture until I towered over her. Juliet thrust her hand out, her jaw taking on the determined slant that drove me to distraction even seconds after I resolved to walk away.

"Mr. Everett," she clipped.

Managing the hand shake and a normal tone of voice took all of my self-control. "Miss Rivera."

She spun on her heel, swaying to the door. I indulged myself one last time and watched her go. What was the harm, I figured. I couldn't have her. Not when she made me lose my grip on apathy. Not caring too much about anything was the only thing that kept me going.

When Juliet reached the door and grasped the handle, she paused, but didn't look back. "Graham?"

Why was my throat bone-dry? The rasp in my voice surprised me. "Yes?"

"I don't think you need the velvet suit," she murmured to the door. "You're a formidable opponent without it. Trust me."

Chapter Seven

January 26, 2017

Juliet

Thursday felt never-ending.

I started the day by convincing myself to wear one of the more daring outfits Abuelita made for me. The beautiful long-sleeved dress had a tasteful V-neckline and a thin gold chain around the waist. The tulip skirt met asymmetrically over my left thigh, giving good range of motion when I had to walk around. All-in-all, it wasn't anything ostentatious.

As long as you liked bright teal.

Which, turns out, Dominic did. *Way* too much.

His unwanted attention started the second he strolled into the legal department, and went on—*unceasingly*—until lunch, when he *insisted* we spend together in his office. I tried to argue that I hadn't had a free lunch all week. I even went so far as to give him some personal details, since I planned to use the hour to draft a letter to Abuelita's employer about his continued discrimination against her.

Dominic would not take no for an answer, though. He insisted I had to eat with him so we could "review our schedules"… which took about three minutes. He consumed the rest of the hour with stories about himself from his university days and all of the high-powered jobs he went through thereafter.

He so clearly believed he had a shot with me, despite our twenty-year age difference and the *literal wedding band* on his hand. He carefully avoided any mention of his wife or his home life, telling tales that cast him as some sort of misunderstood hero. The whole thing was so pathetic that it might have been sort of funny… if his interest didn't jeopardize my livelihood.

Every time his eyes wandered to my bare knees or my chest, I did my best to cover what little skin I had showing. I folded my hands over my crossed legs, held my phone in front of my boobs. After an hour, I practically itched with the urge to escape.

At one point, he alluded to us coming in to work on the weekend. Sick anticipation gleamed in his leer—the hope that I would jump at the chance to be in the office with him alone. I demurred on my upcoming plans, knowing I needed to consult Marco about getting a possible escort from him before I committed to meeting Dominic in an empty building.

By five, the *last* thing I wanted to do was drag myself downtown. But Tris arrived at my desk, bright-eyed and bushy-tailed, five minutes after the day ended.

"Damn," she said, whistling. "How do you make everything you wear look so sexy? If I put that dress on it would be *frump city*. I guess it must be that fabulous figure." She shook her head with mock solemnity. "Bitch."

I giggled, "It isn't me, I promise. My grandmother makes my clothes. Without her help, I would look like a lumpy potato."

Tris blew her auburn side-bangs off of her face with an irritated huff. "Oh don't be *that* girl."

Gathering my things, I followed her to the archway. "What girl?"

"The One Who Has No Idea How Hot She Is," Tris told me, rolling her eyes. "It's so *done*. And besides, that's Ella's whole *thing*. And, trust me, no one does it as well as she does it—because that girl is drop-dead gorgeous and *actually* clueless."

I began to see that Tris had a one-of-a-kind personality and the humor to match. Her jibes usually involved compliments, delivered so cuttingly that they may as well have been insults. Or maybe it was the other way around… I couldn't figure it out, but she made me laugh all the way downstairs and out onto the street.

We huddled into our coats while we waited for her roommate Alice to arrive with our cab. When the car pulled up, the small mousy girl inside surprised me. She didn't seem like the sort who could hold her own against someone larger-than-life like Tris.

While Tris wore another of her daring jumpsuits—this one cranberry, low-cut, with long fitted sleeves and bell-bottom pants—Alice seemed plain in comparison. Her dark blonde hair hung straight around her slight shoulders. In the dim car, it almost blended into the pale gray color of her sweater-dress.

Tris mostly filled the silence on our way to SoHo. She told the story of how the two had met in college and become best friends. Alice quietly cut in every so often to offer a quick joke or slight correction. It was clear they knew each other better than anyone else.

I found myself fighting off a wave of envy. It sounded nice to have friend to take on New York with. The city could be so lonely. I sometimes dreaded the thought of moving closer to work all by myself.

So I resolved to spend the evening turning these friendly strangers into new friends. I figured it couldn't be too hard. I'd taken on Graham Everett. *A few women my own age should be nothing.*

Graham

I could not deal with Grayson's shit.

Specifically, his absolutely sickening adoration for his fiancée.

Who, sure, looked damn fine in some vintage orange mini-dress with flowy sleeves and thigh-high white boots. A look Ella mysteriously carried off without looking like a go-go dancer who charged by the hour.

Admirable. But surely not justification for Grayson's googly eyes.

He watched her saunter across the room and up to the bar, his gaze saturated with devotion and possessiveness. "God. Those boots."

Ella had a well-known penchant for ugly shoes and these were no exception. Straight out of the seventies, the pleather footwear's only redeeming quality fell somewhere around the bare strip of skin at the back of her thighs. Since I wasn't allowed to ogle my best friend's future wife, the shoes found no such redemption in my mind.

"They are hideous," I announced.

Grayson smiled, delighted. "I know. I love them."

Christ. After another sleepless night and another trip to Chris's dorm room at two in the morning—this time with gyros—I really didn't have the stomach for his mooning.

I took a long sip of my drink. "Never pegged you for a shoe fetish."

His eyes glued themselves to her hemline again. "Not shoes. Ella."

Rolling my eyes, I searched for something—*anything*—else to focus on. It was too dark to see shit, though. I knew we had to choose some place quiet and too dark to take photos, since the lovebirds were splashed across every tabloid, lately… but this felt extreme.

Anotheroom—the trendy bar-slash-lounge in SoHo that Ella selected for the evening—didn't believe in lightbulbs, apparently. Small gas lamps barely gave off just enough light to see the faces of whoever gathered around the tabletops or sat at the counter. People walking in the aisle between the bistro tables and the bar were no more than silhouettes.

At least they served decent scotch.

"So have you made much headway this week?"

Grayson's off-handed question felt like a trap. Did I tell him no and play it cool? Or tell him I'd spent the better part of two days banging my head against the wall trying to figure out all my next moves? One option seemed like a good way to appear incompetent, while the other felt recklessly cavalier.

I picked at the seam of my lapel. "I made enough."

Grayson drank his gin and tonic, eyeing me shrewdly. "It's good to admit when you don't know what to do. I had to learn that the hard way a few times. Feigning competence in the name of saving face doesn't get you very far when the rubber meets the road."

Sighing, I downed more scotch. "I did as much as I could. If I'm being honest, I'm a bit out of my depth with the start-up side of the equation. But your contract is done and I have your trades ready to lock in before lunch tomorrow."

"Good." He gave a nod, reaching into the gray tweed jacket of his suit and extracting a folded sheaf of papers from some pocket. "Here. I wrote out a list of everything I could think of to help you get going and included all the contacts I could, and our rates with each. Use my name and you should get the same rates."

In laymen's terms: he was throwing me a lifeline. He'd taken time away from all of his own work… and his fiancée… to help my dumb ass.

The gesture humbled me. I found I couldn't look him in the eye while I took the bundle of information. "Thanks, man."

He clapped me on the shoulder. "You're welcome. Don't get too grateful, though. It's a *shitload* of work. Don't try to do it all at once."

He wandered over to Ella to help her carry our drinks. I watched the two of them without meaning to. It was sort of hard not to stare. Witnessing their relationship in the wild was like spotting a unicorn in the middle of Manhattan. The purity of their connection bewildered me.

An eruption of giggles turned my head. Three women trailed in off the street, pausing to shuck their coats in the doorway. I can honestly say I would not have noticed or recognized them… if not for the one woman on the end of their gaggle.

Juliet.

My body snapped to life instantly. Muscles tightened warily while my prick hardened in my trousers. *Goddamn it.*

Our day apart accomplished nothing. If anything, I wanted her *more*, now.

Especially in that dress.

It wasn't quite as cruel as the red one she had on when we met, but it was close. Another garment perfectly fitted to every delectable dip and curve. The neckline didn't reveal as much, but the divided skirt fell higher on her legs, offering an enticing slash of thigh with each step.

As ever, she walked with purposeful strides and a seductive sway to her hips. As soon as she spotted Ella at the bar, a breathtaking grin broke over her features. She gave an animated wave and Ella waved back before turning and pointing to our table.

To *me*, at our table.

All three girls stopped up short. Beatrice's expression darkened while the wedding planner's—Amy? Ashley? Antoinette? —froze into a careful mask.

For her part, Juliet trailed her eyes down my entire body and back up again, pausing on the details of that day's three-piece suit. Emerald cashmere, with a peacock-feather-patterned vest and matching royal blue tie.

For the seventh day in a row, I'd tucked the red pocket square into the front of the jacket, even though it didn't coordinate at all. I tried not to let myself think about why too much. Though I suspected it had everything to do with Juliet.

The woman made me feel nearly invincible—as though, maybe, *she* could be my one and only weakness. An unsettling notion that gave me more confidence than ever in her absence… and completely fucked me whenever she came into the room.

While the other ladies seemed at a loss for how to proceed, amusement lit Juliet's expression. She shook her head at me and closed the length of the bar between us with slow, languorous steps. The others probably followed her, but I didn't really pay attention.

I was overwhelmed by her sudden appearance at my side. Her long glossy hair caught the dim light from our table's gas lamp, shimmering in a dark curtain that framed the swell of her tits. A thin gold belt around her waist winked at me.

My fingers twitched as I fought the urge to trace them over the metal links. Would they be cold from the wind or warm from the heat of her body? I remembered the way she felt around my fingers—so hot and soft. Perfection. Would she be as wet if I touched her again? Would she grip me the way she did before?

She was the only woman who'd ever taken me to the brink with such ease. I'd spent every night since with my hand wrapped around my dick, imagining what other magic she might wield.

Her sardonic smirk sent a foreign burst of warmth through my chest. "*Pinchao*," she sighed, eyeing my outfit with a look of mock-solemnity. "We have *got* to talk about these clothes."

A smile stole across my face. "You like the green?"

Her topaz gaze glimmered. "You look like you robbed a leprechaun. And how many peacocks had to die to make that vest?"

I took a sip of my drink to hide my grin. "Twelve."

She rolled her eyes at my dumb joke. "*Dios*," she muttered. "It's brighter than any of the lights in this place."

"Not as bright as Ella's boots, though," I pointed out, rolling my head toward the bar. Noticing her hands were empty, I asked, "You didn't want a drink?"

Part of me hoped she'd say no. If she didn't drink, I could stop fantasizing about getting her tipsy and putting my hand back up her skirt. I glanced down at her lap, wondering if she had any panties on.

She squirmed under my regard, smoothing her hands over her thighs before settling them primly at their juncture. "Tris is grabbing me something."

"What do you drink?"

Why did I give a fuck what she ordered? Why did I want to know her favorite drink, her favorite foods, her favorite places?

Juliet seemed to be asking herself the same questions. Her black brows knit. "Red wine." Her gaze dropped to my glass. "Let me guess: scotch?"

I may not have known her, but she seemed to know me. And, for the love of God, how could *that* make me hard?

"It's a fifteen year," I told her, eyeing the drink. "What kind of red wine?"

Juliet shrugged. "I told her I'd drink whatever she wanted a bottle of."

But what did *she* want? That seemed *important*. I was annoyed I wouldn't find out, but swallowed the urge to interrogate her along with another mouthful of liquor.

I tried to chance a glimpse down the front of her neckline, but her bright eyes caught mine instead. True to form, neither of us looked away, each refusing to be the first to back down. The hum of our sexual tension gradually filled the silence settling over us. Like static with a dial that someone kept nudging. Higher… and higher… and higher. Until it blocked out anything but her… and the thick, burning pulse she pushed through my veins.

It eclipsed my self-control. Obliterated all thoughts of maintaining my apathy, staying professional. I knew right then, in one crystallized moment, that my fight was pointless.

Over, really.

I'd already lost.

Her tongue slowly rolled over her lower lip as her gaze roamed over my mouth. I could read every dirty thought flickering in her eyes. She wanted my lips back on hers, my body pinning her again.

I clenched my hand in my pocket, fighting the urge to lunge forward, sweep her up, and carry her out into the alley. Right then, I would have fucked her in front of every person in SoHo, just to show them how badly this woman wanted me. Just to have her once.

Blessedly, the other girls rejoined us a second later. Juliet broke our standoff first, turning just in time for Ella to throw her arms around her like they were old friends.

My best friend's fiancée then set another scotch in front of me. She grinned. "For you, shithead."

Juliet's husky laughter sent a fresh ache through my raging cock. She laughed harder than I'd ever heard before and I found myself staring, unable to look away.

She squeezed Ella's arm. "I knew I liked you," Juliet told her, cutting an electric glance at me.

"It's my nickname for him," Ella replied. "Though Grayson told me you have your own."

Juliet's expression turned sly. Sparks lit her tawny eyes. "Only when he gets under my skin," she returned. "Which is often, I'll admit."

Under her skin. My mouth watered even as I clasped my pocket harder, disgusted with myself. The woman turned me into a rabid beast, literally salivating at the thought of shoving inside her.

I longed to punish her for it, somehow. I almost taunted her by telling the group my pet name for her, but I didn't want anyone else to hear it. The term I meant as a jab had become some sort of twisted endearment. It felt private. Embarrassing, almost.

I missed my moment. Grayson arrived with another gin and tonic for himself, a glass of champagne for Ella, and a bottle of merlot with three glasses.

Tris began chatting away, pouring for herself and her friends. I put concerted effort into focusing on her face—the up-turned nose, her wide smile and unique hazel eyes—hoping that I would experience some twinge of attraction. Anything to distract me from the buzz of energy radiating in the space between my seat and Jules.

No such luck. Tris was hot. I saw it, but didn't *feel* it.

After a few minutes, I caught my peripheral vision tracking Juliet's every move. Her laughter lost his lusty edge as it started to sound nervous. She sipped her wine too quickly and I wondered why. Because of Grayson? Maybe something else happened with her dad? Or a work thing? Or… me? Frustrated, I drained my own glass faster than I should have, too.

After Ella and the wedding planner—*Alice*, as it turned out—squealed over wedding details with Jules and Tris while Grayson dutifully smiled along, the subject finally turned elsewhere. Tris mentioned their new townhome and complimented Juliet on her expedited work.

"She *is* good," I put in, hearing the begrudging tone in my voice even before Grayson's quizzical eyes met mine across the table. I hastened to cover my tracks, "For someone who likes to call me names."

Tris pulled a face, clearly implying that *everyone* would *like* to call me names; most just didn't have the balls. She turned back to Jules.

"Seriously," she went on. "I couldn't believe it when I opened the portal this morning and saw all the documents completed. I came by your desk to take you out for a thank-you lunch, but Dominic beat me to you."

Grayson stilled with his glass halfway to his mouth. His face remained smooth; if I didn't know him so well, I may not have seen the censure lurking in his eyes. "Carter took you to lunch?"

Beside me, Juliet stared at her fingers as she swirled the dregs of her third glass of wine. Tension replaced the sensual energy radiating from her body into mine.

My hackles rose. What did that motherfucker pull? The very first day all week that I wasn't there, and he made her go to lunch with him?

Before I knew what I was about, my left hand crept into the neutral zone between our bodies, resting lightly against her thigh where no one would see it. Her jaw clenched at the contact, but a second later she scooted ever-so-slightly closer as she un-crossed and re-crossed her legs.

"He didn't take me to lunch. He just had some things he wanted to discuss with me in his office," she finally said, offering a tight smile. "Some scheduling issues. I might need to come in to work with him a couple of weekend days. No biggie."

Weekend days? Disgust simmered in my stomach at the thought of the two of them alone in the office. The hand pressed against her leg balled into a fist.

Grayson was pissed, too. Ella noticed the same second I did, then cast me a nervous glance. When she saw my face, her lips thinned.

"I'll speak with him," my best friend announced mildly, taking a long draught of gin. "Multiple people have vouched for your hard work and efficiency, Juliet. If there's so much work to do that you can't get it all done during the workweek, he should delegate to the other juniors or have a conversation with me about hiring more staff. There's no reason for him to drag you in on the weekends. Or your lunch hour, for that matter."

Thank fuck.

I caught Tris shooting Jules a wink. *Huh.* I couldn't shake the feeling that she mentioned seeing Juliet in Dominic's office on purpose, knowing Grayson would correct the situation if he knew. A strange rush of gratitude rose inside of me.

Jesus. Why did I care?

Grayson's arm wound around his fiancée's waist and pulled her closer to him. She offered him a smile, instantly dissolving his frown.

"Alright boss man," she teased, grabbing him by the tie. "I think you and I should scram. Let all of your employees talk about you for a while. It's good for company moral."

Ella truly did make my friend laugh unlike anyone else. "Excellent suggestion, as always," he chuckled. Then, to us, "I left the tab open for everyone. Have a few more rounds on me."

The last look he gave me could only be described as a warning. "See you tomorrow," he said, raising a sharp brow at the hand I had under the table. "Eleven."

Our original meeting was set for eleven-thirty. He wanted me there early. To talk.

Goddamn it.

Juliet

My two glasses of wine turned into two bottles.

Well, not really, since those bottles were shared among three of us. But still, I had twice what I originally planned to drink.

Luckily, I was prepared to blame it squarely on Graham.

Specifically, Graham flirting with Tris, and, occasionally, Alice—though I suspected he only threw her a few grins and compliments to be polite. The fact that he felt he had to bestow equal attention upon Tris' roommate so she wouldn't be upset—because, in his mind, he was *clearly* the biggest catch *ever*—only underscored his arrogant jackassery.

So why did it make me *insanely* jealous?

Possibly because, the more she drank, the more Tris flirted back. By the time we poured out the final three glasses from our second bottle, I realized: her disdain for Graham was only a front. She was attracted to him, too.

How could she not be? The logical part of my brain pointed out that most women would have the same reaction to man like Graham, with his thick, combed-back hair and quick, feral grins.

Not to mention his tall, lean musculature and the elegant way he wore clothes no other man could possibly pull off.

The emotional piece of me, however, was not so charitable. While Tris and Ali giggled over another of Graham's funny stories, I took a bitter slug of my wine and slid from my chair. "I'll be right back," I mumbled.

A line in the narrow hallway thwarted my plan to pop into the ladies' room and regroup. Luckily, I didn't really need to pee; but I waited anyway, biding my time behind several women until I was next, standing alone in the narrow, unlit stretch that led to the back exit. I eyed the door, considering my options, when a voice came from behind me. *Right* behind me.

"You, too, huh?" Graham rumbled into my ear.

My spine stiffened while my throat went dry, turning my words into a rasp. "Me, too?"

"I saw you looking at the exit," he explained, drifting into my line of sight. "I had the same idea. But I suppose I should be polite and let the others down easy, right?"

I did my best to act cool. "A gentleman would," I sniffed, inspecting my nails. Suddenly I was *pissed* and spoiling for a fight. "Unless you wanted to take Tris home. It seems like she would be… willing."

His hands surprised me as they found my hips, then slowly slid up to the gold chain belting my waist. "Now, now, *bijou*," he murmured, leaning close. "No need to break out your claws. You know there's only one woman here that I want to take home."

His thumbs drew circles on either side of my navel, sending a quiver down my legs. "What are you doing?" I asked. "We agreed no more."

Graham shook his head slowly. "We agreed we wouldn't pretend," he argued. "So don't act like you haven't felt this heat building up for the last two hours." He raised one slashing brow, his midnight eyes glinting. "Unless I'm mistaken?"

The question hung between us, floating in the space between his sculpted mouth and mine. An expensive blend of scotch and his usual spice blurred my already-muddled mind. I was too tipsy to remember to act indifferent, especially when his warmth washed over me and pooled between my legs. My chest rose and fell faster as my breathing picked up.

Graham noticed. His gaze, dark and hot, traced over my cleavage. He loomed closer. "Am I, Jules?" he asked, deceptively soft. "Mistaken?"

I swallowed a whimper, not wanting him to hear. "Even if you aren't," I breathed. "It doesn't matter. We work together."

His lips quirked into a ghost of a smile. His eyes trailed down to my collarbone at the same moment he raised one of his hands to the hollow above my sternum. His feather-light touch traced over the ridge of my clavicle, instantly hardening my nipples. An audible breath stuttered out of me.

"Not anymore," he countered, smiling more at my reaction to him. "After tomorrow morning, our business will be over. Once those contracts are signed, you won't have to see me ever again."

My throat clenched closed, trapping the single word that came to mind when I thought of never seeing him: *No*.

"It's still not a good idea," I contended, though I heard my own reluctance.

His hand at my waist slipped around to brush over the small of my back. "My *bijou*," he hummed, moving ever-closer. "Always so sharp and full of fire. Unyielding. I bet you have a lot of rules for yourself, don't you?"

I hated the patronizing drawl in his voice. "No," I spat, lifting my chin to glare at him. "Only one."

Carajo. I hadn't meant to say that out loud, but it was too late. Damn the wine.

"One rule," he repeated, pinning me with his black eyes. "Do tell."

The dark velvet depths were magnetic. Something in them connected with the fluttering sensation stretched taut in my belly. I felt like I'd been hypnotized. Words fell from my lips without much resistance. "I could only sleep with you once."

That shut him up.

He went still, with one hand flat against my tailbone and the other settled into the curve of my neck. His breath gusted against my lips as he stared right into me, completely immobile.

"Come again?"

I smirked at his unintentional double entendre. "That's my whole point: you *wouldn't* come again."

My laughter broke his trance. He finally moved, grabbing both of my hips and pulling me flush against his body while he frowned down at me.

"Only *once*? Dear God—*why*?"

I lifted one shoulder, going for blasé. "One time. It's my rule."

Graham's fingers tightened, biting into my ass. "So you don't sleep with people more than once unless you're dating them?"

My foggy brain thought back through all of the faces of my former lovers—the ones I recalled, at least—checking to be sure I didn't make a liar of myself before I shook my head. "No. That's my point. I don't *date*, because I never sleep with anyone more than once."

He looked incredulous. "*Never*? Ever?"

"Never ever."

I expected frustration or badgering. Instead, consternation filled his features, making him impossibly more handsome. He cupped one hand around my jaw. "Why not, *bijou*?"

I'd never explained it out loud. Most of the men I slept with knew they stood firmly within one-night-stand territory before things ever got physical. We met on dating apps and in clubs. I only went home with them if they had their own places… and I left as soon as we were done, without so much as exchanging last names. Now, I had to come up with something to say.

Because if I sleep with someone more than once, I might start to like them. Because I never want to belong to anybody. Because I watched what happens when women trust men who don't deserve it. And I have to do better.

"It's easier," I offered simply.

"Easier?" He pressed his forehead into mine while his thumb skirted my lower lip. "How could any man only have you once? That doesn't sound easy; it sounds *impossible*."

His flattery sent a new round of flutters through my middle. I didn't know if it was the wine or his proximity, but I couldn't squelch them. I found myself leaning into his hand, enjoying the way his long, strong fingers held my face.

I loved everything about the way he felt, actually. Especially when he shifted, putting one of his legs between mine and grinding his erection into my right hip. The solid weight started a steady pulse in my sex. It clenched, longing to tighten around his length.

Dios mío.

I was in a *bar* with *coworkers*. Why couldn't I care about getting caught or being kicking out? Why couldn't I care about *anything* aside from *him*?

"This is dangerous," I whispered turning my head to graze his palm with my open mouth. "We're combustible."

Graham eyes followed my lips. "Am I the match or the dynamite?"

I knew from the moment I slapped him in the elevator—his antagonism brought out the worst, most volatile parts of me. All the heat I fought so hard to hide burst out. And I'd been working overtime to bottle it all back up since.

"The match."

"You are dynamite," he agreed, brushing his smiling mouth over my cheek.

His stubble made my breasts tingle and I strained closer, trying to rub myself against his chest. His hand slipped back to the nape of my neck. My resistance wavered. I whispered his name.

"*Graham*."

Before I drew my next breath, his lips sealed over mine.

It wasn't like our scorching moment in office Pod C. This kiss didn't plunder or demand. It was a gift—slow and sensuous. Almost… sweet.

Graham coaxed my mouth open and slid inside, gently cradling the back of my head while our tongues met. The luxurious vapor of scotch filled my senses and I stretched up onto my toes, deepening our connection while he licked into me.

My fingers made short work of his jacket buttons and grabbed handfuls of his silk vest. He pressed closer, humming his approval while caressing up the curve of my hip to cup my breast. Tingles trembled through my chest, wracking me with a shudder. I sank my teeth into his lower lip with a punishing nip.

His tenderness evaporated on the spot. He bit me back, then thrust into my mouth with a possessive plunge. I sucked his tongue, refusing to surrender to his carnal onslaught.

My defiance only made him hotter. He fisted the loose hair at my nape and tugged, capturing me for more rough kisses. I let him hold my head still, but squirmed against his body, purposefully rubbing my side into his erection until the steely prod of his cock settled into the sensitive spot between my hip and my sex, his hardness melding perfectly with my softness.

Graham broke away on a groan, panting. "Fucking hell," he growled softly, pulling back to look into my eyes. "We *are* combustible." He teased me with another stir of his hips. "Just give me one night, *bijou*. Let me show how good it can be."

One *night*? How very like him. Never one to agree to a first offer. He had to push for a little more. Negotiating, even when he didn't realize it.

And, insanely, I didn't *want* to turn him down... though I knew I should. As he framed my face with both hands and swept a stray hair off of my forehead, I realized I wasn't even sure if I *could*.

Obviously, I wanted him. Badly. He'd know I was lying if I said otherwise. And what was the point in denying it, anyway? He was right—after tomorrow, we wouldn't work together anymore.

Besides... I felt like I might go crazy if I didn't have him inside of me.

I tilted my head back, eyeing him with all the starch I could muster while enveloped in his arms. "Fine."

His eyebrows lifted. "Fine?"

I gave a single nod. "Yes. I'll sleep with you. For one night. Not tonight, though. It has to be after tomorrow, when our business is concluded."

Graham's cock twitched against my belly. He ground his jaw. "Tomorrow night, then. You'll come over right after work."

My defiant streak reared to life. "No," I countered, just to oppose him. "Saturday night."

I expected an argument, but instead he kissed me again. Another slow, enticing brush of his lips over mine.

The fight drained out of me all at once. Graham gave a low rumble at my surrender, gently combing both of his hands into my hair. His fingertips massaged my scalp while he nuzzled his forehead into mine.

He issued a command, but his breathless voice turn it into a plea. "Come over at seven."

A hopeless laugh escaped me. "At the rate we go, we'll be done by 7:10."

Graham's heated smile melted my amusement. "Oh, *bijou*," he sighed. "I wouldn't count on it. If I only get you for one night, I plan to take full advantage. Come at seven and I'll order us dinner." He pressed a kiss to my temple before leaning back. "You'll need energy for what I have in mind."

With that, he disengaged. After tossing me one last boyish grin, he stalked to the rear exit and left me panting against a wall all over again.

Chapter Eight

January 27, 2017

Graham

I was ready.

Sometime between walking out of the bar the night before and waking up the next morning, it all clicked inside of me. My days of wavering were over.

I was going to close my first deal. I was going to tell my dad where to shove his company. I was going to make Stryker and myself a *shit load* of money. I was going to make Juliet beg to have me more than once.

And I was ready. To. Go.

I dressed with extra care, selecting a navy suit lined with red pinstripes. It was the outfit the now-infamous pocket square originally went with. The crimson coordinated with a matching vest and tie over a white shirt. I knew I'd have to get rid of the damn handkerchief soon—after wearing it for Juliet all week, I wouldn't want to use it anymore if I couldn't see her again—and wanted to give it one last go-around.

I strode into Everett Alexander thirty minutes late and did not report to my father's office for our usual morning pow-wow. When he sent for me around ten A.M., I sat at my desk another fifteen minutes, weighing all of my options.

Should I tell him about G&C at the office? That might cause a scene; with the way assistants and clients gossiped in this town, word could be all over the island by lunch. If I had him come to my place, I wouldn't be able to leave.

I decided to ask him to meet me for dinner Sunday evening. In an upscale restaurant, he'd be less likely to totally lose his shit. I could walk out if I needed to. And, by then, I'd have memories of my night with Juliet to help me forget just how horrible the whole ordeal was.

I caught myself thinking that way all morning. Who cared if I couldn't hail a cab, lost my wallet, broke my phone, or spilled my coffee? It didn't matter if I somehow had the shittiest day of my life—because, tomorrow, I would have *her*.

With all my careful planning, I thought I'd prepared for most possible outcomes. But I did not anticipate my dad being pissed off before I even told him.

"Graham!" he shouted when he heard me outside of his office.

I'd stopped to exchange pleasantries with his assistant—she was yet another twenty-two-year-old blonde who barely knew her own name, let alone a single goddamn speck about finance. From experience, I knew that if she wasn't *already* sleeping with my father, she would be soon. Then we would pay her some sort of settlement, she'd sign a non-disclosure agreement, and, three months down the road, a new blonde would appear in her place.

It suddenly struck me how utterly *fucked* that was.

Grayson would never sleep with any of the women who worked for his company. Even before he found Ella, I never heard him so much as consider it.

I realized I wouldn't, either. Not only was it just plain *stupid*, but the power dynamics of a fifty-year-old executive boning his twenty-year-old assistant were dangerously out of balance. Only a sleaze like dear old dad would get off on such a thing… over and over again.

Bristling with my own indignation, I blew into his office and threw myself down into my usual chair. "You bellowed?"

"You were late," he barked, glaring over the expanse of his antique desk.

I couldn't help but look at the wood carvings for the millionth time. Why didn't I ever notice how garish they were? Why didn't I see all of the pomp and fluff for what it really was—a way for Dad to cope to his own inadequacies, always at the expense of others.

Doesn't matter, my brain pinged. *You'll have Juliet tomorrow.*

"I overslept."

The lie rolled out so smoothly, I realized I no longer felt even a twinge of guilt for deceiving him. I didn't care what he thought of me. I didn't *want* his approval. Garnering it suddenly seemed like a mistake, almost. A great way to end up just like him.

Nauseated by the thought, I swallowed a mouthful of bile and leveled gazes with him, wishing we didn't look so damn similar. Wishing, perversely, that Christian could look more like our father than I did.

Like the coward he was, Dad dropped his stare before I did. "I need those account ledgers back," he snapped at the desktop. "You've had them too long."

Again with the damn ledgers.

Why did he *care*? They were old books, out of use for years. Just busy work…

I thought back to the hours I spent poring over the accounts, trying to understand what should have been simple math. None of it added up. At the time I blamed myself and my inconvenient obsession with Juliet. Now, I wondered…

"Why do you need them back so badly?" I kept looking directly at him, waiting for him to meet my eyes again. "They're just archived accounts, right?"

The old man considered me for a long moment, taking my measure before once more turning his attention to the miscellaneous papers strewn before him. "It's not about me *needing* them, Graham," he muttered. "It's about you meeting deadlines. How can I give you real work to do if you can't even complete simple data entry in a timely fashion?"

A few weeks ago, his question would have enraged me. I'd spent three fucking years doing account reviews, sitting in on meetings, going to bullshit lunches where I couldn't speak unless I was spoken to, like an errant child.

He knew I could do the work. He knew I ordinarily turned every assignment in well before his bullshit deadlines. He just wanted another excuse to keep me out of any real business.

It wasn't the first time.

But it would be the last.

I smiled as I replied, "Excellent point. I'll get them back to you before the end of the weekend. Speaking of which; I was thinking we could grab dinner Sunday night. On me. Maybe Hillstone?" His favorite place to eat and pick up women twenty years younger than him.

Startled by my invitation, Dad balked slightly before gaping at me. "Uh… sure."

I clapped once. "Great. I'll meet you there at five. But right now, I've got to run out. Meeting Grayson for lunch in Tribeca. I'll be back before one."

He nodded as if he had some sort of authority over my plans. I let him think he'd dismissed me and stood up, eager to get on with my day. Eager to get uptown to Juliet.

The meeting, I corrected internally, making for the door. *Eager to get to the meeting.*

Beth waited for me outside the bank of elevators on the fiftieth floor. She stood with her hands together, wringing them in a very un-Beth-like show of nerves.

"Good morning, Beth." I flashed a roguish grin, hoping to earn one of her scolding glowers.

"Mr. Everett," she sighed, her lips thinning. "I'm afraid there's a situation and Mr. Stryker is indisposed. He said you should wait in the conference room."

"Situation?"

My mind whirled back to the last time I saw him, leaving the bar with Ella. He clearly wanted to speak to me in private about my relationship with Juliet. I planned to level with him… sort of.

I would admit that I intended to see her in a personal capacity at some point in the future, when we no longer worked together. I decided I would *not* mention our two make-out sessions, or the fact that "in the future" referred to a point only *thirty-six hours* into said future….

Stryker didn't fuck around where his personnel were concerned. If he cancelled an appointment to discuss his misgivings with me, something bad happened. My thoughts leapt to the worst possible scenario for my best friend.

"Is Ella alright?" I demanded. "Grayson told me he increased her security recently."

Beth paled. "Miss Callahan is… fine," she told me, sounding uncertain. "There was an… incident last night. He's been meeting with police and his security team for most of the morning."

Last night? I watched them leave together. Which could only mean something happened when they got home…

"Can I help?"

I meant to refine the notion before it popped out, but I felt too anxious to fake indifference. Beth's grim expression softened. "No, Mr. Everett," she said quietly. "I suspect he'll be in quite the mood for your meeting, though. Would you like to reschedule, perhaps?"

And miss my chance to see— I edited myself mid-thought. *And miss the chance to seal my deal?*

"No," I determined. "I'll wait."

She stepped aside with a flourish, urging me on. I peered into the executive pod on my way to the conference room, surprised to find Ella sitting at Beth's desk with the most gorgeous woman in existence kneeling at her side.

Jules.

Ella was crying, her small round face scrunched and half-covered by the tissue in her hand. Juliet ran her palm over Ella's arm in long, reassuring pats. Before I knew what I was about, I strode into the pod and crouched down beside Juliet.

"El," I said, frowning at her. "What the fuck?"

Juliet elbowed me, chiding, "Graham. God."

I only got to glance at her beautiful profile for a second before the door to Grayson's office fell open. A veritable army of security people in black suits filed out, including Juliet's cousin, Marco, who saluted us and cast Ella a sympathetic look before rounding up his team and ushering them to the service elevator.

Grayson stood on the threshold, his expression dazed but grave. Ella leapt up and ran to her fiancé. He caught her in his arms, pulling her into an embrace far too intimate for the office. Over her head, his eyes met mine. The veil dropped for just a second—barely long enough for me to catch the sheer panic he projected—before he turned his face to speak into Ella's ear.

At whatever he said, she shook her head against his chest and clutched herself closer to him. Gripping her back with equal force, Grayson lifted his gaze back to mine. "Ella is going to join us for the meeting. Is that okay?"

"Of course." Juliet and I said the words at the same time, reminding me of her presence just behind my line of sight. At the sound of her voice, I turned to her automatically.

My knees almost buckled.

Fuck me.

In a black leather-like pencil skirt and a red blazer trimmed in the same supple material, she looked wickedly sexy. She'd styled her hair in another low bun, showing off her gorgeous facial features. A single ruby stone winked from the hollow of her throat, drawing my eyes to her breasts. They swelled under the simple black shell beneath her cropped jacket, a perfect counterpoint to the decadent curve of her ass. My throat went dry when I noticed the red heels on her feet.

I want those on and nothing else.

Juliet read my thoughts. Her golden gaze flashed to her feet and then narrowed ever-so-slightly at me, as if to say, *"How could you be thinking about* that *at a time like* this?"

I'll admit, it wasn't one of my finer moments. Silently clearing my throat, I swallowed the rising tide of lust and motioned for the conference room. "Shall we?"

Our deal went through without a hitch.

Stryker was, understandably, subdued. He held Ella's hand on the conference table as Juliet and I took turns running through the details in her contract. He nodded along and picked up his pen without hesitation, signing his money away with an inky slash.

He shook my hand, managing a slight smile. "There you go, you greedy bastard."

I laughed while he reached for Juliet's hand as well. "Miss Rivera," he said, "This was excellent work. I will be relying on you for all such future business, if you're amenable."

Juliet glowed at his praise.

I loved it.

"Yes, sir," she agreed. "In fact, I believe Tris has your townhome closing contracts for you today as well. I finished a final review of them this morning and was just coming to let Beth know when I ran into Ella."

Grayson's fiancée sniffled while she smirked. "It's sweet of you not to mention that I was dramatically wailing on Beth's shoulder at the time."

I offered Ella an answering grin, but Grayson's face shuttered. He rubbed his free hand over his neck as he turned back to Jules. "Do you think the closing can wait? Ellie and I want to get out of here a little early today."

Juliet seemed taken aback that he would ask her for her opinion. She bit her lush lower lip. "I'll be honest: no. The sellers were still trying to haggle with Tris on our cab ride to the bar last night. If they have the weekend to change their terms, I think it's likely the sale will fall through."

Grayson sighed, but Ella smiled. "Thank you for being honest," she told her. "I'll be fine to do the closing. Want to come with me to grab Tris?"

Juliet nodded right away. "Absolutely."

She gathered her files and pivoted for the door, casting me one last look before sauntering off. I watched her go, practically drooling.

Goddamn.

Only thirty-one more hours.

Grayson blew out another audible breath, regaining my focus. For a moment, I wondered if he would grill me about Jules, the way he originally intended to. I quickly realized she and I were the last things on his mind, though. Shadows darkened his gaze as he watched his fiancée retreat through the glass doors.

As soon as we were alone, I took the chair next to his. "So, what the hell happened?"

He deflated before my eyes, sinking down into his seat and scrubbing his face with both hands. "Someone broke into my place."

"While you were out with us last night?"

He dropped his hands and stared at me for long, tense beat. "No," he finally muttered. "Before."

My mind reeled. "But how do you know when they came in?" Stryker's apartment building was a company holding. It had all the same modern amenities and safety features as their offices. "The cameras?"

Just then, Grayson didn't resemble the CEO he'd grown into. The look on his face reminded me of a very shitty day, years before, when we were still in school. The day he told me the love of his life had disappeared, leaving him without a trace. The day he thought he'd lost Ella forever.

"Was it…?"

I acted like I didn't want to mention Grayson's son-of-a-bitch cousin out loud for his sake. The truth was, I didn't like to even *think* the motherfucker's name. I still struggled with the fact that a guy I once considered a friend had assaulted countless women. Including our sweet, lovely Ella.

Some of Grayson's strength returned as rage filled his eyes. "We don't know who it was, but it might have been him. He wasn't supposed to make bail… then, we found out this week that some anonymous source scraped it together for him. That's why Marco and I hired more people to shadow Ella when she goes out alone. He tried to convince me to have someone in the apartment with us at all times, too, but I never thought I would need anyone with her while *I* was with her. And, you know, I wanted our privacy…" He rubbed his palm over the back of his neck. "Stupid. I pay him to advise me. I should be listening."

Grayson had a tendency to be too hard on himself. I mumbled, "Anyone would want privacy. You guys are engaged, for Christ's sakes. And you couldn't have known what would happen. What did the security cameras catch?"

He ground his jaw, seething. "We didn't see anything unusual on any of the cameras. Nothing was broken or stolen; and the electronic locks record when they're unlocked and which key card unlocks them. The only people who came into the apartment after I left it yesterday were my cleaning people.

"They come every Thursday, two of them. They didn't see anything out of the ordinary but they did open the sliding door for a few minutes to wipe down the outside of it. One of them told Marco they left it ajar for a bit to air out the room after mopping the floors. Marco says it's feasible someone could have entered a different apartment, used the fire escape to climb up to the balcony below mine and crawled up to my platform, then inside, while the sliding door was unlocked."

What the fuck kind of psycho… "Holy shit."

"Yeah." He swallowed. "I know."

But I knew *Ella*. She'd been through hell. It made her tougher than she looked. If she broke down sobbing on Grayson's secretary's shoulder, something else happened. Something traumatic enough to trigger her... And if someone snuck in while they weren't home…

"They were still in the apartment when you came back?"

I thought Grayson's teeth might be pulverized by the time he finished telling me the story. "Yes," he gritted. "We came home and everything seemed normal. But then we heard running footsteps and the front door slammed. Our system says it unlocked from the inside at 10:09. Whoever it was must have been hiding in my closet, where the penthouse floor's controls are, because they disconnected all of the cameras on my entire floor and my elevator before they left."

I tried to picture the scene. One more question came to mind. "But if you were home when they left and they were coming out of your bedroom, why didn't either of you see them?"

His eyes shifted. "They didn't leave until we were… in bed."

Oh, God. "Like in-bed-going-to-sleep or in-bed…" I somersaulted my hands over each other.

Grayson's expression turned murderous. "The second one."

"Jesus." The curse hissed out of me. "They *watched*?"

The whole thing sounded sick and twisted enough. But, to my horror, Grayson went on. "They were *recording*, we think. Ella… she isn't sure but she thought she saw a red light blinking in the closet. She figured it was something I had charging in there that she just never noticed before. She didn't think about it too hard because we were… busy. And we've been moving things around all week, packing boxes for the move and shit. She assumed some electronics got rearranged. Well, I don't charge anything in my closet. Which means, if she's right…"

Sex tape.

That explained the sobbing.

My blood ran cold. "But how could she see into the closet while you were…?" I asked, grasping at straws, determined not to believe that my best friends could be so violated, once again, by Daniel. *That scum-sucking piece of shit.*

Grayson scratched at the back of his neck again. His cheeks darkened slightly. "She had a, um, decent view."

My mind had no trouble filling in the blanks. *She was on top.* I must have made a sour face because Stryker rolled his eyes at me. "Jesus, you don't have to *picture* it, shithead."

"Ugh," I moaned. "I'm trying not to. Christ."

A humorless smirk pulled at his features. "Well, if someone really did record us, people won't have to picture it."

Recalling Ella's scrunched-up, tearstained face, I sobered immediately. "I'm really sorry, man."

Grayson sighed again. "Thanks." He checked his watch and smoothed out his expression. "Now get out of here and go make us both some money, *pinchao*."

I groaned as I rose to my feet, scowling. "Not you, too."

He gave his first genuine smile of the morning. "I like it. I can't believe I didn't think of it first."

I brushed off my sleeves, busying myself with a loose cufflink instead of looking back at him. "I've Googled it, but I think it's slang of some sort. Or I'm spelling it wrong." I sniffed. "Will you at least tell me what it *means*?"

He widened his grin, pleased by my cluelessness. "You know, I don't think I will."

I turned to go, grumbling, "Whatever. I'm going to go make your trades. But I'll text you if I see your hairy ass on Pornhub."

He shot me one last glare and I snorted. "Too soon?"

"Too soon."

Juliet

Dread chilled my gut while I shuffled against the wind.

After a horrible morning fighting off Dominic's repeated suggestions that we work the weekend together, I spent the better part of an hour trying to comfort Ella.

I still didn't know the details but clearly something very upsetting happened. I'd never seen Mr. Stryker so openly distressed. And Graham… he snapped into friend-mode immediately, softening in a way I'd only caught a brief glimpse of once before, after Tuesday's lobby incident.

Watching Graham worry over Ella worried me. Because I liked it.

Every time I caught little glimpses of the benevolence he hid so ruthlessly, it got harder to convince myself I could sleep with him one time and never see him again.

Dios.

I couldn't… *like* him…? That would be silly.

…right?

A flurry of memories from the past week blew through my brain. Graham crouched at Ella's side; picking non-existent lint off of his arm anytime he admitted he was wrong; taking last week's meeting by storm with his slow-burning charisma and quick confidence. The way he reached for me when he heard me crying. The feral grin that melted my mind. His stupid velvet slippers.

Soon I would know even more about him. After our brief, public encounter during the contract signing, he sent a single text message. Two lines. Liquid heat pooled in my center each time I recalled them.

7pm tomorrow, The Ludlow, unit 20A.

I'll be waiting, bijou.

That nickname. When did I start feeling buzzed every time he said it? It was annoying just days earlier… wasn't it?

Thinking about Graham was a welcome diversion from the ordeal ahead of me. The only other text I received that morning was a barely-coherent request from an unsaved number. My father, the unknown contact claimed, messaging me to demand I meet him for lunch at some hotdog stand outside the MetLife Building. Never mind that it was twenty degrees outside.

But sure enough, there he was, huddled into a threadbare brown coat. He bounced on the balls of his feet as I approached, clearly freezing.

"*Mija,*" he called over the wind. "You keep your *papi* waiting so long?"

I hated to think of him as anything even close to related to me. "I have to stay at work until noon," I muttered, then glanced at the hotdog cart beside him. "I'm assuming you waited for me so I would pay?"

Julio puffed his chest out indignantly. "I can pay for two hotdogs, *mija.* I only thought you would *want* to pay now that you're working."

His claim alluded to an old fight between us. He wanted me to go to work straight out of high school and often remarked that I "freeloaded" off of his mother by living with her while I attended college and law school. Of course, now that I paid her rent and all of her other expenses, he felt he should be entitled to a slice of my income as well.

Rolling my eyes, I reached for the twenty stashed in the pocket of Abuelita's black trench coat. I held up two fingers, peeved beyond words, and handed the money to the vendor. He wordlessly handed back my change and two dogs.

I ducked into the covered archway at the front of the MetLife building, seeking a bench and some refuge from the relentless cold. My father followed, shambling gracelessly behind me. I handed him his food and dropped to sit.

"I'm here," I said flatly, busying myself with a bite of my hotdog. "What do you want?"

I recognized the wounded expression on his face before he started speaking and cut him off. "Don't bother with the guilt-trip, Papi. I'm not giving you any money. I can't believe you would even *ask* me to pay for your *girlfriend's* expenses, considering you're still *married to my mother*."

You gigantic piece of mierda.

A deep frown creased his weathered face. "We are still family, *mija*. Your mother would want you to help your baby brother."

The very mention of my father's love child sickened me. I lowered my half-eaten hotdog and gaped at him. It blew my mind that he had the audacity to use my mother—his *wife*—against me in an argument about his *side piece*.

But then, when I really thought about it, I realized he was correct.

Mami *would* tell me to give him the money. She would be *worried* about him.

Because, even after years of outright abandonment, she still loved him. This pathetic, selfish, weak man owned her heart. She routinely asked after his well-being, and often clammed up when

I mentioned my plans to procure a divorce for her as soon as I got her onto American soil. If she knew he carelessly knocked up his latest girlfriend, it would crush her.

"You think I'm going to mention any of this to Mami?" I hissed. "Hasn't she suffered enough?"

Julio scoffed, sending a stale burst of rum-scented breath toward me. "Your *mami* does not suffer because of me. She had her men and now I have my women."

A burst of fury straightened my spine. "You *know* she had no choice," I spat at him. "*Because* of you. She never would have..." I still had trouble saying it out loud. Even thinking about it, hurt. "...done those things, if you hadn't left her to fend for herself with no other options."

My father ate his hotdog with an unbothered air. "You would like Lucia," he told me, as if we hadn't discussed my mother at all. "She's not much older than you. You two could be friends."

His cavalier pronouncement hit me like a physical blow. To my horror, I felt tears swell in the back of my throat.

No, I roared at myself. *No more tears for this man*. I vowed, then and there, that he would never get another single thing from me. Not a penny. Not a look. Not one single drop of my grief.

I stood, feeling brittle and cold as an icicle as I stared down at him. "I would never be friends with a woman who could sleep with another woman's husband. I am leaving now. Do not call me or text me again. Do not contact Abuelita. And enjoy your lunch. Because it's the very last thing I will ever give you."

I dropped my food in the nearest trash can and strode off blindly, not caring that I would have to go around the whole block to correct my course. I refused to let him see me backtrack.

Fuming, chilled down to my very soul, I had one inconvenient thought I couldn't shake.

At least I'll be with Graham tomorrow.

Chapter Nine

January 28, 2017

Juliet

I'd learned long ago to never reference my dates in front of Abuelita. The mention of a viable man either sent her into a delirious tizzy of matrimonial excitement or down a Catholic Guilt spiral. Since I knew I would possibly spend the whole night at Graham's, I made up a story about sleeping at my new friend, Tris's, place after a night out.

I hated lying to her but it was the only way to explain my outfit and my small overnight bag without incurring her wrath. If I wasn't careful, she'd tuck a Rosary into my coat pocket and cluck about how God was "always watching" me.

Standing before my smudged mirror, I debated changing my clothes for the eighth time. Choosing an outfit for a naked night in was harder than I expected. Our little pre-arranged hookup wasn't really a date, so I didn't want to overdress... But Graham was always coiffed to perfection... and I couldn't show up in sweats.

It wasn't like me to be nervous before meeting a guy—why be nervous when I'd never see them again?—and I didn't like it.

In the end, I forced myself to accept dark-wash skinny jeans and a creamy top as my final selection. The jeans were flattering, at least; and the top's low V-neck gave a decent glimpse of the breasts he seemed to like so much. On a last minute impulse, I chucked my black ankle booties in favor of the red heels I caught him staring at the day before.

There, I thought, slipping them on. *I'll make him sweat a bit.*

Pausing in my door, I watched for a moment while Abuelita stood in her usual spot at her stove, stirring. The image gripped me, sending a bittersweet mix of pride and shame through my middle. I worried I left her alone too much. But I also knew she was too proud to allow herself to feel lonely.

I kissed her cheek while I passed. "*Buenas noches*, Abuelita."

She reached back to pat my cheek absentmindedly. "*Ti amo, muñeca.*"

The gold glitter coat felt too flashy, but I had to keep up my pretense of hitting the clubs, so I took it anyway. I didn't encounter many people, thankfully. At six-thirty on a frigid Saturday, the F train was virtually deserted. I rode it all the way over to Manhattan, through my usual Midtown stop, down the center of the island, then over to the Lower East Side.

After a short jaunt from the Second Street station, I found myself standing in front of The Ludlow. Its impressive façade rose up higher than most around it. The hundreds of shining windows were striking, even in the dimness of dusk.

Of course the pinchao *lives here*, I groused internally, frowning at the doorman who opened the door for me. I took in the modern teak lobby and sighed. There were no buttons to press, so I had to cross the terrazzo floor to the concierge desk. As I gave my name and waited for approval to enter the elevators, I wondered how many other women the people at the front desk buzzed up for Graham. It was possible I wasn't even the first girl that week... or that week*end*.

The thought squared my shoulders.

You don't care, I coached myself. *Even if there was someone else here last night... By the time you're done with him, he won't even remember her.*

I did my best to carry that confidence all the way to his door and gave it three sharp raps. It swung open, revealing a gorgeous half-dressed Graham who silently waved me in while holding his phone to his ear.

"Right," he said to whoever was on the call. "I understand that."

His entryway consisted of a narrow strip of hall, its walls covered in small pieces of modern art. I lingered while he closed the door, inhaling the spicy smell of his cologne and the unique woody musk of his apartment.

My eyes roamed over his clothes, taking note of his open vest and unbuttoned collar. The elegant light grey pants had a fine sheen to them. The luster coordinated with the purple-and-silver-silk paisleys on his vest. Clearly, he started undressing and his phone call interrupted him.

He frowned as he listened, but his eyes fell on mine. A spark ignited in their midnight depths, blazing hotter as he trailed his gaze down my body. When he saw my shoes, his jaw hardened. "Uh-huh," he gritted into his phone.

Spurred on by his reaction, I unceremoniously dropped my coat, turned on my red heel, and made a big show of sauntering down the hallway. On the threshold of the main room, though, I almost tripped over my feet.

Ay Dios mío.

The hall emptied out into a spacious great room with hardwood floors and high, white walls. To my left, a kitchen of snowy granite stone and steel cabinets gleamed under recessed lighting. Beyond the island and barstools, an attractive walnut dining table stood further to the left, covered in papers and a glowing MacBook, with a gold sputnik chandelier hanging overhead.

But all of that was nothing compared to the living room right across me. A large rug of colorful lines complemented an asymmetrically curved sofa as red as my shoes. White leather Eames loungers sat perpendicular to the couch, standing like sentries under the floor-to-ceiling window at the back of the room. Exposed brick encroached on the smooth white walls, along with three stunning abstracts in brilliant hues.

It was *gorgeous*. I found myself clutching my hand to my heart. "Oh my…"

Behind me, Graham made a noncommittal sound. Then he said, "Possibly. I have a few other portfolios I'm considering. Let me get back to you. I have something time-sensitive in front of me right now."

Me. I tossed him a coy look over my shoulder. "Am I time-sensitive?" I mouthed.

His eyes roved over my face, down to my cleavage. A black stare speared me. "Yes."

I didn't know if he meant to answer me or whoever he was on with. Either way, he promptly hung up, sliding the phone into his back pocket and hooking an iron arm around my waist in one smooth motion.

"Yes," he said again.

And then I was against the wall.

Graham

Glorious.

It was the only word to describe finally having Juliet all to myself.

It was the only word for how delectable she looked in her soft white blouse.

It was certainly the one term allowable for the visible swells of her breasts, on full display all for me.

God. Until she was back in my arms, I didn't realize how much I *wanted* her. Longed for her, really. I probably would have been disgusted if I had the capacity to feel anything aside from giddy exhilaration.

Through my shirtsleeves, without a suit jacket, I felt her warmth in a whole new way. I had her backed into the wall before I knew what I was doing, pinning her there with my leg between hers and my arm locked around her torso.

It only took a second for her to respond, tilting her head to get at me the way she wanted. Her hands curled into my hair, grasping at the strands brushing my open collar and tugging until I growled into her mouth.

I'd been hard since I woke up that morning—the entire day was an exercise in restraint as I forced myself to wait for her instead of relieving myself. The business lunch and afternoon phone calls I scheduled to keep myself busy only barely helped. Now, my erection resurged, pressing into her belly while she clawed at the back of my neck and rubbed herself over my thigh.

The feel of her heat branding me through my pant-leg snapped me back to reality. I broke our kiss. "Not so fast, Miss Rivera," I scolded quietly, pulling back. "If I only get one night you better damn well believe I'll make the most of it."

With kiss-swollen lips and heavy-lidded gold eyes, Juliet still managed to glower at me. "You're the one who's already half undressed."

Right, as always.

I'd returned from a late lunch at Tavern on the Green with one of my old Columbia contacts and only got partway through changing out of my suit before phone calls started rolling in.

An hour dicking around with another young executive, Jason McAllister, about possibly transferring his portfolio to G&C had me unbuttoning my collar, rolling up my sleeves, and kicking my shoes off while he grilled me. Eventually, I employed a little reverse psychology by implying that I may not be able to help him out after all before quickly hanging up. I expected he'd call me back Monday morning to make a deal.

And even if he didn't, so what?

Juliet was here.

Finally.

Her fingers traced the row of buttons arrowing down my abdomen, then paused when she reached my waistband. Her eyes shimmered.

"And, besides," she hummed, reaching lower. "You're not the boss of me."

This woman might kill me. She challenged, on every level, my innate masculine instinct to dominate. And I'd never been harder.

Yet my prick swelled even more when I caught another glimpse of her red heels. "I cannot believe you wore those," I muttered, shaking my head. "Bitch."

I expected her to take offense. Maybe slap me again. Instead, she tipped her beautiful face back and gave an equally exquisite laugh.

God, how I loved that sound. Without thought, I tightened my arms around her. And she did the same to me. I set my jaw on the crown of her head and let her turn her face into my throat.

"Are we… hugging?" she whispered, catching her breath.

I didn't want to think about it. Or anything else that might happen between us as the night went on. Juliet did things to me that I didn't fully understand. I liked it too much to try to figure it out. At least, for the time being, while I still had her. Maybe I'd un-riddle the whole situation after she left. Then, I could move on.

"Shh," I replied, not loosening my hold. "Don't speak."

Her surprised breath tickled the side of my neck as she pressed herself closer. The soft peaks and valleys of her body fit into the harder planes of mine. I felt her relax bit by bit and closed my eyes, allowing myself one precious minute to soak in the mutual understanding that passed between us in the rare moments when neither of us spoke.

I would have been content to hold her longer, but she sighed and leaned back. Her gaze seemed cautious. I instantly missed her laughter.

"Alright," I mumbled, dropping my hold on her. "I believe I promised you dinner. So, what will it be?"

She took my measure, wary as ever. "I get to choose?"

Why *did* I want her to pick? I only knew that I wanted to hear her answer. Just like I did at the bar when she didn't get to select her own wine.

"I chose lunch on Tuesday."

There. That sounded… diplomatic. Equitable, at least. I suspected such an explanation would appeal to her practical nature and I was correct.

She gave a quick nod and replied brusquely. "Fine. I'll choose."

Juliet pouted while she considered her options, casting her tawny eyes up to the ceiling as if calling upon divine inspiration. I tried not to smile down at her. For the first time since I met her, she just looked… adorable. Unguarded and indecisive.

"Thai food," she announced.

I loved Thai food. When I told her that, she smirked. "Damn. I almost said Indian."

Then it was my turn to laugh. "Oh *bijou*. Always spoiling for a fight. You should save that energy for later. Come on. I have wine in the kitchen."

She followed me into the main room, the clack of her heels as much of a torment as the jasmine perfume now clinging to my shirt. *Patience*, I reminded myself.

"What kind of wine do you like?"

She slid onto one of my barstools, crossed her curvy legs, and regarded me coyly across the expanse of the island. "What do you have?"

"Everything."

It was true. I tried not to dwell on *why* I added twelve different types of wine to my weekly grocery order the day before. It's not like I wouldn't drink it all myself, if I had to. So, really, it was for *me*, not her…

"Pinot noir," she countered. "Please."

Fuck. I liked that word on her lips. I wanted it again. All night. And—damn her—I wanted pinot noir, too.

I cleared my throat. "Alright."

Reaching for the rack of wine glasses and unused cookware over my island, I pointed my chin across the room to the record table under my TV. "Pick an album, if you want. They're all in the table."

Part of me expected an argument, but she didn't seem *quite* as combative as usual. Maybe because I already had her where I wanted her, and she knew it. After all, we agreed that pretenses were pointless. And Juliet was pragmatic.

So, she wandered over to the music, offering me another mouthwatering view of the way her jeans hugged her thick, tight ass. I paused halfway through uncorking the wine to stare before I remembered myself.

Patience.

By the time I poured wine into the glasses, I heard the strains of a familiar Sylvan Esso song. Another one of my favorites. I hated how much I liked it when our tastes aligned. And the alarming *frequency* with which they aligned…

When she returned, she offered me a small smile. "So you like records instead of Spotify?"

"Not particularly." I shrugged, handing her a glass. "I'm just pretentious."

That earned me another lusty laugh. "I knew that, *pinchao*," she returned, eyes sparkling with mischief. "Your suits were a dead giveaway. And now all of *this*." She gestured around. Her expression took on a teasing gleam while she eyed the pot rack overhead. "*Dios mío*, do you even *cook*?"

I almost lied. But I wanted another laugh. "Nope."

Her giggle didn't disappoint. "Oh boy." She shook her head. "Shameful. Those pots and pans are works of art."

"At least you like them," I said. "You hate my suits."

Juliet took a thoughtful sip of her wine, raking her gaze down my body. "I like that one, actually. Purple is my favorite color."

Purple. Huh. "You never wear it," I pointed out.

Juliet's wry smile sent a bolt of unfamiliar emotion into my gullet. "I look horrible in it," she claimed. "Or so Abuelita says. And she makes all of my clothes, so."

Well, that explained why they fit her like second skin. Still, I couldn't help but look as impressed as I felt. "She *makes* clothes?"

"Yep."

I could tell she expected me to balk. Was I really that much of an asshole? I didn't care what her grandmother did for a living. After meeting her father, I only had the utmost respect for the woman who raised Juliet in his stead. Clearly, she passed on an admirable work ethic.

I offered her my most charming smile, hoping to disarm her again. "So she's to blame for me getting slapped in the elevator last week?"

Juliet thin black brows curved. "She would have slapped you herself if she heard your filthy mouth."

I tried to stifle a smug smile and failed. "It has its moments."

I watched a thrill ripple through her, but she tried not to let it show. Stubborn, beautiful woman. I admired her and lusted after her equally—and both emotions only got stronger each day.

Had it really only been a week? It felt like I'd always known her. Like I couldn't remember what the fuck I was doing before I saw her standing there, in the black chasm of Grayson's lobby, wearing her evil red dress.

She lifted her chin in that maddening way of hers. "*Pinchao*, put your filthy mouth to good use and order our food."

Once I placed our order, I leaned my hip back into the island and refilled our wine glasses. "So," I said, eyeing her over the rim, "Tell me all of it."

She took a long sip, then licked her lips. Torturing me. "All of what?"

"You. Your life story." Keeping my eyes fixed on hers turned my request into a challenge. I knew she wouldn't back down if I dared her.

Juliet tossed her shiny curtain of dark hair back and narrowed her eyes at me. "I told you. I moved here when I was six."

I rotated my hands over each other, prompting. "And...?"

Her golden gaze flashed. "And... I came with my dad. We moved to Queens because that's where his sister and his mother—my *abuela*—moved before I was born. He took a job at a bodega and we got an apartment a few blocks from Abuelita's because she used to watch me at the tailor shop under her place after school. I sat and did homework while she worked. It always took me a few hours because—" She suddenly cut herself off, then made a small coughing noise before finishing, "Because I had to learn English as I went."

I felt a stab of self-loathing for the time I made fun of her reading speed. "No one worked with you at school?"

A bitter laugh tore from her. "Never been to a public school, huh, *pinchao*? They can't even teach the *American* kids to read, in some cases. The teachers pushed me through kindergarten and first grade even though I couldn't speak the language. They thought I was smart enough to catch up."

My mind automatically pictured a pint-sized child-version of Jules. She was probably fierce, even then; but it had to be scary for a kid to get dumped into a new school in a new country where no one understood her.

I asked the first dumb question that came to mind. "How did you make friends?"

It was not the correct thing to say. She kept her head high, but the light in her eyes dimmed. "I didn't."

A painful twinge pinched my guts. I grimaced as I drank more wine, deciding to change tacks. "What about your mom? She didn't want to come?"

Her expression only got worse. *Hell.*

"She wanted to," Jules mumbled, looking down at the counter as she fingered the granite. "It's expensive to immigrate legally. They could only afford one adult and me. My father had family here, so it was easier for him to get the Green Card. He brought me with plans to get a job, work for a year, and then pay my mom's way over. Once we got here, though, he… changed his mind."

Something cold gripped me. I froze with my drink halfway to my mouth. "Changed his mind?"

"Yes." Golden eyes snapped back to mine. "He put my mom off when he started to meet new women. At first I didn't understand who they were… but then, one morning, I saw him with one in our apartment and it was… *obvious.* He started taking me to Abuelita's after that. Eventually, he just didn't come back for a week… then a month. Once, he disappeared for almost three months before he turned back up, drunk like he was when you met him, demanding I leave with him. Abuelita chased him out of her place with an umbrella and told him if he ever tried to take me from her again, she would shove it up his ass and open it."

I didn't know if I was closer to laughing or snapping my wine glass in half. "I knew I should have punched that fucking swine when I had the chance." I realized I'd spoken out loud and pinched the bridge of my nose. "Jesus, sorry."

"Don't be," she replied, shrugging. "He is a pig. What kind of man would abandon his wife like that? All she ever did was love him and trust him."

I hated to ask, but I had to know, "So what happened with them? Did she get a divorce and decide to stay in Colombia?"

Her wide, perfect mouth folded into a tight line. "No. When my father stopped calling her and stopped sending her money... She had to find another way to support herself. In Colombia, back then, the drug trade was horrible and she needed protection, too. She had to do some things... and got a police record. That makes it hard for her to get a Green Card on her own, even if we have the money. Which we will, as soon as I can save it up."

Holy shit.

I spent my life sulking because my father wouldn't promote me while this woman put herself through law school to get a good job and *pay for her mother's immigration*?

I found myself looking around my apartment. The cookware I didn't use. The surround sound system I never bothered to read the instructions for. Cashmere pillows. How much money did I spent on stupid shit? Enough for a hundred Green Cards, surely.

My next thought escaped uncensored. "Can I help?"

Juliet inclined her head, tracing my face with her topaz gaze. "No, Graham," she murmured, quieter than ever. "I'm not your problem. And even if I was, the money isn't the issue anymore. Mr. Stryker pays me well."

I slugged back the rest of my wine, agitated by my own uselessness. "Then what's the issue?"

Jules sighed. "Her record. I don't know if you read the papers, *pinchao*, but this country of yours has some seriously outrageous immigration policies. It's almost impossible for anyone to get in if they have a criminal history."

What had always sounded like a sensible rule now seemed heinously incomprehensive. How could they not look at these situations on a case-by-case basis? I had a hard time imagining Juliet's mother as a violent criminal.

"But she didn't hurt anyone, right?" I pushed both hands through my hair, thinking. "Maybe if we ask Grayson. He knows some senators. Or I'm sure I could figure out a way to get a meeting with the mayor, maybe even the governor. I was going to tell my father about the business thing tomorrow but that can wait a few weeks so I can work some of his contacts—"

The cool brush of fingertips over my forearm stopped my stream of consciousness. Juliet's expression split between surprised and stricken. "Even if you did all of that," she said softly, "No one would help her. Politicians won't be linked to sex workers."

A penny rolled around inside my skull, rattling in the sudden silence. *Oh.* When she said her mom had to 'do some things,' I didn't imagine…

But of course it made sense.

"I'm an idiot," I announced. "I didn't realize…"

Juliet gave one of her regal sniffs and straightened back to her usual forbidding posture. "Yes, well. It's not the sort of thing a man like you *would* realize, is it?"

No. And I'd never been more ashamed. I thought of all the women I lusted after in the Red-light District of Amsterdam… how my prep school friends and I passed through brothels in Thailand as a lark. A funny story to tuck into our pockets and whip out years later, after the fourth round of scotch.

Back then, I told myself that I shouldn't feel bad, that being involved in prostitution was their choice. But how many of those women weren't there because of a choice; but, really, the lack of one?

I wanted to tell myself that "at least" I didn't sleep with any of them… but, while true, it really wasn't much better, was it? I still looked. I didn't help anyone or even ask any questions.

When we were kids, my father always said, *"That's just the way of things."* The tepid phrase served as his go-to explanation for videos of refugees on rafts, homeless people huddled together for warmth in the dead of winter, news of mass shootings. And it was what I told myself when I witnessed women selling themselves to stay alive.

Now I realized just how much I used apathy in my own self-defense. If I didn't care, I didn't have to feel. I could go about my privileged existence without guilt or discomfort. It seemed like the only way to get by, since I always assumed there wasn't anything I could do to help.

But, from the second we met, Juliet made me want to fight. Standing there, taking in the fire glowing in her gaze, I believed. As long as there were people like her in the world, I had hope that things could actually be better.

I even thought that, maybe, I could be better, too.

"You're right," I finally replied, leveling gazes with her. "And that's unacceptable. I'm sorry."

Her beautiful face remained utterly still for a beat. I took the opportunity to re-memorize every little feature. The slope of her nose, the point of her chin, her high, wide cheekbones.

A slow smile pulled at her mouth. "That was a first. You usually fidget when you have to admit you're wrong."

Right again. Damn her.

Frustrated with myself and desperate for her forgiveness, I snatched her glass from her and set it aside, closing the space between us in two strides. "Seriously," I murmured, framing her face with my hands. "I'm sorry, Jules. About all of it. About your mom. And my clueless ass. The way I am… it's not necessarily something I'm proud of."

I thought back on my whirlwind week. All of the realizations I made since meeting her—things about Chris, my dad, my friends, my future. "I'm trying to change," I added honestly.

She assessed my sincerity and seemed to find it sufficient. "Hmm," she hummed, bringing her fingers to my jaw. "I accept your apology. But do me a favor, okay? Don't change *too* much." She lifted one brow. "I don't know many men who could pull off those socks."

I forgot all about my purple paisley socks. The mention of them made me chuckle. "When I decide to go for it, I tend to commit."

Heat bled into her eyes. "Oh, I hope so."

Sexy and smart and strong. *Bijou.* I stared down at her upturned face, wondering why it suddenly felt like I held the whole world between my palms.

How could I convince her once would never be enough?

I leaned down just far enough to brush her lips with mine and whispered, "Count on it, baby."

Juliet sifted her fingers through my hair again, sealing her mouth over mine. I had the strangest urge to sweep her up and settle her in my lap so I could wrap my arms around her, but the intercom on my wall buzzed.

"Dinner," I grumbled, disengaging to stalk to the door. "Hold on."

We ate at my island, which was novel for me. I normally inhaled my dinner over the sink or on the couch. While I shoveled forkfuls of drunken noodles into my mouth, she mixed rice into her penang curry and quizzed me about my family.

I gave her basic information only. My dad's name and the fact that he lived on the Upper East Side. That I had a younger brother enrolled at NYU who I saw often. I hoped she wouldn't notice the omission of one maternal figure. But of course she did.

"And your mom?" Jules asked, looking at me askance before gracefully sipping from her plastic spoon.

What could I tell her? *She left me here with my father when he brought his lovechild to live in our penthouse? She's had so many facelifts we don't even vaguely resemble one another anymore? I haven't spoken to her since Christmas and probably won't again until Mother's Day?*

"She lives in Connecticut," I offered mildly.

Juliet's eyes narrowed in her tenacious way. "You hate her."

A startled laugh burst out of me. "Damn. Don't pull any punches on my account, Miss Rivera."

She lifted her shoulder and offered a tantalizing glimpse down her blouse. *Jesus Christ. Was that… lace?*

"You can tell me," she insisted. "It's not like I'll ever meet her."

She had a point. Even if I somehow convinced Juliet to come back after our night together, I would never want her to meet the cold, bitter woman who fancied herself my mother three-to-four days a year.

"Okay, fine," I huffed. "You're right. I hate her. She left me here when she left my father and only came back whenever she needed more plastic surgery. Now we only see each other for a couple of holidays. She'll probably wind up reading about my company somewhere before I ever get a chance to tell her about it."

Juliet considered my words for a second before her face cracked into a wide grin. "We are quite the pair, aren't we?"

When she smiled like that, I had to smile right back. Besides, she wasn't wrong. "That we are."

As we stared at each other, the energy around us shifted. Outside my picture window, I saw that darkness had fallen.

This is it, I thought. *My one shot with her.*

My appetite vanished. I could tell by the way she set her utensils aside that she was ready for our next move, too.

She kept looking into me and I let her. Every scrap of reason deserted me. Every ordinary feeling evaporated, leaving just one behind: desire.

But I vowed to myself that I would take my time.

An idea came to me. I held my hand out to her, palm-up. "Dance with me."

Juliet

"This is ridiculous."

Standing in the center of his great room, I found myself fiddling with my fingers while he changed the record on his turntable. "Consider it foreplay," he replied airily, adjusting the needle and tweaking the volume. "We can dance and then I'll take you. Promise."

Since when did hearing a man say the word "promise" give me strange flutters through my abdomen? Was I losing my mind or was it just… *him*?

Graham came back toward me with his usual loping stride. His dark gaze glided over my face. Smugness twisted his lips. "Unless you're nervous…?"

"I am *not*." I said it too loudly and too quickly.

He noticed. His predatory smile sharpened, sensing my weakness. "Then just do it."

"Why?" I demanded, still too shrill.

Bit by bit, his amusement faded. He stepped up against me and lifted one of his long-fingered hands to stroke my cheek. Earnest longing filled his eyes. "Humor me, *bijou*."

Dios. Why did I *want* to do things for him? What an absurd, down-right stupid impulse.

An absurd, stupid impulse I immediately gave into.

Huffing, I kicked my heels off to the side and shot him a glare. "Trust me, I'm removing them for your protection."

A sliver of a smirk played at his lips. "I trust you."

The music started off as static, but soon I heard it. A quiet, sensual sort of song. A bossa nova track.

"Besides," Graham added, pulling me back into his body. "We should get used to this height difference before we go horizontal."

A surprised laugh bubbled out of me. He had a point; I'd never been in his presence without the advantage of high heels and, even with the platforms, he still towered over me.

Now, our natural statures almost seemed comical. My face barely reached his sternum. The warm spice of the cologne clinging to his collar tickled my nose.

"What now?" I asked, doing my best to keep my face impassive while I looked up at him.

Part of me expected some sort of set-down. Definitely a joke at my expense. But it seemed I'd misjudged just how intent he was on seduction. Instead of taking the clear opportunity to lord over me, he stroked his hand over my hair and gazed into my eyes.

"All you have to do is come to me."

The rough timbre of his voice sent a wave of goosebumps down my back. Everything in my center clenched tight, anticipating.

"I am," I whispered. "I have."

Graham wound one arm around my waist, bending it to cradle the length of my spine and thread his fingers into the hair at my nape. The other hand reached low, resting on the juncture of my backside and my thigh. He folded me closer and started to sway with me.

"I know, baby," he murmured, bending to lean his forehead into mine.

My rebellious instincts lingered below the surface. I wanted to claw into him, shove him away, put him in his place. Not because I wanted to lower him, but because I couldn't stand all of the *feelings* sloshing through me, battering my brittle insides like storm waves eroding rocks.

My fingers twitched, clutching at his shirt while I attempted to shove down the uproar. He felt it anyway. The hand in my hair tugged gently, pulling my head back to put us face-to-face.

Turbulence shifted in his fathomless depths. He spoke so quietly, I almost didn't hear. "Don't fight me right now. You can rip into me all night. But not now. Just… give me this."

No one had ever asked me for anything with such sincerity before. And he didn't even say please. How very… Graham.

Instead of conceding, I tucked my face against his throat. He didn't speak, either, but his fingers began massaging my scalp in tender circles. My eyelids fluttered closed. The hand on my ass glided higher to press our torsos closer.

On the miraculous occasions when we both managed to shut up, we had an innate sort of intimacy. A foreign flood of heat sluiced down my center, leaving a well of calm contentment in my chest while somehow stirring a molten roil of desire low in my belly. The heady combination weakened my knees.

Never one to miss a trick, Graham pulled my head back with another gentle tug. For one endless second, his midnight eyes were all I could see. And then his mouth sealed over mine.

His tongue coaxed my lips open and skated along mine, rubbing me in the slow, sensual slides that curled my toes. He dipped his other hand into the back of my jeans. Just a bit. Just enough for me to feel his touch play lightly over the back of my thong. The sensation wrung a low moan out of me.

That set him off instantly. His fingers tensed in my hair, yanking harder while he licked deeper. My palms smoothed over his shoulders, feeling the strength hiding under his dress shirt. Without any thought for what I was starting, I pushed at his vest, wanting it out of my way. My fingers flew to his shirt, next, unhooking the pearly buttons until the whole thing disappeared.

I gloried in the feel of his naked torso under my touch. His flawless skin stretched tight over every muscle—the ridges of his abdomen, the lean V bracketing his hips, his wide shoulders and long arms.

I caressed down his stomach, wanting to feel him everywhere. His lips found mine while I trailed my thumb down the line of hair leading from his navel to his trousers. Once, twice—on the third pass he snarled.

"I swear to God," he muttered, running his open mouth down to my throat. "If I don't have you now, I will go insane." His hands found my wrists, spinning me toward the wall. "Get over here."

I gasped, my chest heaving into his. He watched my breasts with dark eyes, lifting both of my hands over my head and restraining them with one of his, clutching tight. The other moved to grip my chin, holding me still for his intense regard.

Sparks ignited in his depths. "I'm going to ram my cock into you until you *beg me* to take you more than once," he vowed, menacing and soft. "And I'm going to make you beg right now."

Never.

I bucked my hips into his body and pulled at his grasp on my hands before letting out a frustrated snort. Graham's black gaze glittered. The heat from his nude skin radiated over my chest as he pressed his erection into me.

"If you want me to let you go, I'll do it," he told me, his voice low and even. "Or I can fuck you. But you'll have to ask me nicely."

Ignoring the pulse between my legs, I ground my teeth together. "Graham."

The fingers gripping my wrists squeezed harder. He slid his touch from my chin to my temple, lightly tucking loose hair behind my ear while he continued to burn his gaze into mine. "Say it, *bijou*. Tell me to let you go. Or say 'please' and I'll take you."

Damn him. I didn't *want* him to let me go. And he knew it.

"Please," I mumbled, dropping my gaze to his mouth.

His feral grin flashed. "What was that, *bijou*? You're muttering."

I refused to let him lord over me, no matter how much I wanted him. Instead of repeating the word, I kissed him. I waited until he surrendered to my tongue teasing his.

And then I bit him. Hard.

He gave a jagged groan, instantly losing all patience and snatching me up. My hands fell to his bare shoulders, clutching the hard ridges as he lifted my body into his arms, settling my legs around his lean waist. He nipped me back, then kissed me deep and hard while he carried me across the great room.

By the time he turned into his bedroom, I was breathless. He broke away to toss me down onto his bed. "Clothes off, underwear on," he demanded, peering down at me in the unlit room. "I'll be back."

Walking stiffly, he made for the door. Panting, I took a second to glance around me—another room with exposed brick walls, a large bed with some huge canvas hanging over it. I shimmied out of my jeans and sat up just far enough to peel my blouse off.

Less than a minute later, Graham returned. His pants and socks were gone, leaving him in underwear that clearly outlined his long, thick cock. I quickly realized the short cerulean boxers were as silky as any expensive tie. The thought of him wearing fancier underwear than I did brought a smirk to my lips.

For a long moment, he stared at me—laid out on his bed, smiling. He reached to the side and pressed a switch on the wall. Soft light swelled around us, bathing the room in a dim glow.

"I have to see you," he rasped, stalking closer.

A flash of red caught my attention—my heels, gripped in his left hand. Before I could tease him about that or his ultra-short boxers, he surprised me by lowering to his knees beside the bed.

Never dropping my gaze, he reached for my ankle, caressing up the length of my leg to tease the back of my knee before skimming his fingers back down to press his thumb into the sole of my foot.

The arousal pooling in my core leaked into my panties, dampening the center while he massaged my instep, his midnight eyes glittering while they skimmed over my wet center. He pulled at each of my toes until my mouth went slack. A small, satisfied small played at his full lips.

With deliberate slowness, he glided his touch up to my hips and hooked his fingers into the thong. "You'll take these off," he told me, even as he shimmied the lace down my thighs himself. "And put these on."

Graham slipped the shoes on my feet before gliding his hands to my knees one more time, bending them so the sharp spikes of my heels rested on the edge of his mattress.

"Spread your legs for me."

When I opened myself to his wild gaze, he muttered roughly, staring. "Fuck. Look how bad you want my cock."

I shivered as he slid his fingertips along the seam, parting me. He bent forward, just barely skimming his full lower lip over the top of my pounding clit.

That one touch made me grab fistfuls of his duvet cover. I barely resisted the urge to tilt my hips up for him. Instead of giving me what I wanted, though, he paused, raising his slashing brows at me. A cocky smile flirted with his features. "I still didn't hear the magic word."

The smug bastard. I swallowed hard, ignoring the ache deep in my belly as I silently tilted my head, refusing to give an inch.

"Mmm," he hummed, gazing up at me. "I see how it is."

A breath later, he slid his hand under my hip and flipped me. Gasping, I landed on my elbows, bent over the edge of the bed. Before I could even turn my head, his palm connected with the back of my ass, delivering a sound spank to the juncture of my thighs and my sex.

Once his hand landed there, he left it, rubbing a slow circle. I stifled a moan while every nerve in my core smoldered.

"Now, tell me," he murmured, his voice black silk, "What was the magic word?"

Panting with outrage and maddeningly turned on, I cut him a severe look over my shoulder. "Fuck you."

He spanked me again, sending another echo through my core. Inclining his head, his arrogant smirk deepened. "No, that wasn't it." His midnight eyes narrowed, daring me. "Try again."

"Graham, I swear—"

Whap.

Something about the way he reacted—without a speck of hesitation—excited me. Restless from the wetness slicking my thighs, I shifted, sticking my backside out further.

His mouth pulled into a grin at odds with the dark heat burning in his eyes. "Is this what you wanted, that day, in the elevator?"

The first time I saw him, I thought I hated him. Was it really that I just wanted him so badly that it infuriated me?

The thought of Graham bending me over in the elevator and spanking my ass left me breathless. Still, I denied it.

"No."

Whap.

I panted. His free hand reached up, looping my hair around his wrist and pulling my head back. With my back arched, I saw that he'd removed his boxers. His hard, naked body strained behind me. His solid length bobbed every time he skimmed his palm over my rear.

"You know what I think, *bijou*?" he murmured, his obsidian gaze following his fingertips as they trailed down to the collect some of the moisture seeping from my center. "I think you put up a good fight, but you like it when I win."

Images blurred through my lust-addled brain. The day he snapped me up and shoved me into the wall of Pod C; how he coaxed me into his arms when I cried in the stairwell; the fact that he convinced me to give him a whole night instead of one single hook-up.

Dios mío.

He brought his fingers to his mouth, licking them clean. He groaned quietly while greed tightened his expression. "Christ, you taste good."

A lascivious spark settled into his features, quirking his lips in the feral grin that scorched my blood. "I already knew that, though. I licked you off of my fingers the first time I touched you, after our first kiss."

Recalling the way he reached up my skirt and swirled his fingertips over my pussy sent a clench through my core. My legs parted of their own volition, tottering on my heels as I leaned back to brush my ass against his erection, teasing him. The fist in my hair constricted, pinioning me with more force while Graham muttered curses under his breath.

Another stinging slap bit into my rear. I gasped, so turned on I felt dizzy. Without preamble, he snapped the back of my bra open. It fell onto the bed, leaving my tight, tingling breasts bare. A second later, two fingers plunged into my heat, curling the way I loved. I moaned, the sound garbled by the mattress pressed against my cheek.

Whap.

Graham stepped closer, pressing his scorching-hot hard-on into my hip. "Let me give it to you, baby," he tempted, his voice softer. "All you have to do is say—"

"*Please.*" The word finally vibrated out me, echoing through the room.

And then he was on me.

He flipped me with a hard yank. One arm snaked under my torso, positioning me close as his free hand flew to my aching breasts.

My nipples hardened into points, pressing into his palm while he kneaded each one in turn. He pinched me hard, rolling each peak until they lengthened under his touch. His eyes burned like hot coals, branding me as they looped over my bare body.

"Goddamn you," Graham hissed, his lips finding mine. "You're so beautiful."

He was, too; all hard planes of muscle, lean and warm to the touch. I raked my nails down his broad back, enjoying the way his erection twitched between us.

While he cupped both of my breasts, I gripped his length and gave a gentle tug.

"It's all for you, baby," he rasped. "Take it."

For a beat, I just stared, mesmerized by his perfect package. The long, thick cock was shaved bare, giving me a perfect view of his entire shaft and the full balls drawn tight at its base.

My teeth sank into my lip while I imagined trying to fit it into my mouth. There was no way *that* would possibly work, but I'd have fun trying. While my mind raced with the possibilities, I gripped his naked length and stroked him. His head fell back on a pant.

"Jules. Fuck. Go slow."

I didn't let up, showing no mercy as I twisted my fist over his wide, pulsing head. "Funny," I said, piercing his gaze with mine. "I didn't hear the magic word…"

My teasing snapped his control. His mouth caught mine with bruising force, biting my lower lip while his hands slid down to my ass, gripping it roughly.

I continued pumping his cock in and out of my hand, working him until a snarl tore from his chest. He snatched my wrists up, drawing my hands over my head like he had in his living room.

"You'll ruin me," he gritted, settling over me. "I knew it the second I saw you and I had to have you anyway."

He trailed his lips and his teeth down to my neck, nipping and sucking me while I ground my soaked pussy into his throbbing erection. He adjusted his hips to press his length right into my clit, wrenching a broken moan from me.

Graham plucked my taut nipples, moving rhythmically against me until my sex clenched in anticipation, desperate to feel the same thrusts inside. Another cry floated out of my mouth as I realized that I was about come from those practiced rolls of his hips and nothing else.

"Yes, baby," he praised, hoarse, biting at the tender slope of my shoulder. "You're so wet. I can feel you throbbing. You're going to come now, aren't you?"

"*Graham*." His name sloughed up my throat as my clit pulsed, sending tingles through my core and arching my back.

His tongue teased mine in long, hot strokes that nearly made me come twice in as many minutes. Before I could help it, I whimpered into his mouth.

I expected him to shoot me some version of the gloating grin I loved so much despite all my efforts not to. But Graham silently released my wrists, instead entwining his hand with one of mine. His eyes closed as he pressed our foreheads together and dipped his other fingers into my folds, earning another gasp.

"Christ," he muttered, stroking into me while my sex eagerly clasped itself around his fingers. A fresh arrow of need sailed through my middle. "Juliet."

My hands roamed up his back, into his thick, overly-long hair. I combed the strands back to their usual order and tugged on the roots as he touched me. When he had me trembling and mewling beneath him once more, he suddenly rolled away.

Condom, I realized, hearing the slide of a nightstand drawer. He couldn't wait anymore.

I sensed that he was beyond the need to tease and torment. I was, too. Instead of denying him, I moved further back onto the mattress and opened my legs eagerly, offering myself up.

With his protection in place, Graham kneeled between my thighs. He brushed the backs of his knuckles over my cheek in a surprising, tender gesture that sent a slick rush through my sex and a burst of wetness to my eyes.

"Like this," he said quietly, grasping my left leg to hook my red heel over his shoulder, lifting my ass from the bed to align our centers.

I stretched my arms overhead, finally surrendering to him. *Just for tonight.*

It was all we could have. And I wanted it so badly.

With one last pass of his molten gaze, he locked eyes with me, wrapped his strong hands around each of my hips, and pushed inside.

Graham

Heaven.

Delirious, delicious perfection that could only mean I died, somehow, and found my eternal reward between the thighs of the world's most beautiful woman.

I had never felt any swirl of sensation as wondrous as pressing my body into Juliet's. The way her pussy gripped me, her soft skin, the image of her bountiful curves laid out before me.

I shoved myself into her again and again, savoring the plush cushion of her full hips against mine. Her round tits rocking with every thrust. The way she moaned and whispered to me, saying my name, begging for more, telling me how much she liked my cock.

I'm sure I said things, too. I couldn't focus on what came out of my mouth. Juliet captivated my focus completely, holding me in her thrall while our bodies screwed themselves together.

It took some time, but I finally worked all the way in. Flames climbed up my spine while pleasure radiated up my center. I fucked her hard and slow, then faster. She unraveled, her sighs and whispers mixing with moans and dipping into her native language.

As she lost herself, I stroked my cock into her melting core. The tight clasp tugged at the head of my dick on every thrust until I couldn't take anymore. Coming, an animal roar ripped out of me as I gripped her ass, tilting her just so and driving into her harder.

Juliet cried out. Her body bowed off of the bed as another orgasm rolled over her, sending a series of spasms echoing through her body, milking me until I collapsed on top of her.

I managed to part her luscious legs and flick the heels off of her feet before I fell forward, landing in her softness and turning my face to the jasmine-perfumed crook of her neck. Her arms floated down from their position over her head, banding around my shoulders.

A deep vein of contentment suffused warmth through my middle. Satisfaction dulled my mind. Gratitude and awe shimmered around the edges of my consciousness like carbonation.

For a blissful moment, I felt everything and didn't think about any of it. And then I heard it.

Silence.

The shell-shocked, loud-as-hell kind. It pressed down around us, underscoring everything inside of me. Gradually, my feelings sank through the haze of ecstasy. And, for a minute, I swore I actually *heard* my dismay ricochet through the soundless room.

Dear God. What have I done?

I fucked Juliet Rivera.

And now I was in love with her.

CHAPTER TEN

January 29, 2017

Graham

I didn't sleep for shit.

Partly because I was too busy having Juliet every way she would let me until well after three A.M. On her back, on her front, in my lap. Come morning, I could still taste her—nectar and musk.

Every time, I told myself I would fuck her once more, just to prove to myself that I wasn't in love with her—that it was just her wet heat and her sexy-as-fuck curves and that was *it*.

And every goddamn time I made a liar of myself when the riot of foreign affections grew stronger as soon as we finished.

Juliet finally fell asleep in the wee hours of the morning. She refused to cuddle, of course, preferring to present me with her naked back. Which is how I normally liked to sleep with a woman, when I had to. Only, this time, I spent the rest of the darkness staring at the slope of her spine and memorizing the dangerous curve of her hip… wishing I had the right to roll closer and pull her back into me.

I dozed off some time after the first stirrings of dawn touched my bedroom's picture window, but woke shortly after to the sunrise. More determined than ever.

Juliet and I couldn't be a one-night thing.

I had to figure out a way to get her come back.

By seven, I gave up on sleep and slid out of the bed. Finding my boxers on the bedroom floor and my phone in the pocket of my abandoned pants, I trudged to my kitchen and set to work cleaning up our mess from dinner.

Moving around made it easier to think, somehow, so I decided I would continue and make breakfast. I figured it couldn't be too hard. I had all the kitchen equipment, after all. And wasn't French toast just, like, bread and eggs? Easy.

Half an hour on YouTube later, I had butter browning in one pan and bacon in another. I sipped my third cup of coffee and stared into the foaming fat, considering.

Maybe I'm not actually in love, I reasoned, adding the battered brioche to one pan. *Maybe it's infatuation. That's a thing. Not a thing I've ever experienced* after *fucking someone, but I've* heard *about it happening, at least.*

It didn't seem likely that feelings as strong as the ones Juliet invoked could possibly die down, but perhaps that was the point—something so brilliant couldn't possibly blaze on forever. It would burn itself out eventually.

So I just had to buy myself some more time with her. Long enough to learn her flaws and have my fill of her charms. Then I would be able to leave her alone.

I flipped the French toast, marveling at the golden brown crust. *Well, shit.* If I'd known actually cooking something would be so easy, I would have done it a long time ago.

I shook my head, frustrated with myself. Why did it feel like I didn't recognize my own life anymore? One week with this woman and I was making French toast, starting my own business, and angling to extend a clear one night stand.

Why didn't I recognize *myself* anymore?

And why did I like *this* version better than the old one?

I was surprised to find that my frustration didn't overwhelm me the way it ordinarily did. I just felt… thoughtful. Calm.

Jesus Christ.

I felt *good.*

Even with no sleep, after a night of Juliet, a low-grade sort of euphoria hummed in my blood. And, moreover, cooking her damn breakfast *relaxed* me. I looked down at my own hands, disgusted and fascinated.

Was she a witch? A goddess?

I heard something over my shoulder and turned to find Juliet hovering on the edge of the great room, wearing a mauve dress shirt she clearly pilfered from my hamper.

A slow, seductive smirk lit her features. "Good morning, *pinchao.*"

Juliet

When I woke up alone in Graham's bed, a bracing stab of hurt pierced me.

All the things we'd done left one thing clearer than ever: we had a connection. Rolling over to find his place beside mine empty somehow felt like a betrayal.

Why do I care*?*

Why am I even still here*?*

Wounded and alarmed, I drug myself up and shook out my hair, hoping to straighten my thoughts. *At least he's not watching me freak out.*

Gratitude soothed the sting of abandonment. I realized I needed the time alone that Graham had granted me. I wondered if he did it on purpose—if he'd understood what I needed, because it was also what he needed. After a whole night with him inside of me, I could honestly say that it was uncanny how often our thoughts aligned.

So, sure, I had to get myself together before I faced the man who had me in such a state. But maybe, just maybe, he felt the same way about me.

It didn't matter, really. Graham had his one night.

And he *used* it. And used it.... And used it. To unwittingly tear down every last defense I spent the week building.

He took what he wanted, sure. That part didn't surprise me. *Pinchao*. He was a confident, dominant man, clearly used to getting what he wanted.

What *did* surprise me, though, was how much he *gave*. Nuzzles, whispered praises, massages and lingering kisses between every round.

Graham Everett could be... *sweet*.

And—*ayúdame, Dios*—the memories brought an involuntary smile to my face. One I couldn't control, even as I tiptoed into his bathroom and found myself ensconced in a black marble chamber bigger than Abuelita's kitchen.

I rinsed my mouth out and ran my fingers through my limp hair, smirking at the array of men's grooming products neatly lined up between the two shallow sinks. My reflection peered back at me from the room's wide mirror, my eyes flickering to the love-bites clustered on my neck, my shoulder, the top of my left breast.

Huh. I guess there *was* a lot of biting. Mutually enjoyable, it seemed. Yet another thing he and I had in common.

Shaking my head at myself once more, I used the hair tie around my wrist to knot my hair into a low bun. With my clean change of clothes all the way across the apartment, I settled for a lavender button-down I found tossed on top of his laundry hamper.

It smelled fresh and looked as crisp as the rows of shirts I spotted in his walk-in closet. He clearly tried it on with yesterday's purple ensemble and then abandoned the clean garment to be dry cleaned instead of simply re-hanging it.

Men.

Buttoning the shirt and rolling the long sleeves, I made my way out to the great room. Where I stumbled over my own feet, halting on the threshold, shocked.

Spoiled, overly-coiffed Graham was… *cooking*? Breakfast? For… *me*?

A quick glance told me he prepared more than enough food for both of us. *And he told me he didn't eat breakfast.* The thought brought a smug twist to my lips as I greeted him.

"Good morning, *pinchao*."

He cracked a crooked version of my favorite boyish grin. "*Bijou*."

His gaze slid down my body, clearly filling in all of my covered parts from memory. His eyes met mine for one brief moment before he nonchalantly turned back to his work, flipping what appeared to be a piece of French toast.

"Far be it for me to disagree with Abuelita," he said mildly, not looking up. "But I think purple is lovely on you."

I recognized the strained undercurrent in his voice. Concern. He worried about the compliment, even as he gave it. So did I. He shouldn't have been so kind to me and I should not have liked it so much.

But I drifted into the room anyway, drawn to his side by the sight of his hard body in his silky underwear as much as the mouthwatering scents of bacon and strong coffee.

When I reached him, he pulled the pans off of the burners and set them aside. Grabbing his coffee in one hand and a matching stone mug in the other, he pivoted to face me and leaned his hip into the counter, offering the second mug to me.

The brew turned out to be *very* strong, bordering on abrasive. Just the way I liked it. He watched me take a sip and then chuckled at my startled expression.

"You know me—never one for subtlety."

I do *know him*. My eyes flashed down to the bulge in his boxers. *Very well.*

"Hmmm," I muttered, distracting myself from his package with another mouthful of coffee. "I must say, I've never hooked up with a guy who wears fancier undergarments than I do."

I felt his hot gaze trail over my face. "Not all of us can be connoisseurs of quality, I'm afraid."

The quiet cadence of his voice took the edge off of his taunt. A second later, his fingertips grazed my temple and swept a stray lock of hair behind my ear.

I had to resist the urge to jerk away. Affection after-the-fact was a strict no-no for me. It made things blurry in the most ordinary of circumstances… and whatever Graham and I had going on was already far more muddled than any of my past hook-ups.

Overreacting would only show him how much he affects you, I told myself, holding still as he skimmed his thumb down my jaw and touched my chin once.

Our eyes collided. Brooding bewilderment roiled in the black velvet irises staring back at me. "Will you stay for breakfast?" he finally asked.

My focus slid to the side, where a plate of French toast sat innocently beside the pan of crispy bacon. It really did look delicious…

"Yes."

His perfectly impassive face didn't move, but the tumult in his eyes shifted. "And then you'll go?"

The notion filled me with equal measures of relief and dread. I lifted my chin and forced my shoulders back, faking certainty I did not feel. "Yes."

Something about my bearing amused Graham. His lips curved sardonically. "That was our deal, I suppose." He turned to retrieve the food and nodded at the dining table. "Let's use that. I've never eaten there before."

A giggle bubbled out of me. "Didn't you tell me you've lived here for, like, two years?"

Graham shrugged one of his bare shoulders, sending a fluid ripple of muscle down his back. "I don't entertain much."

If the array of work papers scattered over the wood surface was any indication, he didn't entertain *ever*.

I swallowed my observation with another gulp of coffee. Helping myself, I stretched across the stove to grab the carafe off of the coffee maker and refill my mug. Graham's hot gaze followed my every move, glued to the backs of my naked thighs.

I had to tamp down a smirk, then a wave of self-loathing. *Carajo*. Since when did I *like* him leering at me?

Clearly, the man made me lose my mind. I needed to get out of there ASAP.

Graham retrieved two heavy stone plates that matched our mugs. His silverware turned out to be *gold*. Of course.

I rolled my eyes at him and he caught me, flashing a sexy grin. "Fancy forks to match my fancy underwear. Naturally."

"You're ridiculous," I told him, laughing. "I've never been more certain I chose the perfect nickname for you than right now."

Graham swept half of the table's-worth of papers into a neat stack and set them aside. "I noticed that nickname was nowhere to be found last night."

As he spoke, he doled out our place settings and arranged the food in between the seat at the head of the table and the one directly to the right. He cocked an eyebrow at me as we sat down. "Could it be that I pleased you somehow?"

A flush rushed to my cheeks before I could control it. I focused on smoothing my napkin over my naked lap, sniffing as I replied, "You did fine, *pinchao*."

We both knew that was an understatement of the highest order.

Graham gave a snort. "I seem to recall one round that lasted almost an hour. And I wasn't *counting* or anything, but I believe you thought I was doing more-than *fine* multiple times."

As he served me French toast, his hand contorted around the fork to flash the number four.

Four times in one hour. Carajo. He was right.

Hot color blazed along my cheekbones. "So you *were* counting, then," I groused, snatching bacon up from the pan before he could offer me any.

He grabbed his own side and turned to frown at me, his expression bordering on confounded. "If I was, it's only because I'd never experienced anything like it before." He dropped his eyes to his food as he started to cut his toast. "But maybe that's typical for you…"

Why would he ask that? Did he want to know if what we'd shared was… special? Was it possible he felt the same searing connection I did?

I studied his profile for a beat before carefully admitting, "No. Not typical."

My heart gave a pang at the dash of vulnerability that darted over his features. He stared into his plate. "I don't know why, but that's good to know."

I could feel him working up to another question. *What if he asks me to stay? Or come back? Am I really going to walk out of here and never see him again?*

Until I felt certain I could definitely turn him down, I opted to change the subject. Searching for inspiration, I glanced to the side and skimmed the nearest document. A list, penned in his bold, slashing handwriting. More chaotic than his usual work, with unnumbered items piled haphazardly on top of each other and notations cramped into the margins. The first—and most legible—line read, "*Insurance contract review.*"

Gracias a Dios. Something I could actually talk about.

"What's this?"

Graham froze. His fork hovered between his plate and his mouth as he stared at the paper in my hand, obviously debating how much to tell me. When his features filled with rueful amusement, a silly flutter trembled low in my belly.

"It's a list of all the business shit I don't know anything about," he admitted. "Grayson suggested that the most important thing for my start-up would be recognizing when I need to ask experts for help, so anytime I start to think I'm in over my head on a particular subject, I write it down." He shoved a large bite into his mouth and talked around it. "Only, now, the list is like two pages long. Clearly, spending four years in business school accomplished fuck-all."

Chuckling, I made my way down his litany of unknowns. Items like "*Hiring—fuck me, I don't know—non-compete clauses? Background checks?*" and, "*Drafting agreements for clients who don't have thirty in-house lawyers like Stryker.*"

"Eight," I corrected absently, waving the list before flipping it over to read the back. "We only have eight attorneys in-house."

"Which is eight more than most people," he shot back, biting into a strip of bacon. "I can't count on all of my clients having sexy lawyeresses for me to work with. I'm going to have to draft standard contracts for such mere mortals."

I bit the inside of my cheek, warding off a giggle and debating the wisdom of the first reply that came to mind. "You know…" I started reluctantly, "That contract I wrote would probably work in most cases. If you changed the names and dollar amounts accordingly."

I expected some measure of surprise, but Graham kept eating without so much as a flinch. "I know," he said. "Your contract—sans Stryker's information—is exactly the sort of thing I need. But I would never dream of using your work without paying you for it."

He suddenly pinned me in place with his bright, black eyes. "Unless you'd be willing to let me pay you for it...?"

The offer was exactly the sort of thing I was afraid of. "I wouldn't feel right selling a contract template I designed for Mr. Stryker, especially since he already paid me to create it in the first place."

Graham tilted his head slightly, his expression carefully blank. "Why not? You wrote it. It's your work. If anyone is going to make money off of it, it should be you."

I couldn't disagree… "If I were to want to sell it as a template to another party, I would rewrite the whole thing. Even if it wound up being similar… re-doing the work would keep my conscious clear." Sensing the dangerous bent of our conversation, I hastened to add, "But, like I said, Mr. Stryker pays me well. I don't need to do any freelance work."

He bored his gaze into mine, undeterred. "But you *could,* right? Stryker mentioned that your non-compete doesn't apply to me since I'm not a competitor."

I knew he was feeling me out, trying to sense how open I would be to working with him. I shoved a big bite of French toast into my mouth to buy some time while I chewed. "Surely, even if it's technically allowed, Mr. Stryker would be less-than thrilled by anyone doing work for another company on the side."

My barb missed its mark. Instead of looking discouraged, Graham's lips turned up at the corners. *Maldición.*

"Not an issue. I spoke with him about it last week and he offered to lend me one of his in-house counsel. After hours, of course, and on my own dime. But he specifically said he's cool with me hiring one of you for freelance shit. He suggested Dominic, but I'm thinking I have the perfect person for the job right here. If past performance is any indication…"

The suggestive gleam in his eye was not lost on me. Nor was the strange somersault in my stomach.

Clever *pinchao.* He devised a way for us to spend more time together in a professional capacity, likely because he knew I would be more apt to entertain a working relationship than a personal one. It might have worked, if I wasn't so peeved at his presumption.

"Keep dreaming," I snorted, draining my coffee and rising to refill the mug.

Graham leaned back in his chair, unmoved by my denial. "Why not? It will only take a couple of weeks to get all of the things I need sorted out. And I'll pay you. A lot."

Part of me—the thrifty, desperate part that still washed out plastic bags to reuse them—paused at that. *How much?* I wondered.

Would it be enough to hire the immigration lawyer now? I had a savings plan to allow me to reach our goal by the end of the year... but what if Graham's money could get my mother here *now*? How could I say no, then? Especially if Mr. Stryker *really* didn't mind...

Staring down into my fresh cup of coffee, I realized he'd tricked me into contemplating an offer I shouldn't even *consider*. The bastard.

Pissed, I shot him a glare from across the room. "Do I seem like the sort of person who would abandon their principles for *money*? I told you that you could have one night and you had it. We're done now. I'm not going to become your legal-counsel-concubine. I don't care how much you offer me."

Graham crossed his arms over his chest, the bare pecs and biceps flexing. He narrowed his gaze at me. "Who said anything about sex? I want to hire you. To *work*. Because you're very good at what you do. And, sure, we fucked. And that will be there, between us, I guess, but you've made your boundaries exceedingly clear. One night. And I agreed."

His brows arched. "Do *you* think *I'm* the sort of person who would ignore a woman's boundaries? Or go back on his word? I want you, Juliet, but I respect you, too. We made a deal for last night and we can make another one if we work together."

My teeth ground as everything inside of me split down the center.

The louder, panicked part sounded alarm bells. Like a cornered animal, I had a sudden, frantic urge to do *anything* to flee. It took a moment for me to get ahold of my fear and smother the voice shrieking at me to *get out now*.

After a few deep breaths, my rational side crowded in; and it argued in Graham's favor.

Admittedly, he made several good points. And I did trust him. After spending the night with him, I was more certain than ever about his capacity for goodness. He simply reserved those rich depths for people he cared for.

And I'd begun to suspect that I may have been one of those people.

I thought of the way he listened to my mother's story. The shame in his expression, how he instantly tried to offer help, even though he didn't know what that help might look like. The way he watched me while we were in bed together, paying his undivided attention to my every cue. How he got up and made breakfast without even a word, with no expectation of anything in return.

I believed him; he did respect me. He wouldn't fight me on a firm boundary.

Which made the practical part of me wonder—why couldn't I work with him? As long as we agreed not to break my one-time rule, I could still make a clean get-away… it would just be a few weeks later and I would be a few thousand dollars richer…

The exact amount suddenly felt vital. A little extra cash wouldn't be worth putting myself through the temptation of working so closely with a man I still wanted every bit as much as I did before we slept together. But if the money would truly make a difference in my plans, I'd force myself to muster more self-control and soldier through.

So I came back to the dining table and stood at the opposite end, locking gazes with Graham. "How much?"

He eyes turned to cool fire, somehow regarding me with smoldering sensual interest and business-like detachment simultaneously. "Every night after work and possibly some time on the weekends for two weeks. Fifty thousand dollars."

Fifty.

Thousand.

My tongue felt numb and thick in my mouth. "I'm sorry—*what*?"

Graham's gaze held steady. "You'll come here every night after work and maybe one afternoon each weekend for two weeks. Less, if we finish up early. Either way, I will pay you fifty thousand dollars."

The staggering amount sent my mind reeling. It was almost half of my annual salary. More than enough to retain an immigration expert for Mami… maybe even enough to pay for the entire Green Card appeal process.

Graham watched me reach my decision within seconds. Triumph glimmered in his eyes. "So what do you prefer, *bijou*—cash or check?"

Graham

By all accounts, I was a very bad man.

In twenty-four hours, I had seduced a woman who had no intentions of pursuing a relationship with me, fucked her so many times I lost count, and bribed her into a business arrangement that could only be described as precarious, at best.

Then, after we finished our breakfast and she made her hasty exit, I wasted most of the day sleeping instead of preparing for dinner with my father.

I intended to spend my afternoon typing up an official list for Juliet and I to work from and finishing up the damned account log

I still needed to input for Everett Alexander. I figured I would return all the books to my father over dinner, then drop the bomb about leaving the business once he had all of their company property firmly in his possession.

But the second Juliet breezed out my door—dressed in a black sweat suit she magically produced from her big purse, only pausing to briefly glance back and ask, "Tomorrow at seven?" before leaving—I all but collapsed from exhaustion.

Hours of sleeplessness and my newfound emotional turmoil left me depleted. And watching Juliet go without so much as a farewell kiss sapped what little energy remained.

So, I went back to my bed and spent about ten minutes hating how strangely wide and open and—ah, hell—*empty* it felt. The jasmine lingering on the pillow beside mine didn't help. But I finally turned away and drifted off.

When I woke up, light no longer slanted in through my eastern windows, which meant it was well after noon. I only had enough time to shower, dress, and do a cursory review of the delinquent Everett Alexander account book. In a disgusting display of sentiment, I actually started to put on the lavender dress shirt Juliet had worn before I caught myself and chucked it back into the hamper.

Goddamn it.

The woman had me under some sort of spell. I made a big show of leaving the button-down behind and chose a color on the opposite end of the spectrum—a yellow shirt with navy slacks and a navy-and-white striped bow tie.

Satisfied, I brewed another pot of coffee and sat down at my kitchen island with the green account binder. *Why green*, I wondered. I'd been doing data entry for three years and the only other green binders I ever saw here my father's personal files, in his office closet. How the hell did one of our account records end up in a green sleeve?

I didn't have time to dwell, though. I had just over an hour to take one last run at the review before hauling ass uptown.

Turned out I didn't need that long.

Because it only took minutes for me to see what I hadn't been able to comprehend all week.

Fraud.

Who knows why it suddenly made terrible, perfect sense. Maybe my endless lust for Miss Rivera ran even deeper than I allowed myself to believe; and I was so distracted by wanting her that I couldn't really focus on what was clearly sitting in front of me. Maybe, now that I'd satisfied my need for her—if only temporarily—I could finally *see.*

The numbers didn't make sense before because they *couldn't* make sense. Because they were *wrong.*

False. Fiction.

Millions from about two dozen different portfolios had been funneled into various high-yield IPO's… but the returns reported in the green ledger were significantly lower than the actual pay-outs should have been. Meaning someone lied to several clients and skimmed the excess returns on those investments off the top.

And who knew if these books were the only ones that person had cooked…

My gears spun, conjuring up an image of the cramped, cluttered storage room I used as my office. There were piles and piles of books there that I never even touched… Did they all hold similar evidence that someone swindled our clients? Or just the green ones?

The ones Dad keeps. His personal clients. Locked up in his office.

My father was the only other person who had access to the book laid out in front of me. And he spent the better part of the week nervously hassling me about returning the records to him.

The realization hit me with the accuracy and alacrity of a bullet.

My father was a con-artist.

Hillstone boasted a dark, moody sort of ambiance, along with some of the best martinis on the whole damn island.

And thank God.

After my one night with Juliet and the shocking revelation that my family business was basically a criminal operation, I needed a goddamn drink. I downed two while I waited at the bar, trying to smooth my frayed nerves before I faced dear old Dad.

I had no idea how to approach the situation. Should I jump down his throat immediately? Play it cool and act like I hadn't noticed anything at all? Let him go on his merry, duplicitous way and just jump ship immediately?

Could I go to jail for knowing about the fraud but not reporting it? Could I be implicated because, as CFO, I *should* have known all along?

What would happen if I *did* tell the feds? Would Dad… go to prison? Would Everett Alexander be mine? Or would the whole damn business crumble into dust once people realized what my father had done?

And, for that matter, what *did* he do, exactly?

I only had one falsified ledger in my possession… but if his locked closet was full of the same sorts of books… The implications were staggering. He'd likely lose everything. Unless he could pin it all on some poor fool.

Upon further inspection, I saw that, although the clients were his, the trades weren't done under his usual broker number. He probably used lower-level traders' numbers when he planned to report false returns on a transaction, just in case he got caught. It made sense, in a sick way… but, in that case, I'd expect him to change the broker numbers over time, in keeping with the whoever we employed. That meant multiple employees could be implicated, if the other green books told similar stories to the one currently stashed in my briefcase.

In order to test that theory, I'd have to put off my defection from Everett Alexander for a few days, maybe a week. Just long enough to get into the locked closet and look at the other binders in there. Every trade accounted for in the volume I currently possessed listed the same trader number… one I didn't recognize.

Fuck me. At least it wasn't mine.

I wished I found that reassuring. If my father truly intended to pin the false books on someone else, it would have to be someone high enough within the agency to reasonably take responsibility. That really only left me and my dead grandfather; but I knew Grandfather's broker number and it wasn't his, either.

Unless, Dad used a random person's number instead? That seemed… clumsy? Stupid. Then again, how smart could the guy really be? He defrauded people instead of working hard and didn't even possess the competence to keep it hidden from me.

I downed my drink. I needed a plan and I had no time to make one.

Taking a deep breath, I closed my eyes and wished, stupidly, that I could call Juliet. She would have legal answers to all of my questions, of course, but it was more than that. I knew she would also have the pragmatism and good sense to form a workable strategy.

My fingers twitched toward my phone, but a voice behind me interrupted the movement. "Hey!"

I resisted the urge to cringe by reaching for my fresh martini.

"Started without me, huh?" Dad chuckled, slipping into the stool beside mine. "It's fine; I had two at the club before I came down here."

He signaled for a bartender and ordered a scotch on the rocks. My usual drink. Another similarity we shared. Today, it nearly made me flinch.

I had to repress the urge again when he clapped me on the shoulder and started jabbering about the menu. Listening to him debate grilled artichokes versus spinach dip doubled the queasiness seething in my stomach. How could he just sit there? Blathering on? Acting innocent?

Jesus Christ. How many similar meals had I sat through without even a speck of suspicion? Had I ever gone out with him and one of the people he fucked over?

All of his bluster and bullshit started to make more sense to me as he went on, oblivious. None of it—his reputation, his status, his relationships—was *real.* There *wasn't any substance* beneath anything he projected. No talent or character. The man was a paper tiger.

And I'd almost ended up just like him.

Luckily, he was also obscenely self-absorbed, and didn't even recognize my horror while I sat, marinating in all of my newfound insight, staring at him.

He flashed the famed Everett grin. I felt sick.

"So what do you think? Artichokes? Spinach dip?" His smile widened. "Hell, let's get both. You're buying right?"

Chapter Eleven

January 30, 2017

Juliet

If I didn't already feel guilty about accepting Graham's deal against my better judgement—without Mr. Stryker's specific approval—I did when I walked onto the executive floor and ran right into my boss and Ella.

He cut a formidable figure in his navy suit, even with his head bent over his fiancée's. She looked to be masking some anxiety… poorly. Her eyes were wide, her lips pinched around the small smile she offered him.

Mr. Stryker didn't buy it. He cupped his hand under her face and traced his thumb over her mouth, frowning at her expression. "Ellie…"

"I'm really fine," she insisted, full of forced brightness. "I have things to do today, Grayson. I'll be okay!"

I spent the weekend so wrapped up in my own drama, I completely forgot about their security issue last week. It occurred to me that Marco's absence from Sunday supper probably had something to do with the breech.

How didn't I put that together before? Was I *that* out of sorts? From…what? Sex with Graham? *Dios mío*. The man truly did scramble my brains. It was a miracle I'd gotten through the preliminary pre-up work I did on Sunday afternoon.

Mr. Stryker's thick brows furrowed, but Ella turned toward me, relief passing over her face. "Oh look, it's Juliet!"

Her obvious bid for distraction brought a smile to my face. It really was impossible not to fall in love with Ella. I saw, once again, why a man who could have anyone so clearly adored her.

She looked as lovely and oddly-dressed as ever in bell-bottom jeans and a thick mustard sweater with a floppy cowl neck. A pair of clunky green clogs peeked out from the wide denim legs of her pants.

For a moment, I was almost jealous. The ugly shoes looked very comfortable… especially when facing the prospect of a long day at the office in platform heels. Not to mention the trek down to Graham's after work and my eventual journey back to Queens.

"See!" Ella crowed, waving one unpolished hand at me. "I told you she could help. Juliet knows how to choose colors. Look at that dress."

Another of Abuelita's creations. The fitted blush frock had sharp, exaggerated shoulders, long sleeves, and a tapered skirt. The slit up the back reminded me of Graham's long fingers, trailing along the backs of my thighs. Flushing, I ran both hands over the fitted sheath and looked down to hide my overheated cheeks.

Thankfully, Mr. Stryker didn't even glance my way. His eyes narrowed at Ella as he glowered. "Ellie. You're changing the subject. It won't work."

Ella pinned me with a beaming grin. "Ignore him. He needs to get to work and quit fretting over me. And *I* need to make a final decision on colors for the wedding. I'm driving Alice crazy changing my mind every week. Last week, I was *sure* I wanted to do shades of yellow but now I'm thinking about purples…"

Sighing heavily, Mr. Stryker tucked his babbling fiancée under his arm and finally faced me. "I'm just uneasy about leaving Ella alone after everything she's been through recently," he explained. "And she thinks I'm being over-protective."

Ella's sapphire eyes rolled. "Because he *is*. I have *Marco* following my every move. What kind of lunatic would ever want to take *him* on? That's like starting a bar fight with the Incredible Hulk."

Mr. Stryker and I laughed—me loudly, him with reluctance.

"She has a point," I chuckled. "Marco will take good care of her, I'm sure. And wedding colors are very important. They set the whole tone."

Ella smacked my boss's chest with the back of her wrist. "I told you so," she said, then twirled back to me. "Jules, can I add you to my wedding group chat? Tris and Ali are in there, along with my little sister, Darcy, and my best friend, Maggie. I want your opinions on the swatches Alice shows me today!"

I thought of Dominic breathing down my neck. I still had to catch up on all of the "work" he wanted me to come in for over the weekend. Since I denied him, he'd surely be in one of his moods… and checking my phone every so often would probably just make him angrier.

But my momentary trepidation was no match for Ella's genuine enthusiasm. At the sight of her glowing expression, I had to grin. "Of course." My eyes slid to Mr. Stryker. "As long as my boss doesn't mind me looking at swatches on work time, of course."

Mr. Stryker shot me a slight, grateful smile. "Project approved, Miss Rivera. If Dominic gives you any grief, tell him you're working on another personal assignment for me. Offer to send him my way if he requires confirmation."

He turned his face back to Ella. "You'll stick close to Marco and listen if he tells you something is risky? And text me? A lot?"

She stretched up to kiss his cheek. "Yes. Promise."

And then I'll take you. Promise.

Graham's vow echoed through my mind. For a second, I swore I could almost feel his palm sliding against mine, pulling me into his arms for our dance. A tingle shivered down my spine.

Ella stepped away from Grayson and squeezed my upper arm on her way past me. "I'll add you to the text," she bubbled, smiling, then cast one last adoring, amused look at my boss. "Do try to keep him busy today, will you? If he keeps worrying like this, he'll have grey hair in all the wedding pictures."

Mr. Stryker and I watched her stroll to the elevators. He was still smiling widely when the doors slid closed. He shook his head. "She's not wrong. I know I've been overbearing all weekend. It's just hard to let her out of my sight when things are so…unsettled."

Thinking of how I might offer support, I reached into my work bag. "Maybe this will help. I finished the draft of your marriage contract yesterday. It's on your personal portal, but I printed one out to drop in your inbox, too." I handed him the document. "Maybe you can give the hard copy to Ella and get it all locked down before your vacation next week."

But Mr. Stryker grimaced as he took the contract from me. "Can't really say I'm happy to see this. We'll spend all week arguing about it."

Arguing? He basically planned to gift her half a billion dollars.

Images of Ella's handmade sweater and hideous rubber shoes came to mind. The way she didn't have her nails done or carry a name-brand handbag…

"She doesn't want any of it," I realized out loud.

A deeply sardonic smile stretched across Mr. Stryker's handsome features. "Not a blessed thing. I spent half my life worried someone would only want me for my money… and now that I have someone I *want* to give things to, she hates it. Ironic, right?"

I smirked. "Well, I hope she doesn't give you too much grief. But at least you'll have a week off to make up?"

Mr. Stryker's green eyes lit. "Excellent point."

He held the contract up as he started back toward his half of the floor. He suddenly paused. "Thank you for this, Juliet," he added. "I know the turn-around was tight. I really appreciate it. And thanks for taking the time to look at those color swatches. Ella admires your style and I know she'll value your opinion."

He really was a great boss. A good person. Somehow, knowing he chose Graham as his best friend raised my opinion of the man I'd come to know intimately.

Although, Ella does *call him "shithead"...*

It was never simple with Graham. I couldn't seem to grasp his true nature. Was he kind? Arrogant? Apathetic? Bold or secretive? Romantic or a total brute?

I couldn't decide. The more time I spent with him, the less sure I felt. I had no idea who I should expect when I showed up at his door after work—the fierce, sensual man who held me so gently while taking me to my absolute limits all night long... or the polished, conceited urbanite with only his best interests at heart.

I didn't have much time to ponder it.

Because Dominic turned out to be the *real* shithead. He barked my name the second I stepped into our pod and glared from his office while I unpacked my things.

Grabbing my tablet and phone, I squared my shoulders and jaunted his way, refusing to scamper for him. He was a grown-ass man, after all. And my boss, not my emperor. He could wait while I walked at a normal pace.

"Good morning, Dominic," I said, making a show of looking him in the eye and speaking in a calm, even voice. "How was your weekend?"

His scowl pulled tighter at his square features. "No time for pleasantries, Miss Rivera."

His eyes skimmed over the high neckline of my dress. I'd chosen with care, making sure not pick anything that might tempt Graham into tempting me. The blush color seemed demure; and the boat-neck covered everything, skimming straight across my throat, just under my collarbones. As with all of Abuelita's clothes, the dress fit me well, but the shape wasn't skin-tight. I'd half-clipped my hair back, too… though my hairstyle didn't seem to matter much to Graham.

Dominic, on the other hand…

It was ridiculous that I had to worry about being just-sexy-enough-but-not-too-sexy every day. The other attorneys at Stryker certainly didn't spend their mornings assembling professional-yet-alluring ensembles to avoid getting snarled at.

His frown deepened when he took in my appearance.

I wanted to spit at him. Report him. Anything.

But how could I report a feeling? He hadn't crossed any lines or violated company policy. He was always careful not to take his ogling or his comments too far.

Dominic was an ass, not an idiot. I almost wished he were stupid enough to be obvious. Then I might have something to prove my suspicions weren't just paranoia.

I watched him decide I wasn't enticing enough for him today. Any trace of interest blinked out of his eyes, leaving them flat and hard.

"We have a lot to catch up on," he continued, waving me into his office. "Since you were unwilling to pitch in this weekend."

I bit the inside of my cheek when I felt his gaze drop to my ass. *Carajo*—the slit up my skirt. But how else was Abuelita supposed to make dresses that were long enough to be appropriate and fitted enough to flatter? She knew I had to totter around in heels all day. If I didn't have some range of motion, my nude pumps would put me on my ass every time I stood up.

I took the nearest seat across from his desk, eager to get my butt out of sight. “Oh?” I asked lightly, deciding to play dumb. “You had to come in?”

Dominic dropped into his desk chair. I knew the answer even before he refused to meet my gaze. “I was able to work from home,” he hedged.

I forced a smile that made my stomach twist. “Me too. I had a personal assignment from Mr. Stryker that took up most of Saturday morning and Sunday evening.”

Dominic’s expression hardened further while he focused on me. “I assume it’s finished? You really should have had a copy on my desk before I got in. I’ll need to review it before Mr. Stryker sees it, of course.”

I did my best not to let my face fall. “I already gave it to him, I’m afraid. I wasn’t aware he asked you to review it, so I sent it to his secure portal as soon as I finished it. He needed the document by the end of the month, which is tomorrow, so I wanted to get him the draft as soon as possible, in case he has any revisions.”

And he specifically told me not to breathe a word of the pre-nup to anyone.

Dominic narrowed his eyes into slits and leaned across his glass desk. “Let’s get one thing clear right now, Miss Rivera. You work for *me*, not Mr. Stryker. *I* ensure your place at this company. You would do well to remember that going forward, and act accordingly.

“If I ask you to work on weekends, you will work on weekends. If anyone gives you an assignment, I will check it before you turn it in. You are junior counsel and I am your senior. There will be no need for you to meet with Mr. Stryker anymore. From now on, I will handle all legal matters with him one-on-one.”

Indignation filled my mouth with a thick wash of saliva. The edges of my vision clouded. The last time I felt so irate with a man,

I slapped him across the face. Of course, *that* wasn't an option. Neither was backing down.

I decided on a half-truth. Surely, he wouldn't object to my continued work with Mr. Stryker if it had already been assigned. And our CEO *did* ask me to help his fiancée with the swatches…

I brushed my hands over my lap before forcing myself to look back at him. "Mr. Stryker has already personally assigned me a couple of other—"

Dominic cut me off by slashing his hand through the air. "Are you not hearing me? Do we need to involve HR in this conversation?" A chilly smirk twisted his face. "Maybe a disciplinary memo in your file would help you remember your place here."

My throat felt oddly tight. Miraculously, I swallowed my mouthful of spit instead of hocking it at him. "How should I communicate to Mr. Stryker that you've decided to reassign me?" I asked, keeping my features still as stone. "And what shall I direct my energy to this week?"

I could tell Dominic expected some sort of scene. He seemed slightly miffed when I didn't give it to him. "I will speak to Mr. Stryker. No need for you to tell him anything."

Mierda de toro.

I nearly guffawed. There was no way I would ever trust Dominic to communicate with our boss on my behalf. I also wasn't about to argue with him about it.

Besides, helping Ella with color choices couldn't possibly be a threat to this asshole…

Deciding to send Mr. Stryker an email later in the day, I nodded as if agreeing with Dominic. "And my work for the week?"

I could see he didn't have an answer. His gaze flickered around his desk, finally landing on a pile of folders in the corner. "This," he determined aloud, shoving the stack at me. "Proofread them."

Proofread? Like a secretary? I *did not* sit in law school for three years to be a paralegal.

But when I opened my mouth to protest, Dominic simply spun his chair away from me, turning to the window behind him. "Have them all back to me by Wednesday. That will be all, Miss Rivera."

"But, Dominic, I—"

"Mr. Carter," he corrected sharply, tossing a disdainful look over his shoulder. "Now get to work. It's after nine. You're late."

Que gonorrea.

Graham

The plan would work.

I was about ninety-two-percent sure.

I straightened my bright white tie—the same one I wore the previous Monday, when I wound up defiling Miss Rivera in office pod C—and refolded my collar.

Damn.

Okay, ninety-five-percent sure. Because fuck if I didn't look *good* in pink. Light pink, to be specific. With a rosy vest under the jacket and a striped pink-and-white shirt beneath that.

I usually reserved the outfit to annoy Stryker. Of all my colorful suits, he hated the pink one the most. I couldn't understand why. He used the word "obnoxious," if memory served.

In any case, the blush suit always served me well. Yeah, it was flashy and maybe a touch unprofessional, but I knew for a fact that I carried it off.

Plus, women *loved* that shit. I never struck out while wearing the pink suit.

And I banked on that for my plan.

"Good morning."

I leaned my hip against the desk in front of my father's office, grinning down at his assistant, Lacey. I let my eyes roam over her low-cut red blouse, feigning interest while my mind jeered at me, *Not as hot as Juliet by half.*

She truly wasn't. With forgettable blonde hair and an average figure, the woman's singular appeal lied in her clear blue eyes. It was easy to overlook the rest of her to focus on those. I pretended to gaze into the molten honey irises I'd grown so infatuated with, and projected intent interest as sincerely as I could.

"You look lovely today." The words rolled out smoothly, without invoking even a flicker of feeling in me. "Did you have a fun weekend?"

Lacey's gaze went wide as she gaped up at me. Shocked, no doubt, that I'd suddenly taken an interest in her after months of treating her like another piece of office furniture.

"Uh… yeah. I mean, yes. Sir. Mr. Everett."

I affected a charmed chuckle. "You don't need to call me Mr. Everett. Graham is fine. And I'll call you Lacey." I tilted my head, regarding her as warmly as I could. "Deal?"

"Yes, sir. I mean, Graham," she stammered, turning red. "Did you need help with something?"

I glanced down at her desk to see if my father's schedule happened to be penciled into her desktop calendar. No such luck. Damn.

"I was just planning a meeting for later this afternoon and wondered if there were any prior commitments on our schedule," I told her, still grinning.

She blinked, dazed, and then visibly swallowed. I saw a flash of fear move through her eyes.

Bingo.

"Just a long lunch," she mumbled, dropping her gaze while the color in her face darkened. "We—*he* should be back by two."

I had a hunch the two of them would sneak off at some point. After all, they hadn't seen each other in two days. I felt certain that a long lunch was just code for a rendezvous. I knew I could sneak a locksmith in and out of his office during that time, to unlock the closet.

Just to be extra sure, I asked, "And do *you* have lunch plans as well?"

She thought I was asking her out. I watched her pause, considering her options—the elder, sleazy Everett with all the money… or me.

"Yes," she decided. "I do."

My lips twitched. *Just as I thought.*

I worked to keep smugness out of my smile. "Pity. Well, thank you, Lacey. Enjoy your lunch."

Striding back up the hall, I sent a text to the locksmith I procured earlier that morning. He was waiting for my instruction, ready to drop by at any point after noon. I told him twelve-thirty just to be sure my father and his secretary would be well on their way by the time he arrived.

Staring at my inbox, my fingers itched to message Juliet. I tried to come up with something professional, but wound up going for droll.

So help me God, I wrote. *I hope you left those red heels at home.*

Juliet

Despite my entirely shitty day, I almost had to laugh when Graham opened his door and I saw that our outfits essentially matched.

I swallowed my amusement for two reasons—first, he looked way too good in that godforsaken pink suit. It somehow made him even *more* wickedly sexy than any of his other ensembles. Perhaps because it displayed his unshakable confidence as much as it contrasted his dark, masculine features.

But, second—and more importantly—I couldn't so much as giggle once I saw his face.

His skin looked ashen, his eyes solemn. He wore an expression somewhere between grim acceptance and true, helpless sorrow. I'd never seen him so serious. Raw, without even a shred of his usual indolence.

"Juliet," he murmured, standing in the doorway, staring down at me. A flash of relief eased the tightness around his eyes for a moment. "I forgot you were coming, but I'm glad you're here."

He sounded… sincere? Not taunting or flirting or insinuating a thing. Not Graham-like at all.

I hesitated, suddenly unsure of myself. "I can go…? I thought we had work to do."

"No," he replied softly. "Stay. I—God, I forgot dinner. Do you want food? I'll order food."

"I brought dinner," I told him, holding up my lunchbox. "Two of those sandwiches you liked last week. Abuelita made more steak yesterday."

He seemed so disoriented. I reached over the threshold to touch his arm, hoping to help him focus. "Graham? You look sick."

Graham blinked. "Sick?" He glanced down at himself, as though checking for some sort of stab wound or other injury before answering. "No. Not sick. Although…"

Without thought, my hand drifted up from his arm to cup his solid jaw. I saw that he'd shaved that morning, but a thin layer of stubble still pricked my palm. Our gazes collided. His echoed the pain pulling at his features.

"Did something happen?" I asked him.

Graham's eyes fell shut for a long second. I swore he leaned his face into my hand slightly. "Let's just say it's a good thing I hired a lawyer."

My stomach clenched. "Well, technically, you haven't retained me yet," I replied, trying for a teasing tone I didn't quite achieve.

Graham's expression froze over. He pulled my hand from his face and used it to tug me into his apartment, locking the door before dragging me into the great room. While I set all my things down in one of this chairs, he reached for a slip of paper on the island and presented it to me. "Here."

A check. For fifty thousand dollars. Made out to me.

I balked. "You don't have to give me the whole amount to retain me! What if I die before your work is finished? Or if I quit? Or do a bad job?"

Graham's face didn't even flicker. "I told you I trust you. So take it. Because, believe me, you're going to earn it."

"Graham." I found myself glancing nervously around the room, looking for signs of a grisly murder or some other heinous crime. But the only new addition since the previous day was a file box in the center of his coffee table. "What did you *do*?"

A sudden burst of manic energy twitched through him. He started pacing, spinning his phone in his palm while he muttered, "Not me. I didn't do anything. I don't think. I mean, if I did, I didn't *know* about it. What is that called—*plausible deniability*? So I have that, at least. Except, maybe not any more since I *know* now... You're the lawyer, you'll have to tell me."

He suddenly stopped cold and rotated to me. As soon as our eyes met, all of the fight drained out of him. He slumped forward, holding himself up by pressing his hands into the edge of his white stone countertop.

"My father has committed fraud," he finally said to the granite. "Multiple times. For three years, at least. I found one book he cooked... and I thought maybe it was fluke or a mistake, but today I got into a closet he always keeps locked and there were...." He swallowed, his gaze flitting back to the file box over his shoulder.

"*Dozens*," he rasped, squeezing his eyes shut and shaking his head. "Dozens of falsified accounts."

My mind whirred, trying to process his confession and its implications. My criminal law knowledge was theoretical, but I studied many such cases over the years. I knew the right questions to ask. I actually—much to my own surprise—had answers.

"And you had no prior knowledge of these accounts?" I verified. Though, even before he nodded, his demeanor betrayed genuine shock. "Then you can turn him in under whistleblower protections."

I stated the fact immediately, without really thinking it through. When my brain caught up to mouth, I bit my lip. *Turn his* father *in?* For *dozens* of counts of stock fraud? Amounting to millions, probably… Surely enough to close Everett Alexander down.

What if he didn't want to report it? What if he wanted to act like he'd never seen it?

"Or…" I chose my words very carefully. "Are we having a different conversation?"

Graham straightened, pinching the bridge of his nose as he only did when he reached the end of his rope. "Jesus. *I don't know*. I'm leaving the company either way… I guess I could just… slip away? And not tell anyone? But then, am I complicit if he ever gets caught by somebody else?"

My empty stomach heaved. We were discussing how to let his father continue defrauding people… so he could make a clean getaway.

I had a difficult time discerning how I felt about that. On the one hand, greedy men like Mr. Everett deserved no mercy, in my opinion. And what Graham proposed would allow his father to continue stealing from people indefinitely.

But I was a lawyer. And Graham was my client. His interests had to be my priority. Legally. I was obligated to answer his questions honestly and forbidden to breathe a word of our discussion.

After a deep breath, I reached for a pen in my purse and pulled out a Starbucks receipt. Jotting quickly, I wrote a note and slid it to him. *Are there cameras or recording devices in this apartment?*

He read it and blinked at me, visibly thrown by my train of thought. "No," he replied aloud. "Neither."

Gracias a Dios. It never occurred to me to ask about a camera when I stripped both of us out of our clothes on Saturday night…

I forced myself to focus. Rolling my shoulders back, I straightened my spine. "If you're asking me how to get out of this situation without repercussions for yourself or your father, then I will say this and only this: we will have this conversation one time and never speak of it again."

Graham's jaw hardened. "I don't know if that's what I'm asking you. But I want to hear how it would go, should I choose that route."

I nodded. "Alright. But, like I said, I'm only going to say this once, so pay attention."

With a sigh, I looked over at his box of files, then down at the phone in his hand. "If you've used your phone, laptop, or work computer to Google any of this, it's too late. If you've texted, emailed, or spoken with anyone else about it, it's too late. If you've implied that you know anything to your father, it's too late. But if I am truly the only living soul who knows, apart from you, then you may not have to turn him in to save yourself. You could pretend you never saw anything.

"If you go that way, you will return the materials you found to their original places, after wearing gloves and wiping them down to destroy any fingerprints you left on them. You will destroy any copies you made, as well as any notes.

"You will go to your father and tell him your plans to leave the company. You will never tell him you know about the fraud. You will never *imply* that you know. You will follow his company's usual termination practices and return all of his accounts to him. I would advise leaving as quickly as possible without arousing suspicion—two weeks is a standard amount of time. I would also advise avoiding any work for clients from Everett Alexander in the future, just to keep things clean. We could say it's an integrity move—not wanting to take clients from your own father.

"If you're ever questioned, you will tell them you had no knowledge of any of it. Never saw the books. Never touched the accounts. Never brokered any of the deals. You will act appalled and make it clear you always intended to open your own firm for personal reasons unrelated to your father or his business practices. Then you plead the Fifth. Forever. And I mean refusing to answer a single question. There will be no evidence to incriminate you; so as long as you don't implicate yourself, they won't be able to charge you."

Graham and I stared at each other. An endless silence stretched between us, thick and heavy. I watched the gears turn in his mind, processing.

His throat worked on a swallow before he replied, "And if I want to report him?"

A wave of relief washed through me. My knees trembled with the force of it. I gripped the nearest barstool, hoping I didn't look like I was about to wilt.

"Then we need to do it as soon as possible. If we go to the FBI and tell them you want to blow the whistle on Everett Alexander, we should do so immediately. You've done nothing illegal, yet. You only become complicit if you sit on the information. How long have you known?"

Graham's jaw hardened. "I got the original tainted book last week, but I didn't realize what I had in front of me until yesterday afternoon. I saw my father at dinner but didn't confront him or act differently. I gave him back the book in question this morning, at his request. I didn't know about the other accounts until this afternoon, after I took the books out of his office closet, copied them, and reviewed the results."

A chill ran through my blood. "Did you scan them or photocopy them?"

"Photocopy," he mumbled, picking lint off of his sleeve. "I used our oldest copier, in the back storeroom. It's from the eighties. It doesn't even hook up to a computer. No virtual copies and it doesn't store memory."

He was smart. I tended to forget that when I thought of his flashy clothes and gorgeous face and general nonchalance. All of that pretty packaging hid an exceptionally sharp mind.

But I was sharp, too. I quickly spun through both scenarios, looking for loopholes and pitfalls alike. One stood out above all the rest.

"If you blow the whistle," I told him. "And the FBI finds out you started your company after you knew about the fraud, then they could claim your new business and its profits as fruit of the poison tree. At the very least, it would taint your reputation to future clients and put you on every government watch list for the next two decades."

His posture deflated slightly. "Goddamn it. How is that even fair? I haven't *done* anything."

I knew how he felt, having been screwed over my own father's pitiful choices more times than I cared to count. I had to leash the part of me that longed to rail against the injustice of it all in order to think clearly.

"Unless you can prove that you planned to start your company before you had any knowledge of the fraud. Meaning, if we had a witness or some paperwork to show that the plan was already in motion before your father ever assigned you the original account review; then we show that your choice to leave Everett Alexander had nothing to do with any wrongdoing."

Graham shook his head again, the motion stiff. "No. I don't have anything to prove that because it isn't true. The truth is: I *did* decide to leave before I knew there was fraud… but *after* he gave me the fraudulent ledger. And I did originally hire you to help me with my new company, not this issue. Even if all the timing looks suspect, my story is true. They can give me any test they want."

"This isn't CSI," I said gently. "They won't polygraph you. If they can't prove you're lying—which they *won't*, if you're telling the truth—then they'll just… try to screw you. Watch you. Possibly forever."

Graham's mouth rolled into a tight line. "Waiting for me to fuck up... Not to mention, I'll have one hell of a time finding anyone who will hire me after all of Manhattan finds out my father's been lining his pockets at his clients' expense."

My entire being cringed away from that concept. "So you don't tell anyone."

Some color finally returned to Graham's face as he scowled. "And he just gets away with it? For the rest of his life? While I go on pretending I can still look at him without wanting to retch?"

"No," I snapped back. "While you go on to have a successful career and make your own reputation, separate from his. I don't—"

I don't want you to suffer.

I caught myself just in time. It was an unprofessional thing to say to a client. And why did I want to argue with him? In favor of *his father*?

I blew out a breath as quietly as I could. "You'll have to make your own decision, of course. I can advise you either way."

Graham crossed his arms over his chest, glowering. "But, basically, my options are to tell on my father so he gets punished, possibly ruining my own future in the process; or, let him continue to steal from people while I do my best to distance myself from his shit and possibly live a long and very wealthy life without anyone finding out I ever knew anything?"

"Yes," I admitted.

Graham's tense features tightened. "But if he gets caught later and I'm implicated, then all of my work in the interim would be taken from me?"

A pang of pain shot through my chest. "Yes," I whispered.

His color drained again. He dropped his arms to his sides and just stood there, in his pink-striped shirtsleeves and socks, in his gorgeous apartment, looking somehow desperately adrift despite all of his charms.

Our gazes locked again. And though his expression seemed eerily still, his eyes were turbulent. His voice cracked as he asked, "How much time do I have to make my decision?"

"I'll have to research some precedent to be absolutely sure," I mumbled, more to myself than him. "But I would say—off the top of my head—two weeks sounds reasonable."

He seemed like such a solitary figure all of a sudden. I wondered why it had never occurred to me to ask if he had any other good friends, aside from Mr. Stryker. He obviously wasn't close to his family the way I was... and if he *had* been close to them, he likely wouldn't be going forward.

When Mr. Stryker got married and—one way or another—Graham left Everett Alexander, he probably wouldn't have anyone to turn to. No one would comfort him or stand by his side.

And he stood to lose everything... even his own name.

The pressure building at the back of my throat reminded me of the last time I shed tears. In the stairwell, that day at work. When Graham offered me his handkerchief and insisted on giving me solace.

Before I knew what I was doing, I stepped toward him. My heels clicked on his wood floors as I closed the distance between us and threw my arms around his neck, just catching the flash of disbelief on his face before pulling myself into his chest.

He caught me instantly. His arms came around me in a vice so tight, I couldn't move. A gust of breath ruffled my hair as he tugged me closer and exhaled into my neck.

"God," he said softly, bringing one hand up to hold the back of my head. "Jules."

I felt him shake and started to stroke my hands down his back. "Shhh," I whispered, hoping to calm him. His body shuddered hard, and I wondered if he'd eaten anything all day. Or had any water.

"Come here," I told him, my tone brokering no argument. "Sit. I'll get our food."

I knew he must really be in bad shape when he listened and did as I said. I recalled where his plates were from the day before and made my way across the kitchen. When I turned back, I found him blatantly staring at my body.

He sighed. "You really are beautiful, Jules."

I tried for a joke. "So are you, *pinchao*. I think it must be the pink."

I set his plate down and unpacked our dinner within seconds. "Now eat. This is a fine mess you've gotten us into and I, for one, will not suffer a weak partner in crime."

The ghost of a smile tilted his lips. "Fair enough, *bijou*."

CHAPTER TWELVE

January 31, 2017

Graham

I gave Juliet a key to my place in case drinks with Jason McAllister ran long Tuesday night.

A purely practical decision that, of course, brought out the fight in her.

We went seven rounds on the goddamn thing, with her claiming it had some "unspoken significance" and calling it "egregious" while I argued, over and over, that it was a temporary measure to keep my neighbors from thinking I left my women standing around in hallways.

She, naturally, objected to being one of "my women;" I pointed out that, like or not, she *was*.

Stubborn *bijou*.

Even after eating our incredible sandwiches in silence and working quietly on my couch for two hours… even with my mind so clouded with issues and my gut full of fear… I still wanted to fuck her the second that little chin tilted up.

I managed to rein in my impulses long enough to talk her down. "It's just a key, Jules," I growled, pressing it into her palm for the tenth time. "A meaningless sliver of metal. And, look, it even has a monogramed fucking keychain on it. GE—Graham Everett. It's *mine. My* spare key. Not yours. You're just using it for *one night.*"

She finally took it and left in a snit, muttering in Spanish. I wanted to ask Grayson for a list of curse words—ones I knew I wouldn't find in any respectable dictionary—but thought better of it when I realized such a request might give us away.

We'd determined we would wait until after his vacation to tell him about our work arrangement. Better to inform him after he spent a week in his fiancée.

I mean, in *Aruba.*

I spent Tuesday huddled in my cramped office, never daring to leave lest I do anything remotely suspicious to tip my dad off. After wasting seven hours staring at my computer screen without entering a single keystroke, I left at four to meet the creative director and heir-apparent of The McAllister Group at a bar in Tribeca.

Drinks did, in fact, run long. So I was feeling particularly smug when I shoved into my apartment…

And all haughtiness evaporated at the impossible sight of a gorgeous woman, dressed in my clothes, blasting music on my speakers, barefoot, in my kitchen.

Holy. God.

What had I done? Why did I *like* it?

Juliet's ponytail swished as she tossed a look over her shoulder. A loud laugh burst up her throat.

"*Ay Dios mío, pinchao.* You should see your face." She shook her head and turned back to my stove. "Worth it."

I couldn't tell if she meant that her work making dinner was worth the look on my face or if she implied that her meal would be worth the panic that ran through me at the sight of a girl in my kitchen. In my *clothes.* Either way, her cocky little remark made me smirk.

"For someone who didn't want the damn key, you certainly used it to help yourself."

I tossed my own keys onto the island and leaned my hip into the counter, crossing my ankles as I stared at her backside. She was a sight for sore eyes, even in my burgundy joggers and black tee shirt. She'd rolled the ankles on my pants to her knees and tucked the back of the tee shirt into the sweat's waistband, but she still looked adorably small and soft engulfed in my clothing.

She moved from the stove to the mess of chopped vegetables on the nearest stretch of counter. Using the back side of a blade, she scraped them off the cutting board, into the stock pot, where they made a satisfying hiss. With a slight shrug, she pointed the knife over her shoulder and said, "I didn't want to wreck my dress."

I'll be damned.

The red fucking dress.

My cock went from semi-erect to stone as I spotted the garment draped over the edge of my sofa. Her matador's cape. She wore it to work again. Then wore it in my apartment. And *took it off.*

Torture.

I had to clench both of my fists to keep from snatching her up and pinning her to the counter. "Naughty girl," I commented, forcing an even tone. "You knew I wanted to take that off for you and you did it without me."

She laughed again. "Keep dreaming, buddy."

For the first time since Sunday morning, a wide smile pulled at my face. The unfamiliar swirl of satisfaction and gratitude whirled in my center, warming me. *Christ.*

She was so beautiful. And funny. And brilliant.

And *here*. With me. Cooking?

After giving her veggies a good stir, she turned and faced me. For a long moment, she worked her eyes up and down my body. Liking what she saw. She pressed her luscious thighs together and lifted her jaw just so.

"You wore the purple again," she commented. "After my stroll through your closet earlier, I thought you must have a new suit for every day of the year."

I stalked a bit closer before hesitating. "And I thought you had a different dress for every work day. Guess we're both outfit repeating."

Juliet canted her head, her shrewd gaze staring me down. "Fancy that."

I wondered why she chose the now-infamous dress for her day. Did she want part of me with her, too?

I didn't ask. Instead, I nodded to the food behind her. "What is it?"

She tossed back a word I didn't understand, then grinned at the confusion on my face. "Ah-yah-co," she repeated, taking mercy. "It's Colombian chicken soup. For truly bad days."

Bad days. The tepid notion nearly made me laugh. "Got anything for bad *weeks*? Bad *lives*?"

A flash of sympathy tightened her fine features. "This will help," she replied, almost sounding gentle. "It's my favorite when something upsetting happens." She winced at the pot. "Abuelita usually makes it… But I had a hell of a day and I figured you did, too, so I guess you're stuck with my version."

I hated the idea of her having a hellish day. "What happened, *bijou*?"

My nickname seemed to soften her. Her lips fell into a slight frown while she bit the inside of her cheek and spun away, hiding her eyes.

"Dominic," she grumbled.

My fists tightened. "I'd *love* to kick that guy's ass. He's such a prick."

That earned me a sly, amused look over her shoulder. An expression that was quickly becoming one of my favorites. I wished I had a picture of it.

"Marco and I think he has penis problems," she smirked, adding a pile of pulled rotisserie chicken to the pot. She poured a whole quart of chicken broth on top and backed away from the range.

With a sigh, Juliet floated over until we stood face-to-face. For a second, my impulses got away from me; I reached over to tuck a loose strand of hair behind her ear. "Tell me what he did," I murmured, not wanting to let it go.

Juliet's posture stiffened. "I can handle him."

My fingers had a mind of their own. They traced a slow path from her ear to her chin. "Never said you couldn't," I replied mildly, examining her beauty up close. "But I want to know what he's up to."

Her topaz gaze narrowed. "Why?"

She probably worried I'd go running to Grayson. Most women would have tried to take advantage of my connection with their boss. For some, it would be a major point in my "pro" column. But Juliet seemed to consider it a mark against me. She wanted to make her own way. I'd never take that away from her.

My touch glided up her cheekbone, back to hair. I blew out a long breath, loathing myself for what I was about to say.

"Because I care."

Her face became so wary, it felt like an affront to my character. "*You* care?"

I almost laughed at her incredulity. "Yes. And it disgusts me."

That seemed to mollify her. A dazzling grin lit her features. "Why does that make me *so* happy?"

I didn't know, but her delight delighted me. I found myself smiling widely, too, even as I pushed back. "Your gorgeous smile will not get you out of my question."

She composed herself within a second, smoothing her face back into its stunning mask of obstinacy. "It really wasn't anything major," she told me, flicking her ponytail back in an agitated gesture. "He just… he's an asshole who doesn't want anyone to upstage him."

I thought back over the few times I interacted with Dominic Carter, including the meeting where Juliet's cool competence made him look like a pedantic moron. "And you upstage him all the time, I bet."

She hadn't pulled away from my touch, so I took a small step closer and slid my hand around to massage the back of her neck. Another fleeting spark of vulnerability softened her expression.

"I don't mean to," she mumbled, looking down at her bare feet. "I just want to do good work. I'm trying to learn as much as I can, you know? And the best way is through experience. So, when Mr. Stryker gives me something new to do, I jump at it. But Dominic feels threatened."

Fucking piece of shit.

What did he care if Juliet flourished? It would just make him look like a good manager if his juniors excelled. Ego was his only reason for trying to keep her down. I flattened my lips together, actively holding the stream of expletives I longed to spit out.

Juliet went on, still staring at her toes while they drew circles on my wood floor. "He told me yesterday that I wasn't allowed to contact Mr. Stryker directly anymore and that I had to route all communication through him. So I sent an email to Mr. Stryker letting him know that I'd be doing just that, in accordance with 'the new policy.'" She threw up air quotes and snapped her fiery honey eyes back to mine. "I didn't even *mention* Dominic by name, because I had a feeling Mr. Stryker would be annoyed with him if I did..."

But I knew Grayson. He'd see right through Dominic having Jules do his dirty work. And he'd be *pissed.*

"Shit," I muttered. "What did Stryker do?"

Juliet exhaled, deflating. "He's angry with both of us, now. He spent ten minutes nailing Dominic to the wall of his office and then called me in to 'clarify the chain of command.' I could tell he didn't like that I obeyed Dominic's orders when they contradicted his own. I guess that was stupid. I just—" She broke off mid-thought.

"You what?" I demanded.

Her eyes darkened along with her expression. "I got intimidated, okay?" She spat it like I was responsible, somehow, then ranted on, "I didn't go to Harvard or Yale or whatever, Graham! I don't have fancy business clothes or debutante etiquette training. My only previous work experience was waitressing in high school and restocking shelves at a Rite Aid in college.

"And Dominic and all the other guys in my department are, like, fourth-generation attorneys who went to Ivy League schools and started temping at firms the summer after they graduated high school! They have credentials I will never have. And despite all of that *mierda*, on my good days, I *know* they're all idiots who are full of hot air. But, sometimes, when I make a mistake or when they get in my face like Dominic does, I start to wonder if maybe *I'm* the one who doesn't belong and maybe I have it all wrong."

I started to step up against her body, moving to hug her, but she shoved at me with both hands, rejecting any comfort I tried to offer her. A hot knife of chagrin stabbed me. Embarrassment turned to defensiveness. It bled into my concern. Both roared through my blood, pounding in my ears, begging me to snatch her hands and haul her into my arms. But I just glared down at her.

Seething.

Yet another similarity we seemed to share: we both got mad when we felt vulnerable.

I understood all too well. Sometimes, true weakness seemed like an unforgivable sin. And Jules was a fighter, like me. She would claw and snap to protect her pride.

As I stood there, I realized she wasn't mad *at me*. And I knew what she really needed.

Reassurance. That I didn't lose respect for her after her outburst. That I still found her formidable, despite her weaknesses. That I would always think of her as the mysterious, wondrous creature who kept me up all night on Saturday… and each night thereafter, if I was honest with myself.

After my dark revelations the previous evening, I spent the entire day craving the same reassurance. I wanted to know she still wanted me, still thought me a worthy opponent. I only knew one way to show both of us that nothing had changed.

I slipped my light gray jacket off, meeting her eyes with a challenging look. "Your shirt. Give it to me."

Her chest heaved. Color rushed to her cheeks. "*What?*"

"Your shirt—or *my* shirt. Whatever. Take it off."

Golden slits flashed at me. "*Why* would I do that?"

I yanked on my tie and toed at my socks and shoes before stalking toward her, leaning my face down into hers. "Because you want me to flatten you on this island and ram my cock into you until you forget all about your shitty day. Because I'm going to show you how powerful and beautiful and brilliant you really are. So fucking perfect that I can't keep my hands off of you, even when I know I should."

We stood chest-to-chest. I watched her swallow. She glared up at me. "You are the cockiest, most spoiled, insensitive, entitled, *vulgar* son-of-a-bitch who's ever lived."

I smiled, knowing it would goad her. "And you hate me, right?"

"Yes," she spat.

"Then say no."

She wouldn't. Because she already had my button-down fisted in her little hands, tugging it out of my pants. Her fingers unfastened it, along with my alligator-skin belt. She whipped the latter off of my waist with a flourish. Grabbing it from her before she got any ideas, I snapped the belt once before stepping back against her.

"Let me show you," I whispered, grabbing her chin roughly. "I'll show you how potent you are. How crazy you make me. The things you make me want to do. I'm a fucking *savage* because of *you*."

She tilted her head back, silently panting while we locked eyes.

"Yes or no, baby?" I asked.

I felt her push at the sweats until they fell to her ankles. "Yes."

Juliet

The smoldering sensuality in Graham's dark gaze proved too much for my self-control.

Because he was right. I *did* want him.

The way he looked at me when I argued with him—like some fearsome goddess he wanted to fuck senseless—*did* make me feel powerful.

He didn't waste any time. Within seconds, he had my tee shirt on the floor, along with his pants and shirt. A black pair of silk boxer-briefs showcased his erection. The thick bulge ran down his in-seam, so long I swore I caught a glimpse of his cockhead before he tugged my body against the length of his lean hardness and kissed me deeply.

It occurred to me, in some distant corner of my mind, that I should have freaked out. I'd never hooked up with a man more than once. But the second I asked myself why I didn't feel panicked, I knew… that same small piece of my sub-conscious accepted, from the first time, that there would be more. That there *had to be* more, as long as I kept Graham in my life.

As wrong as it was, this moment between us almost felt… inevitable.

Our tongues slid together, sending tingles to my breasts and a liquid ache between my thighs. Graham broke away too quickly and turned his hot gaze down to my body. He groaned at the sight of my red demi-cup bra.

"Was *this* under that dress last week?" he rasped, tugging the cups down. My breasts spilled out. His expression turned black. "You know what? I think I hate you, too."

He had a way of making me want to laugh and claw into him simultaneously. Insanity. That's what it was. What it had to be. He made me insane.

In that moment, as his throbbing cock pressed into my belly, I didn't care. With the scent of his cologne filling my nose and his hands roaming over my nakedness, it got harder to think by the second.

Turned out I didn't need to. He had other plans for me.

"Your hands," he said, brandishing his belt once more. "Put them out in front of you."

I started to argue, but then he snapped the leather again. The sound instantly took me back to Saturday night, and the sound his palm made when he punished me for denying him. A burst of wetness spread through my panties. I stretched out my hands.

Grinning, he gave one last crack of the belt. "I'll have to remember this trick. It seems to have quite the effect."

His smile disappeared as he looped the strap around my wrists, knowing just how to fasten it into a restraint. I pulled at the binds to test them, finding that I could only move my arms slightly before leather bit into my skin.

He took a step back and made a big show of looking me up and down, obviously committing the image to memory. Picturing what he saw, I wished I'd worn matching panties that morning instead of throwing on the faded navy thong I found at the top of my underwear drawer.

The self-conscious thought made me shift on my feet. His eyes instantly snapped to mine. He frowned.

"Hmm," he murmured to himself. "Alright then."

He hooked his index finger through the looped belt and tugged me into his arms. One hand fell to my ass while the other reached for something on the island. He leaned down close to my face like he was about to kiss me, brushing our lips together until my nipples pebbled, teasing me.

"Not yet. Turn around."

He spun me toward the island before I could comply on my own. I loved his impatience. It showed me how much I affected him.

He was right—even though he was ostensibly the one in control, I felt more powerful than ever.

Graham's hard warmth flattened my hips into the counter's edge. His arms came around me to wrap his purple paisley tie through his makeshift belt-cuffs. I felt the ridge of his dick rub over my ass when he stretched up, pulling my hands over my head and then forward. He knotted the tie around the rack of pots and pans overhead and stepped away, leaving me tethered, with my body bent over the island and my back arched.

"Jules," he growled from behind me. "You look so fucking hot. I'm never going to be able to eat at this island without getting hard again."

His hand followed the slope of my spine in one long caress. "What do you think?" he hummed, pressing himself into my hip and nuzzling my shoulder. "Can you take it like this?"

"Yes," I said, breathier than I intended. "Stop playing and give it to me already."

I felt his smile against my neck. "I don't know," he replied, his voice low. "Maybe I'll leave you here while I have dinner."

I pulled at my restraints. The pans clattered. "Graham, so help me *God…*"

He bit the place below my ear, making me hiss. When he heard the sound, his cock twitched against me. I realized if I wanted him to take me right away, arguing with him wouldn't help. I had to entice him.

Sticking my ass out further, I ran the front of my right foot over the back of my left calf. The motion sent my hip swaying into his groin. He nipped me again, punishing me for goading him, then swirled his tongue over the sting.

Graham's hand slipped into the front of my panties, feeling my wetness. With a growl, he started pawing at the lace with both hands, pushing it off. He spun me effortlessly, once more putting my backside against the island. Above, his rack clanged.

"This way," he grunted.

Graham sank to the floor and tore my thong away from my ankles, leaving me bare. With his hands wrapped around the backs of my thighs, he caressed up to my ass. All while staring at the juncture of my thighs as if it was all he could see.

I wished I could run my fingers through his hair. When I inadvertently tugged at my bound hands, Graham's black eyes leapt up to mine. I expected him to gloat or look away, but he didn't. He let me stare right into him, making his point without words.

I was the one tied up. But he was on his knees. For me.

"Do you see?" he asked, holding my gaze.

Before I could form an answer, he planted a kiss on each of my hip bones and turned his attention to my sex. He skimmed his lips over my clit so lightly, I huffed in frustration. Graham's grin curved against me, taunting me with the prick of his stubble. I grumbled louder and his fingers clutched me tighter. He gave me another teasing kiss.

"Gorgeous." *Kiss.* "Impatient." *Kiss, kiss.* I tried to push myself closer, but he held me in place. "Stubborn," he muttered. *Kiss.*

His fingers slid around to spread across the tops of my thighs. His thumbs skimmed over my folds, rubbing me before spreading the lips, revealing me to his hungry eyes. With a quiet snarl, he tilted his head and sucked my swollen bud into his mouth. Sensation spiraled through my core, arching my spine as I cried out his name.

He liked that. Yanking my legs apart, he slung them over his solid shoulders and pulled me tight against his open mouth, licking with a muffled curse. His tongue slipped into my opening, tormenting me with short, shallow strokes and then spearing deeper. My body spasmed around him, right on edge. A second later, he broke away.

"You're so slick and ready," he murmured. "Tell me you want it."

My pride refused to beg him. But then he burned his midnight eyes into mine and bent forward to blow a cool stream of air right on my clit. Squirming, I pulled on my bound hands. His pots and pans rang out again.

With a self-satisfied smile, he lifted me down from his shoulders. Standing, he ground his silk-covered erection into my trembling sex. "Do you want it, Jules? Right now?"

He stepped back and shucked his own underwear, then grabbed my left hip and flipped me around again, bending me over the island. I nearly convulsed when he pressed his bare package against my ass. Reaching around, his hand cupped my sex. I writhed.

"Say it," he demanded hoarsely, pressing the heel of his hand against me. "Tell me."

Delirious, I bucked against him. "*Graham.*"

He moved his hand just out of my reach. "Say it," he rasped again, grinding into my ass.

The heat of him felt like a brand. Everything between my thighs pulsed, needing that steely length to quell the ache. "I want it now," I bit out, pushing back against him. "Please."

He gave me more pressure against my clit while his other palm smacked my ass with a loud *whap*. "I want to hear that again."

Just like the belt snapping, the sound aroused me. I moaned, beyond shame. "Please. I want it now."

Another *whap*—this time while two of his fingers plunged into me. "Again, Juliet."

Ay Dios mío. What was he *doing* to me? Trussed up, nude, panting and wriggling, literally *begging* for him. Shameless, all I could only feel the ecstasy he pushed through my veins with each pump of his hand.

His thumb slipped over my clit while he fingered me. The rack clanged above me. My thoughts scattered. Mindless, I pleaded, "Please, Graham. I want your cock *now.*"

He made a feral sound and went still for half a second before disengaging. I almost cried out at the loss of his knowing fingers, his body heat. A drawer opened and slammed shut behind me, where I couldn't see.

"I wish I could feel you," he muttered, but held a condom out long enough for me to see it. I heard the foil rip and felt his blunt head press into the cleft of my ass a second later.

The completely insane part of me wanted to tell him to take the rubber off. I was on the pill—and I wanted to feel him, too. Much to my dismay.

I shoved all such insanity aside and swished my ponytail while I swayed my hips, silently taunting him. Graham curved his body against mine, until every line of my back touched the planes of his torso. His arms banded around. Holding me, he spread one hand over the base of my throat. The other rolled my nipples in turn.

A long, keening cry escaped me. His cock twitched at the noise as his body tautened. His fingers stroked over my breasts again, eliciting a whimper that time. "Shhh," he whispered, tugging them again. "You like that?"

Too much. So much that I felt a foreign ache throb somewhere near my heart. "Graham," I moaned, out of finesse. "Please. I need you."

His erection pulsed against my ass. "Mmm," he murmured quietly, running his open mouth over the nape of my neck while he held me closer. "Yeah. I *definitely* hate you."

But it didn't feel like hatred. It felt tender and erotic and precious. A lot like…

His hands floated down my body until he gripped both hips. With one tug, he pulled me back and bent me forward, open to him. Before I took my next breath, he shoved in. Deep.

We both called out—me with a broken moan, him in a vicious curse that echoed off the high ceiling and curled my toes.

Groaning, he rolled his hips, stretching and filling me completely. With one more yank, he positioned me just so. His balls hit me every time he thrust inside, tapping my swollen clit with just enough pressure to drive me crazy.

Then he really started to move. Pumping like a piston, he held me in place while he took me higher and higher. Relentless. Maintaining a tight, insatiable pace, never letting up for even a second. I could barely breathe.

With Graham clutching my hips and my hands tied above me, I felt almost weightless as I soared closer and closer to my climax. When I was seconds away from coming, he suddenly pulled out. I screamed in protest, but he just delivered another hard slap to my ass.

"Hush," he whispered, rubbing away the burn.

A second later, he lifted and spun me once again, putting me on the counter to bring us face-to-face. His expression sucked all the air out of my lungs. It was fierce. Feral. Beyond the realm of any ordinary lust. He pushed between my open thighs and fisted my ponytail, pinioning me where he wanted me. His other hand started stroking his cock.

"This is what you do to me," he thundered, roving his hungry black eyes over my body while I strained to get closer to him. "Even when I have you in knots, you fucking *own* me."

Graham slid my ass to the edge of the granite and ran his fingers down the front of my body, to the pulsing bud at the top of my folds. As soon as he touched me, I moaned again. My head fell back into his hand. He pulled my hair harder, positioning me to peer into his eyes.

"I'm going to shove back into you and come instantly. I don't want to. I'm not ready. But I won't be able to stop because it's *you*. Do you *see*, Juliet?"

He started to slide into me, but I couldn't look away from the roiling depths of his gaze. The velvet turmoil. His fingers swirled over me. "Do you see what you do to me?"

"Yes," I cried, not sure if I was agreeing or praising. Not sure of anything except him.

Yes—yes to Graham.

That was all he wanted. Slamming forward, he thrust deep. The thick length of him was enough. I came hard, nearly sobbing his name.

Graham held me immobile, watching, working me over the edge. When my body gave a final clutch around his cock, he sloughed out a desperate breath and lost control. His fingers tightened and his head fell back on a groan as he finished.

He pulled me into his chest right away, squeezing me tightly before reaching up to unfasten his necktie. My arms felt like dead weight. Still cuffed together, they fell over the back of his neck. His own hands followed, chasing the numb tingles with kneading fingers.

And he was still inside me.

It all felt so good, I couldn't stifle the small whimper that slipped up my throat. Without a sound, Graham bent to put our foreheads together. He rubbed his nose along the length of mine.

Our gazes held. In the quiet, I heard everything he didn't say. Saw that he felt every bit as lost and awe-struck as I did. My instincts recoiled, begging me to shrink away from the intimacy. But I held still. I wouldn't back down as long as he didn't.

The meaningful silence stretched on and Graham didn't blink. His swirling eyes memorized mine, shifting with all the words neither of us spoke. A searing flash of clarity tore through me.

This is more than sex, I realized. *He means something to me.*

I hated it. After years of swearing to myself that I would never form any romantic attachments, I couldn't believe I allowed myself to develop such true feelings for a man. A man like *him*.

Shame filled my eyes. Fear, thick enough to choke, swelled in my throat.

Graham's expression broke. Consternation streaked through his gaze. "Hey," he murmured, seeing my tears. He held me closer, running both hands down my back. "Was I too rough, baby?"

I did my damnedest not to cry. But his simple, honest affection unhinged some part of me that I'd kept welded shut for a very long time. I sniffed the tears back, pinching my lips to stop them.

"No," I blurted. "I have no idea what's wrong with me. Just ignore me."

Graham gave a grim smile. "I think I've demonstrated that's impossible."

He slid his hands up my forearms and un-looped the binds while my wrists hung crossed behind his neck. He let the belt fall behind him without a care, bringing my prickling fingers to his lips for a series of soft kisses.

His face seemed more solemn by the second. "I'm sorry, Juliet. We made a deal and I pushed you anyway. This wasn't what we agreed to."

I hated his apology even more than I hated losing control. I didn't want to be something he regretted. Not when I couldn't quite manage to summon proper remorse within myself.

With another sniffle, I tossed my lopsided ponytail back and did my best to brazen it out. "I'm not," I told him honestly. "We wanted each other. And we promised we wouldn't ever pretend otherwise, right?"

Graham sighed heavily, dropping our entwined hands to my lap. "Do you have to argue with me about everything? I upset you and I didn't mean to. I'm sorry about it. Let me be sorry."

"No," I refused, scowling at him. "I don't *want* you to be sorry."

He moved to grip the edge of counter on either side of my bare thighs, leaning down into my face. "Well, I *am*," he replied, earnest. "So I guess you don't always get what you want, *bijou*."

The foaming urge to fight rose within me. "You do if you make it happen," I shot back.

Amusement sparked in his black eyes. "And how, exactly, do you plan to *make me* stop feeling sorry?"

I kissed him immediately. Hard. Slipping my hands up his neck and into his hair, I brought our naked bodies together. When he gave a frustrated grunt and tried to pull away, I bit his lower lip hard enough to taunt.

That did it. He grabbed me, clutching my arms with bruising force, holding me as if he didn't know whether he should push me away or yank me closer. I deepened our kiss, sliding my tongue into his mouth and then sucking on his.

I knew I had him when he let out another groan and moved to frame my face with his long fingers, positioning me just so and sealing his lips over mine. Between us, his cock came back to life. I stroked both of my hands down his abdomen, resting them lightly just over his groin.

He suddenly ripped his face away. Panting, he glared and rubbed his thumb over my mouth in an angry swipe. I opened my lips just in time to suck it into my mouth and lick the pad before nipping it. A shudder ran through him. Under my hand, he hardened into stone.

"Are you still feeling sorry?" I asked, trailing my fingertips down his length.

His obsidian depths glittered. "You're the devil, woman."

"But you're not sorry anymore, right? You want to do it again?"

Graham exhaled through his nose. "Yes," he gritted.

I slid down from the counter and out of his reach. Knowing he would watch my naked ass, I bent to pick up the clothes. "It's too bad dinner is ready," I taunted. Tossing his boxers and dress shirt over my shoulder, I righted my bra and stepped back into his sweatpants. "And I'm the devil."

Graham

She left me standing in the kitchen with a second hard-on and a pot of soup ready to boil over.

After the initial shock wore off, I had to admire her technique. She was right—I no longer had a shred of remorse. If what happened meant I got to keep fucking her, I couldn't regret even a second of it.

Who was I trying to fool, anyway? I'd shuffle across hot coals on my hands and knees to have her. Of course she knew that. I was the one struggling to accept it.

Muttering curses at myself, I trashed the used condom and put my underwear back on. *Fuck the shirt.* I'd work in my boxers. I was in my own goddamn house, after all. And all professional decorum had gone out the window. Clearly.

I kicked my rumpled suit into a pile beside my bedroom door and turned the stove down before stirring the contents. It looked good. Like a traditional chicken-and-vegetable soup, with potatoes and a medley of chopped herbs that smelled delicious. The broken ears of corn bobbing on top surprised me. I was poking at one when Juliet emerged from my room, having clearly washed up and adjusted her hair.

Her bare face made my heart seize up in my chest. So fucking gorgeous, it hurt. I instantly tugged her into my side and dropped a kiss on her forehead.

She stiffened in my embrace. Her troubled expression seemed more pensive than upset, though, so I decided not to ask. Golden eyes skimmed down my other arm, to the spoon in my hand.

"The corn is good," she mumbled. "Trust me, *pinchao*."

I felt relieved that she used her irreverent nickname. That usually meant things between us were okay. I had no idea what "okay" meant, anymore, though, so I couldn't be sure.

Leave it to Jules to be two steps ahead of me. Her brooding expression started to make sense as questions flooded my mind. She broke her one-night rule… was this really the first time? What did this mean? Would we keep having sex? Maybe just while we worked together and then we would stop?

Could we stop? And, if we did, then what? I'd just see her in passing at Stryker's? Wave and walk on? The thought depressed and panicked me in equal measures.

But what was the alternative? *Never* stopping? And then that would mean… a relationship?

I didn't do those. Neither did she. So that wouldn't happen.

Why did I want her more every time I had her? Infatuation didn't *work* that way, in my experience. Sex usually dulled the desire over time. Until, eventually, it died off.

This felt like the opposite. Each time she looked at me, smiled at me, gave herself over to me…. I just wanted *more*. And then more of that more.

Christ. My own thoughts didn't even make sense.

"Do you have any capers?" she asked quietly, not looking up. "Or sour cream? The bodega was out of capers and I always forget the cream."

I padded to the fridge and found it just as blank as I remembered. I did have plain yogurt, though. "No capers, but can you use this?"

She shrugged. "Sure."

Wordlessly, Jules ladled her soup into two bowls and spooned yogurt on top of each. She topped both of them off with half an ear of corn. If the air around us didn't feel so heavy, I may have teased her about the odd assemblage. As it was, we both took our seats at the island and dug in without speaking.

"Mmm." An appreciative grunt escaped me before I could stop it. "Damn it, Jules. This is amazing."

She smirked around her second bite. "Not as good as Abuelita's, though."

I shoveled another scoop, pondering how I might get an invitation to eat some of her grandmother's food in person. The lady had to be a marvel. Just like her granddaughter.

Before I knew it, I hit the end of my bowl and sat back. As delicious as it was, the soup also accomplished exactly what Juliet claimed it would: I felt better. Settled.

With a stomach full of warm comfort food, my mind cleared. I remembered why she was in my apartment in the first place.

"So, did you find any precedents to tell us how much time I have?"

Juliet exhaled. "A month. Maximum. But there were more favorable outcomes for whistleblowers who waited less than three weeks."

"Jesus." I had a guillotine hanging over my head. With a timer on it.

Juliet's spoon clattered into her empty bowl, drawing my eyes to her tense expression. When she spoke, her soft voice didn't carry a single hint of judgment. "Which way are you leaning?"

I didn't have an answer. My self-protective instincts told me to take all the dignity I could and run to higher ground without raising any alarms. It would be cleaner and *way* easier. Not to mention all the motherfucking *money* I stood to earn with an untainted reputation.

Truly, the notion of getting some sort of twisted revenge from turning my father in didn't appeal nearly as much as just getting the hell away from him. Every time I considered it, though, one thing haunted me.

The broker number.

He used the same one for every single fraudulent transaction. Not his. Not mine. Not *anyone's* as far as I could tell. None of our employees—past or present—had the same ID.

But I knew he wouldn't have gotten the trades past the system without a valid number. Did he pay someone to make a whole false identity and then pay someone else to get the fake person a broker number? And, if so, how did he get the money he stole back out of that fake account and into his own without raising any eyebrows?

"To the left," I deadpanned, not having any other answer.

Jules' lips twitched, hiding mirth. "Graham."

Damn her. This beautiful woman could scold me anytime she liked. I couldn't keep scowling when she looked so amused and disapproving.

A grin broke over my face. She surprised me when she brushed her warm fingertips over my cheek, tracing a laugh line.

She sighed, shaking her head. "You *are* handsome, *pinchao*, I'll give you that."

Her compliment only encouraged my smile. "I'm aware."

"Walked right into that one," she muttered to herself, rolling her eyes. Then, louder, "Should we work? I do have to go back to Queens eventually. And you did already pay me. A lot."

I hated the thought of her trekking back to Queens alone, late at night. Especially in that red dress. Unfamiliar anxiety clawed at my stomach. "I'll call you a car."

Another eye roll. "I can hail my own cab, Graham."

I stood up and gathered our bowls, balancing them in one hand while using the other to tug lightly on her ponytail. "You're doing it again," I pointed out. "And I didn't say 'taxi.' I said a car. As in, I'll call my service."

Fire snapped in her gaze; the same blaze that stole my breath the first time I saw her. "Doing *what* again?"

I set our dishes in my sink and lifted my bare shoulders, shrugging. "Arguing with me for no reason."

Her lush lips flattened. For a long moment, she stared back at me and I watched her war with herself. "I don't mean to," she finally admitted. "I think I do it when I feel off-balance."

Now we're getting somewhere. "So apologies and hired cars put you off-balance. What else?" I wanted to know, but I worked to keep my tone offhand. She seemed uncharacteristically skittish.

Glancing down at her hands, Juliet mumbled, "I don't know. I've never done this before."

That answered one of my questions and led to another. "Why?"

Her thin black brows creased while she glared at her own fingers. "I always figured that sleeping with someone wasn't the problem—no offense, but most men can't fuck their way out of a paper bag. I knew I wouldn't have any issues walking away from *that.* It was all the stuff *after.* So, I made my rule, to avoid ever getting caught up in… drama."

She almost said "love," but she stopped herself. It made me wonder…

"You don't believe in love at all, then?"

She grimaced slightly, considering. "No, it's not *that.* I'm sure it's *real…* as in, I'm sure love *exists.* I just—" Agitated, she tossed her ponytail back and huffed out breath, turning her narrowed gaze on me. "What about you? Do *you* believe in it?"

My stomach dropped. *Well, I* didn't, *two weeks ago….*

But was that really true? I thought of the way Grayson looked at Ella in her hideous boots. The way she always knew exactly what to say to get my hard-ass friend to laugh at himself.

Pursing my lips, I tried to explain it to her and myself. "I guess I believe in love the way I believe in God or flu shots or emotional support animals. Great for other people, I'm sure. I've just never felt the need for it in my own life."

Until now.

I told the hissing voice in the back of my head to shut the hell up. I wasn't *in love* with Juliet, after all; only *infatuated.*

More infatuated *every fucking second...*

As if to prove my thoughts correct, Juliet's beauty hit me all over again. Her eyes glowed as she rested her chin in her hand and offered a small, commiserating smile. "We're both bitter."

"And sexy," I quipped, hoping for a giggle.

Juliet managed not to give in, though I caught a flash of laughter in her eyes. "And procrastinating." She glanced at her work files, all neatly stacked next to her dress, on my couch. "Shall we?"

I followed her over to the red sofa, unable to keep my eyes off of her. She explained some of her research and handed me a stack of preliminary information to review. Meanwhile, she slid a laptop out of her tote bag and situated herself with the computer in her lap and her legs stretched out. Before I could talk myself out of it, I lifted her feet and sat with them in my lap.

Our gazes met, hers quizzical, mine impassive. In the end, she didn't back down and move away. And I wound up massaging her feet with one hand while I used the other to hold the documents I needed to read.

A moment later, she scooted slightly closer. I redoubled my efforts, making sure to pay extra attention to her instep. I had to swallow a chuckle when she gave a contented hum, then coughed to cover it up.

After I finished my reading—which, God, only made me like her even *more* because she was so fucking brilliant and thorough—I tossed the sheaf of papers down on my other side and asked, "Anything you're in a hurry to get to? I could order the car now or we could put the TV on for a bit."

A new softness melted Juliet's expression. Her golden eyes blinked at me, fluttering her thick black lashes. The warmth in my middle smoldered.

"We could turn the TV on," she agreed slowly, clearly suspicious. "As long as you don't choose anything annoying."

Always scolding me. Why did I like it?

"Deal." Smirking, I used my phone to fire up the smart TV, navigating to the menu. "Alright, *bijou*. What qualifies as 'not annoying?'"

She watched the screen flicker while I watched her face. When disgust contorted her features, I automatically turned to see the source, expecting some gore. But it looked like an old kids' movie.

"What's wrong with this?" I snorted. Another quick glance confirmed that I'd stumbled upon a classic: *Sleeping Beauty*.

Her nose scrunched. "I *hate* fairy tales."

The vehemence struck me. I didn't usually get anything out of enchanted love stories, either. But I didn't *hate* them.

I watched the animated swirl of pinks and blues for a beat. *Fairies*. So harmless. Loathing seemed like overkill. "Why?" I asked.

Juliet gave a slight shrug. "I just always have."

My brows rose. "Even when you were a little girl? Didn't you want to be a princess?"

She gave one of her deep, gorgeous laughs. "Never. I always thought they were so *dumb*. Whining and singing and swooning. Ugh. No wonder all those evil queens and wicked stepmothers wanted to off them."

I smirked. "So, when you were a little girl, you related to the bitter old ladies and not the young, pretty princesses?"

"Yeah, yeah. I know." A wry smile curved her full lips. "I'm bitter and evil and I have daddy issues. Laugh it up, *pinchao*."

Only… I didn't want to, anymore. Images of Juliet's face on that cold grey morning when her father turned up at Stryker's flowed through my thoughts. I remembered the way she shrank back when he bent toward her, how her eyes filled when he insulted her mother.

My guilt returned, running stronger and deeper than before. How many times had I gone out with a group of guy friends and snickered about desperate women with "daddy issues"?

Christ. Ella nailed it. I was an absolute *shithead.*

I looked back at the screen, watching while the fairies waved their magic wands. Juliet watched, too. When a prince appeared in his armor, she sighed as if giving in to the film. "*Dios,*" she muttered to herself, not looking away. "*Perdiendo la mente…*"

I didn't know what that meant, but I knew her husky voice sounded even sexier when she spoke Spanish. While she faced the screen, I studied her profile, committing the moment to memory. I didn't know when I'd started doing that—stashing little pieces of her away, as if she was some vital resource I knew I only had finite access to.

I didn't just *want* to remember her. I *needed* to.

Because she was changing me.

I didn't want to go back to the man I was even two weeks before. Mocking people, chasing skirts, moping around Everett Alexander like an entitled prick, complaining about all the things I thought my father owed me. Letting Chris slowly kill himself because I couldn't get in Dad's face without losing my inheritance. Planning to lie to my best friend just to prove myself to the father who didn't deserve anyone's respect.

Now, I spent my days actively considering a decision that would cost me everything—my family, their money, our name. All to do the right thing. All because of this gorgeous, fiery, jewel of a woman, with her sharp edges and unyielding strength.

It seemed impossible. But there I was.

"Jules."

Her name rasped out of me before I thought better of it. She turned to look right at me, offering a smile so slight, I knew it must have been involuntary.

"I'm glad you're here."

Even as I said it, I couldn't quite believe it. In more than a decade of hooking up with women on a regular basis, I'd never found myself craving the company of any of them *after* sex…

Juliet obviously felt just as torn. She flashed her teeth, somewhere between a grin and grimace. But her feet pressed lightly against my thigh, silently asking for more attention. "Me too."

CHAPTER THIRTEEN

February 1, 2017

Juliet

For the first time in a week, I found Marco at Abuelita's kitchen table.

It wasn't a good morning for him to drop by.

Our grandmother slammed every cabinet while she moved through the room, mumbling Spanish reprimands as she fried *arepas* in a pan. The second I stepped out of my room, Marco shot me a *somebody's-in-trouble* look. His bushy eyebrows nearly curved to his hairline.

"*Buenos dias, prima.*" The slightest hint of a smirk settled into the grooves around his mouth. "Late night?"

Mierda.

She told *Marco*?

Throughout the years, she never told anyone in the family about any of our fights regarding men. But, then again, I guess I'd never come home after midnight, in a man's clothing, without any of my makeup on, either.

It was stupid for me to assume she would be in bed. I forgot she often stayed up late on Tuesdays to make *arepas* for her Wednesday evening Bible study. At this rate, I'd be lucky if she didn't tell all of her old bitty friends that her granddaughter needed extra prayers to ward off promiscuity.

A drawer clattered. "*…esa vaina.*"

A mess.

Well, she wasn't wrong. I *was* a mess.

I woke up with pictures of Graham blurring through my brain. Graham in his pink suit, almost unfairly handsome. Graham's serious frown while he worked with one hand and massaged my feet with the other. Graham's sexy body in those short silk boxers.

Ludicrous. Always so infuriating and unexpected and audacious and colorful and just…

Graham.

Perfectly natural, I coached myself while I put on my makeup. *He's hot. He wears nice clothes. He has a great smile. Any woman would feel this way about a man like him.*

But the lie chafed. Because my heart knew that the flutters weren't just about his appearance or his money or even his sharp tongue…

No. It was something more to do with how he always cupped the back of my head when he held me. Or maybe his insistence on slow dancing before we hooked up for the first time. The handkerchief, perhaps. Or the foot massage? The French toast?

Ay Dios mío. My blood ran cold. *Do I like it when he's… loving?*

To avoid panicking, I put on the first black dress I could find and distracted myself by braiding my hair into as intricate a bun as I could manage. Ordinarily, I would have gone out for coffee and conversation to help clear my head, but I was too chicken to face Abuelita's wrath on my own. I waited for Marco on purpose.

While I took my usual seat, my cousin slid a cup of Colombian roast across the table. His expressive brown eyes snagged mine. One look said it all.

I was in for it.

Marco was a former cop. Answering his questions all the way to Manhattan without arousing his suspicion would be impossible. My queasy stomach lurched again.

Without warning, Abuelita spun on her heel and pointed her spatula at Marco. "You," she said, speaking English for his sake. "Tells Julieta. Tells no mans want *la vaina*."

He glanced back at me for a translation. "Mess," I mouthed, wincing as I gulped down my coffee.

"Juliet isn't a mess, Abuelita," he replied in the warm, stern way he seemed to reserve just for her. "She has a good job and she works hard."

Waving her utensil, Abuelita launched into an abridged tirade. "She home late. In mans' clothings. No makes-up. Hairs no done. *La vaina*."

Her lined face was so severe, neither of us even bothered to correct her grammar. Marco waited until she whirled back to her stove to toss me an amused expression. "Boyfriend?" he murmured quietly.

I grit my teeth and gave a firm head shake, not daring to deny it out loud. If Abuelita knew I'd been out half the night with a man, mussing myself up, wearing his clothes… and then overheard me say he *wasn't even my boyfriend*, she would definitely drop dead.

Disapproval darkened Marco's features, too, but he didn't say anything else. He nodded at the door and lifted his brows, silently asking if I was ready to leave.

I downed the contents of my mug, ignoring the tweak of protest in my gut. Abuelita tensed up when I drifted to her side. She pushed my lunchbox at me without a sideways glance. "I make more lunches. You no home for dinner."

I knew she wouldn't complain once she found out about the money. I wondered why I hadn't brought myself to tell her about it yet. I'd already told Mami, omitting all of the details about the man I made the deal with… but lying about Graham to my grandmother felt worse, somehow. Especially now.

Sighing, I hugged her side. "*Gracias*, Abuelita. *Ti amo*."

A few minutes later, Marco and I slid into the day's Mercedes. As he put the white sedan in gear, he grunted, "So tell me."

Pouting, I crossed my arms over my chest and fell back into the leather seat. "I was with a guy last night and it ran later than usual."

I had to be careful not to give too much away. Marco was quick and intuitive—a human lie detector. Loyal to his work, too. I assumed as soon as he knew about Graham and I, Mr. Stryker would know also. Then again, he did delete that elevator video for me...

Marco's suspicious face grew more intense. "But you came home in his *clothes*? Are you insane?"

As a matter of fact, yes.

"No," I snapped, fidgeting with my hem. "I'm a twenty-five-year-old woman! I can go out with a man if I want to! And if I want to borrow some sweats so I don't have spend the forty-minute ride home in my work clothes, then I will."

He slid on a pair of aviator sunglasses, blocking the one window into his thoughts. "Huh. Okay. So you were in the city, not Queens. Forty minutes away from Abuelita's puts you in... Midtown? No, it was nighttime. No traffic. So lower. Lower East Side. If you were driving. The subway would have taken way longer at that hour. But I know you would never call a cab or an Uber for yourself when you could take the train, so he must have called you a ride. Lower East Side, hired car—"

He stopped right in the middle of his sentence and snapped his head to the right. Even with his sunglasses on, he looked furious. I didn't even want to know what his eyes were doing.

"Jules," he growled. "*No.*"

He knew. I knew he did. I could tell from the snarl marring his face. "I don't know what you're talking about," I lied, mumbling to my lap.

"Graham. Everett." Marco scowled ferociously. "He lives in The Ludlow. He has a car service. And I know you two worked together in close quarters after that elevator incident.... Jules, tell me I'm wrong."

What was the point? He figured it out. All from one lousy sentence.

"Don't tell anyone," I replied, muttering. "It's just a temporary work thing. He's starting a new company and I'm doing some contract work for him."

Marco clutched the steering wheel with white-knuckle force. "*Contract* work? That requires you to *take off your clothes*? How stupid do you think I am?" His thick jaw clenched as he stared out the windshield. "Damn it, Juliet. I thought we talked about this. Now I have to tell Stryker."

Panic leapt into my throat. "No you don't," I insisted. "It's nothing. Just a..." *Can't say one-night-stand. Can't say friendship.* "Fling."

That word didn't fit at all. Flings were supposed to be light and carefree. Things between me and Graham were more... complicated. I broke rules for him. My own, my company's. And I didn't even know why. Until I was in a room with him... and then it all miraculously made sense again.

"There's no reason for you to mention it to Mr. Stryker," I went on. "It's not like we're in a relationship."

Marco guffawed. "Great. Perfect. So you're sleeping with Graham Everett and working for him on the side; but I shouldn't concern myself, because you're just *screwing* and not dating at all? You're right. I feel so much better now."

Well, when he put it like that...

"No wonder Abuelita freaked," he muttered, frowning at me. "And she'll tell your mother. And *my* mother. *Carajo*. I know you're smarter than this. What happened?"

I couldn't tell if he wanted to know why I stupidly wore Graham's clothes home or why I was even with Graham in the first place.

I didn't have an answer, apart from another silly, fluttery flip in my chest.

"He's..." *Different. Fun. Brilliant. ...Good? To me, anyway.* "Not what I expected."

Marco cast me another sideway glance, still shielded by his Ray-Bans. "What does *that* mean?"

I wanted to groan. Because I didn't *know*. I didn't want it to *mean* anything, but I knew it did. "I'm still... figuring that out."

Considering my face, Marco pursed his lips to the side. "How many times?"

My face heated while my brain started to tally. "I'm not telling *you* that."

My cousin nodded once, as if he expected my reply. "So more than once. And do you guys *talk*? Or eat meals together?"

... "Yes."

Marco's lips twitched. "And you actually get work done, amidst all of the other stuff?"

I nodded, hoping my face didn't register my own surprise at that fact. I assumed we wouldn't get anything done once our clothes came off the night before, but Graham proved me wrong once again. He was a hard worker, dedicated to tasks once he set his mind to them. And he read faster than anyone else I'd ever met.

With a deep sigh, Marco loosened his grip on the wheel. "Does he make you laugh?"

I recalled his insane velvet slippers. His witty banter. "Yeah..."

He blew a breath out of his nose. "And he respects you? Your thoughts? Your... wishes?"

Heat blazed over my face. "Yes," I gritted, mortified. "What's with all the questions? I'm telling you, he and I are not a big deal."

The lines between stern cop and protective older cousin blurred all over his face. "I'm trying to determine if he's decent, *prima*. If there's going to be a man in your life, I want to be sure he makes you happy."

"He isn't '*in my life*,'" I sneered, every bit the bratty baby cousin. "He's just…"

"The man you're falling for," Marco stated, like a fact. When I opened my mouth to argue, he glared over the top of his shades. "Don't bullshit me. I used to interrogate people for a living. And I know you. You like this guy."

Carajo. He was right.

Choking fear stabbed my gullet. Pissed at myself, I crossed my arms tightly over my chest and turned to peer out the window. Queens streaked past as I blinked frustrated tears out of my eyes.

"Juliet." The quiet stillness of Marco's voice made me look back at him. I found his sunglasses gone, his brown eyes on mine. "It's okay to like him."

Only it wasn't okay. Because falling for a man always led to trouble. It did for my mother and our grandmother. Marco was just about the only trustworthy guy I knew… and even he couldn't hold down a relationship.

"Where could it even go?" I blurted, asking myself as much as I asked him. "It's not like people actually *stay* together, happy."

His voice dropped to a whisper. "My parents did."

That was true. His Colombian mother and Syrian father met at an immigration office. They didn't speak the same language or know any of the same people. They didn't even know where the other came from… but they spent the whole morning staring at each other across the waiting room.

Six months later, they got married. They stayed that way until his father died three years ago.

I swiped at my watering eyes, irritated. "Yeah but they were, like—" *A fairy tale.*

I used to think that, as a girl. I would watch the two of them at family potlucks. Always the outcasts, they often sat in their own corner, whispering to each other.

No one else bothered to try to learn enough English to talk to Marco or his father, including Abuelita; so Marco wound up on the sidelines a lot, too. We bonded over that—I often stuck to the fringes because the old ladies *loved* gossip…and my parents gave them plenty to cluck about. While minding my own business, I occasionally caught one of my aunt and uncle's exchanges. The way he looked at her was something straight out of a Disney movie. And when he had his eyes on her, she glowed.

"They were just people," Marco told me, interrupting my reverie. "Two people who found each other."

I sniffed back all my feelings. "It still seems like a miracle to me. They were so different."

Marco's smile looked sad. "People always assume that. I guess because they were from such different places and spoke different languages. But, really, they always made perfect sense to me. Their hearts were the same."

The depth of his simple statement struck me. All of my anxious musings and stomach flutters and doubt came to a screeching halt.

Their hearts were the same.

"My father used to claim that he knew she was the one on their first date. He said they didn't speak more than ten words over the course of two hours. Just 'hello,' 'where are you from,' and 'goodbye.'" But by the time it was over, he knew."

Normal Juliet would have argued that no one could possibly know something so important so quickly. But whatever messed up version Graham created only whispered, "How? How did he know?"

Marco rolled his massive shoulders. "He never told me how. He just *knew*."

"And that lasted for almost thirty years." I couldn't wrap my mind around it. "They never fought?"

He laughed. "Of course they fought. They were from two totally different cultures. Different traditions and backgrounds and religions. They fought all the time. But they just… I don't know. They *understood* each other."

Like me and Graham.

The thought closed my throat.

Panic must have been written all over my face, because Marco shoved his hand thorough his hair. "Look, I'm sure it's nothing if you say it's nothing. I'm probably wrong about everything. As you know, my knowledge in this area is purely theoretical."

Marco's lone-wolf attitude was a notorious thorn in Abuelita's side. She constantly tried to fix him up and marry him off. It usually amused me, but, at the moment, I couldn't even feel my own face.

He cleared his throat, clearly chagrinned, and murmured, "I won't tell Stryker, Jules. I can't do that to you. But just… think about it, okay? Because if you and Graham *get* together… then our boss is going to find out eventually."

Brushing his hair back another time, Marco made a discouraged sound. "Damn it. I got way off track. Listen, there was a reason I wanted to pick you up today. I needed to talk to you about some stuff… about my mom."

My father's sister, Esmeralda, and I never had the closest relationship… I always sensed she felt ashamed of her brother's actions and maybe avoided me to avoid her own embarrassment. But she was a great mother to Marco and a much better child to Abuelita than Julio.

"What's wrong with Tia Esme?" I demanded, anxious.

"Nothing," Marco said, too quickly. "I mean, you know… I've been living with her since my dad died because she doesn't want to be alone. But, with everything going on, Mr. Stryker wants to move the fleet to a garage near his new home and has some new job duties for me. *A lot* of new duties for me, really… and a new salary, with a housing allowance."

He paused to let that sink in for a moment. "You're moving?"

Guilt pulled his lips into a cringe. "It just doesn't make sense for me to live all the way in Queens anymore. I can afford a place in the city… And with all of the things Stryker has me doing… I'm in Manhattan every day until midnight, then I have to drive back to the borough. Then I'm up at five to work out. I barely get any sleep, Jules. I need a place in town where I can just crash."

I examined him, noting the red around his eyes. "Yeah, you do look like *mierda*."

Marco's quick smirk melted back into a frown almost immediately. "Anyway. I wanted to talk to you about moving my mom and Abuelita into a place of their own. That would get Abuelita out from under Junior's thumb and give my mom some company after I'm gone."

I felt my eyebrows rise halfway up my forehead. "The two of them? Alone? They'll nag each other to death."

Huffing out a sigh, my cousin gripped the wheel tighter. "Well what are we supposed to do?" he asked quietly. "We can't just live in the Heights forever. We both have careers in the city. This commute is murder. And I think… look, after what happened last night, I think you would agree we could both use some more independence. *Carajo*, Juliet, I'm almost thirty. I can't be my Mami's security blanket for the rest of my life."

I knew he had a point. I'd had the same thoughts myself. Except… "I feel like *la grande mucosa*."

"Jules," he groused.

"A big brat," I translated. "How can we just leave them out here?"

Marco stared right ahead as we sped into the tunnel. "They love it in Queens. It's their home. But if they want to be in the city, I'll make it happen."

While we surged through the dark, his meaning sank in. "You're going to pay for their place *and* your own? *Dios mío, primo*. How much money is Stryker giving you?" Before he could reply, I waved my hand. "No. Don't tell me. I don't want to know. And I don't want you to pay for Abuelita alone. Let me pay for half of her rent, at least. And maybe her other living expenses, too. Junior gives her a pittance, so I'm mostly paying them anyway. It won't make much difference if she quits."

He didn't like that idea. I wondered again just how much more he made, if he felt prepared to support three grown adults in Manhattan.

Pride swelled inside me. Just a few years ago, he was the family's black sheep. He couldn't speak Spanish, couldn't hold down a relationship. He quit the police force, took a job as a lowly chauffeur. Now he ran security for an entire corporation. All because he saw something in Grayson Stryker and stuck by him.

"We can work it out," he replied. "But, in the meantime, you'd be okay with me mentioning it to my mom and Abuelita?"

I couldn't argue—his plan made sense. It was what I wanted, too, in a lot of ways.

"Yeah," I said. "It's a good plan. But if Abuelita doesn't want to move, I don't want to make her, okay?"

We emerged from the tunnel. Light flooded the car. I could see my cousin's face, reflecting my own guilt back at me. "Agreed."

I spent the rest of our ride deep in thought, pondering all of Marco's revelations. By the time we pulled up outside Stryker & Sons, I was so distracted I didn't even notice Ella standing on the curb with an older gentleman dressed exactly like Marco.

More security.

I had to swallow my surprise when the man opened my door and looked past me to my cousin, awaiting instructions. "I'll take Miss Callahan, Barnes," Marco told him. "You can stay with Mr. Stryker."

The weathered, white-haired man gave a slight nod. I got the sense he rarely smiled, though his frown did flicker when Ella squeezed his arm and offered him a grin.

The moment she saw me, though, her dark blue eyes narrowed. "You," she snapped, crooking her finger to beckon me out of the car. "How could you do this to me, Jules?"

Placing one foot on the pavement, I spied a document rolled up in her other hand—the pre-nup Mr. Stryker warned me she would hate. I winced while I slipped out of the Mercedes.

"I am so sorry."

Ella folded her arms and stomped her green-clog-clad foot at me. "I expect this kind of nonsense from Gray. But *you* are sensible like me!" she cried, waving the contract under her arm. "You *know* this is nuts!"

Still cringing, I could only murmur, "It's what he wanted."

"Do you tell him that he's *crazy*?" she sputtered. "A lunatic! *Four hundred million dollars?!* I don't need a single penny! He already got us a townhouse. An army of cars and drivers. Grocery and food deliveries. He sends me shopping on his dime *all the time*. I don't even have to touch my own wallet, most days. What could I *possibly* want with that much *money*?!"

Wow. Grayson knew his fiancée well; Ella really *was* going ballistic. While she ranted, she waved her arms, causing her homemade, rainbow-hued poncho to swing around her jeans.

"He wants to protect you," I replied, reaching out instinctually. "He knew you would be upset and he knew you didn't want anything. He just…"

How much could I say without breaching attorney-client privilege? One look in her wide, panicked eyes sent a pang through my center. "He wants to make sure you're taken care of," I whispered, careful not to let anyone overhear us. "It's all that matters to him."

All of her manic energy drained away at once. "I *know.*" She heaved out a sigh. "That's how Grayson's always been. Gallant and generous. Just a smidge too bossy and *way* too handsome. Drat him. But… *this*?"

Sensing a sure victory, I offered her half of a smile. "He knew you would be mad. He worried about it the whole time. He hates the idea of fighting with you, but he wanted to go ahead anyway. The contract must be really important to him."

Ella's pretty features thawed into a murk of indecision. "He usually indulges me, but this time he's so *adamant*… I know he wants to protect me more than anything."

I bobbed my head, eager to agree. "Absolutely. And think of it this way—if you don't want the money and won't use any of it, then it's a just a number. An abstract. Banks don't even carry that kind of cash on hand. It's not like you could ever *get* it. So, really, is it even *real*? No. It's just… a concept."

Ella glanced down at the rolled-up document. Her lips pursed as she studied it, then me. "I can't tell if I'm annoyed at you for being so crafty or grateful to have you on our side."

A laugh bubbled out of me. "Isn't that the hallmark of a good lawyer?"

She giggled, too. "I suppose it is." Her gaze flashed over my face, assessing my sincerity before slowly giving in. "…Alright. I'll sign your ludicrous contract. I might have to tattoo 'just a number' on the back of my hand so I can talk myself down twelve times a day, but I'll sign it."

I did my best not to grin like the Cheshire Cat. "Excellent. My work here is done, then."

With a good-natured eye-roll, Ella smirked. "Yeah, I'll say. Grayson better give you a raise or something; you just saved him *tons* of arguing and we're due to leave the day after tomorrow. Oh!

Speaking of—drinks again tomorrow night? I thought we could make Thirsty Thursday a thing."

I smiled, happy to be back in sweet Ella's good graces. "Sure! We should do a girls' night this time, though. You know, make him sweat a bit."

Ella's eyes lit up. "You really *are* brilliant. Tris told me so. Graham, too."

My heart fluttered at the mention of his name. *And he said I was brilliant.* Biting back another grin, I started to back toward the building. "It's what I do," I joked and nodded at the car. "Keep Marco in line for me!"

Ella's laughter was enough to keep me warm all the way up to the fiftieth floor… where the temperature plummeted immediately. Dominic tore through our pod the second I reached my desk.

"Miss Rivera," he clipped, dragging his eyes down the front of my demure black frock. "You're late."

The read-out on my espresso machine said 9:04. I decided not to argue over the margin.

"I'm sorry, sir," I replied automatically. "Miss Callahan caught me downstairs. She had some questions about a legal document."

He wouldn't object to that; not after the way Mr. Stryker reprimanded him the day before. Still, he regarded me with obvious contempt. "She isn't our priority. Mr. Stryker is."

I knew for a fact that our boss would disagree, but nodded along. "Understood, sir."

Dominic leaned back and looked me over a second time, leering. The dress—while professional and colorless—fit as tightly as all of Abuelita's other alterations. I'd compensated for the high neckline with a pair of dangly gold earrings and my thin chain-link belt. When I selected it, I wondered if Graham would wind up fingering the slit up the skirt's back when I saw him after work.

"There will be a lot to get done while Mr. Stryker is out," Dominic went on, eyeing the gold belt with renewed interest. "I may need you to come in next weekend."

Damn. Well played.

Ten days' notice meant I could change any other plans, if I had them. And Mr. Stryker wouldn't be around next week to rain on his parade. Neither would Marco, since he planned to travel with the Strykers for security purposes.

"Let me look at my schedule and get back to you on times," I replied, diplomatic.

My acquiescence surprised him. He thought I'd put up a fight. Well, *I would.* But I'd fight smarter, not harder.

Wide-eyed, Dominic nodded curtly. "Fine."

With nothing else to berate me over—*yet*—he stomped back to his office. I collapsed into my chair, ready to bury my face in my hands. *Ay Dios mío, this fucking day.*

And it was only 9:06.

Graham

I felt like an over-wound toy. *Tick, tick, tick*ing with every hour that passed.

My entire life had become an ongoing muddle of anxiety and dread. I felt physically ill every time I confronted the decision hanging over my head. And, in the rare moments when I wasn't consumed by the choices ahead of me, I worried about Christian.

I tried to call him on my way into the office, but his phone bounced me straight to voicemail. Last week, he called me twice in four days.... But now I hadn't heard from him in seven.

Did that mean he was okay? Better, maybe? Or much worse? I really didn't know.

Tick, tick.

Amidst all the uncertainty, I had only one thing to look forward to.

Juliet. Counting the minutes until she would walk into my apartment kept me sane. I found myself keeping track way more than I should have.

Sometime around lunch, Grayson texted asking if I wanted to go drink the following night and informing me that Ella planned a "girls' night." The thought of not being able to run home to Jules after work the next day pissed me off. I told him I'd get back to him and spent the rest of the afternoon stewing in self-pity.

By the time work ended, I had gone from an angry and nervous to exhausted and depressed. I shuffled from the elevator to my door, not even bothering to pick my feet up off of the ground. I secretly hoped Jules would be there, again; in my clothes, humming to music she chose and stirring some new, questionable food on my stove. Instead, cold silence greeted me.

Tick, tick, tick.

I stood on the threshold of the great room for a beat, looking around at all of my shit, feeling hollow inside. Aside from the mad dash to get out the door for work every morning, I realized, I hadn't really been alone in my place since Saturday. Without Juliet invading my space, the apartment seemed as empty as I felt.

"Graham?"

Instant, blessed relief erupted through me as I turned to find Juliet on my threshold, looking polished and beautiful in a simple black dress, her raven hair swept up in a series of shiny braids.

Spinning blindly, I scooped her into my arms and flattened her back into the wall of my hallway before the front door swung closed behind her. Leaving her bags on the floor, she melted into me without hesitation. Like she knew I couldn't take a fight; or maybe she couldn't, either.

Our mouths met that same second, open and desperate for each other. Jules' moan vibrated against my lips and sent a bolt of lightning down my spine. Our tongues slid together. My cock hardened into stone.

Her hands curled into my hair while mine roamed up her body and fit around the swells of her breasts. Even through her dress and bra, I felt her nipples tighten. Wild for her, I shoved her coat down her arms and fumbled for the zipper at her back.

Garments fell away piece by piece. Her panties hit the floor. She un-looped my yellow tie, shucked my navy jacket and vest. I pushed her dress down to pool around her belted waist and lifted her up, wrapping her legs around my naked torso.

A groan rumbled in my chest when I felt her wet heat against my abs. "Juliet," I whispered, nearly delirious. "Thank God."

She ran her fingers through my hair again, softly this time. Her next kiss came slower than the last.

"I'm here," she murmured, somehow understanding everything I couldn't say. Her fingertips trailed lightly over my brow. "I want you. Put yourself inside me. Please."

With an incoherent growl, I reached between us to find her soaked center and rub my thumb over her until she gasped. As soon as a burst of molten wetness slipped over my fingers, I lost all control. Her legs tightened around me while I opened my trousers and fumbled for my wallet—specifically, for the condom stashed inside of it.

Juliet splayed her fingers over my navel, halting me. "You don't need it," she whispered. "I take birth control. And I just went for a checkup last month. There hasn't been anyone else."

Our eyes met for one breathless moment while her meaning sank in. She wanted me bare, without a barrier to separate us.

She trusted me.

I hated to deny her. And myself. But I hadn't been as circumspect as she was. Sure, I felt reasonably certain I was clean. Not 100% though. And as much as I wanted what she offered, I absolutely refused to risk her health.

I laid my hand over her fingers, staring into her. "Next time," I murmured back, "I promise."

I'd go to a clinic the next morning. The city had dozens of same-day testing sites. I could get tested and write a donation check to cover every patient they saw that day.

Juliet seemed to read my thoughts. She bit her full bottom lip, but still didn't argue. "Okay," she whispered. "Do you want me to turn around?"

That would have been easier to maneuver. Ordinarily, I'd drop to my knees to lick her, then flip her around to take her from behind.

But that thought did not appease the pulsing ache in my chest. I wanted her *close*.

"No," I confessed, staring into her eyes. "I don't."

If I'd ever worried we weren't on the same wavelength, I never would again. She knew exactly what I meant. Understanding flashed through her features, leaving her eyes wide and her lips trembling. For a moment, she hesitated, on the cusp of shrinking back.

I wasn't exactly a godly man, but I found myself *praying* she wouldn't, this time. Because—ah, hell—I *needed* her. Not her body. Not her pussy. Not her perfect curves.

I needed *her*. Her face. Her eyes. The way we connected when she looked into me.

Juliet gave me all of that and more, gazing at me as she lightly brushed her lips over mine and then took the condom from me without another word.

Reaching between us, she slid the rubber onto my throbbing member. The feel of her fingers gliding over my shaft nearly made me pant. I clenched my teeth, trying to get a grip before slamming into her.

Juliet's touch skimmed over my tense jaw next. "Hey," she said softly. My gaze flickered back to her molten honey depths. "I'm here, Graham. I'm right here." Her cool hand caressed my face, gentling the riot inside of me. "I want it like this, too."

I couldn't breathe. My lungs tightened to the point of pain while I positioned myself. A ragged moan tore out of me when I pushed inside, finally bringing us together.

Juliet cried out, arching her body into mine. "*Graham*," she gasped, gripping my hair to tug my mouth back to hers. I kissed her deeply, rocking into her with the same desperate urgency that made me grab her in the first place. When I strummed my thumb over her clit, her groan broke our kiss.

Our torn breaths mingled. I pressed our foreheads together and watched her face, reading her cues while I stroked her. Tension evaporated from her brow. Her lips fell slack. I knew I found the right spot when her pussy clamped around my cock on every plunge.

She murmured something against my cheek, slipping into her native language. I loved that. I took it as the highest compliment that I could fuck her right out of her mind. Even though I didn't understand most of it, I caught one word clearly. One she said melodically, sighing while her eyes fluttered closed.

"*Amado*."

It sounded sweet. I nuzzled my nose against her temple and pressed on her clit. Her body tightened down on mine while I murmured my own endearment back to her. "*Bijou*. Christ, you're so beautiful. You make everything better."

My voice sounded tight. From the delirious pleasure licking up my spine or the hoarse lump in my throat, I didn't know. Both, probably.

A second later, it didn't matter. Juliet reared up slightly, moving to adjust the slide of my cock. I felt her quicken instantly and went wild, surging into her snug heat with renewed abandon.

She sobbed out more unfamiliar words as she came. Unable to tear my gaze from her face, I fucked her until she went limp in my arms, then pushed in as deeply as I could and lost it.

The feel of her stroking my hair brought me back to earth. I realized I'd buried my face into her neck. The warm spice of jasmine filled my nose while I brushed my lips over her skin.

I love her.

For the first time, the revelation didn't make me recoil in panic. I nestled deeper into Juliet, letting her hold me; and stillness washed over me.

I love her. So damn much.

I felt complete and crushed all at once. How did this happen? Did I have to tell her?

The thought gave me a giddy wave of nausea. How would I live if she didn't feel the same way? Could she possibly? We just established that she didn't even believe in love. And I thought I didn't either.

Yet there I was.

I leaned back just far enough for us to look at each other. Glowing gold eyes roamed over my face, seeing more than I bargained for. Her lips rolled into a tight line while she cast her gaze to the floor. "We should…"

Right. I was still in her.

Disengaging, I lowered her safely to her feet and rolled the condom off before re-doing my fly. While I stalked into the kitchen to toss the rubber, Juliet righted her dress.

She left her heels among the wreckage and floated into the kitchen after me. "Could you…?" she mumbled, presenting me with her open zipper and a glorious glimpse of her naked back. Wordlessly, I zipped her up, bending to drop a kiss on her nape before the gold clasp sealed fabric over it.

For a second, she seemed uncharacteristically nervous. Almost like she could sense everything I wasn't saying, despite my best efforts to keep the intrusive thoughts from my features.

But, then, my *bijou* returned. Hard as stone, sharp as glass. She tossed her head back and lifted her stubborn little chin at her work bags.

"I have *arepas* for dinner if you'd like some," she informed me, all business. "I've written a few very rough drafts for you to review. I also brought over research on various topics. It's a lot. I probably should have gone to a print shop. I felt bad using Stryker & Son's ink for all of it."

Equally impressed and exasperated by the way she reverted to crisp professionalism, I snorted. "I think Stryker can afford it."

In fact, I knew he could. The money I invested for him a mere five days before had already appreciated by about four-percent. Four-percent of five million dollars amounted to quite a chunk of change.

Rubbing my palm over my forehead, I shut my eyes. "That reminds me, I have to do some broker work tonight. Adjust some of his holdings and lock in tomorrow's trades. Jason McAllister finally agreed to sign with me; I have to finalize the plan for his portfolio, too."

Juliet smiled widely. "As in, The McAllister Group? Nice work, *pinchao*. We'll work on his contract first, then."

The pride beaming in her expression nearly weakened my knees. *Christ. I need a drink.* I grabbed two glasses, only allowing myself one word lest my voice give me away. "Wine?"

She nodded absently, moving to fetch her things from the threshold. "Maybe a cabernet?"

As I uncorked the bottle, I watched her kneel in my living room and carefully unpack her files, laying them in straight piles spread over the rug. I found myself wondering what my life would be like if I could keep her there with me. Would we spend all of our nights like this? Drinking wine and bouncing work issues off of each other;

loudly making love all over the apartment and then sharing our meals in quiet contentment?

She would move her clothes into my closet and we would probably end up fighting about it. We would argue about a lot of things, I suspected. And she would just keep blowing me away with her brilliance and her fire.

Would she eventually let me hold her through the night instead of turning away? Would I tell her about Christian? Would she let me help her mother? Meet her famous Abuelita? Would we make family meals here, together?

The ferocity of my longing staggered me. God, I wanted all of it. So fucking bad.

Still shirtless, I did my best to keep my stride loose as I delivered her wine to her, dangling the glass over her shoulder. "Here, baby."

Thankfully, she didn't glance back and see the yearning all over my face. She accepted the glass right away, not thinking anything of my casual pet name. "Oh, perfect."

I lowered myself to the floor, drinking down half of my glass in three gulps. *Mellow out*, I told myself. *You don't want to scare her off.* When I neared the bottom of my drink, I found it a little easier to breathe.

Juliet set to work unpacking our *arepas*, placing three foil-wrapped bundles beside me. She sipped her wine and licked her lips, oblivious to the way I stared.

"Okay," she started, grabbing the stack of paper closest to her. "The first order of business..."

Chapter Fourteen

February 2, 2017

Graham

By one A.M. we found ourselves on our backs, and not in a fun way.

With our heads nearly touching and our bodies sprawled in opposite directions, each of us clutched a different document in our limp hands.

Jules turned to blink sleepily at me. "You called the car, right?"

I was so tired, I almost couldn't remember. "Yeah. I'm sorry to keep you here so late. Again."

"S'okay," she mumbled, barely coherent. "You're just getting your money's worth."

A small smile pulled at my mouth. She looked adorable when she was so drowsy.

Between hours of work, we managed to eat dinner and have several conversations. We talked about the contracts, her plan for girls' night out, my on-going indecision about Everett Alexander.

She told me stories about Colombia and Queens. I told her about being Grayson's roommate in college, a few of our travel anecdotes. We both laughed until we were breathless when I revealed that my most embarrassing moment—involving an ill-placed jellyfish sting—happened on one such trip.

All of our conversation somehow inspired me work harder. She got into a groove, too; the woman banged out three more finalized drafts before night bled into morning.

I knew she had to go, but I hated it. On impulse, I reached over and tucked a hair behind her ear, meeting her tired eyes.

God, I love her.

"Think you might be willing to cut me another deal for this weekend?" I asked, doing my best to affect a teasing grin. "I want you in my bed all night."

She pursed her lips to the side, considering. "Depends. Will you throw in dinner? And another foot massage?"

My intercom buzzed, indicating her car had arrived. We both drug ourselves upright. "Those sound like reasonable terms," I conceded, sweeping her papers into a stack and handing them over.

Juliet nodded as she stood. "Alright. Deal." She tossed me her sexy scolding look. "But no fairy tales this time."

The irony was all-too real. That time, I didn't have to make myself grin. "Oh I wouldn't dream of it."

Juliet

I woke with a bubble of warmth in my chest. The same tentative joy that simmered inside of me all night—from the moment Graham joined me to work on his floor, all the way back to Queens.

Every time I remembered Graham's intensely focused frown, his quick smiles, his very capable fingers drumming over the side of his wine glass or scratching notes into margins—I smiled into my pillow like a lovesick idiot.

Like one of those insipid singing princesses.

Ayúdame Dios. I *wanted* to sing.

In fact, I had to actively stop myself from humming while I brushed out my hair and applied my makeup. But the songs still played in my head, running on a loop of silly childlike glee. My foot tapped while I flicked through my work dresses. I chose the sunniest one—a long-sleeved yellow sheath that reminded me of Graham's tie the night before.

When I closed my eyes, I saw the way Graham stared at me before he took me up against the wall. In that moment, I knew in my soul that he had never looked at anyone else that way. The completely insane part of me hoped he never *would*…

Even Abuelita appeared to be in a good mood. Yesterday's upset seemed a thing of the past. She smiled at me when I came into the kitchen. "*Que linda, muñeca*."

I was pleasantly surprised. Usually, Abuelita stewed for days. Much like myself, her temper burned so bright it often took a while for the flames to die down once she got heated. And even longer for all the residual smoke to clear.

I poured my coffee and silently debated which coat to wear. A moment later, a plate full of breakfast appeared in front of me. *Empanadas*. My favorite. And not necessarily easy to make…

Surprise turned to suspicion. "Abuelita… is something going on?"

She paused just long enough for me to know I was on to her. Then she lied. "*Ack*! No's thing go on!" she snapped, acting offended. "I make for you."

I crossed my arms at her. "Yesterday you were mad at me."

She waved a dismissive hand. "No's I was."

"Wasn't," I muttered automatically.

"Is what I said!" Abuelita retorted. She started scrubbing a pan in the sink. I looked over her shoulder and realized it was already clean.

"Abuelita, *que esta pasando*?" I demanded, plucking the soapy brush from her hand.

She scowled at me. "No's things," she repeated, digging her heels in. She whipped a roll of foil out of a drawer and started to wrap up my breakfast. "You has work. *Vamos.*"

I didn't want to leave but she had a point. Marco couldn't drive me and my train left in twelve minutes. I gathered my things, rolling my eyes when she changed the subject before I left.

I finished my food on the way to the subway, then spent the forty-minute ride to Midtown resisting the urge to text Graham. I didn't have anything to say, really. I just…

I miss him.

The impossible truth made me shake my head. I had to bite my lip to stave off a grin when his name appeared on my phone screen a minute later, along with a video clip and text message caption that read, *All your fault, bijou.*

The video started off as a shot of a bowl of cereal. I recognized the snowy granite counter, the grey stone bowl, the gold spoon. *He's eating breakfast,* I realized, unable to stop my smile.

The clip panned over a short strip of countertop. Colors blurred from white to tan. *Muscled* tan. His thighs. Then silky red. *His underwear.* Specifically, the huge bulge in his underwear. All the muscles low in my belly thrummed at the image.

His camera flipped, showing a glimpse of his wry smirk while he shook his head, appalled with himself. Before I could squelch it, I giggled.

Wasn't I just doing the exact same thing? Shaking my head at myself because I couldn't believe what he'd done to me in a matter of weeks.

Which part? I typed back, dodging fellow commuters as I stepped onto Madison Avenue. *The breakfast or the boner?*

My phone buzzed in my hand a moment later. I swiped to answer his call without even considering letting it go to voicemail.

The second I picked up, he replied to my text without letting me say hello.

"Both."

I heard the bustle of the city behind him and all around me. It made me feel closer to him, somehow. A new burst of happiness shimmered through me.

"That was quite the video, *pinchao*. I may have to review it again later."

His laughter warmed my bones and gave me chills at the same time. "Review away, Miss Rivera."

My heels pounded the pavement beneath me, releasing some of my jitters. "So this is new," I commented, hiking my bags up on my shoulder. "I usually spend my walk to the office reading *The Wall Street Journal* headlines."

"God. I knew you were the perfect woman," he flirted evenly. "I'm calling because I won't see you tonight. Girl's night and whatnot… right?"

Why did it feel like my answer held more weight than it should?

"Ugh. Yeah. That. I'm always making plans to do fun things and then regretting it." I paused to consider why. "I think I work too hard and then I'm exhausted at the end of the day."

"You do work too hard," he agreed. "You should definitely blow Ella off and come to my place instead."

As smooth as his boxers. No wonder my stomach kept doing flips.

"I told you I'd make up the work this weekend," I replied as airily as I could. "And you have the contracts you need for McAllister, right?"

A rueful edge crept into his voice. "Work is not what I had in mind, baby. Although…"

Dios. The man made me smile like a moron. And why did I like it so much when he called me "baby"?

Maldición. He was becoming my boyfriend without permission and *I liked it.*

Wanting to retaliate, I shot back, "Careful, Mr. Everett. If you make me wet, I'll have to take my panties off before I get in the elevator."

"Christ, Juliet. I'm going to start tracking how many erections you give me every day and then spanking you accordingly," he threatened, his voice like rough velvet. "By my count, you already have three strikes against you today."

"Three?" I laughed. "The breakfast boner and right now would only make two."

A horn blared on his end of the phone. "There was one when I woke up that I'm blaming you for, too. You spent half the night at my place and the other half running through my dreams," he replied conversationally. "Took care of that one myself, though."

I instantly pictured him fisting his big cock. My insides did another somersault. And I was *blushing*. On Madison Avenue? *Carajo.*

"What's the matter, *bijou*? Have I finally stunned you into silence?"

"Not at all," I shot back. "I was just wondering why I got a video of your cereal when you could have sent me the sausage."

Graham laughed harder than before. "I swear to God," he chuckled. "I almost spit coffee on myself just now. Which would have been a travesty because this suit is Italian merino."

"What color?" I inquired, wanting to picture him.

"Blue. Like that suit you wore the first day we worked together. The one with that slit up the back… Goddamn it. I'm going to be hard all day, aren't I?"

Stryker & Sons loomed up ahead, distinct from the other buildings around it because of the inspired concrete garden gracing it's grounds. "Definite possibility," I returned.

Graham grumbled. "I can't have that, Miss Rivera. I have work to do… decisions to make…"

My heart panged at the thought of all of his impending legal issues. I didn't want to stress him out, though. I wanted to give him a reason to smile. "Lucky for you, you'll be free of me all evening. Plenty of time to think… and wrangle your boners."

My joke did not have the desired effect, though. Instead of chortling, he grew quiet. I thought I heard a sigh. "I'm going to miss you," he finally murmured.

I would miss him, too. In fact, I suspected that might be the true reason for my reluctant attitude about girls' night…

"You sound possessive, *pinchao*," I teased weakly. "Almost like a boyfriend."

The word sent another sparkle of giddiness through me. It almost felt… well, if not *right*, then *correct* at least. We fought and fucked, spent time laughing and talking. The night before, he all but committed to getting tested so we could dispense with condoms.

I wanted to fight the word. I didn't want it to make sense. But the lawyer in me liked precise definitions. And I had to wonder—if he wasn't a boyfriend, what else could he be?

Graham only paused for a second before he answered. "Eh. I'm currently deep in denial about that fact. I'm assuming that doesn't bother you."

It would have bothered me to talk about it. Denial with undertones of mutual understanding sounded like a heaven-sent relief from the constant catalogue of questions I couldn't stop asking myself.

"Not at all," I said, as brisk as could be.

"Naturally." He went on, "Besides, I believe in order to be in an official relationship, one would typically have to participate in traditional milestones like meeting the family… and actual, you know, dates."

More stomach flips. By then, I was beyond trying to decide if the flutters indicated anxiety or glee. "But you're going to the doctor?" I confirmed.

"Right now," Graham volleyed back. "I made you a promise."

"So that means…" I figured he wouldn't bother getting tested unless he planned to remain monogamous. I couldn't bring myself to say it, though. I'd look like an idiot if I was wrong.

But Graham answered immediately again, reading my thoughts. "Yes," he said, his voice gentler. "That's exactly what it means."

For two people who didn't really say much of anything, our phone call told me a lot. I said my goodbye and walked into the building feeling more settled.

Settled and happy. Because of Graham Everett.

Que milagro.

All morning, my yellow dress seemed to ward of negativity like a talisman.

Dominic had an appointment outside the office, so he didn't hassle me and he wasn't there when Mr. Stryker dropped by my desk to personally thank me for convincing Ella to sign their pre-nup.

While it was nice to get recognition in front of all of my co-workers, the wide grin on my boss's face was the true reward. I liked being able to help a good man who wanted to do the right thing. So far, that was the best part of my job.

Graham and I kept up our conversation, texting each other sporadically while we worked. With every returned message, I felt myself relax more and more. He always replied. I wasn't sure why, but that gave me as much security as finding out he actually went to the clinic.

By the time Tris asked me to grab sushi for lunch, I was truly having a kick-ass day. I should have known better. But, because I didn't, we bounced into the lobby at five after noon.

I didn't see my father at first. He stood off to the side again, facing the glass wall, looking out at the street. My heels screeched against the black marble under me when I jerked to a halt.

Tris had been babbling about which bar we should choose for girl's night out. She stopped in the middle of a sentence and followed my gaze. "Someone you know?"

Not really, my mind jeered. In the years since he left me with Abuelita, my father gradually grew into a stranger. Greasy and haggard, he appeared to sway on his feet while I watched.

When he leaned too far to the left, I saw that he wasn't looking out at the street around the building, but down at someone he had with him. Someone small and round… dressed in a red maternity dress.

My insides lurched when I put the situation together. *He brought* her *here*. The baby mama.

But, why?

"I'm going to have to take a rain check on lunch," I told Tris, speaking through numb lips. "I'll see you upstairs later, okay?"

Tris's smooth porcelain forehead crinkled between her auburn brows. "Okay… are you sure you don't want me to come with you?"

I shook my head, inhaling deep into my nose. "I'll be fine," I told her… and myself.

My new friend frowned, but gave my forearm a slight squeeze. "If you say so. How about I bring you something to eat? California roll?"

My appetite had vanished, but I agreed to move her along and then waited for her to make it to the doors before I turned back to my father.

A burst of fury slammed into me. I told him last week that I was done with his manipulation. Abuelita told him to fuck off, too.

Abuelita… Her strange behavior at breakfast made sense, now. She knew there was a chance he would show up and she felt bad.

How dare he come back here? With her*?!* The audacity of parading his pregnant mistress right in front of me… at my *job*.

I should have simply walked out of the building without so much as glancing at him. But that revelation didn't hit me until it was too late. He already saw me coming… and he smiled.

"*Mija*!"

There was a time when I spent days staring out the windows of Abuelita's apartment, waiting to hear my dad call that endearment from the sidewalk below. Back before I understood that he left me there by choice; back when I still believed that he loved me and would always come back for me.

Now, the word left me cold.

I stepped up to the unwelcome pair, refusing to speak either of their names. My mind wouldn't stop repeating hers on a loop, though, trying to attach the sunny word to the worn-down woman in front of me.

Lucia. It meant "light."

Ironic.

My father was correct on Friday. She looked young enough to be one of my friends. Young, but definitely not a typically carefree woman in her twenties. This girl was small, with raggedy brown hair, sallow skin, and horrible posture.

As I took her measure, the woman drew back slightly. Her hand fell to the pronounced bump under her grubby red dress.

"This is Lucia," Papi said. "I told you about her, remember? She's going to give you a baby brother."

The rage roaring in my ears trickled down my back, leaving my neck hair standing on end. Instead of staring at his girlfriend, I focused on my dad. "I told you not to come back here. You both need to leave. Immediately."

His face pulled into a sneer. "Not without what I came for, *mija*. Didn't you talk to your *mami?*"

How did he know about the missed calls from my mom? And so quickly? It hadn't even been an hour since I saw my mother's voicemail…

Fear joined the anger and revulsion pounding through me. "No," I gritted. "Not yet. I texted to tell her I would call her after work and she told me that was fine. Is she okay?"

And he *laughed.* "She is fine, *mija.* I spoke with her so we could catch up. We talked about your fancy job and all of the money you're making. I thought she might agree with me about the best way for us to use it."

It felt like someone had sucked my insides out with a vacuum. "No," I mumbled. "You didn't call her. You never call her."

"She calls me once a week," he gloated, as if it were a cute thing—like a child who drew him a picture at school. "I know she doesn't tell you. She thinks it would make you upset. I usually can't answer, anyway."

I didn't want to believe him… but it sounded like Mami. She knew I disapproved of her abiding devotion for the man who abandoned her. And I knew that my feelings had no bearing on her feelings for him, despite everything he'd done. It wasn't hard to imagine her secretly calling him, even if he never answered or got back to her.

"So this time you picked up?" I demanded, crossing my arms at him. "Why?"

He canted his head, regarding me as if I was obviously absurd. "I needed her help. To convince you to do the right thing. Once I explained Lucia's condition, she agreed right away. She wants you to give me the money instead of saving it for her."

It had to be a lie. My mom knew how hard I worked for her. I often told her about my mission to find the right immigration experts and provide the necessary funding…

"No," I said, hearing a tremor in my voice before I felt it wrack my body. "You're lying."

My father's smile turned indulgent. "Oh, *mija.* I knew you wouldn't believe me. That's why she's been calling you, to tell you for herself."

It made sense in a horrible way. My father was clearly desperate. After I turned him down twice last week, he turned to the one person he knew he could manipulate without fail. The only person he thought could ever sway me in his favor.

"Well your little plan backfired," I hissed. "If I wasn't going to give you the money before, I'm *definitely* not giving it to you now that you've upset Mami and tried to manipulate us both."

He had the nerve to act affronted. "No manipulation, Julieta," he drawled, looking wounded. "I only told her Lucia's happy news. And your *mami* decided she no longer wanted to come here."

That made sense, too. I only barely understood my brand new feelings for Graham, but if he knocked up another woman under my nose, I would never want to be in the same room as him again. I could only imagine how I would feel if I'd loved him for half of my life and spent decades believing we would somehow find our way back to each other.

For a moment, I thought my chest might actually cave in. My hand flinched toward my purse; I needed to call Mami immediately. But then my father said the one thing that could stop me in my tracks.

"She told me about the fifty thousand."

The betrayal pricked at my throat. *I told her not to tell anyone.* Particularly my father. *After all these years and all the sacrifices I made for her, would she really sell me out to him just like that?*

My brain refused to accept the information. But my heart *knew*. It heaved painfully under my breast, laboring my breaths.

"I think that should be more than enough," my father continued. "Since your *mami* doesn't need it anymore, she wants me to have it. She'll tell you so herself."

Pleased with himself, Papi snaked his arm around his girlfriend's waist. She, at least, had the decency to look embarrassed. Her eyes remained on the floor between our feet.

I wanted to scream at her. How could a woman sleep with someone else's husband, then condone him shaking his own daughter down for cash?

It enraged me, but it also made me wonder… how did she end up with a man like him? She wasn't a great beauty by my estimation, but she wasn't *hopeless*… why would a young girl shackle herself to a forty-something alcoholic loser?

"Do *you* have anything to say?" I asked her, too loudly.

A man walking past shot me a glare. *Carajo*. If I wasn't careful, we'd have security all over us.

Lucia cast my dad a lost look. "Julio said you would want to meet me," she said. "He told me we would all go to lunch."

Exhaling through my nose, I worked to keep my tone even. "He lied to you, Lucia. He probably also told you he could provide for you and that baby. I bet he didn't mention it would be *my* money, not his. Maybe he also neglected to mention that he's *still married* to my mother. Or perhaps he told you all of that, but made it seem like you two could show up here and all would be forgiven. Either way, he's a liar. I told him last week I would not give him a dime and I meant it. I don't care how much he tries to manipulate my mother. I won't be giving you any money."

Lucia's chin shook as she gazed up at my dad. "Julio?"

"You could both start by getting jobs," I snapped at my dad, annoyed by the tide of guilt rising in my throat. "Considering all the time you've spent hounding me over the last week, I have to assume you're not working much."

A spiteful expression twisted my father's face. He spoke to Lucia instead of replying to me. "I don't know what we will do, *amada*. If my daughter will not help us to bring her brother into the world, it might be best for us to give the baby up. Or get rid of it."

My body jerked, physically balking. Lucia's features crumpled. "No!" she shrieked, hugging her belly. "He's already—I already—How could you *say* that, Julio?"

My father pinned me with a vicious smirk. "It isn't right to bring a child into this world if we can't provide for him. If Julieta won't give us the help we need to get back on our feet, I really don't see any other option..."

Stomach seething, eyes stinging, I staggered back a step. I wanted to yell and stomp and rage, but at the moment I couldn't even breathe.

Lucia whirled on me with tears streaming down her face, looking every bit as horror-struck as I felt. For an awful second, our eyes met. I felt so ashamed and disgusted, I swore I would be sick. My hand flew to cover my mouth. They both stared at me—Lucia sobbing and my father just... waiting.

Because he knew he would win. He knew I wouldn't be able to live with myself if... if...

I couldn't even think it.

My gaze traced Lucia's pronounced baby bump. She had to be nearly eight months... How could he even make such a threat? Against his girlfriend? To his daughter? Did he love *anyone* or *anything* aside from his own damn self?

I couldn't even look at him. But I also couldn't walk away.

"How much do you need?" I asked his girlfriend.

When he opened his mouth, I waved my hand in his face to silence him. "Not you, *cerdo*." Staring the other woman down, I whispered, "*Her*. Lucia, how much do *you* need?"

She blinked twice before catching on to my meaning. My father tried to pull her against his side again, but she stayed firmly planted with her arms around her belly. "I—I don't know. Julio said—I'm not sure how much *I* would need, but..."

My entire body shook. I knew I didn't have much time left before I completely lost it. "Figure it out," I muttered to her, "and then come find me. Not here. Come to my grandmother's, please. Julio has the address."

Without sparing my father another glance, I spun, blindly striding to the exit. I only made it into the alley twenty steps away before my legs gave out, and I fell.

Graham

"Graham?"

I went from scowling at my phone to scowling at my dad. "What?"

He gave me an assessing once-over. "You've been looking at your phone since that conference call ended twenty minutes ago. Is everything alright?"

No, damn it. Because I'm supposed to be acting normal and evading suspicion but I can't make myself act calm when I haven't heard from Juliet in six hours.

"Yeah." I quickly weighed the risk of mentioning a woman versus leaving him to conjure up his own reasons for my distraction. No contest. "There's just a girl I'm hoping to hear from."

That perked him right up. He grinned his charming, deceitful, son-of-a-bitch grin. "Got a hot one on the hook?"

Ugh. I hated that he thought we were bonding. Over Jules, of all things.

Doing my best to hide my distaste, I sat back in his uncomfortable chair and crossed my ankle over my knee. "She's very hot," I allowed.

A perverse gleam lit his eyes. "Got a picture?"

My jaw snapped shut. "No."

Dad shrugged, acting noncommittal. "I guess I'll believe it when I see it, then. You know, you've never been one to bring the ladies home. If I hadn't seen your picture in half a dozen tabloids with various socialites, I might be worried."

I picked at my sleeve and tried not to take the bait, but wasn't quite able to resist. I fixed him with a steady stare. "Worried? Why? Because I might be gay? Would that be upsetting somehow?"

A trace of pink crept up his neck. "Well, *no*, but…"

"But?" I knew I was being rude, but I didn't give a fuck. *Why hasn't Jules answered me?*

"I didn't mean 'but,'" Dad argued. "I didn't—all I said was—"

Suddenly unable to stand him for another second, I stood. "I'm just screwing with you," I mumbled. "I'll see you tomorrow?"

Having made my exit, I stalked down the hall and hailed the elevator. I glanced at my phone again. *Goddamn it.* It wasn't like her not to answer at all. For the first few hours I figured she might be in a lunch or a long meeting… but half of the day? I even sent a work-related question I already knew the answer to, just to see if she'd reply in a professional capacity. No dice.

I forced myself through a workout and a protein shake. I called Christian and tried not to panic when his phone rang six times and then told me his voicemail box was full. By nine, I gave in and texted them both one more time. I told Christian to call me when he could and asked Juliet, *Everything okay, bijou?*

When my cell vibrated ten minutes later, I jumped at it. But the number scrolling over the screen wasn't familiar. I answered anyway, not wanting to chance missing a call from Chris or Jules.

"Everett."

A tense pause swelled over the line. "Yes," a deep voice clipped. "Everett, this is Marco Amir… Grayson's head-of security."

And Juliet's cousin.

Overwrought by anxiety, I pinched the bridge of my nose. "I know who you are, Marco. Christ. What's wrong? Is it Grayson or…"

Helpless panic rose, inflating my chest like an over-filled balloon. I didn't want to out our relationship without Juliet's permission, but I needed to know if she was okay.

"Grayson is fine," Marco cut in brusquely. "I'm calling regarding a personal matter. Have you spoken to my cousin, Juliet, this evening? Is she with you?"

The panic morphed into full-blown horror. Stifling silence pressed down all around me, highlighting how very alone I was.

"No, she's not here. What the fuck happened? I've been trying to reach her since noon."

Another sickening pause. "I was hoping you might have an idea," Marco admitted. "None of us know where she went."

I started to pace. "What do you *mean*?" I practically shouted. My mind reeled, whirring through all of our texts, searching in vain for something amiss. "She was perfectly fine this morning! I spoke to her on her way to the office, so I know she got there safely. Her asshole boss wasn't in, so it can't be him. She said she had lunch plans with Tris…"

Hearing my alarm, Marco's voice thawed. "Yes, I know. Miss Dunn is the one who alerted me to the situation when Juliet didn't return from lunch. She found me first instead of reporting to Mr. Stryker. She said they were on their way out the door when Juliet saw someone in the lobby and sent Miss Dunn along without her."

I froze mid-stride. *Her father. That fucking bastard.* What did he do this time?

Before I could ask, Marco went on. "Miss Dunn expected her back after lunch, but she didn't return. Mr. Stryker then informed me that he received an email from her about some sort of family emergency. He granted her the rest of the day off, but I wasn't aware of any family emergencies so I reviewed the lobby security footage to see who threw off her original plans. The video showed her having some sort of… altercation with her father. She just walked out and never came back."

I couldn't imagine Juliet walking out of work. "She wouldn't do that," I muttered. "Unless something was *very* wrong. He came to the lobby last week, too. She got upset but she still went back to work after lunch…"

Marco's grave tone implied that he agreed with me. "I know this is out of character for her. When I called our grandmother; she insisted Juliet must be with '*el pinchao*.' That's you, right?"

My heart sank at Jules' taunting nickname. *She has to be okay. I love her.*

What if we couldn't find her? Where would she go? Why didn't she come to me?

"She was going to girls' night tonight," I told him. "Otherwise, she would have been here, with me."

He grunted. "I just drove Ella home from their girls' night out. Juliet didn't show. All of them tried calling her, but she didn't pick up. She never went home to our grandmother's. I tried tracking her cell phone but she turned it off." He blew out a frustrated sigh. "I know she's been with you most nights, so I thought..."

"She should have come here," I growled, torn between outrage and fear. "She has a key. She knows she can come to me..."

Fuck. I was giving way too much away, but I couldn't bring myself to stop. I didn't care if I had to marry the damn woman tomorrow, with Marco holding a shotgun to my back; I needed to find her.

"Do you know where she would go?" Marco demanded. "I've checked a few places already, but they're mostly her old law school hang-outs. I don't think she's been anywhere in Manhattan over the last month except for work. And your place."

I resumed my pacing. "She mentioned being worried about her mom over text. I guess she missed some of her calls. Would she call her mom back, maybe? I know they talk a lot."

Marco made a skeptical sound. "I can try her. But even if they spoke earlier, it's unlikely she'll know where Juliet is *now*."

Closing my eyes, I did my best to think like Jules. She was on her way to lunch with a friend when she changed course. That meant she probably didn't have any of her work with her. She wouldn't do well sitting idly when she felt she should be working. And if she didn't return during office hours because she didn't want anyone to see her upset, then there was a chance she went back after the others left to get her stuff...

"Do you have access to Stryker's cameras right now?"

"I *always* have access," Marco grumbled. "Why?"

"Look at the ones in the legal department," I directed.

He grunted again. "The office is closed. The elevators stop running up to the executive floor after six unless you have a key-card. Besides, she left. She didn't want to go back, or she wouldn't have emailed Grayson."

All of that made sense… for a normal, non-workaholic. But I had a sneaking suspicion she wasn't trying to avoid her work when she stormed out of the building; she wanted to be sure no one at the office saw her distraught. Besides, I knew for a fact she wasn't above taking the stairs, after what happened the day we met.

"Just look."

I heard him tap at his screen. A second later he exhaled loudly. "I'll be damned. There she is."

My lungs expanded for the first time in minutes. "Thank God. Is she okay?"

"She's… working." Marco sounded dumbstruck. "Just like you said." His ragged sigh filled the receiver with static. "I'm going down there."

The urge to go to her surged through me, too. But I knew she wasn't answering messages for a reason. If she needed time, I didn't want to rush her.

"Don't," I bit out. "Work helps her calm down. I'll send a car for her. The driver will wait outside until she's ready to leave. You can watch her on the cameras, to make sure she's okay."

I could tell he didn't appreciate my input. He also didn't disagree. "Fine. I'll apprise you of any changes."

The call clicked off. I immediately tapped into my texts and sent her one last message. *I don't know what your dad did this time*, I wrote, *but I know he messed with the wrong woman.*

When my phone trilled a while later, surprise flashed over my face.

She only wrote three words, but it was enough to tell me she would be okay. And if I wasn't already in love with her, I would have fallen right then and there.

Bet on it.

Chapter Fifteen

February 3, 2017

Juliet

Mr. Stryker sent out a company-wide email on Thursday evening giving everyone a surprise day off for Friday.

By the time I caught up on all my work, it was after midnight. I called Marco back as I shut down my workstation. He swore our boss always planned on offering his executive employees the surprise long weekend. In his words, "Grayson said that if he doesn't have to show up, he doesn't think everyone else should have to either."

But his voice sounded off, even through the phone; and I suspected that our "long weekend" was Mr. Stryker's way of giving me a personal day without singling me out.

I shuffled out of the office and found one of Graham's cars waiting for me on the curb. I called Marco again, ready to yell at him for dragging Graham into our family nonsense. He once again insisted I had it all wrong and told me Graham figured out where I was and what I was doing without his help. He also claimed that Graham insisted on using his own car, even when Marco offered to drive me himself.

I understood right away. It was a message. A way for Graham to be there for me even when I wouldn't let him physically be *with* me.

Just twelve hours before, the gesture probably would have given me butterflies. Now, I only felt the hard knot of dread in my center pull tighter. How long did I have before I had to tell him that I couldn't see him anymore?

I spent my whole afternoon sitting in a café, trying to reach my mom and thinking about what I needed to do. I couldn't make any decisions without speaking to Mami… except for one.

I couldn't see Graham anymore.

I let myself get carried away with him for too long. Seeing my father with Lucia, hearing all the ways he manipulated her and Mami because of how they felt about him… it brought the whole issue into a new light. Or, really, an old one.

My whole life, I operated alone for a *reason*. I didn't date. I didn't have repeat hook-ups. I didn't make men a part of my future, because they couldn't be trusted. And women in love didn't make good choices.

Numb with exhaustion, my heart full of cement, I went to sleep without an alarm for the first time in months. When I woke up Friday morning, I spent a few minutes hiding under my covers, avoiding the sunny day outside my window. Eventually, I finally sat up and took a look around me, daunted by my cramped surroundings.

Abuelita knocked on my door and called out in Spanish, telling me Marco would be there soon. I forgot he threatened to come have breakfast with us before he joined Ella and Grayson for their trip.

Yelling back to her, I threw on the nearest yoga pants I could find. In a moment of weakness, I also slipped into Graham's black tee shirt and sniffed to see if any trace of cologne remained.

Sighing, I scraped my hair back. *I won't see him again*, I told myself. *I can call him or text him to tell him the deal is off and arrange a time to return his check. Or possibly just offer to shred it. Maybe an email would be more professional…*

I didn't know what I would tell Mami. Or how I would help Lucia. But I'd figure it out. Maybe, once Marco had Abuelita and his mother settled, I could live somewhere really, really cheap to save up extra money faster. Maybe I'd be able to afford Mami's expenses *and* Lucia's.

Trudging out of my room, I ran smack into Marco's broad back. He wasn't in his usual secret service suit. Instead, he wore a black thermal, black jeans, and an expression darker than his clothing.

"*Prima*." The word contained a wealth of disapproval.

"I know, I know," I said, offering a passing pat on his shoulder. "I'll never go off the grid again. Abuelita already tore me a new one last night."

"What I tear-ed?" Abuelita asked, not understanding the idiom.

Instead of throwing me a life raft the way he normally would, Marco fixed me with a taunting look. "Yeah, *prima*? What did she tear?"

"*Es nadie*, Abuelita," I demurred, glaring at my cousin. "I just mean I'll always answer my phone from now on."

With her own reproachful look, Abuelita shuffled over to the table and dropped our plates in our usual places. Marco sat across from me and started to eat. He glanced over with his mouth full. "Did you talk to your mom?"

I shook my head. "Colombia is an hour behind. I'll call in a bit."

Truthfully, I didn't want to. My awful suspicions had not abated. And I had no idea how to react if everything my father told me turned out to be true.

But leave it to Marco to not let me—or *anyone*, really—off the hook. His brown eyes regarded me steadily. "Doesn't she work at nine? It's eight-thirty there now."

Carajo. Why did my cousin have to be an ex-cop with mad interrogation skills?

Abuelita started muttering under her breath, slurring my father's name in with some choice insults. Yet, for all her grousing, I didn't hear anything to suggest she thought he had lied about my mother offering him my money. The knots in my gut tweaked tighter. My appetite evaporated.

"Fine," I bleated. "I'll do it now."

I thought I knew what Mami would say. Yet, even as I told myself, again and again, that my father's hold on her made his story plausible; I didn't realize how much hope I clung to until she dashed it. Within moments of answering my call, Mami broke down. In a desperate stream of high-pitched Spanish, she admitted to telling Julio about the fifty-thousand dollars.

"*Tienes que dárselo*," she sobbed, hysterical. *You need to give it to him.*

My temper erupted. For the first time in as long as I could remember, I yelled at her. I asked how she could do this to me, why she continued to choose a man who didn't care about anyone over the daughter who would give anything for her.

When I started to shout about how I would never give away the money I'd saved for her to anyone, let alone my father, she gave a sob that stopped me cold.

"*Mi amorcita, no puedo ver.*"

I cannot watch.

Her agonized confession sank into me, connecting directly with the dread swirling in my center. And I realized that I'd known, all along, that this would happen. That as soon as she heard about Lucia and her baby, she would refuse to come. Because, as I suspected, she couldn't watch the man she loved make a family with another woman.

She won't ever be with me.

As reality set in, I sat on my bed and pulled my knees up against my torso. My heart ached. Tears rolled over my cheeks and splashed onto my stolen tee shirt.

"Mami. *Por favor.*"

Suddenly, I was nothing more than a little girl who wanted her mommy. How long had it been since she gave me hug? Twenty *years*?

Twenty years of waiting and plotting and clawing and scrimping. I felt like I'd been fighting for her my entire life. How could I stop now that she didn't want my help? How could I keep going against her will?

Her whole existence revolved around doing what other people wanted her to do. And I always hated that. I wanted better for her. My whole world centered on earning that better life. But if bringing her here would only make her miserable… what if I had it all wrong?

I spent ten more minutes begging her to see reason before she had to go to work. She cried along with me, apologizing for her feelings but never wavering. Mami also pleaded on Lucia's behalf, calling the baby in question my 'little brother' over and over.

Hermanito.

Each time she said the word, my lungs squeezed. At the end of our call, she told me she loved me and then murmured, "*Nos veremos algun dia.*"

We will see each other one day.

With those words ringing in my ears, I buried my face against my pillow and cried for a long time. Without the distraction of my job, it was easy to slide right from dismay to depression.

At my mother's defection, all of my carefully-crafted plans sifted through my fingers like dust on a breeze. I laid in my bed all morning, staring at the shifting sunshine overhead, watching all my hopes dissipate along with the morning light.

Marco and Abuelita both tried to knock, but I kept my door shut. By noon, they both gave up. Marco left. The clouds rolled in shortly after, and a cold rain lashed my window. Feeling wrung out, I closed my burning eyes and fell into a deep, troubled sleep.

A sound woke me hours later. The scent of fresh food floated around me while I blinked away blurred images from a dream.

The time startled me. I jackknifed upright and then heard the noise again. Laughter? It was deep… and warm… and familiar.

Dios mío. It couldn't be…

I clipped my hair back and rushed to my door, throwing it open to reveal our kitchen. At first, nothing seemed amiss. Abuelita bustled past me; the familiar aromas of *bandeja paisa* filled the air.

And then I saw him.

Sitting in my usual place at the small breakfast table, dressed impeccably, with his ankle crossed over his knee and a wide grin on his face.

"Hello, *bijou*," Graham crooned. "Nice of you to join us."

Graham

I had no idea what I was doing, but it had to be something right, because it only took about half an hour for Juliet's grandmother to take to me.

I liked her, too. She reminded me so much of Jules—her fire and no-nonsense attitude, somehow blended with nurturing warmth.

When I first showed up at their door, the elderly woman recognized me immediately. I knew her right away, too. She looked a lot like Juliet, only stooped and creased, with much darker eyes and braided grey hair.

I felt like an idiot, but I'd practiced what to say all the way to Jackson Heights. "*Hola, Señora. Yo soy Graham Everett. Juliet es mi amiga. Está ella en casa*?"

Abuelita fixed me with a scathing scowl, flicking her eyes down over my three-piece suit. *Damn it to hell.* I knew I should have changed after work. But by the time I decided to ambush Jules, I figured I better go before I lost my nerve.

I looked down at my own clothes, examining the fine black fabric and red pinstripes through her eyes. I chose it because the suit matched the cursed red handkerchief folded in my breast pocket… along with my crimson velvet vest, an onyx shirt and tie. Hindsight being twenty-twenty… I now realized I looked like the rich, arrogant super villain from a comic book.

Instead of insulting me, though, the elder Ms. Rivera pursed her lined lips and asked, "You suit—it is silk?"

If she felt self-conscious about her broken English, it did not deter the ferocious frown on her face. I liked her instantly. With a wry smirk, I raised an eyebrow at her. "*Sí, señora.*"

But she didn't smile back. She pinched at my shoulder and made a *tsk* sound. Her silver brows folded together. Stepping over her threshold, the woman waved me in. "You come. I fix."

Like her granddaughter, she seemed to know exactly how to throw me off my game. "Um…" I stifled a chuckle and forced myself to nod. "*Sí, señora.*"

Yes, ma'am seemed like a safe response to most things. I said it again when she wrestled me out of my jacket and once more when she pointed to a seat at her kitchen table.

As she busied herself with my (apparently ill-fitting) suit, I took a moment to soak in my surroundings, hoping to find more clues to understanding the woman I couldn't seem to stay away from.

Her jokes over the weekend about her entire apartment fitting into my living room weren't exactly an exaggeration. The place started in a pressed stretch of hallway, cluttered by a coat rack and two closed doors. The short hall ended in a small room with a low ceiling. A partial brick wall stood opposite the entrance, cabinets filling the space. On the other side of the partition, I spied a sitting area just big enough for a love seat and a small TV on a card table.

I sat at the scarred wooden table pushed into the wall across from the kitchen area. My fingers glanced over its edge, imagining what it would have been like to grow up with a family table. Did they sit there and tell stories? Was it always just the two of them?

Less than five minutes after taking my jacket, Abuelita returned it with an impatient flourish. Before I could slip it on, she grimaced and pinched my shoulders again.

"This. *Un problema*," she fussed. "You no eat. Tall man. *Necessita comeda.*" She waved the jacket at me. "Put in. I fix."

Blinking, I did my best to interpret her words. Put *on*? I slid my jacket back on and she gave a firm nod.

The fit felt better already. She fixed it in five minutes—talented and bossy, just like her granddaughter. "*Gracias*," I told her, meaning it.

A second later, cabinets started to open and close with rapid-fire determination. Before I knew what was happening, she had food out. Tons of it. Beans and beef and eggs and an array of produce appeared in haphazard piles all over her counter.

She spared me a look over her shoulder. "You *forte*," she told me. "Here."

In French *forte* meant "strong," so when she waved a meat mallet in her hand, I figured she had some sort of manly kitchen duty for me. I shucked my jacket for a second time and started to roll up my shirtsleeves.

When I took three steps and reached the place beside her, she whipped an apron off of a hook and tossed it at me. "Silk stain. *No bien.*"

Not good. See? I could do this.

I smiled while I donned the apron. Silk did stain like a bitch. The woman knew her fabrics, clearly.

"*Plátanos*," she said, shoving a stack to me. They looked like small, oddly-shaped bananas. Plantains, I realized. "You cut. Mash. I fry."

Simple enough. I got to work peeling and cutting the plantains into chunks before squashing each piece with the mallet. I did half of the pile before I realized I never even got an answer about whether Juliet was even home.

I chanced a glance at her grandmother—who worked twice as fast as me, turning a heap of fresh herbs into precisely minced mountains in minutes—and pondered my next question carefully, choosing words I thought I could get right.

"*Como esta,* Juliet?"

That was all I really cared about, anyway. I didn't need to know where she was every minute, but I needed to know *how* she was.

Abuelita slowed her knife and gave a small, discouraged shake of her head. "She sleeps," the woman murmured quietly.

Telling. Juliet wasn't one to crawl into bed and hide. She must have been in serious pain.

Her grandmother noticed when my face registered shock. She sighed. "She work *todo su vida*. And now—" she slashed her knife through the air in front of her. "*Nadie*."

It took me a second to comprehend. My chest clenched. *Her mother*. Whatever her father said must have had something to do with her lifelong plan to bring her mom to America.

I hit the next plantain with unnecessary force and said a word I ordinarily would not have said in front of my girlfriend's grandmother. Abuelita's soft, wrinkled hand flew up, grasping my chin and turning my head. I braced for a dressing-down. But she simply tilted my face one way and then another, her dark eyes narrow and sharp as they traced my features.

"*Un pinchao*," she grumbled. "*Pero tu amas a Julieta*."

There was my nickname again. I still didn't have a precise definition, but it didn't matter so much anymore. It was Juliet's word for me and I would always like it. I'd grown to accept that I may never understand the meaning.

I couldn't understand anything else Abuelita said, either, though.

Seeing my confusion, her expression melted into compassion. She patted my cheek softly. The maternal gesture touched a place inside of me that I never even knew I had.

"*Julieta*," she murmured, "You love."

She still had my face in her hand. It wasn't like I could lie. And I didn't really *want* to. Just like Jules, something about her grandmother inspired me to be an honest man.

"*Sí, señora*."

If I expected some sort of welcoming embrace, I was doomed to disappointment. She dropped her weathered hand and frowned some more. For a long moment, she stared. Then, she tapped her chest. "Abuelita. You call me."

I bit back a victorious smile. "*Sí*, Abuelita."

Twenty minutes later, we had all of the food prepped and on the stove. Abuelita snatched my apron and sent me back to the table. I watched her make coffee and listened as she told stories about Juliet as a girl. She spoke a dizzying mix of Spanish and English, but I followed along better than I thought I would, possibly because her inflections made her easy to read.

Sometime halfway through coffee, with seven different foods frying on the stove, Juliet appeared.

Everything inside of me sighed, simply relieved to see her after two days. I grinned when I recognized my black tee shirt hanging off of her petite shoulders.

With her hair clipped up against the back of her head, spilling over the side of a claw, and a super tight pair of yoga pants, she looked as disheveled and gorgeous as she did the morning she woke up in my bed. When she stepped into the light, though, I noted swelling around her eyes and red lining their lids.

My smile vanished. I drew to my feet instinctually, forgetting we weren't alone until I stood half a foot away from her and saw her panicked face. Her eyes flashed to her grandmother, then glared at me.

"It's okay," I said quietly. "I haven't totally screwed anything up yet. She even let me mash *plátanos*."

Juliet's brows lifted. "She let you help her?"

She looked cold. I wondered if I could touch her without incurring Abuelita's wrath. "Yes… she asked me to."

"She literally never—*never*—lets anyone help her," Juliet mumbled. "Marco tried once and she swatted him with her metal spatula."

I knew my sexy lawyeress. When she said "never," she meant it. Another swell of fondness rose in me as I smiled at her grandmother's profile. "It's not my fault that the Rivera women seem to take a particular shine to me."

Her mouth wobbled, torn between amusement and disapproval. "What are you doing here, Graham?"

She didn't use her endearment for me and I noticed. My fingers twitched while I repressed the urge to reach out to her. "You didn't come to me," I replied, looking into her gold eyes. "So I came to you."

Juliet lifted her pointed chin, even though it trembled. She looked ready to fight through her pain, but the second our gazes connected, she stilled. Her eyes widened. Her skin blanched. For a moment, her guard slipped. And she looked so lost, pain struck my heart.

Before I could stop myself, I took her hands in mine and brought them up to my lips, drawing closer. "Whatever it is," I vowed against her knuckles. "I'm going to help you the same way you're helping me."

Fire snapped in her ocher eyes. I gave a severe look, halting her argument before it began. "I came all the way to Queens," I went on. "In my silk suit. Do I seem like a man who will leave without getting what he came for?"

She pressed her lips and her thighs together at the same time, then nervously flicked her gaze to her grandmother again. It didn't seem likely that the elder understood my double-entendre, but I took the hint.

With one last crooked grin, I tugged Juliet over to the table and pulled out a chair for her. She dropped into it with an indignant huff, never taking her wary eyes off of my face.

Even with a little old lady in the room… and ready-to-bolt rigidity stretched taut through Juliet's posture… sexual tension crackled in the air between our seats. I couldn't keep myself from reaching for her hand again. "I have no idea what we're making, but it smells amazing."

Apprehension seeped into her features as she ran her eyes over mine, frowning. "*Bandeja paisa*," she informed me.

Abuelita burst into the conversation, waving her spoon and firing off a stream of Spanish so fluid I realized she'd majorly dumbed it down for me before Juliet came in. My *bijou* listened. The corner of her lush lips pulled up in a reluctant smirk. Then she gave me a wry once-over.

"She says you're too lean for your beautiful suit and you need to eat more. Apparently she told you 'in plain English' that she would fix it."

"The suit, right?" I clarified.

Her lips twitched again. "No. *You*."

I tried for another teasing smile. "Many have tried and many have failed. But if anyone could do the impossible…" My eyes slid over to her grandmother, cooking up a storm. "It's you two."

She canted her head, her hair swishing to the side. "Seriously," she whispered. "Why are you here?"

I'd already told her the truth, so I tried to explain. "The week is over… and as soon as I walked out of the office, there was only one person I really wanted to see."

Because I love you, woman.

She honestly couldn't believe me. I watched her try, but even as her eyes widened hopefully and her lips fell slack, those thin black brows stayed puckered. "That's it?"

"*Sí, señorita.*"

A giggle bubbled out of her. "Your accent is *awful*."

Abuelita's laughter surprised us both. Our heads swiveled in unison, turning to witness the stern old lady erupt in hearty chuckles.

Juliet's beaming smile melted the last of my stubborn pride. I'd be the butt of any joke if I got to see that smile. And, in that moment, with the two marvelous Rivera women mocking me, I was the happiest I'd ever been.

Juliet

I could tell Abuelita was secretly overjoyed.

Graham not only ate his entire platter of Colombian delicacies, but half of mine as well. I didn't mind. I had trouble shoveling food in my mouth while translating our entire conversation both ways; though, after her outburst, I suspected maybe Abuelita understood a lot more English than she ever let on. After all, they got along without me for who-knows-how-long before I woke up…

I still didn't believe she even let him in.

I couldn't exactly blame her for falling under his spell, though. In his pinstriped pants, velvet vest, and rolled-up shirt, Graham looked sinfully handsome. He had his hair combed back the way I loved. The weeks' stubble darkened the sharp slash of his jaw. Truly, the man was as dark and charming as the devil himself.

A devil who did *dishes*.

Without any prompting, he suddenly whisked our plates into a stack and carried them to the sink. He pushed his rolled sleeves up his muscled forearms… and started cleaning.

Abuelita's jaw dropped. She blinked at his back, astonished. Men from her generation, in our culture, rarely did housework. It occurred to me, then, that he'd done the dishes every single time we ate together at his apartment, too; including the morning he also cooked for me.

For the hundredth time since I found him at my table, I wondered if letting him go would be a mistake. He clearly wasn't the spoiled misogynist he pretended to be. He knew where to find me last night when no one else did. He knew I needed support today. He even knew how to get on Abuelita's razor-thin good side.

By all accounts, he truly cared for me.

But I'm sure my mother thought the exact same thing about my father, once.

Moving with his usual slouchy elegance, Graham scrubbed the dishes and arranged them on the drying rack. Abuelita eventually turned back to me, her face conveying a wealth of meaning. She didn't want to like Graham, either.

But she did.

As soon as he finished his task and returned to the table, she made a big show of covering a supposed yawn. "You fed," she said, using her stilted English. "Bed now."

I watched Graham bite the inside of his cheek, holding back laughter at her unintended innuendo. Glowering at him and my grandmother in turn, I argued, "Abuelita, it's only eight."

She shrugged as she stood and touched her shoulder. "I old woman. Needs sleeps." She paused between our chairs and fixed Graham with a sharp look. "You go soon, *pinchao*."

Graham's devastating grin always gave me a little buzz, even when it wasn't directed at me. "*Sí, señora.* Thank you for dinner. And fixing my suit."

Her eyes flicked down over his outfit, then over to me, and back again. "*El traje es hermoso. Debes cuidar las cosas hermosas.*"

My heart squeezed. She patted both of our cheeks and shuffled down the hall to her room. I noticed she left her door ajar and felt my lips curve even as my chest throbbed.

Graham's midnight eyes met mine. "What did she say?"

"That your suit is beautiful," I sighed. "And you must take care of beautiful things."

He stared into me steadily. "I'm here, aren't I?"

Before I knew what hit me, he grasped both of my wrists and tugged me into his lap. His arms enveloped my body, pulling me tight to his torso. I was too confused to fight him, especially when it felt so good to turn my face into his neck and breathe in his cologne. He arranged us comfortably and skimmed his hand up my spine to cradle my nape.

"What happened, baby?" His low voice sent a flurry through my abdomen, settling in a pool of heat between my hips. His fingers began kneading the base of my skull. "Tell me."

I was weak. Weaker than I ever thought possible. As his other hand found the curve of my jaw and his lips brushed over my forehead, I sank right into him.

"My dad," I said, not even bothering to stem the tears clogging my throat. "He came to the office again."

"Marco told me," Graham murmured. He rested his chin on the crown of my head. "What did your dad say?"

I couldn't even get mad at him for talking to my cousin behind my back. I knew he only did it out of concern for me. And, at the moment, his comforting embrace was just about the only thing holding me together.

I spilled the whole sordid story, rehashing it all word for word, including my father's insistence on getting the fifty-thousand.

Beneath me, Graham's body stiffened. "I'm assuming you told him to go to hell?"

"Yes," I whispered to his collarbone. "But he…"

His fingers clutched me tighter. "Did he threaten you?"

I shook my head. "The baby. He basically implied that if I didn't give them money to pay for the baby that he would make Lucia give it up. Or end the pregnancy. And she looked horrified. She's got to be almost to term; they picked out a name for him already." I huffed. "I know I shouldn't feel any sympathy for my father's mistress but it isn't just her it's… My father is basically acting like his own child is a dog he can have put down just because he doesn't want to pay to feed it anymore."

The same way he treated me like a pet he could desert at the pound.

"So give him the money," Graham growled. "I told you, I'll help your mom. Hell, I'll help your dad, too, as much as I hate the bastard—and then you can keep the money *you're* earning for *yourself*."

His generosity touched me. I sniffled again. "Thank you for offering, but it's not necessary. I called my mom today, and she doesn't want the money because she doesn't want to immigrate here anymore."

A tremor snuck into my voice. "I thought she wanted to move here to be with *me*, but now I understand—she wanted to come to be with *him*. And she knows if she comes now, she will have to watch the man she loves raise a baby with someone else. After the way he abandoned me and her… she can't take it."

The sad, stark truth sent a shiver down my back. Graham chased it with his hand, murmuring one question. "She's not coming, is she?"

Crying in earnest now, I barely got out, "No, she's not," before collapsing into sobs.

Tears soaked into Graham's fancy shirt and vest. And I didn't stop. I wept into his shoulder like an absolute loser and couldn't even feel embarrassed about it. Because Graham held me with fierce protectiveness and hummed calming words the whole time.

It felt like I cried for hours. When I finished, his hand at my nape released the claw clip in my hair and combed through the tresses for a long time. Eventually, he gave a gentle tug and brought us face-to-face. He pressed a series of kisses over the tear tracks wetting my cheeks. His dark eyes roamed across my features, consternation clear in their depths.

"I'm sure I look great," I mumbled, snorting back snot.

Graham's sensual mouth quirked into a ghost of a smile. He pitched his voice low for privacy. "You are truly the only woman who could cry for an hour and still look beautiful enough for me to fuck you senseless."

A watery laugh escaped me. He always knew what to say to instantly put me back on my game. His flirting sent a surge of confidence through me. I tipped my chin up to meet his eyes. "Is that a promise?"

Heat sparked in the black pools, but the rest of his expression remained wry. "Here? Abuelita would beat me to death with her spatula."

He had a point. Yet—even without the remote possibility of sex—he dragged himself all the way out to my borough, after a long week of work and in the midst of his own personal crisis. Gratitude rolled over me. My fingers gripped his velvet vest.

"Thank you for coming out here."

Graham flashed a wide, white smile. "I like it here. The food is *fantastic*." He fingered a strand of my hair. "Nice view, too."

He considered me a moment longer. "You look tired, though." His face softened while he skimmed his fingertips under my left eye. "Come on."

Holding me in his arms, he stood so suddenly, I had to swallow a squeal. In five strides, he crossed into my bedroom. There on the threshold, he paused and looked around.

"Huh. I thought it would be purple."

No mention of that fact that it was smaller than his master bathroom. Or how none of the furniture matched. Or even my yellowed lace curtains.

He took me to my bed, depositing me on it before pulling my covers over my lap and perching on the edge of the mattress. He gave a bone-deep sigh and a shake of his head. "I can't believe I'm tucking you in without even copping a feel. Who am I?"

That was a good question. Because he wasn't the man I met in the elevator anymore.

He held me when I cried, washed my dishes, listened to every word I said with an intensity that made my heart skip.

But, on the other hand, he was still every bit as intriguing as the dark-eyed, audacious stranger who riled me. The suits, the feral grins, his impatience and dominance.

How would I ever send him away? I didn't want to. I wanted... to let myself love him. To let him love me. I just had no idea how to do either while I felt so terrified.

I didn't have any answers for myself, but I knew exactly what to say to him. I picked up his hand and brought it from my lap to my boob. Placing it there, I raised an eyebrow at him. "You're Graham Fucking Everett."

The very best version of smile—a boyish, heart-stopping one—spread over his face. His fingers curled around my breast, giving me a sound squeeze. "Bet on it, *bijou*."

Chapter Sixteen

February 4, 2017

Juliet

"*Qué carajo estoy haciendo?*"

I muttered curses at myself while I rushed around my bedroom, looking for the gold dangly earrings I thought I wanted. *Or maybe the hoops… What if I wear my hair down instead of up? Maybe. But the ponytail looks good because of the zipper…?*

I had no idea what I was doing.

A *date*? I did everything in my power to *avoid* dating. More importantly, to avoid what dating *meant.*

This date, in particular, meant a lot.

Graham said as much the night before when he tucked me in. "So, I got tested yesterday," he told me. "And I'm healthy. You know there's no one else. I met your grandmother. Didn't we say that exclusivity, meeting the family, and going on real dates were the pillars of a relationship?"

I narrowed my eyes at him. "Yeah…"

Graham brushed my hair back one last time and then stood. He did that thing where he picked at his shirt, indicating he felt uneasy. "Then I'll pick you up tomorrow at eight."

I started to protest. "Graham—"

Having unfolded his sleeves and re-buttoned them, he focused on me so intensely that the look sucked all the air out of my lungs. "Jesus, woman, give me a shot," he said, tossing in a crooked grin for good measure. "We had a deal for this weekend anyway, remember? Let me take you out. If you don't want to do it again, we'll revise our terms."

Then, having thoroughly obliterated all of my plans for *ending* our relationship—and, somehow, conned me into make the whole thing even *more* legitimate—he walked out.

I thought I'd wake to a hangover of regret, but I didn't; and as Saturday bled from afternoon to evening, I actually felt… excited.

Jesucristo.

Posing in front of my mirror, I admired the way my dress's gold zipper molded to the curve of my back. I knew Graham would like that—it was like an arrow to my ass. I imagined he'd also approve of the hot pink hue and the way the stretchy material hugged every curve from the middle of my thighs to my shoulders. I bent over to test the neckline. My breasts didn't fall out, but they certainly spilled over the top of my bra and were clearly visible where the bright fabric V'ed over my cleavage.

One desperate look at the time convinced me to leave my hair up. It was too late to take it down and straighten it, so I hooked the dangly earrings into my ears and sprayed perfume on my exposed chest. With my nude heels on and the sparkly gold coat closed carefully over the top of my ensemble, I stepped out of my room.

Abuelita looked up from her book and raked her eyes over me. "*El pinchao*?"

"*Sí.*" I made a bee line for my purse, checking its contents for a pair of flats and clean panties to wear home later. Coming back in sweats and pumps clearly hadn't worked out last time; and I doubted the G-string I had on would survive Graham.

"Abuelita," I muttered, hoping my face didn't look as hot as it felt. "I might stay at Tris's again… so I may not make it home tonight. If I don't, don't worry about me, okay?"

She gave a disapproving huff, but I swore the side of her mouth tipped up slightly. "*Dios siempre está mirando.*"

Ugh. For His sake, I hoped God was *not* always watching.

After dropping a kiss on Abuelita's cheek, I made my way downstairs, unfastening my coat as soon as I hit the stairs. Graham was on the street, leaning indolently against his town car with his ankles crossed and his phone in his hand.

He looked too handsome, again; this time, in a grey suit so fine the threads shimmered, lending it the silvery quality of a storm cloud. His tie stood out against the lavender shirt underneath—an eye-catching pattern of deep purple and bright pink poppies.

Dios. The outfit made me want to laugh and jump him all at once. And we almost… matched. *Again.* Why didn't that utterly mortify me?

When he heard my heels on the pavement, he glanced up… and froze. His dark gaze snaked down my entire body and then up again. He wordlessly slipped his phone into his pocket. Before I could even take a step, he charged me.

Right there, with faded twilight overhead and the Heights bustling on the sidewalk around us, Graham locked me in his arms and dipped me into a stage-worthy embrace. Cradling my head in one hand and my ass in the other, he suspended me over the ground and ravaged my mouth with a mind-melting kiss.

The second we connected, languid heat flowed through my center. I'd missed the feel of his lips on mine so much more than I let myself believe.

Too soon, Graham righted us. Releasing me, he glared at my face. "*Infuriatingly* gorgeous," he rumbled, piercing me with his black stare. "How am I supposed to sit through dinner when you look like this?"

I saw an opportunity to get out of the date without sending him away altogether. "We could just skip dinner and go to your place…"

The hunger in his gaze flared. "Oh no you don't," he replied, reaching for my hand. "We're going on a date. Even if it kills both of us."

I made a face and Graham chortled. "Yeah, I know," he said, pulling me to the car. "It's gross for me, too. I *think* I managed to plan something tolerable. It's a gamble, though."

Running my eyes over his tie and back up to his face, I glowered sarcastically. "Odd. You're not usually so bold."

Graham held the door open for me and I slid into the car. "You just keep honing that sharp tongue, *bijou*," he taunted, leaning down to flash a grin. "I'm going to need it later."

Graham

I planned the evening with military precision, single-minded in my goal.

Juliet Rivera would be my girlfriend by the end of the night.

I would wow her within an inch of her life and then put the whole thing over the edge by spending the rest of the night making her come. My impatient dick couldn't *wait* for that part of the plan. Three days was far too long to go without her.

She shot me a dirty-yet-amused look when she saw the name of our first destination—one of the trendiest cocktail lounges in the Lower East Side: Make Believe.

Jules' hot pink dress went well with the rosy velvet booths and blush up-lighting. Sometime between her second and third drinks, she even let me take a picture of her. The second I hit the button, freezing the moment, I knew it was a photo I'd never delete. Holding her coupe glass in one hand, eyes shining, with her head canted and a sassy smirk on her lips…

She was perfection.

"Any good?" she asked, sipping her drink some more.

"It's…" *Everything.* "…great."

She didn't seem to care much. I knew a lot of girls who would demand to see the snapshot. They would critique it and themselves, obsess over posing and preening.

Jules simply shrugged one of her shoulders and looked down into her half-empty glass. "These are dangerous," she muttered. "I almost just asked to take *your* picture."

I discovered that tequila made her flirty. The botanical concoction of añejo, orange liquor, and pineapple juice had her rubbing her foot along my calf under the table. I got my revenge a moment later, stretching my arm across the back of the booth and brushing my fingertips against the exposed nape of the neck until she shivered.

We tortured each other all through drinks and our meal at Dirty French. We also laughed a lot. Juliet had a dozen hilarious anecdotes about Abuelita and her antics. Images of little Abuelita slapping butchers and railing at men who gawked at Jules on the subway cracked me up, but they also touched me. The Rivera women spent so long taking on the world together—I could tell their bond ran deep.

After hearing about her childhood with Abuelita, I was in awe of everything Jules did for her family. While I was taking bong hits and scoring on sorority girls, she had two jobs just to save up for college and a third gig babysitting to send money to her mom. The fact that such a noble, brilliant woman saw *anything* worthwhile in me was humbling.

Yet she did.

She asked endless questions about my career, specifically interested in the ins and outs of a broker's day-to-day tasks and the way I tried to predict market trends. For the first time in my life, I wanted to impress my date. Every time her brows arched or her mouth fell open, triumph surged through me.

Juliet also loved my stories about Europe and asked specific questions—she clearly read a lot about travel, but had never been anywhere. I wanted to fix that, one day.

She argued with me over the check, just enough to get my blood up. I didn't even want her to *see* how much we probably spent. Between the wine and three courses apiece, I estimated it had to be somewhere around three hundred bucks.

I finally got the leather booklet away from her long enough to slide five hundred-dollar bills into it. That shut her up, though she seethed all the way to the door.

The tension followed us out of the restaurant, into the wintery air blustering down Ludlow Street. With an agitated movement, she shrugged her sparkly coat on, but didn't belt it. Before I could smooth things over, she took off toward my apartment.

Goddamn it. I didn't have one fucking clue how to deal with a pissed off girlfriend. And I still had a whole plan set up for her at my place. I needed to get back on her good side. Quick.

"You're going to get cold," I commented, taking a few long strides to catch up.

Her pissy expression pinched. "It's not even two blocks."

I shrugged. "Still. You should close your coat."

She looked to the street and then back at me. Her stance reminded me of our elevator encounter—the way she stuck her chest out and tipped her head up. The heat simmering in her eyes ignited into an inferno.

"Make me."

Just like that first day, I couldn't think rationally. I only knew I had to have her. Now. I bent and threw her over my shoulder. Then I hauled us both into an alley.

Sliding the length of her body down mine, I tackled her into the brick wall at her back. She didn't even bother to put her feet on the ground. Instead, her ankles locked together at the small of my back while she fisted my lapels and pulled my mouth to hers.

I couldn't blame her. Three hours of non-stop teasing, a decent buzz, and multiple days without her body had me on edge, too. Obviously, I wasn't the only one stretched past the limits of my control.

Grunting, I flattened our torsos together. Even in the cold, I felt the damp heat from her core. My hands finally slid up the back of her skin-tight skirt, finding the bare, bountiful curves of her ass.

Is that a G-string? Fuck. This woman is going to kill me.

Her dangly earring brushed my forearm as I tugged on her ponytail, licking into her mouth until she moaned and tightened her legs around me. She reached between our bodies to tug on my fly.

I leaned back just far enough to let her, panting. "You want it *now*?"

My disbelief made her smile. She liked throwing me off. Without a word, she unzipped my pants and slipped her hand into my boxers.

Fuck me. Her touch felt incredible. Burying my face against her throat, I bit a tender spot while her fingers slid over my shaft. When I started to pulse in her hand, she stroked me harder.

"Jules," I groaned. "If you don't stop, I swear, I'll fuck you right here."

"Do it," she dared, skimming my jaw with her teeth before biting my lip. "Now."

I weighed our options, knowing I should do my best to hold off until I got her home. I wanted to make her wait, drive her wild.

I had surprises for her… a whole plan of attack. And someone could see us, there…

While I wavered, my phone started to buzz in my back pocket. I ignored it, but the ringing picked right back up a second after it cut off. With a frustrated growl, I ripped the cell out and glared at it.

Damn it. Christian.

I ground my teeth together and forced myself to set Juliet down. "I'm sorry. If it was literally *anyone* else, I'd ignore it. But I really need to get this."

Worry crowded into her features. The smoky sensuality in her eyes evaporated. She fussed with the front of her dress and the belt of her coat while I stepped back to answer.

"Chris?"

Static filled the line, followed by ominous silence. A chill prickled through my blood, cooling it. "Christian?" I tried again. "It's Graham. Are you there?"

Street noise swelled behind him. "Graaaam?" he slurred, then groaned. "I think I—*ughhhh.* I need helsh."

"Help?" My back straightened. I took two more steps away from Juliet. "Where are you?"

"Dunno," he mumbled, "Itsh code."

Cold. Outside. "Okay look around you. What do you see?"

"I can't *see.* Itsh cold. It hurtsh."

Fuck, fuck, fuck. I'd already sent my car off. Needing a taxi, I grabbed Juliet and drug her out to the street. She caught on quick; her hand flew up to hail the first cab she saw.

"Can you send me your location? Go to the Maps app."

"It hurtsh. Graammm. Itsh not supposssedd t-to *hurt.*"

He means the drugs. God only knows what he took. "I'm coming to get you," I promised. "But I need a location."

I heard him fumble with his phone while we got into the cab. "Sstreet-t," he garbled. "Near sc-school. Thersh a flop. On Th-th-third."

It sounded like the phone hit the ground. "Christian? Chris!"

Panicked, I pulled the screen away from my face and blinked down at it, trying to think. Juliet's hand fell on my forearm, but I couldn't feel it.

"He dropped the phone," I rambled, opening the Maps app and zooming in on NYU. "I need to find him. He said he's on Third?"

She glanced at my screen, then over to the rearview mirror. "Head toward the Village, please," she told the driver, all business. "We're in a hurry; it's an emergency."

The car glided forward. She refocused on me. "Okay. He said Third. He goes to NYU?"

"Yes. He—he said he was at a flop? Or outside one?" I didn't even really know what that meant. My mind reeled.

Juliet's features tightened. "I know there's a place some NYU kids go on East Third Street," she whispered. "A few girls I knew went to parties there..." She gave a delicate shudder. "Did he think he was near campus? This place was only eight blocks away or so. East Village."

Hell, it was as good a place to start as any. I nodded and she gave the driver our updated destination. I tried to call Christian back twenty times, but the phone rang to his full voicemail inbox every time.

Juliet didn't question me or try to make conversation. She kept her hand on my leg, silently offering support while we sped uptown.

The cab spat us out on Avenue C and she took charge again, leading me up Third Street, constantly glancing around as she tried to get her bearings.

"I never went there myself," she mumbled, frowning at our surroundings. "But the girls mentioned something about a nearby bar... That was four years ago, though. Do you think maybe it isn't a motel but one of these gardens? There are half a dozen on this block... maybe if one of them is abandoned or condemned, people might use it to meet up..."

She made sense, but I couldn't think. Panic obliterated all my wits. An ambulance screamed by us, driving slower than most. *Going somewhere close by…*

And, deep down, I *knew*. It was for him. Someone called 911.

Fresh horror lanced through me. I dropped Juliet's hand, pausing just long enough to say, "I'm so sorry, Jules. Really, I am." And I took off running.

Chapter Seventeen

February 5, 2017

Juliet

The emergency room seemed shockingly busy for the late hour.

I sat hunched forward in one of the only hard plastic chairs available. On one side of me, a homeless man snoozed with his mouth hanging open; on the other, a woman wiped at her bleeding chin, looking like she lost some sort of fight.

Bending over my own lap, I dropped my face into my hands. A dozen prayers and promises fell from my lips, inaudible whispers to the God Abuelita swore was watching me. Most of them didn't make much sense.

I couldn't get certain images out of my head. The flicker of the burned-out street light across from the alley we found Christian in. The way his arms bobbed limply while Graham hauled him off of the pavement. The tint of his skin—blue from the cold, bathed in flashing red ambulance lights.

I hailed another cab to follow them to Mount Sinai, despite Graham trying to push his keys into my hand and send me home to wait for him comfortably. I couldn't bear the thought of him sitting in the hospital alone, especially if his brother didn't make it.

The EMT's believed he'd been dosed with fentanyl, an illegally-manufactured opioid that dealers often tried to pass off to junkies.

Apparently fentanyl OD's were actually more deadly than other narcotic overdoses.

Graham came jogging in from the ambulance bay, wild-eyed. His beautiful suit was ruined, with dirt and alley sludge ground into the knees and something else smeared over the jacket's shoulder pad. He rushed up to the front desk and started emptying his wallet, flinging cards and cash down onto the counter. I hustled to his side, hurrying to block his wad of cash from the rest of the waiting room.

"*Dios mío pinchao*, the last thing we need is for you to get rolled on our way out."

He didn't hear me. "I can't find the goddamn insurance card," he growled, ripping out more cards. "He didn't have his ID—I don't know if he's an organ donor or not and—"

I placed my hand over his, stilling him. "Shh. It's okay. I can look through your wallet for the insurance card, but sometimes they're online now, so there's a chance you have it on your phone already. Did you call your dad? He might know about the organ donation thing."

Graham gritted his teeth through multiple deep breaths. His eyes snapped shut. "I don't want to call him until we know what's going to happen. If he finds out about this, he'll stop contributing to Christian's tuition."

Curse words exploded in my head, but I held my tongue. With a nod, I gathered his cards and cash together and scanned through them. "Here." It was an insurance card; no way of knowing if it was expired or if it covered his brother, too, but it would get the administrators off his back. The nurse at the desk took his cards before turning away.

"How was he on the way here?" I asked.

Graham pushed both hands through his hair and pulled on the back of his neck. "His heart stopped," he rasped. "Twice."

"Oh, Graham."

I threw myself at him without thought, winding my arms around his neck and holding him close. His returning embrace squeezed all the air out of me.

"It's late," he rumbled with his face against my hair. "Go home and get in bed. I'll come as soon as I can."

Home. He meant his place. I didn't even want to correct him.

Reaching up, I stroked my palm over his cheek. "Trying to get rid of me already? I just became your girlfriend forty-five minutes ago when our date ended."

With a snort, he nestled his nose behind my ear. "Jesus, our date. I had all these plans... God, now I fucked this whole night up. I'm sorry, baby." He let out a ragged breath, then muttered, "If Christian lives, I'm gonna kill him."

A doctor called from one of the automatic doors. "Everett?"

We followed him down a short hallway into a triage room. There, under the fluorescents, I got my first real glimpse of Graham's little brother.

They looked strikingly similar; same height, same built, same dark features and straight nose. He was much thinner, though. Gaunt and pale, with shaggy unwashed hair shorter than Graham's. He also didn't have his older brother's penchant for flair—his grimy cargo shorts and navy tee shirt were as boring as they were impractical on a freezing New York night.

"He's in a medically-induced coma," the doctor said, rounding Christian's cot to check the IV attached to his hand. I almost asked why they hadn't used his arm, but then I saw the track marks and bruises filling the creases of his elbows.

I found myself clutching my hand to my heart, trying to cover the ache blooming there. At my side, Graham's jaw ground audibly before he asked, "Is that absolutely necessary?"

"Yes," the doctor nodded. "Mr. Everett had an acute overdose. There's no way to know how long his brain went without oxygen during his periods of unconsciousness and subsequent codes. Keeping him under for twelve to twenty-four hours is the standard of care for such cases because it gives his brain the best chance at recuperation. It also allows us to keep him stable while his body comes down from the high and enters withdrawal."

Graham blew air out of his nose. "I guess it's going to be a long night for me."

The doctor scowled. "Family isn't allowed in triage. You'll have to wait out in the waiting area unless you'd like to go home and come back. He won't be taken off the coma meds until after noon."

I watched Graham consider this. He bit the inside of his cheek and stared at Christian for a beat before casting his gaze over to me. He fixed the doctor with a penetrating stare. "You're sure he won't wake up? At all?"

He nodded. "Certain. Of course, we have your contact information if there's any change in his condition."

I took Graham's hand in mine and gave it a squeeze. "I'll go home with you," I offered.

Our eyes met for a long moment. Gratitude swelled in his midnight depths. "Fine," he agreed, hushed. He shot the doctor one last glare. "Call me."

We didn't speak the whole way back down to the Lower East Side. When we made it to his apartment, I finally took a deep breath. I didn't know when or how, but his place had come to feel like our shared reprieve from all of the insanity surrounding us. At the island, I kicked my heels off and unhooked my earrings while he slid out of his jacket, vest, and tie.

I had an idea. "Does that big tub in your bathroom work?"

Graham seemed distracted. He frowned at his cufflink while he tried to undo it. "I've never even tried it, but I assume so. You want a bath?"

I swept my hair over my shoulder, presenting him with my zipper. "We're both amped up and stressed. I thought we could take one together, unwind a little before we try to sleep."

My dress gaped open at the back. He slid his hands in, roaming them over my sides and then wrapping his arms around my middle. His forehead fell to my shoulder. "That sounds like heaven right now."

In short order, I filled his tub, added some bath oil I found in his linen closet, and laid out a stack of towels. He joined me in the bathroom, wearing only a pink pair of his signature short silk boxers.

He paused on the threshold, drinking in the sight of me in my panties and bra. "One day," he said quietly, coming toward me. "Will you wear that outfit for me again? I want a chance to strip you out of it the way I fantasized I would all night."

I ran my hands over his naked chest, up to his shoulders. "Yes," I whispered, enjoying the broad strength under my fingertips. "Unhook me?"

He undid my bra and watched me shimmy out of my panties, his gaze hot despite the tense lines marring his forehead. When I lowered myself into the foamy water, he stripped and climbed in behind me, pulling me into his lap and nestling my ass against his erection.

One arm curved around my belly while the other hand spread up over my throat, tilting my head to give him a place to rest his. He murmured into the crook of my neck. "Thank you for coming out with me tonight. And being here, now. And for saying you were my girlfriend. Though I'm sorry the circumstances were… regrettable."

I sighed. We had so much to figure out. His brother and my father. My changing living situation. His company hanging in the balance. My job. His friendship with the Strykers.

How would I tell my boss? Maybe Graham would want to tell him alone? Or with me? I knew we had to say *something*, now that Graham and I were… whatever we were.

For the moment, though, I just wanted to breathe. I knew Graham needed that too.

His lips brushed over the top of my shoulder as his fingers found the indentations my thong left embedded in either hip. His thumbs rubbed over the marks in gentle circles. When I shifted on his naked lap, he rumbled.

"Jules," he grunted quietly. "Stay still."

I almost dared him to "make me," but I didn't want to bait him while he was down. Instead, I turned my face to snag his gaze. One hand slipped back up to the column of my throat. It tightened slightly as he stared back at me. An unfathomable look filled his eyes.

"What?" I asked.

"Tell me, sexy lawyeress; after the events of tonight, if I say something crazy, do I get to plead temporary insanity later?"

I couldn't quite squash my smile. "Possibly. Depends on exactly *how* crazy it is."

He matched my half-smirk. "In that case, I don't think I'll take my chances. I had hellish luck this week. And this"–he hugged me closer—"is one thing I'm not willing to gamble on."

Joy shimmered through me. The flurry of sparks melded into the thick cloud of apprehension crowding my lungs. Filled with a bittersweet slurry, I pressed my forehead into his.

"Me neither," I whispered back, wrapping my arm over his. "*Pinchao*."

Graham

By the time we dried off and dressed—both in boxers, with Juliet also wearing a borrowed tee shirt I wholeheartedly objected to—it was nearly three AM.

The adrenaline finally drained away, leaving my mind a bottomless blank and my extremities full of lead. I groaned while I collapsed onto my pillow.

Jules slipped into the other side of the bed and arranged herself the same way she did last week. I wanted her closer, but after all that she'd done for me already, I decided not to push it. Instead, I dropped a soft kiss on the back of her head.

"Good night, *bijou*."

"Good night."

The room fell into silence. For some reason, it took that long for all of it to hit me. Memories from the alleyway—my *brother* slumped on the concrete like garbage—washed over me. I did my best to fight them back, hoping they wouldn't stay so vivid forever.

One particular moment clung to me. After Christian coded for the first time in the ambulance, they used shock paddles to get him back. When the jolt hit his chest, his body bowed off of the gurney. His eyes flew open and rolled back into his head. The ice-cold hand gripped in mine went completely slack. And I believed, in my soul, that I was watching him die.

No. He's not going to die. I breathed deeper, tamping down my emotions. *He's not going to die.* But no matter how hard I tried, I couldn't stop picturing his eyes, lolling sightlessly.

Fuck. I refused to cry like a bitch while lying in bed with the sexiest woman alive. My eyes watered anyway. My next breath shook. *Fuck, fuck, fuck.*

"Graham?"

Juliet's face appeared, hovering over mine. Her golden eyes roved over my features. Pain streaked across hers.

She opened her mouth to comfort me, but I couldn't take it. I knew if she said one kind word, I would break. So I touched my fingertips to her lips, saying with my eyes what I didn't dare try to say out loud.

Her gaze pierced mine, telling me all of the things I wouldn't let her say… seeing everything I didn't want to confess.

I love you.

I almost said the words, earlier, in the bathtub. I knew she saw it, now, burning in my eyes. And I could swear I saw those flames reflected back at me.

She blinked away a sheen of tears and slowly laced her fingers into mine, moving my hand to the side of her face. Instead of speaking, her lips brushed mine. Sweet and enticing. Irresistible.

Juliet kissed me until I couldn't think of anything but her warmth melding into me. I caressed her back, her hips, her ass. Losing myself in the feel of her skin, the way her curves filled my palms.

Our mouths and bodies communicated without words, giving everything we had and taking what we needed in turn. At some point, I stripped her shirt off and pulled her all the way on top of me. She clutched herself closer, stroking my hair. Her tenderness made my chest ache along with my cock.

"God, baby. I need you."

That spurred her on. Juliet pushed my boxers off and rolled onto her back, guiding me on top of her. She lifted her arms over her head and stared up at me, offering her submission. Giving me exactly what she knew I loved.

Suddenly, I remembered: *no condom.*

Fuck yes.

A burst of raw need erupted inside of me. I kissed her possessively, wrapping my hands around her wrists. Eating at her, I aligned her hot, wet sex with my erection.

She moaned, tipping her hips up to let me in. "Please," she whispered. "Please, Graham."

Pressing my cheek against hers, I nuzzled her face. "What do you want? I'll give you anything, Juliet."

"You," she murmured. "Just you."

Flattening her arms under my hands, I slowly pushed the first inch of myself into her. I'd never felt anything so amazing. Her pussy was everything perfect about her body, concentrated in one place—her heat, the plush softness, the way she pulsed for me.

While I panted against her temple, her head tipped back on a groan. Hearing her abandon frayed my patience. Cursing roughly, I thrust all the way in, screwing my hips against hers. A jolt of pleasure rocked down my spine.

"*Graham*," she cried. "Oh my *God*."

I almost smiled. *No Spanish yet.* That meant I had work to do.

Rotating my cock inside of her on every plunge, I gathered her wrists in one hand and roamed the other down to her breasts. Rolling her nipples between my fingers earned me another sharp cry. She ground her snug heat over me, a perfect counterpoint for each of my drives.

I reached for her clit next, finding the bud swollen and wet. Circling my fingers over her, I grazed my teeth against the cords of her neck. She moaned out a stream of unfamiliar words as I bit down just hard enough to leave a mark. Her pussy gripped my cock tighter.

Suddenly, I just wanted her to hold me. I slipped my hand from her wrists, releasing her. Dropping to my forearm put us face-to-face. I curled my bent arm around her head, brushing her hair back. She lifted her face to kiss me. Without prompting, her touch skimmed over my back. I felt her nails bite into my shoulders when I thrust into her and pressed down on her clit at the same time.

More words tumbled out of her mouth as she came. My own orgasm built—a persistent pressure at the base of my dick. But I didn't lose my grip until Juliet hugged me closer, burying her fingers in my hair while I groaned into the crook of her neck.

Pleasure pulsed through and out of me, filling her. She brushed kisses over the side of my face, gentling me after I shuddered in her arms. Her legs locked around my body, keeping me inside of her when I collapsed.

With every last one of my defenses lying in rubble, I closed my eyes and let her hold me. The next time I opened them, sunlight filled the room.

And Juliet was gone.

Juliet

I tapped my foot while the people in front of me slogged forward.

With a line so long, Froth—the overcrowded and typically-trendy coffee shop around the block from Graham's—seemed to supply most of his yuppie neighbors. I normally hated upscale coffee places; but I needed a reason to get out of the apartment and a coffee run seemed as good an excuse as any.

I woke up naked and warm, nestled in my boyfriend's embrace. For one blissful moment of half-consciousness, I couldn't believe how happy I felt.

It all came back a second later. *Christian will wake up soon…I hope. What will I tell Abuelita when I get home? I should probably call her if I'm going to back to the hospital with Graham to check on Christian. Who knows how long all that could take…*

When will Marco talk to her about moving? Do I want her to move? Being in the city would be so nice, especially now that I'm with Graham.

I am with *Graham, aren't I? Dios mío. I'm going to get fired when Mr. Stryker finds out. What if Marco gets fired, too? He wouldn't do that. Would he? No… But he might fire* Graham *when his father's fraud gets out… No one could blame him. Who wants a broker who's linked to theft?*

Maldición… what if no one will work with him? What will he do for a living? Can I handle being with someone who can't work in their designated field? I just got away from a life of counting every blessed cent. I don't want to go back…

One by one, our issues swarmed. Black as crows. Flocking to our fledgling relationship, shaking it. Because Graham and I weren't a sturdy old oak tree. We were new and green and fragile. I wasn't sure how we could ever get through everything facing us.

My restless anxiety carried me into Graham's massive closet, where I found a pair of burgundy joggers and a Columbia hoodie buried in the bottom of his built-in drawers. How very like him to hide his casual clothes, even from himself.

Even if we weren't together, I mused while I shuffled into his bathroom and splashed water on my face. *We would still have to deal with all this mierda. Except for the issue of telling Mr. Stryker… and lying to Abuelita… and this choking feeling in my throat that happens every time I think the word "boyfriend"…*

I'd never been so conflicted. My mind and my heart both agreed that I wanted to be at Graham's place. But some crude, baser part of me screamed at the thought of committing. And as I stood at the foot at Graham's bed—staring at the man I very much feared I could fall for—that part panicked, plain and simple.

I took my borrowed set of keys and my cell phone, stuffing both into the hoodie's pocket and sneaking out of the apartment as quietly as I could.

Outside, it was a beautiful winter morning. Cold, clear, and crisp. Inhaling, I held the frigid air in my lungs and counted to ten. That helped a bit, so I kept it up on my way to Froth.

Standing in line, I wondered what to order for Graham. Did he like drip coffee no matter what? Or would he prefer something else from a shop? He didn't strike me as a chai kind of guy… definitely nothing blended…

Checking my phone, I wondered if he had woken up yet. *Probably not. Best to just pick for him.*

He mentioned something about *café au lait* in France, so I ordered two whole-milk lattes and some croissants for good measure. By the time I made it back to his place, almost an hour had passed. I breezed in and froze, surprised to find Graham seated at his island with his head in his hands.

As the door closed behind me, he bolted upright. "Jules. You're back."

Oh. He thought I just… left? Do I seem that heartless?

I scowled at him. "Of course I am. I just went for coffee." *And a casual panic attack.* "You thought I left without saying anything?"

He scrubbed his hand over his face. "I don't know. Maybe?"

We stared at one another, both wary and wounded. After the searing passion we fell asleep to, this felt like a particularly cruel reunion. And it was my fault, really. I got up and slipped away without even waking him because I couldn't handle my feelings. Though it still stung that he instantly assumed the worst of me.

Clearly, neither of us knew how to do this. As a peace offering, I held up the bag of croissants and the lattes. "*Café au lait*, right?"

He visibly swallowed. His voice sounded rough and sexy from sleep. "Yes. Thank you."

I pushed the cup at him, along with the pastries. He kept his eyes on my face as he accepted both. "I think it's obvious I have no idea how to be a boyfriend," he admitted. "Probably should have mentioned that before I talked you into letting me try."

I tossed my hair back and gave sniff. "Well, I'm not exactly a relationship expert, either, so…"

Something about my face made his lips quirk. "I do have something for you, if you want to see it. I planned on showing you after dinner last night but that got derailed…"

He threw on some sweats and wrapped us both in coats before gathering our breakfast and leading me out into the hall. When he opened the door to the stairwell, my brows knit. Why would we walk upstairs? He lived on the top floor…

Sure enough, we only went up one flight before Graham balanced our lattes in one hand and pulled a key card out of his coat pocket with the other, swiping at the electric pad beside a big metal door. With a subtle beep, the slab gave way, revealing the rooftop.

"Graham," I gasped, stepping out into the bright, chilly air. "What did you *do*?"

The set-up occupied an entire corner of his building's roof. A large oriental rug, covered in pillows of every shape and size, laid out in front of a projector screen.

He took my hand and tugged me forward, picking our way through the burned-out Moroccan lanterns surrounding the whole arrangement. He gave one of his signature shrugs. "I meant to surprise you last night, but we never made it."

Speechless, I followed him into the middle of the semi-circle. He sat down on an artfully-arranged stack of cushions and patted the place next to him, offering half a grin. "You'll have to sit close to stay warm. That was part of my evil plan."

I couldn't even roll my eyes as I dropped down next to him. I kept blinking at the scene, sure it would shimmer and dissipate like a mirage. "Graham… This is…"

Way too much?

If being called his girlfriend terrified me, then *this* certainly should have, too. Only, I didn't feel even a pinch of panic. Only… awe.

I could tell he thought out every last element. The brilliant fuchsia-and-violet rug; sumptuous velvet and satin cushions; a fluffy down comforter rolled up beside us. Up close, I saw that the lanterns were carved. In the dark, with their candles lit, I imagined they cast intricate shadows.

"It's really beautiful," I whispered, taking in the details. My gaze trailed up to the blank projector screen. "What were we going to watch?"

Graham cast me a wolfish smile. "*Beauty and the Beast.*"

My throat felt thick. From the cocktail bar—*Make Believe*, a reference to my hatred of enchanted love stories—to the restaurant—*Dirty French*, like his nickname for me—and now this.

Beauty and the Beast. Because he was such a beast when we met. And he thought I was beautiful.

He brushed a piece of hair behind my ear. "I thought I'd see if I could change your opinion on fairy tales," he murmured. "Guess the universe had other plans, though."

Sitting there, surrounded by his grand romantic gesture, watching the way the sunshine lit his dark eyes, I felt like I could float. "I wouldn't be so sure. The day we met I swore I hated you… but you have a way of changing my mind."

"Bet on it, baby," he flirted, once again using my own words against me. He winked and I wondered *how* he was the only man in New York who could pull off such a cheesy move.

With an eye-roll, I settled myself into the place beside him and started in on my latte. The over-priced coffee tasted delicious, much to my annoyance.

Graham tipped his head back as he watched the sky overhead, his expression contemplative. Thinking about his brother, I suspected.

"Tell me about him," I said quietly, leaning my head against his shoulder. "Christian."

He cupped the back of my head, sweetly stroking my hair, and gave a deep sigh. "I guess I sort of gave you an… *abridged* family history last weekend. The whole story is a lot more dramatic, but the short version is: my dad and mom had me and a few years later my father knocked up his latest lady on the side.

"He didn't tell my mother and lived in denial for the entire pregnancy, so the other woman eventually sued him and the court made him take a paternity test. She won, obviously. I guess being a dancer didn't pay well, especially after giving birth. He had to pay her child support, got shared custody of Christian. The story was in every gossip column in the city. My mom was humiliated. My parents got divorced. And I got a little brother."

As an adult, finding out I would have a half-brother horrified me. Maybe I would have felt differently twenty years ago, though. Graham certainly didn't seem bitter towards anyone aside from his father.

I could honestly relate.

Cuddling closer, I brushed a kiss under his ear. "Did you guys get along?"

Graham rested his cheek on my crown. "Always. It wasn't hard to, though. He only came over two weeks a month and he went to different schools than I did. Plus, the age difference. I taught him how to sneak out of class, how to get money from Dad's wallet without him noticing, where he hid the good scotch. Eventually, I took him out to drink, tried to get him laid." He shrugged around me. "Big brother stuff."

I could picture the two of them, out on the hunt. The image filled me with equal parts jealousy and amusement. "I can imagine you taught him everything he knows… except how to dress? I noticed his cargo shorts."

Graham grimaced. "Trust me, I have *tried*, but he's hopeless. Too serious."

For some reason, the word surprised me. I tilted my face back to look at his. "More serious than you?"

He cracked a crooked grin. "No one's ever accused me of being staid before. I think working with you has been a good influence on me. I have to buckle down to keep up. But Christian was always quieter, smarter, more dependable." Pain sliced through his eyes. "Ironic, huh?"

My fingertips traced his bottom lip, hoping to dispel his frown. "You know it pains me to compliment you, *pinchao*, but I have a hard imagining anyone being much smarter than you are."

Instead of chuckling, Graham widened his eyes earnestly. "No, really. Chris is brilliant. Much better at what my family does than I'll ever be and he doesn't even have formal training. He just… knows things. He reads constantly and his instincts are great."

A small, sad smile flickered over his mouth. "When he was eighteen," he went on, "I was twenty-two and about to graduate and start at Everett Alexander. He helped me study for my broker licensing exam a few nights a week after our dad blew me off. Well, when you take the exam you can put down the name of the company you're trying to certify for. Obviously, I put down Everett Alexander. So I took the test and a month went by. The results came to the office… two sets of results."

Graham smirked fondly. "My little brother took the damn exam without telling anyone and he *passed.* That brilliant asshole got a higher score than *I* did."

Pieces of the puzzle fit themselves together in my mind. "So he's the 'C' in G&C Capital? You were saving a place for him?"

"Yes." He blew out a breath. "Our father always treated him like a second-class citizen, but I know he can be as successful as me. More, even. I didn't see it back then, but as soon as I realized Dad never planned to bring him into Everett Alexander, I started plotting my own company in the back of my mind. I didn't want the family business if Christian couldn't have it, too."

Why would a guy like Christian with such a great big brother and so much to live for start doing drugs in the first place? *Unless…* "Does he know all of this?"

"I wanted to get everything up and running before I told him or anyone else," Graham replied, smiling without an ounce of humor. "Great plan, right? Now he's in a coma and I'm most likely going to lose everything our family's ever had."

You won't lose me. The vow sat on my tongue for a long moment, but I choked it down. I couldn't make that sort of commitment to him… not when both of our futures were so uncertain.

Instead, I curled closer. "I'm sorry, Graham. About all of it. I feel like I gave you bad luck. It seems like everything was going fine until I slapped you."

Finally, he laughed. "No, *bijou*. It wasn't all fine. My dad had already committed fraud; my brother was already doing drugs. I needed to get my shit together and grow some balls. I was just in denial. If anything, that slap woke me up."

"You deserved it," I grumbled into my latte, fighting a smile. "Pig."

"Viper," he shot back without heat, tucking his arm around me.

Companionable quiet settled over us, punctuated by the squeal of taxis and the hum of the city coming to life below. I melted into Graham's side, letting his body warm me. The temptation to let the rest of our issues go proved too strong. I gave in, closing my eyes and soaking in our surroundings, the proof that I meant as much to him as he claimed.

Graham

I sent Juliet home in my car before hiking up to the hospital. The second her gorgeous ass sauntered out of my apartment, all of my compartmentalized anxiety erupted. For the first time in years, I left the house in sweat pants, pulling on the Columbia hoodie Jules borrowed so I could smell her perfume whenever I wanted to.

I didn't have the patience for traffic, so I took the damn subway. After ten minutes on the dirty platform and ten more stuffed into a tin tube like a roll of instant biscuits, I wondered what the hell Grayson liked about it. He used to ride it weekly in college.

Tried the subway, I texted him, using my phone as an outlet for my restlessness. *And confirmed you're fucking crazy. What were you thinking?*

I stalked up the sidewalk, toward the looming hospital on the corner. My cell buzzed. A photo of Grayson and Ella in swimsuits, lying on the beach, appeared. *Worth it*, he wrote back.

Right. He met Ella on that subway. It boggled my mind that the most important person in his life started out as a chance encounter. If he'd taken an earlier train… or even a different car on the same train… they never would have seen each other at all.

Like me and Jules. I wasn't even supposed to be at Stryker & Sons the day we met. I didn't have permission to make any deals; but I went rogue.

What if I hadn't? Or if I arrived two minutes later? Or if she wore a different dress that day? If Juliet and I hadn't shared that one elevator ride, would everything be different, now?

Christ. I sounded like a lovesick sap, even inside my own head.

After harassing two nurses, I found Christian in his own room on the convalescent floor. True to the doctor's word, he was still knocked out. I checked my watch—*almost noon*.

"I was wondering when you'd turn up," someone snapped.

A nurse bustled in, half my height and twice my width. Her scrubs swished while she flitted to Christian's other side. Before I could open my mouth to question her, she fixed me with a pointed look.

"He ought not be left alone. He almost died, young man."

Guilt stabbed at my center. "The doctor told me family wasn't allowed in triage. He said the coma meds would keep Chris under all night."

The woman met my eyes immediately, her scowl fearsome. "Well, he'll be waking up shortly. He needs people around him who love him." Her blonde eyebrow arched. "I *assume* that's you."

The gall. I almost flinched. My eyes dropped down to her name tag. "Sandy." Goddamn. Schooled by a middle-aged nurse with a mom haircut named Sandy.

"He's my brother," I replied. "Yes."

That quelled some of the disapproval in Sandy's expression. "Good. People like your brother need family. Love. It's the only thing that will help his condition."

"The coma?"

"The *drugs*," she spat, her face severe. "Addiction is nasty business, young man. It won't be enough for you to pop in whenever it suits you. He needs someone who can really be there for him. He needs a good in-patient program, a mentor, and a safety net."

Sandy put her fists on her hips. "Where are you boys' parents, anyhow? Mr. Everett here isn't even out of college and you can't be older than twenty-five."

"Twenty-six," I said automatically. "And our parents—" I realized I was about to explain our whole sordid family dynamic to a stranger and balked. "Who *are* you, anyway?"

Sandy wasn't here for my shit. The lines of disdain around her lips tightened. "*I'm* the one who's been caring for your brother," she sniped. "Now, are you going to listen and learn how to do it yourself or are you going to leave him here to fend for himself again?"

I clenched my jaw, struggling against the tide of shame rising inside of me. "I would have gotten him help before if I knew he needed it. I knew he'd been… partying. But he's in college, so I didn't think—" The lie died halfway out of my mouth. I *knew* when I didn't hear from all week. I just added that knowledge to my growing list of denials and hoped for the best.

Sighing, I looked down at Christian's ashen face and finally let the guilt pour through me. Nausea flipped my stomach inside out. "Look, he's my kid brother," I rasped, staring at him. "I love him. I didn't want to believe he had a problem like this. I always hoped he knew when to stop. I guess that was stupid."

"Very," Sandy agreed with a sound nod. "Addicts *can't* stop. They need *help*."

Her concise critique stung. It also took me back to the recent night in Chris's dorm, when I offered to let him move in with me. He said it wouldn't matter, because he'd still be himself. An addict.

Was that him trying to ask me for help? How did I not see all of this coming in that very moment?

"What do I do?" I asked her. "I'll do anything."

Sandy straightened. Her formidable posture, so at odds with her stature, reminded me of Juliet. "Now you're talking," she chipped. "I'll call for the doctor. And you should find some paper and a pen. You're going to take some notes."

Chapter Eighteen

February 6, 2017

Juliet

"Jules!"

Tris waved me down the second I stepped off of the elevator and onto Stryker & Sons' executive floor. In another of her signature jumpsuits—rose pink, this time, with a matching shade of lipstick highlighting her wide smile—she looked bright and polished.

For a second, I worried she might bring up the way I bailed on our lunch last week, but then she fell into step beside me and gave a conspiratorial look. "Seems like *someone* has a not-so-secret admirer."

I felt my brows arch. "Really? You do?"

Tris scoffed. "Please. I wish. No. *You*, silly. I saw Beth whisk a *very* impressive floral display into the legal department. And we all know you're the only badass bitch in there." She bumped her arm against my shoulder playfully. "So how did you get a man to make such a grand gesture? And a *full week* before Valentine's Day, too. Maybe he's just getting warmed up. I wonder what will come for the day-of."

I laughed a little too loudly. I'd never gotten a Valentine in my life. "*Please*. There's no way those were for me. I'm sure one of the guys ordered them for his wife or something. Maybe Dominic finally decided to stop flirting with me and devote his attentions to someone who actually *wants* him."

Carajo. Internally, I cringed, knowing I'd said too much.

But Tris spared me a telling sideways glance. "Before you it was Grayson's father's personal assistant. She left when he retired last year, but Dominic used to look for reasons to hang around her desk all the time." She shuddered. "Skeevy perv. Isn't he, like, married?"

I rolled my eyes. "According to the ring on his finger and the photos on his desk, yes."

Pausing outside my pod, Tris gave my arm a squeeze. "Let me know if you need any back up. You have my extension. Lunch tomorrow?"

Relieved, I grinned at her. "You're on. I think I owe you one."

"Or two," she winked, breezing off. "I'll text you!"

That reminded me*: Graham didn't text me yet this morning.* And the fact that I noticed at all made me feel so disgustingly *girlfriendish*—to use one of his fake words—that I wanted to slap *myself.*

I couldn't exactly blame him, though. I knew he spent Sunday afternoon with his brother, arranging to have Christian transferred to a very expensive rehabilitation program in the city where he would continue working on his degree remotely while he got treatment.

From what Graham told me when he called me before bed, the whole process was exceedingly complicated and emotionally draining. Christian didn't want to go. Graham pleaded with him for hours before Chris's withdrawal hit and he basically agreed under duress.

Graham had to oversee the actual move this morning, then figure out an excuse for his tardiness at Everett Alexander, because both boys agreed not to tell their father about any of it. That meant that my *pinchao* must have paid for the whole program with his own trust fund.

Wincing at the thought, I swept into my department and nearly tripped over my own feet. A gasp slipped out before I could help it.

Tris was right. The flowers awaited me on my desk. At least a hundred blooms, in every shade of purple. Orchids, azaleas, hydrangeas, and lilacs, mixed in with creamy roses and snow-white snap dragons, all bursting out of a colorless crystal vase.

My hand floated out to touch them, sure they couldn't be real. I'd never seen an arrangement so beautiful before. *They can't possibly be for me*, I thought. *Graham would never send something to me* here, *would he? And when did he even have time, with everything else he has going on?*

My fingers trembled as they gently freed a white notecard from the center of the bouquet. *Bijou*, the handwritten note read, *Since it's Monday, you should take your panties off for me... if you're wearing any. -G*

I grinned so big, it hurt my cheeks. Outrageous man. Exasperated with him and myself, still smiling, I shook my head. But I couldn't resist holding one of the roses to my nose.

A fellow junior attorney strolled in, whistling when he passed my desk. "Damn Rivera," Chad chortled, "You must have had some date this weekend."

Bristling, I straightened away from the flowers and started to unpack my work. "Not really," I demurred.

He sat at his own desk, still smirking. "Well, all I know is, I'm not sending something like *that* to a woman unless she's the one."

A flutter quivered through my belly. "It was one date," I muttered, more to myself than to him.

Chad didn't buy it, but turned toward his computer anyway. I did the same, booting up the MacBook and arranging the vase in the corner of my desk where I wouldn't accidentally knock it over. While my laptop loaded, I tried to come up with something witty to send to Graham.

I wound up taking a photo of the bouquet and typing out, *Graham Everett. You are in so much trouble.*

He texted back a moment later. *You're welcome, baby. I assume you got my note?*

Crossing my legs under my cream sweater-dress, I clamped my thighs together, hoping to stave off the tingles at their apex. *I did. Guess you'll have to wait until tonight to see if I comply…*

Something to look forward to, he wrote in return. *I need that today.*

My heart squeezed for him. I started to think of ways I might surprise him after work, aside from the panties. I'd have to decide what to do about those, too. He seemed to like it when I disobeyed him… but he also liked it when I finally submitted.

An evil idea occurred to me, one that would involve a shopping trip over lunch. *The nearest store is about ten minutes away, if I walk… Which gives me about thirty minutes to actually shop, if I grab something to eat from a cart on the way…*

I was so busy plotting, I didn't notice Dominic hovering behind me until he reached into my line of sight and plucked Graham's note off of my desk. All of the warmth and excitement inside of me plummeted into an ice bath. Before I could think better of it, I instinctually snatched the card back.

Jesucristo. Who does this asshole think he is? He can't read my personal correspondence. Thank God Graham didn't sign his whole name…

Glaring at Dominic, I slid the notecard under my keyboard. "Mr. Carter," I clipped. "Can I help you?"

An inscrutable expression covered his face. Something between scorn and… hunger? *Que gonorrea.* He was *jealous.*

The realization sickened me, but I drew myself up straight, staring him down. "Sir?"

He stayed silent just long enough for me to wonder how much of the note he'd read. Then, lightning-quick, he glanced at my lap. Specifically, I suspected, my panty-line.

Carajo. Bile welled behind my teeth.

A perverse gleam shone in his grey eyes. "Miss Rivera," he finally replied. "I hope you had a *relaxing* weekend. I'm afraid next weekend you won't be so lucky. We'll be working on a project that needs to be completed before Mr. Stryker returns next week."

My instincts screamed protests at me. "I'd be happy to get started on it right away," I hedged. "I'm sure I could finish the project by Friday. My week isn't too busy yet."

An arrogant smirk twisted his thin lips. "Unfortunately, mine is. I won't be able to begin the work until Saturday and it's your job to assist. I'm afraid I have to insist."

My job? Pointedly, I glanced around at the three other junior attorneys in our pod...none of whom ever had to meet him one-on-one after hours.

"That's fine," I retorted, cool, "Who else will be joining us? I'll take everyone's coffee orders and pick up them up on my way in."

Dominic's sick excitement dimmed. "Too many cooks in the kitchen may be counter-productive."

The bastard. "I agree. Maybe it would be best if you just bring Chad in, then? He was just telling me he doesn't have any Valentine's plans. Of course, I'd still be willing to alter mine to come join you two." I threw in a blasé, very Graham-like shrug. "Just let me know."

He ground his jaw. "I'll do that, Miss Rivera," he gritted, looking down at my thighs one more time. "Now get to work. If your gift distracts you too much, I'll have it removed."

Graham

I barely made it through my day from hell.

It started with a five A.M. alarm, followed by a workout I didn't have energy for, then running out the door to get to the florist before racing to the hospital for Christian's discharge at the eight A.M. shift change.

Sandy was there to help manage the whole transition. On a whim, I decided to bring her a bouquet of flowers, too. Her help turned out to be invaluable—by nine, Chris was settled into his new digs at the Chelsea treatment center. I promised I'd come back after work to have dinner with him, but he hardly heard me. Withdrawal symptoms had him curled into a ball under his covers.

I felt intensely guilty about leaving, but he made me swear that Dad wouldn't find out what happened. As such, I had no choice but to show up for work and continue maintaining the status quo.

That was its own sort of torture. I spent hours inputting data, all the while debating the fraud issue through a new lens. With Christian counting on me financially and Juliet counting on me personally… did I really even have the option of turning my father in and losing everything?

Christian didn't want to eat dinner. The clinic gave him some non-addictive sleep aid to knock him out, but I still went back to Chelsea to sit with him for a while. It was important for him to know I was there.

After promising to come back in the morning, I finally made it all the way across town for the third time, arriving at The Ludlow an hour later than usual. I shuffled into my apartment, pleasantly surprised when the strains of a lo-fi album greeted me. I didn't find Juliet in my kitchen, though. Just a pizza warming in the oven.

"Jules," I called. Rolling my neck, I tugged at my black herringbone tie and unbuttoned the matching tweed jacket. "Baby?"

God, I couldn't *wait* to see her. Not even a minute. Stripping out of my emerald vest, I strode to the back of the apartment, into my bedroom.

Good. Sweet. Lord.

Juliet leaned casually against my big picture window, her body silhouetted by the street lamps outside. When she saw me, she straightened away from the glass and stepped into the soft light from the bedside table.

Fuck.

Far from panty-less, my beautiful *bijou* had on a full lace teddy. The dark crimson color complemented her glowing caramel skin while the ribbons lacing up the front turned her curves from magnificent to miraculous.

"Turns out I'm not so good at following instructions," she teased. "But I didn't think you'd mind."

I threw my clothes somewhere. "To hell with my instructions." I crooked my finger, wanting to watch her walk. "Come here."

Still wearing heels, her slow saunter did not disappoint. Nor did the small smile on her face when she reached me. Her hands slid up my black shirt, moving to undo the buttons. Mine instantly settled at her nipped waist, skimming lightly over warm lace until she shivered.

My cock hardened into stone against my inseam. My mouth watered, longing for a taste of her. Juliet pushed my shirt off and started on my belt, whipping it off and then snapping it at me.

"Take your pants off and sit down," she told me, smiling coquettishly. "I think I'll be in charge."

That idea sounded embarrassingly appealing. I'd been making huge decisions non-stop for *weeks*. And now this sexy woman wanted to wear lingerie and order me around?

Sold.

I ripped open my fly and let my pants drop, not giving a fuck that my dick practically hung out of the bottom of my boxers. Today's pair was as green as my vest and pocket square. Jules seemed to like them. Her eyes glinted in the half-light while she stared at my package, running her tongue over her top lip.

"These, too," she whispered, running her fingertips along the silk waistband.

I complied, then allowed her to push me backward, onto the bottom edge of my mattress. Nude, with an erection big enough to stretch up past my navel, bobbing under its own weight, I leaned back on my hands and cast her a challenging look.

Juliet raised one brow back at me, silently answering my dare. She swept her hair back into her hands, securing it with a hair tie. Like she was about to go to *work*. My cock throbbed from that thought alone.

In a graceful crouch, Jules went to her knees, moving to settle herself between my legs. Her touch trailed down the line of muscle bisecting my abs, teasing me until I shuddered.

"Tell me," she purred, eyeing my dick. "How am I supposed to fit this *whole thing* into my mouth?" Her other hand cradled my balls. Tingles shot up my spine. "Never mind," she whispered. "I'll figure it out. I like to learn on the job, anyway."

With her taunt issued, she bent over my lap, offering a perfect view of her back and her red-lace-lined ass. My lips fell open when she stared right up at me, lust sparking in her golden eyes, and sucked me into her mouth.

Wet heat enveloped the head of my cock. I pulsed between her lips, as aroused by the sight of her working my length in as I was by the feel of it. Her tongue caressed the underside of my shaft in a long, slow glide. A breath burst out of my lungs.

The hand cupping my sack squeezed lightly as she sucked harder. I groaned, tilting my hips up to push into her throat. She clamped her lips around me, giving more friction.

While she pumped my shaft with her mouth and her fist, the pads of her slender fingers tormented me, kneading and rolling my scrotum until it drew up. Another wave of pleasure rolled over me.

"Juliet," I rumbled. "Goddamn it, you're so good."

She hummed her approval, her mouth vibrating around my member. My hips twitched every time she pulled her lips up to the swollen head, restless for more.

A moment later, she shifted a bit, twisting her lower half to press her pussy against the side of my leg. I felt her wetness brand me and nearly convulsed. "You're soaked for me," I growled, sinking my fingers into her hair. "Does sucking my cock turn you on?"

A breathy moan vibrated over my dick as she took the entire thing deep into her throat. Beyond any modicum of control, I fisted her ponytail and thrust up into her mouth. Frenzied, my gaze roamed over her gorgeous face and the long arch of her neck, stretched tight to accommodate me, committing the sight to memory before I lost it.

Juliet wrapped her free hand around the base of my shaft and went back to working her fist up and down alongside her lips. My orgasm struck me like lightning, bolting through my core. Unable to stand her onslaught one minute more, my head fell back as I bucked up into the wet heat of her suction and came so hard my vision blurred.

She swallowed everything I gave her and waited for the last shudder to subside before pulling back. Dragging her sex up over my thigh, she straddled my hip and brushed her swollen lips over my temple.

"Thanks for the flowers."

I almost snorted. *Was that her way of being sweet and showing gratitude—a teddy and a world-class blow job? Where has this woman been all my life?*

"Mmm." I turned my face to capture her mouth with mine. "My pleasure. Literally." My hands roamed up her curves. "Please tell me you took some pictures in this thing before I got home."

She smiled into my kiss. "Take them yourself," she shot back.

Pulling her all the way on top of me, I plunged my tongue into her mouth. She tasted salty from my cum, which only turned me on all over again.

"Maybe I will, after dinner. But I think I want dessert first."

I flipped her onto her back and pulled her to the edge of the bed, slinking down to the floor. Her surprised squeal made me smile for the first time all day. My fingers traced over the lines of her lingerie while I admired my present.

So lovely. So un-fucking-believably sexy. I had my proof; no matter how shitty my days got, coming home to Juliet always turned them around. I knew I still had a lot of things to worry about. But, in that moment, with my beautiful jewel laid out just for me, I felt grateful.

And I was about to show her just how much.

We wound up on my living room floor again, eating pizza and outlining every possible approach to my Everett Alexander issues. As with most topics between us, the discussion devolved into a debate pretty quickly.

It seemed like no matter which side I took, she had an endless stream of questions to undermine it. I knew that was her *job*, but, goddamn it, the woman infuriated me as much as she turned me on.

To make matters worse, I found I hated to spar with her right after sex. Our connection seemed so precious when we were in bed. Going straight from mutual adoration to a knock-down-drag-out was like being dumped out of a warm bath, into a snow bank.

Nevertheless, we argued in circles. If I said I wanted to turn Dad in, she had twelve reasons not to. When I considered simply cutting my losses, that didn't sit well with her, either.

"Jesus," I cursed, falling back against the couch and shoving my hands into my hair. "I can't win with you!"

"It's not about *me*, Graham," she snapped back. "I'm playing devil's advocate here so you're forced to defend your position over and over again. Because *that's* what you'll have to do every single day, in your own mind."

It made sense, but I was beyond reason. Pissed, I scowled at her. "So this has all been some sort of mental exercise? Because my day wasn't shitty enough?"

Most girlfriends might have some sympathy. But not my firebrand. Of course.

"I'm trying to *help*," she shot back. "Trust me, I have *actual work* I could be doing right now. So do you! But we have to *deal* with this. You only have until next week to decide."

The low-grade panic constantly climbing my insides roiled to a fever pitch. "*You think I don't know that*?" I demanded, shouting. "You think it isn't every third thought that passes through my mind? It is, Jules. I know the stakes here. I could lose everything."

I could lose you.

It wasn't the first time the thought had occurred to me. Our relationship being so new and Juliet being so skittish, there was always the chance that she would bolt. And it got harder to imagine living through *that* every single day.

My outburst quieted Juliet down. She sat back on her heels, sighing. "Let me ask you something, Graham. What do your instincts tell you to do?"

I didn't want to answer that. Because my instincts were selfish, born of years of loneliness and cynicism. But I also refused to lie to my girlfriend.

"Honestly? I want to cut and run. Slink off. Leave him to his misery and hope karma gets him one day… far from now… when I've had the time and resources to build up my own reputation and defenses. At least, then, if the feds ever come calling, I'll have some credibility to fall back on. Not to mention, you know, *money*."

That worried me, too. Echoes of my old pessimism whispered that perhaps Juliet wouldn't be interested in me without my wealth. I knew, if I turned Dad in, I would still be able to keep my apartment and my trust, but the rest of my funds fell into murky territory. The trust would only last… maybe five years? If I kept spending like I currently did. Not to mention the expense of Christian's care.

"I don't even have precise numbers," I grumbled. "I can't exactly call my accountant. He works for Everett Alexander."

Juliet crawled over to me. I wished she hadn't put her dress back on, especially when she straddled my lap a moment later.

"I'm sorry if I'm making this decision harder for you," she murmured. "I think I feel compelled to push because… deep down, I have the same instinct. But I feel guilty about it. I *want* you to cut and run. Even though I know it's wrong. Because I'm scared for you."

With our admissions hanging between us, our eyes locked. What she suggested was out-right illegal. Colluding to hide a crime was a crime in itself. She stood the risk of being disbarred.

But her gaze stayed steady on mine. Cunning and fearless. So very like her.

Something inside of me clicked. She was in this with me… and as long as I had Jules on my side, I could do anything. "Then I'll cut out cleanly," I decided. "And hope like hell I make it to higher ground before Everett Alexander implodes."

Juliet released a shaky breath. "Alright," she agreed, nodding once. "Let's talk next steps."

I raised a brow at her, aroused and amused as ever by her bossiness. My hands slid up the backs of her thighs, cupping the luscious curves of her ass in both palms. "I suddenly find myself distracted."

Her eyes snapped with heat. "Get serious, *pinchao*. You have work to do."

I cocked my head, loving our banter. Loving *her*. "You know what, *bijou*? Make me."

Chapter Nineteen

February 8, 2017

Graham

On Wednesday, I decided to go shopping.

It always worked in the past. Anytime I started to feel like a bad son for never calling my mother or a bad employee for plotting my own independent trades, I found myself cruising Bergdorf's or looking at Rolexes. A holdover from my childhood, no doubt; when an endless parade of nannies attempted to buy my favor with their Everett charge cards.

Now, a trip to Fifth Avenue sounded therapeutic. I figured adult angst called for a bigger budget.

Besides, I wanted to buy some things for Juliet. She worked at my place until after midnight Monday and Tuesday before riding all the way back to Queens. It seemed ridiculous for her to go all the way home just to turn around and hike back to Manhattan seven hours later.

She'd get more rest if she just stayed the night. That meant she needed work clothes to keep at my apartment. And underwear. Maybe a watch. Or two…

I'd be lying if I said I wasn't perversely pleased by the thought of dressing my gorgeous girl. I usually just spent money on myself. It was refreshing to think about someone else for a change. And I'd always appreciated fashion. Colors, lines, textures. It was art, in its own way. Just like Jules herself.

The more I shopped around, the more I found I had a pretty clear sense of her style. At Bergdorf's, I selected enough pieces to build a basic capsule wardrobe. Mostly skirts with slits up the back and blouses I looked forward to unbuttoning.

Agent Provocateur provided a selection of bras and panties and some negligees. By the time I walked out of there, I was practically salivating. *Damn.* I couldn't wait to see her in all of it.

I knew it was time to stop, but my subconscious had other ideas. My feet carried me further down Fifth. Until I found myself loitering outside Tiffany & Co.

I convinced myself I needed a new tie clip. Or maybe a chain to wear on my suit vests… *Or a Valentine's Day gift.*

The thought stopped me cold, right in front of a case of sparkling diamonds. *What am I thinking? I can't get her jewelry from Tiffany's. We've been dating for five days. She'll freak out.*

But the thought only made me pause long enough for one particular bauble to catch my eye.

Fuck me. It was beautiful. Perfect.

A sales associate noticed my interest. Her eyes worked down my body, noting my *Blancpain* watch. Interest lit her gaze. "Something you'd like to see, sir?"

I didn't mean to point, but my hand didn't feel connected to my body. "That one."

She pulled the velvet tray out of the case, placing a selection of sparklers in my line of sight. My fingers clasped around the one that caught my eye, bringing it closer for inspection.

"That one is a beauty," the girl chirped. "Three carat center stone, five total. Emerald cut with a cushion and pave band. I have the papers for it, if you're interested."

Yes. But, unlike my thoughts, my mouth actually made sense. "I'm not really in the market."

That wasn't "no," though, and she saw her opening. "The setting is platinum, of course," she went on. "Virtually indestructible."

Like Jules.

I balanced the ring in my palm, weighing it. Heavier than it looked. Even more exquisite up close, too. The center stone glimmered as I twisted my hand, reflecting its fire at me.

I'm only planning for the future... This is pragmatic curiosity. No harm in asking... "How much?"

The salesgirl's smile turned coy. "Does it really matter?"

No. If I was going to buy Juliet a ring—which, I *wasn't*... because that would be *stupid*—I'd pay any price for the right one.

For *this* one.

My heart pounded against my ribs while tingles raced over my scalp. *I could buy it and just... hold on to it. Indefinitely. Besides, if my net worth ever does wind up taking a hit, I'll have a gorgeous diamond ring to sell...*

All manner of lame explanations ran through my mind. All sorts of logic and justifications to keep myself from having a stroke when I heard my voice say, "I'll take it."

I stashed the ring in the office safe, not trusting myself to have it close at hand in my apartment.

Clearly, I'd lost my goddamn mind. Who knew what I would do if she flashed me that beautiful smile one-too-many times? Or got on her knees for me again...

Luckily, I the ancient safe at Everett Alexander had a combination no one but myself and my father knew, in theory. Though, every year, when we changed the code, he refused to write it down and always wound up asking me to unlock it for him the next time. Because six months had passed since we last reset it, I felt fairly confident I was the only living soul who knew how to get in and out smoothly.

While I was in there, I helped myself to the stack of documents on the safe's bottom shelf. Most were boring, standard fare. Insurance shit, some tax returns, licenses. I slipped them all into my inside jacket pocket, figuring I'd review them to get a better sense of what I needed to procure for G&C. Then, I hid my little blue Tiffany's box behind some gold bars, and locked the whole thing back up.

My father caught me coming back down the hall. I noticed him tucking his shirt into the back of his pants and glanced behind him, where his secretary busied herself with rearranging her necklace.

Jesus. The old man could at least *attempt* discretion.

When he spotted me, he faltered. "Graham. You were in the safe?"

"Yes." Pointedly, I flicked my gaze from his to his secretary. *You don't want to piss me off, Dad.* "I bought a new watch and it needs to be sized at the repair shop three blocks from here. I'm storing it in the safe overnight so I can take it in tomorrow."

Mollified by my blatant lie, he nodded. "I can never remember the damn combination," he muttered, glancing nervously behind him. "Anyway. Dinner this week?"

Knowing our days were numbered, I said, "Yeah why not? Seven on Friday?" Then, just to be a dick, I added, "I can pick Christian up if you want to include him."

As far as Dad knew, his second-born was at NYU, studying. He had no idea Chris was actually in rehab in Chelsea, three days through opiate withdrawals. Still, he grimaced. "Eh, leave the kid at school." He punched my arm. "Grown-ups only."

I stood completely still, staring at him. The motherfucking asshole who slept with his twenty-year-old assistant during lunch and then had the nerve to call himself an adult. For one insane moment, I pictured burning his entire life to the ground, just because I could. And it felt *great*.

Clenching my jaw, I swallowed the rage and gritted, "Fine."

But as I pictured sitting across from him for another cordial meal, I realized I wouldn't be able to do it. Not this time—not with Chris in the state he was in. Not without help.

"I'm going to invite my girlfriend, then," I told him, deciding on the spot. "Assuming that's alright with you."

Dad's features filled with bemusement. "Your *girlfriend*? I'll be damned. Is this the same woman we discussed last week?"

I tugged at my shirtsleeves, focusing on the black paisley material so he wouldn't see the hatred burning in my eyes. "Yes," I clipped. "The very same."

He leaned closer, intrigued by my ambiguity. "Anyone I know?"

"No." *Thank God.* "She's an attorney, from Queens."

I added the last part as a test. He failed. His mouth folded into a frown. "*Queens*?" His disapproving inflection turned the word into an expletive. "How did you meet an attorney from Queens?"

My skin itched as outrage bubbled in my blood. "She works in the city."

I couldn't say any more. If he knew we met in a meeting, he would ask which one. If I told him she worked at Stryker, there was a chance he'd mention it to Grayson's father the next time they crossed paths.

Goddamn it. Jules and I would have to come up with a fake meet-cute story… presuming she deigned to attend the dinner at all. *She's going to be so pissed.*

I already knew she'd be mad about the new clothes… now this. I pictured her tossing her hair back and lifting that stubborn, pointed chin at me. I nearly twitched, equal parts anxious and aroused.

My father observed me carefully. His expression took on a wary note. "Alright… well I'd be happy to meet her, I suppose. I haven't heard you call anyone your girlfriend in years."

I tried to remember when I'd ever given another woman that distinction, but came up blank. Maybe he had me confused with Chris.

He settled his hand on my shoulder in a paternal gesture. My stomach seethed. "Little tip—Valentine's Day is next week. Let me know if you need help getting a reservation."

The irony of the man giving anyone relationship advice brought a sardonic smirk to my face. *Way ahead of you, asshole.* I remembered the rock in the safe, then dismissed the thought instantly. "I've got it handled."

Juliet

The office felt unnaturally quiet without Mr. Stryker.

I could tell Beth didn't know what to do with herself. She offered to change the water in my flowers three times before lunch and one more time at the end of the day.

Apparently, Marco was as bored in Aruba as Stryker's personal assistant was in New York. I imagined his job description for the week involved a whole lot of looking the other way while the happy couple made out. He passed the time by emailing me potential properties for Abuelita every few hours.

I copied the links and forwarded them to Tris, asking for her professional opinions. She vetoed four of the seven, so I sent back the three remaining candidates and told Marco to choose. By close of business, he informed me he set up tours at each, never once mentioning the prices.

For the dozenth time, I wondered exactly how much money my cousin had to work with. Before his promotion, he already seemed pretty comfortable. Lately, though, I noticed that some of his new clothes were designer brands. He stopped mentioning some of the things he'd always wanted to save up for—a particular car or fancy sound system. I wondered if he had finally purchased the items for himself and just decided not to tell anyone.

In any case, he seemed to have the real estate situation handled. I had a nauseating feeling *I* would wind up dealing with Abuelita, though. It didn't escape my notice that he left town without mentioning the potential move to her.

On my way to the subway, Graham texted to tell me had a surprise for me. I spent the entire ride to the Lower East Side imagining what it might be—and most of my musings did not involve clothes.

But, alas, when I finally burst into his apartment, he was most assuredly still dressed. Today's ensemble made me shake my head the second I saw it. "*Pinchao*," I moaned, eying the stark blazer and its black velvet trim. "These *suits*."

He paused in the middle of uncorking a bottle of wine to trail his gaze down my simple blue sheath. Amusement gilded his handsome features when our eyes met. "This one?" he asked, holding his arms in front of him. "It's not even colorful."

True, apart from his red tie... and the handkerchief. "But a white jacket? In February? Isn't there some sort of rule about white before Memorial Day?"

"Easter," he corrected automatically, then cracked a sideways smile. "And this isn't *white*, baby, it's *winter* white. Entirely different thing."

Scoffing, I set my bags on one of his barstools. "If you say so." I noticed something boiling on the stove behind him. And, in a separate pan, spied some pancetta. Incredulous, I asked, "Did you make dinner?"

Graham brought a glass of wine to me, bending to brush his lips over my temple. "Working on it." He nuzzled my hair and made a low, contented sound in his throat. "Come here for a second."

His arms brought me close for a slow, chaste kiss. Then another and another after that. His hands went to their usual places—one behind my head and the other cradling the curve of my ass.

"You always hold me there and there," I mumbled against his mouth, pushing back into his palms.

His lips smiled against mine. "My two favorite things. Your gorgeous ass and your brilliant brain. What more do I need?"

Warmth bled through my chest, melting down to form a puddle in my panties. Too soon, he leaned back. A small smile touched his lips as he gazed at me, his dark eyes transparently adoring. "I missed you today."

Joy shimmered in my chest, along with a wash of chagrin. He was so much better at this whole relationship thing than me. I wondered how many times he'd done it before…

"Me, too," I confessed. Tracing one of his thick brows with my fingertip, I decided to try for a compliment. "You look very sexy in *winter white.*"

He snuggled me closer, grinning. "You're very sexy, always. Do you want your surprise now or after I've subdued you with pasta and sex?"

Had I ever been so… *happy*? I couldn't think of another single occasion when I felt too ecstatic to catch my breath. And all over… what? Spaghetti?

To distract myself from the concerning bent of my thoughts, I slipped my hand between our bodies and began to glide it down to his fly. "I don't know," I murmured. "I'm pretty hungry…"

We didn't make it to his bedroom. Graham took me on the dining table instead, sweeping his papers off of it before setting me on the polished wood and yanking my panties down to one ankle. Our clothes hung off of us—my dress unzipped and pulled off of one arm to give access to my breasts, his pants bunched over his thighs and vest gaping.

When we both fell over the edge, one of our poignant silences settled between us. Graham gathered me up in his arms and carried me into his bathroom. Wordlessly, he removed the rest of my work clothes and cleaned both of us up before retrieving a robe from his closet. A women's robe, with tags on it.

I fingered the silky violet kimono, my gaze questioning as it met his. Instead of answering, he kissed me deeply one last time and nuzzled his nose into my hair for a long moment. After a couple deep breaths, he left me sitting on his black marble sink, naked, holding what I assumed must be my surprise.

Though I didn't like him purchasing things for me without occasion, it was too beautiful to reject. So I put it on and turned to my reflection. The dark purple color seemed to complement me well enough, though I saw Abuelita's point about the way it clashed with my black hair.

I swept my locks into a haphazard ponytail and stared at my face, startled by the expression I found staring back at me. Bright eyes, a glow tinging my cheekbones, some unfamiliar softness around my mouth…

It can't be… I refused to even think the word.

Sex, I corrected internally. *It's very,* very *good sex. Nothing more.*

The lie sent a stab of shame into my center. Because I knew it was a betrayal—of Graham, of course, but also of myself. My true feelings.

Ayúdame Dios.

If I wasn't already falling for the man, I would have been after watching him make carbonara in his underwear.

He seemed to enjoy cooking in the same meditative way I did. He frowned absentmindedly while he stirred his finished product in a pan, staring off into the space in front of him. I sidled up against his back, reaching around to offer him two pasta bowls. "Here."

"Thanks." He flashed a grin, but his eyes still seemed far away. "Should we eat at the table tonight?"

I chuckled. "Well, it's already cleared..."

I retrieved the wine while he served the food. We settled into the spots I'd come to think of an "our usual." He always sat at the head of the table and I always took the place on the right.

"How's Christian today?" I asked, tucking into the meal. His presentation looked a bit clumsy, but he had a natural knack for seasoning. It tasted perfect.

Graham's expression darkened while he chewed. "No better, no worse. The addiction specialist I spoke with today told me the first four days are the worst. He should start improving tomorrow."

I wondered if I should offer to go visit with him. That seemed suitably girlfriend-ish… "I could come with you after work."

Warmth filled his midnight eyes. "I would love that, trust me, but I think he'd probably be embarrassed. Maybe this weekend, if he feels more normal. We can bring him bagels or something."

His suggestion amused me. I'd noticed that Graham was New York City through-and-through. He often mentioned bagels, pastrami, slices of pizza, street food. He could hail a cab with a casual flick of his wrist and effortlessly navigate a crush of bodies on busy city sidewalks. His unparalleled style and confidence somehow managed to be both brash and elegant in one brush, much like the city itself.

My *pinchao*. I loved all of it.

There was something sexy about the idea of letting a man like him squire me about. Excitement flurried in my stomach when I pictured the two of us around town. With his new venture looming, he needed someone suitably sophisticated and intelligent on his arm. I wanted to be that woman.

Maybe that's why, an hour later, when he pulled me into his closet and presented me with my actual surprise, I managed not to faint.

Instead, I snapped, "Absolutely *not.*"

Graham crossed his arms and shrugged, unbothered. "Yeah, I figured this would be a fight. Glad I got laid first."

Que gonorrea.

I guffawed. "Because you know this is insane!" I shouted, spinning away before I got sucked into the beauty of the various outfits hanging on a recently-cleared corner rack. "And insulting. Is there something wrong with the clothes I have? You seem to like them well enough when you're taking them off!"

He raised one winged brow. "Are you finished?"

"No! If I wanted new clothes, I'd go buy some! I may not have a penthouse in Manhattan but I'm hardly *destitute*. I don't need your high-handed hand-outs, Graham."

His jaw hardened. He waited for me to stop panting and then asked, "Is it my turn to speak? Great. I didn't buy these clothes because I needed to or thought *you* needed me to—I got them because I wanted them for you, here. It doesn't make sense for you to keep shoving flats and spare underwear into your purse every day just to have something to wear all the way back to Queens at two A.M. Especially since you work just uptown and staying over would cut your commute in half."

Damn him. I hated it when he made sense. But part of me didn't quite believe he'd drop thousands on clothes for pragmatism's sake. "So this was a *practical* decision?"

He regarded me steadily. "Naturally."

I glanced at the rack now dedicated to me. My heart gave a stupid pang that I dismissed. Of course I didn't care that his gift was more sensible than romantic. I didn't *want* him to want me in his space.

Did I?

My hand floated up to touch the long-sleeved emerald dress closest to me. It was gorgeous. They all were. And, secretly, it thrilled me that he went out of his way to personally choose things for me.

I thought of how Grayson sent Ella to a personal shopper and almost laughed. Not my *pinchao*. He wanted to select every last item, down to my underwear.

As if on cue, he pointed his chin at the built-in drawers beside my rack. "Third drawer. I got undergarments, too. And stuff for you to sleep in. Oh, and some shoes. Just three pairs."

My teeth ground together. "Graham."

His posture unwound. He loped over, boxing me into the closet's wall with both hands on either side of my head. "They're just clothes. Having some stuff here will take packing up off your plate and give us more time together."

I glanced over again. A particularly fetching periwinkle blouse caught my eye. I sighed, defeated. "How much were they? I'll write you a check."

Indignation sharped his gaze. "Like hell you will."

Embers smoldered in my middle. "You know, sometimes, I just want to slap you. Again."

Lust glowed in his black eyes. "Oh *please* do. I'd *love* to show you how I *wanted* to react the last time. I very nearly slammed you into the wall of that elevator and ripped that goddamned dress off."

I remembered the unfathomable way he stared at me. *Feral*, I called it. He had the same wild energy to him now. My untamed urbane beast. Why did the thought make me pulse?

"You're an animal," I spat, glaring and gripping the wall behind me to keep from swinging at him. "No wonder I hated you so much."

He leaned his face closer, his black gaze burning into mine. His voice was deceptively soft. "How much?"

My restraint snapped. I clutched his hair in both hands and yanked hard, bringing our mouths together. "This much."

Chapter Twenty

February 10, 2017

Graham

I winced slightly as I shifted in the chair at Christian's bedside. Lucid for the second day in a row, he actually noticed. "Did you hurt your back or something?" he asked, talking into his hoagie.

Or something.

The memory of Jules riding me, hell-for-leather, on the floor of my closet, sprang to mind. I took a bite of my own sandwich and spoke around it. "Rug burn."

For the first time in ages, I watched amusement seep into my brother's blue eyes. His lips twitched up. "No shit?"

The abrasions all over my ass delighted Jules to no end, too. When she stripped my clothes off after work the night before, she laughed at the raw skin for two full minutes. She felt I'd earned it after my "high-handed hand-outs."

"Your place doesn't even have carpet," he contended.

"Bedroom closet," I told my brother, shrugging a shoulder.

Chris snorted. "You couldn't have walked ten steps into your bedroom?"

I remembered the fire crackling in Juliet's eyes, the way she pulled my hair at the roots; and decided out loud, "Not a chance."

Instead of laughing, he creased his forehead. Always so serious, my baby brother. "What was a woman even doing in your closet? Isn't that, like, your Fortress of Solitude? I thought you didn't even let the maid in there."

I cast him a glower. "Fuck you. The maid got Pinesol on my favorite loafers last year. I'm not risking another."

We both ate in silence for a moment. Christian surprised me when he decided to probe. "So who's the girl?"

I wasn't sure if rubbing my new relationship in his face was a good idea. We still hadn't discussed what happened Saturday night, or how Juliet happened to be there with me. I suspected he didn't remember any of it and worried he'd be embarrassed if I told him. On the other hand, it was the first time he'd asked me a coherent personal question in *months*. And I figured I better start getting used to telling people… since I had to face Grayson soon.

I answered reluctantly. "Well, she's sort of… my girlfriend. Her name is Juliet."

Christian stared at me. "Your girlfriend. Like, a woman you date *exclusively*?"

I cast my eyes down at my lunch. A vision of the engagement ring flashed through my head. "Something like that, yeah."

"And you aren't fucking *anyone* else?" he asked, his voice dead even. "Not even one other person?

The notion of being intimate with any other woman sent a chilling prickle over my scalp. I scowled at him. "No, I'm not. Jesus. Is that so hard to believe?"

His steady regard remained solemn. "You once told me that it didn't count as cheating as long as the other woman lived in a different borough."

Fuck me. I did say that. And now I was in love with a woman from Queens.

"Let's just say, karma has firmly caught up with me," I muttered, aggrieved by the memory. "And she gave me an ass full of rug burn."

"Karma or Juliet?"

I smirked. "Both. She was mad at me at the time, actually. I bought her a bunch of shit without her approval."

"Hell of a way to express anger." Christian chewed thoughtfully for a moment. His earnest frown returned. "I thought you said women liked presents."

"They do," I assured him. In fact, Juliet wore one of my gifts into work that morning. And I got to make love to her in the shower beforehand. "She's a proud woman, though. She doesn't like the idea of anyone keeping her."

Normally—and only if necessary—I spilled my guts to Grayson over drinks. It was exhilarating to talk about the woman I loved; sober, and in the light of day.

I'm proud of her, I realized. I wanted to brag. I wanted everyone to know how wonderful she was. How she picked *me*.

Christian's gaze flit over my face, searching for something. Insincerity, I guessed. When he didn't find any, he finally said, "Huh. Can I meet her?" Some dark thought crossed his expression. "I mean… does she know about me?"

He thought I'd be ashamed of him. I found myself gripping his forearm. "Yes. Of course she does. She—" I almost admitted that she already met him, in that godforsaken alleyway. Swallowing, I reworded. "Juliet asked if she could come with me tomorrow, actually. We'll bring breakfast."

He agreed and we said our goodbyes. On my way out, while thinking of Jules meeting my family, I had a flash of inspiration about Valentine's Day. My watch informed me I only had thirty minutes to make it happen before I had to return to work.

Between that errand and everything else, my afternoon somehow wound up jammed. I took back-to-back calls from McAllister and another friend from prep school who wanted to meet up and discuss their new IPO.

Jules texted me intermittently, stressing about our dinner with my dad. I offered to send my car for her so she could go back to my place to change, but she decided to come straight from the office, since the restaurant was only a few blocks off of Madison.

I took the ride instead, using the extra hour of time to stop for more flowers. Pink, this time, like the blouse she wore out of my apartment that morning. With time to spare, I made it home around six and arranged the bouquet on the island along with a bottle of wine we could crack open after our meal. I had a feeling we'd need it.

The concierge delivered dry cleaning while I was out. An envelope pinned to the plastic bag caught my eye as I strode into my closet. Ripping it open, I found a note from my cleaners', telling me they discovered some papers in one of my jackets.

Damn it. The shit from the safe.

I forgot all about it when Jules undressed me on Wednesday. Thankfully, everything was attached to the note, unscathed. The envelopes on top looked oddly familiar. I plucked one up on impulse and scanned its contents.

It was my broker licensing information and the certificate that arrived after I passed the exam. I moved to open the second, identical envelope, thinking I might have Christian's certificate framed for him as a gift.

Maybe having a reminder of his accomplishments hanging up in his room would be good for him…

I slid my eyes over his credentials, considering. A familiar series of digits snagged my attention. My blood froze.

There, under his name, social security number, and passing grade, I saw it.

His broker number.

The exact broker number listed on every fraudulent trade I discovered in my father's files… belonged to Christian.

Which meant that our dad didn't just steal millions of dollars. He framed his son for it.

Juliet

I would have to kill Graham.

Bad enough I was forced to meet his father, the criminal. Even worse that I had to be nice to *el cerdo*. But Graham had apparently decided to delay the whole ordeal by showing up late for our coveted reservation.

How he even managed to get a table in the first place was beyond me. I'd heard of the famous restaurant, Butter, multiple times, but the press didn't do it justice. Inside, modern ambience mixed with the mouth-watering aroma of French fare. My stomach rumbled while I shifted on my feet, glancing at the door again.

Where *was* he?

I'd checked my shimmery coat the second I came in. Glancing down at the outfit Graham purchased, I smoothed my palms over the nude pencil skirt. I had no clue how the *pinchao* somehow found something the exact color of my skin without actually having me with him, but the piece truly was flattering. At the very least, I looked good.

Another man walked in. For a second, I swore it was him—but then I saw the extra girth around his middle, the lines banding his thinner lips, the way his hair line receded. It had to be Mr. Everett, though. The resemblance seemed too strong to be a coincidence.

I weighed my options and decided it would be beyond awkward for us to hover near each other for who-knew-how-long until Graham arrived. And I needed to act as if I'd never even heard the word "fraud" in connection with "Everett."

"Sir?" I said, extending my hand. "I'm Juliet Rivera, Graham's… girlfriend."

Recognition sparked in his eyes. They were dark, just like my favorite pair. And, also like Graham's, moved down over my body in a way that felt altogether indecent.

"My, my," he chuckled, holding on to my hand for a second too long. "I see for once my son didn't exaggerate. You *are* very hot."

Clearly, my boyfriend neglected to mention my penchant for smacking men who objectified me. Blanching, I withdrew my arm. "Did he say that?"

Now I really *would* kill him. Painfully.

Mr. Everett had a charming grin, not unlike his son's. "I may be paraphrasing," he admitted. He gestured to the hostess stand. "Shall we? Graham is probably stuck in traffic."

Anxiety knotted my guts as I arranged myself in my seat. I felt prepared to sit through a meal with Graham and his asshole father… but dealing with him one-on-one made me feel sick.

Mr. Everett ordered a double scotch and I got a glass of rosé, wanting to keep my wits about me. I also requested a single-malt for Graham.

"So," his dad said, eyeing me across the tabletop. "How did you two meet?"

I glanced toward the door again, desperately willing him to appear one last time before I gave the answer Graham and I discussed. "We met at a bar in SoHo," I lied, then added some truth for good measure. "It's sort of hard not to notice him. His clothes always catch my eye."

The waitress set our drinks between us and he immediately picked his up, downing half of it. A sheen of interest glinted in his eyes. "I find it hard to believe he could get a woman like you without some tricks up his sleeve." His gaze fell to my cleavage, tastefully displayed by the blush blouse Graham selected for me. "You are clearly out of his league."

I nearly recoiled. He didn't even *know* me. And how could say something so rude about his own son?

"If he were here, I'd agree with you just to goad him," I replied, sipping my wine. "But since he's not, I'll plead the Fifth."

"Ha!" he crowed. "He told me you were a lawyer."

I attempted a tight smile. "Yes. That's true. I graduated from NYU School of Law last spring and recently took a job as in-house junior counsel for a development company."

Mr. Everett opened his mouth to reply, but cut himself off. His eyes followed some movement behind me and he smiled, standing.

Graham. Gracias a Dios.

I swiveled to shoot him a severe save-me-now look, but the second I saw his face everything inside of me lurched. My spine stiffened. Instinctually, I clutched my purse in my hand, ready to leap up.

Lord knew I made Graham plenty angry, but I'd never seen him *enraged.* His eyes narrowed into slits while they tracked his dad. He sailed through the crowd, intent on his mark.

I witnessed the entire scene unfold in slow motion. The way Graham's hands clenched into balls before he even rounded the table. The moment he cocked his fist back. His arm snapping out to cut cleanly across his father's face. The sick crunch of cartilage cracking.

Mr. Everett went straight to the floor. The entire restaurant fell utterly silent. Graham stood over his dad, glaring down.

"You sick son of a bitch," he growled. "I will *bury you.*"

Without looking away, he extended his other hand to me. Bewildered, I grabbed his fingers in my own and let him whisk me into his side. Fifteen seconds later we were on the sidewalk. He dropped me as if I'd burned him and started to pace, shoving both hands into his hair.

"What the fuck did I just do?" he muttered. "Jesus Christ."

I felt like he stole my line. Panicked by the scene he just caused, I sprang into action, raising my arm to hail a cab. "We should go. Now."

Graham nodded, but didn't speak. Seething, he followed me into the taxi and slammed his door. "Lower East Side. The Ludlow," he barked.

"Please," I added, pointedly.

Turning to give him a baffled scowl, I demanded, "What the *hell* is wrong with you? Have you lost your mind?"

His jaw snapped audibly. "We'll discuss it at home."

Pissed by his attitude, his actions, my own confusion, I crossed my arms and huffed. "First, I don't live at The Ludlow so it isn't my 'home.' Second, I'm starving. I skipped lunch today because Dominic gave me attitude and I was looking forward to this amazing dinner we were supposed to have. So, third, maybe *I* don't *want* to go to your apartment right now."

Grinding his teeth, Graham regarded me with hot, black loathing. "Then *why are you here*? Get out."

I sat up straight, leaning closer to his face, refusing to back down. "Why am I here?" I shrieked. "*You asked* me to come. If you recall, I didn't even want to meet your father! I only agreed to attend dinner *for you.* I sat there and let that disgusting excuse for a man eye-fuck me... *for you.* I just fled the scene of an assault without my favorite coat *for you. I am here for you*, you ingrate!"

He stared, not blinking. Gradually, the color drained away from his face. I watched the column of his throat work over a hard swallow. "Tell him to pull over," he murmured, hoarse. "Now."

Mutinous, I glared at him. His coloring went from white to sallow. "I feel sick," he whispered, stone-still. "Please."

Sloughing out a curse word, I bent forward and asked the cabbie to stop the car. Ordinarily, Graham had his wad of cash out before our cabs ever stopped. This time, when I looked over, I found him jumping out.

"*Loco hijo de puta.*" Muttering to myself in Spanish, I extricated my own wallet and paid five dollars for the two-minute ride. Then I stepped onto the pavement just in time to witness Graham vomiting into the gutter.

Graham

"The flowers are very beautiful."

After I completely lost my shit at Butter, and then proceeded to thoroughly mortify myself on Park Avenue, Juliet bought me a bottle of water from the nearest street stand and hailed another taxi without a word. While we rode downtown, I pressed my pounding head against the window, hoping its chill would numb my brain.

We made it to my place without another incident. She followed me inside and stayed quiet while I ditched my dirty clothes and turned on the shower. Part of me hoped she'd join me again, but I wasn't surprised when she didn't.

Full of dread and self-loathing, I scrubbed myself clean, brushed my teeth twice, and found a fresh set of burgundy sweats. Normally, I preferred not to get dressed at home, but putting a barrier between myself and the world appealed to me. And I felt oddly cold.

Juliet had the same notion. Wearing her new navy yoga pants and a matching tank top, she joined me on the couch and thanked me for the floral arrangement. Leaning my head back, I gazed up at the ceiling without seeing it.

"Glad you like them."

My voice sounded foreign. Clogged and rough. I felt her hand land on my arm—one warm spot amidst all my cool numbness.

"Do you feel okay?" she asked.

Did I feel *okay*? The question brought a bitter smirk to my lips.

"I can't talk about it right now." I set my hand on top of hers and let my eyes drift shut. "I'm sorry about losing my temper in the cab. I understand if you want to leave. I'm not going to be good company tonight. Or even this weekend, probably."

Or ever.

Because I knew what I had to do, now. And, after my display at the restaurant, I couldn't change my mind even if I wanted to.

Jules gingerly settled into my side, resting her head on my shoulder. She sighed. "I can take you, *pinchao*."

Her words from the taxi chose that moment to return to me. *I am here for you*, she said. It seemed she really meant it.

A burst of gratitude washed over the icy lump of dread sitting in my center. I let my head rest against hers. "Thank you. For staying. For not getting out of the car. I'm sorry I ruined dinner. Did you order something for yourself?"

She turned her hand over, lacing our fingers together. "For both of us. Smoothies."

The appreciation swelled through me again, so strong my next breath shook. *Jesus*. Were my eyes watering? What the fuck had become of me?

I turned to press a kiss into her crown, distracting myself with the scent of her hair. "I don't deserve you," I mumbled, speaking my unfiltered thoughts. "You should run. Now. Far and fast. I'm a ticking time bomb. When it all blows, I don't want you caught in the crosshairs."

"It already blew," she argued lightly. "All over Park Avenue."

I would have laughed if I wasn't so busy groaning. I scrubbed my free hand over my face, horrified. "Christ. People *know* me on Park Avenue. Someone could have seen."

She giggled quietly. "Well, you may have flown under the radar if you hadn't worn your insane leprechaun suit today. I swear it matched your complexion by the time we stopped the car."

I leaned back to look down at Juliet, unable to bear another minute without seeing her face up close. Cupping her pointed chin in my palm, I turned her toward me and stared right into her eyes.

"Seriously, *bijou*," I murmured. "I'm sorry for snarling at you. Forgive me. Please."

Her mouth wobbled, torn between concern and reprimand. "You don't want to tell me what happened? The last time we talked about your father, we made a whole plan. Something clearly altered it."

I had to tell her. But I found I couldn't do it right at that moment. After, everything would change. I wanted one more peaceful night with her before I told her I had to blow up my life after all.

Brushing her hair back, my regard hardened. "I said I'm sorry," I repeated. "Forgive me?"

Her golden gaze softened into liquid honey. "Yes. I forgive you. But I still think we should talk about what the hell caused you to lose your mind."

"We will," I mumbled, dreading it. "Tomorrow, okay? After we visit Christian, if that's alright with you."

Juliet didn't like waiting. She was impatient by nature, like me. I suspected that was one reason why we'd defiled half of the surfaces in my apartment in the span of two weeks. But she nodded mulishly. "Fine."

An hour later, after eating—or drinking, really—dinner, I rested my head in her lap while we watched TV. Jules picked a crime show with lots of courtroom drama—and made faces whenever someone said something unrealistic. She steadily combed my hair while she explained the legal inaccuracies.

I loved the feel of her fingers and the sound of her voice. It was the first night we'd spent together without sex or work, but I felt more content without either than I ever dreamed I could.

My phone buzzed on the floor beside the couch. When it went off a third time, I groused and fumbled for it. There were three texts from Grayson. Two photos and one message.

The images were dark, fuzzy frames. Blurred. I squinted closely.

"*Fuck.*"

Pictures from Butter. One of me with my fist cocked; another of my father on the ground. Thankfully, Juliet wasn't visible in either.

I see telling your dad about your new company didn't go well, Grayson's message read. *We're wheels up in ten but the jet has Wi-Fi service. Call me.*

Instead, I typed back. *Where the fuck did you get pictures? It just happened two hours ago.*

I sat up when my phone started to ring. "Hold on," I muttered to Jules. "It's Grayson. I have to take this."

I went to my bedroom and paced. *He doesn't know anything about Juliet. He doesn't know about Christian overdosing. He has no clue my father committed fraud or that I have to turn him in.*

I cursed again and swiped right. "Hello."

"We took off early," Grayson said by way of greeting. "I wanted to talk to you ASAP. There's someone you need to call. Immediately."

"Wait a minute," I interjected. "Back up. How the fuck did you even get those pictures? Do you have security following your friends now?"

He gave a bleak laugh. "No. I hired a PR person last week after the whole break-in/possible-sex-tape fiasco. She works exclusively with paparazzi all over town and buys photos from them directly, to destroy them or release them for her clients on her own terms. She knows you're my friend so when one of her sources told her he had pictures of Graham Everett knocking out an old guy at Butter, she called me."

A PR person. The idea was nauseating and brilliant. I felt disgusted that my friends had to hire a professional to monitor their reputations because of some sick fuck trespassing on their privacy. But, on the other hand, I wondered how hiring a PR professional for my own situation never occurred to me.

"Who's your girl?" I asked. "And how much do I need to pay for her to make those pictures disappear?"

Grayson paused just long enough to make me suspicious. The hairs on the back of my neck rose. "Fuck me," I groaned, doubly ill. "Stryker. Tell me you didn't hire *her*."

He sighed heavily. "She's the best in town, shithead."

But not even my second-favorite moniker could quell my dread.

Ava Morgan. Kill me now.

"She's a raging *bitch* is what she is. I cannot believe you're *paying* her. Where do you send her checks—the seventh circle of Hell?"

"Otherwise known as the corner of Seventy-Fifth and Park." He laughed darkly. "Yes, I hired Ava. I didn't want to, but Ella and I met with five people and she's the one Ella chose. She's started a whole campaign to win public favor for our relationship and it's *working*. In one week, we've had three photos I personally chose appear in tabloids as 'candids.' Next month, she's booked us interviews with *People* magazine and *Architectural Digest*. The woman is seriously connected. And, listen, I know you two have history, but—"

I cringed at the thought. "Grayson. Come *on*."

He knew the stories. I didn't want to relive them. Especially with my girlfriend in the next room.

"I know, I know," he sighed. "But think of it this way, Ava took all of her Upper East Side venom and socialite social capital and put them to good use."

Ugh. I wanted to moan. "So you're telling me I have to call *her* to kill the photos? She's literally one of four phone numbers I have blocked."

"I already had her kill the photos," Grayson replied. "So you're welcome. She has all the copies and she won't release them without word from me or you. But, listen; she had an intriguing idea. I won't pitch it for her, but you two really should get in touch."

My skin crawled. "I'm having the month from Hell, Grayson. I can't take her shit."

I heard him murmur to someone. Ella, probably. Then, to me, "Yeah, I sort of figured there was more to the story than your new business venture. I thought we'd grab a drink this weekend. I saw the portfolio stats you emailed yesterday—I owe you a round."

His stocks rose another three percent that week. Up a total of seven in less than a month. My brain spit calculations out at me automatically. *$350,000.*

But I couldn't even enjoy our success. I knew I'd have to tell him about everything *else* when we met up. Anxiety flattened my lungs.

"Yeah, sure," I managed, defeated. "I'll text you tomorrow."

I turned to find Juliet hovering on the threshold, looking nervous. I tossed my phone on the bed and reached for her, relieved when she came right into my arms.

"Does he know?" she whispered into my chest.

About us. "No. But I think I'll have to tell him tomorrow."

She clutched herself closer. "What if I'm not ready?"

"He's my best friend. I can't keep lying to him," I told her. "He called because he just saved my ass once again. He deserves the truth, but it's more than that. I need him to know because this—you and me—is important to me. I *want* him to know."

I also wanted to kiss her. To get in bed with her and make us both forget the whole shitty day, week, month. To show her she was the one bright spot in all of my darkness.

But Juliet stepped away. Her gaze dropped to her feet. "I understand," she muttered, then pulled at her shirt. "I was thinking… I'm really tired. Mind if I go to sleep?"

I remembered the way I woke up without her last weekend and had to work to swallow. "Will you be here in the morning?" I asked, trying for a joke.

My attempt fell flat. Her expression remained solemn as she nodded. "Of course."

Juliet

I knew it was wrong to eavesdrop on Graham's conversation, but I did it anyway.

While I tossed and turned in his bed, I replayed pieces I overheard. Something about pictures? A girl Graham didn't like… for carnal reasons, I inferred. A girl from his past he had to call, now…

I hated how much I cared. As I loomed outside his bedroom door, I despised myself for how invested I'd become. I never wanted to date anyone because I never wanted to deal with feeling the way I did in that moment—jittery from jealousy and squeamish from suspicion, with an ache pounding where my heart should have been.

He never told me why he lost his ever-loving mind and decked his own dad in public. I couldn't bring myself to push him after watching him get sick, but I also suspected there were a lot of things he kept hidden while we watched TV together.

Why wouldn't he just tell me? He told me everything else… didn't he?

Dios mío.

What if there was more?

When I thought about the tender way Graham held me, the way he gazed into my eyes… I didn't want to believe it. But he didn't tell me about his brother's addiction. And he went back on our plan for dinner with his father without so much as a heads up.

Did I really want him to risk my job by telling my boss about our relationship when he couldn't even be up-front with me?

I rolled back and forth for hours, frustrated and heartsick. I didn't realize until well after three A.M. that Graham never came to bed at all.

Chapter Twenty-One

February 11, 2017

Graham

Recent events should have taught me to trust my gut.

Hindsight, in so many instances, revealed that I knew things were fucked up all along. Christian's drug problem, my father's deceit, the nagging feeling that there was something too familiar about that damn broker number…

In every case, my subconscious turned out to be more correct than any of the rationalizations I fed myself in order to sleep at night.

So. Why I chose to—once again—ignore the alarm bells clanging in the back of mind is a mystery to me. Yet, when I woke to find myself prostrate on my sofa sometime in the wee hours of the morning, I did just that.

Before I even opened my eyes, I knew something was wrong. I blinked, disconcerted by my surroundings until I remembered that I intended to give Juliet some space. *I must have accidentally fallen asleep in the living room.*

Then I felt it—the cool brush of her fingertips, sifting through my hair. "Graham?"

Turning my head, I found her standing beside me. Completely naked.

Instead of feeling aroused, another prickle of apprehension pulled at my shoulders. "What's wrong?" I asked, gruff. "Are you okay?"

She smoothed her hand down my spine. "I came to find you… I want you, Graham."

My body warred with itself. My cock swelled. My heart pounded. I rolled to the side, facing her. "Right now?"

I didn't know much about relationships, but I knew we didn't end the evening on good terms. So this seemed… random, at best. Almost ominous. But how could I resist her, when I loved her so much I couldn't breathe and she came to me, wanting me?

…completely naked.

I let her guide me into a seated position and pull off my hoodie. She tossed it aside and straddled my lap. Moonlight slanted over her features, making her more beautiful than ever. "Kiss me."

Her breasts were the closer than her lips. I brushed my mouth across her dark rose nipples in turn. "Like this?" I murmured between her tits.

She gasped quietly, straining closer. "However you want," she breathed. "I want you take me however you want."

My cock thoroughly approved. Blood rushed through my ears, drowning out the last of the warnings ringing in my mind. I skimmed my hands down her sides, relishing the restless way she shifted over me.

My erection tented my sweats, insistent. Her warm, soft flesh filled my palms. *God.* Had anything ever felt as good as she did? Or looked so luminous in the semi-dark?

"You're so beautiful," I rasped, unable to think of anything else. "Have I told you that?"

Her golden eyes glistened as she softly trailed her fingertips over my cheek. "You tell me every time." Some errant thought moved across her expression. She clasped both hands on either side of my face. "Will you tell me one more time?"

The emotion beaming from each of her features made me weak. "I'll tell you forever."

Her wet gaze gleamed in the darkness. She whispered my name; part plea, part lament. "Graham."

The words I swallowed a dozen different times came up, then. Who knows why. I didn't. I only knew that they were suddenly too big for me to contain.

"Juliet," I murmured, locking eyes with her. "I love you."

Her chin trembled against my palms. Tears slipped over her cheeks, melting into my fingers while I held her face. "Graham," she cried. "Don't."

"I can't stop," I sighed. "I have *tried.* I've tried every minute since the first time I kissed you. But it's fucking useless. So. *I love you.*"

With a quiet moan, she tackled me into the sofa, banding her arms around my head and plunging her tongue into my mouth.

Her kiss said more than any words could. She poured all of her fear and longing into it; and, like always, I understood her perfectly.

Wild, Juliet nipped my lips and tugged my hair. Punishing me for loving her, for making her care about me. I understood that feeling, too.

She ate at me. Scratching, tugging, biting. I let her have her way, holding her tenderly and whispering to her whenever I could. I said the words again and again, meaning them more each time. When she finally ran out of steam, she pressed her forehead into mine and panted quietly.

I nuzzled my nose against hers. "Shhh. It's alright, baby. Rip into me all you want. I'm not going anywhere."

Adoration and trepidation fought for space inside her eyes. More tears slipped over her face. "I want you now," she murmured, hushed. "Please."

She seemed lost. I let my instincts guide me and fisted her hair, pinioning her head in place, taking control again. "Do I still get it the way I want it?"

"Yes." She quivered, her nipples tightening. "Anything you want."

I guided her hips with my free hand, pulling her body into mine and pushing my sweats off. She tried to move back and sink down onto me, but I tightened the fist at her nape. "No. Stay here."

Face-to-face, where I could stare right into her. I watched her features break when I licked my thumb and reached for her center, stroking over her clit. She rocked into me, her frantic breaths gusting across my cheek.

I turned and caught her lips to give a deep, slow kiss; matching the swirl of my tongue to the whirl of my thumb. She moaned into my mouth. The ragged sound sent a throbbing pulse through my dick.

"Touch me," I ordered, moving to suck on the side of her neck.

Juliet used both fists to pump my cock. Grinding restlessly, she rubbed her tits against my chest while she stroked just hard enough to make me desperate. Snarling, I flipped her onto her back and spread her silken thighs. With one thrust, I buried myself to the hilt. Her snug heat pulsed around my member until I groaned her name.

She cried out while I drew back to slam into her again. "*Graham!*"

I loved my name on her lips. I loved her hands clawing down my back to grip my ass and pull me in deeper. I loved her body opening up to welcome me.

I loved *her*.

I told her again, mumbling the words in an incoherent stream of praises I murmured into her breasts. When I slipped my hand between our bodies to touch her again, she mewled a stream of Spanish. Her nails dug into my shoulders. I felt her body tightening around me on every plunge, bringing her closer to her release.

Lifting my head, I held her gaze and watched her fall apart. So epically gorgeous, she made my chest ache. "Yes, baby," I praised, resting my forehead against hers once more. "You're so beautiful. I meant what I said—I'll never stop. Forever."

My thrusts grew sloppy as I lost control, pouring myself into her on a loud groan. Juliet held me close while I came. She pressed sweet kisses to the side of my face and let me linger with my head on her shoulder.

"*Amado mío.*"

Amado. She used the word before. I didn't know it, but it had the soulful cadence of an endearment. Turning my nose into her neck, I inhaled her jasmine warmth and shifted my weight into the sofa, holding her body against mine while I rolled us onto our sides.

Silence settled, so different than the first night we ever had sex, when she blew up my entire world in one fell swoop. Now, instead of a relentless roar of uncertainty, the quiet covered us like a duvet.

Juliet massaged my scalp. Every few minutes, I felt her lips brush my forehead and constricted my arms, hugging her closer. I dozed for a while before Jules shimmied down to put us at eye level. She gave me one more light kiss. "Come with me," she whispered. "Let's go to bed."

Too weary to banter or put my clothes back on, I complied without a word. Still nude, we both slipped into my bed and naturally cuddled close. For the first time ever, she fell asleep in my arms.

I never would have guessed that the first time might also be our last.

Juliet

I spent most of the night in Graham's arms, reflecting on all that had passed between us and mourning what I knew daylight must bring. When my eyes weren't clouded by tears, I stared at his chiseled, gorgeous face.

I'd miss his quick smiles, the dark heat of his eyes. I never wanted to forget anything about him or our time together.

How did I end up here?

When I went to him earlier, I didn't have any intention of leaving. Doubts filled my mind to the brim while I tossed and turned alone. Finally, I went out to him, unable to think of any other way to banish the fear gathering inside of me. I didn't know what I wanted, only that I needed him to give it to me.

But Graham understood. Even when he confessed his love and I started tearing into him, he understood. He always did; just as I seemed to connect to his thoughts and feelings in a way I never had with anyone else.

Which is why I knew he'd decided to turn his father in.

As well as I knew Graham, though, I also knew myself. I would never forgive either of us if I stayed with him through his upcoming legal battle and one or both of us lost. I could be disbarred for ever entertaining the notion of covering up a crime. My entire career—my years of studying and saving and schlepping hours into and out of the city would be wasted—then.

Without my ability to practice law, I had no earning potential. And the savings I'd managed to amass so far—which did not include the fifty-thousand-dollar check I couldn't bring myself to cash—would only last us a few months…

I had to consider my family. Abuelita relied on my income, now. If Mami planned to stay in Colombia, I needed to factor in her eventual care, too. Not to mention Lucia and the baby I wanted to protect against my better judgment.

There were many practical reasons for me to end things before Graham told Stryker about us. Reasons that benefitted him, as well. He would need all of his focus to fight his father *and* the feds. Christian required round-the-clock support. Plus, if he never had to admit to our fling, he wouldn't jeopardize what I now suspected was his only true friendship.

Marco wouldn't lose his job, either.

And yet, despite all of those sound rationales, I found the one reason that influenced me most was not logical at all. In fact, it veered dangerously close to irrational.

Fear.

Terror that seized my heart every time he said he loved me. Dread from the very idea of the word "forever." And downright desperation at the concept of winding up like my parents.

Amado. I murmured the word to him in a moment of sheer insanity, with his body inside of mine and his loving outpour filling my heart to a painful burst. In Spanish, it meant "beloved."

And it was the exact term I heard my father call Lucia last week.

The same one he used to call my mother.

The second I heard the word fall from my mouth, I knew I had to leave Graham. Because it was a lie. Or an impossibility, really. No one could be *beloved* with everlasting faithfulness, as the word implied.

Not my mother. Not me. Not even Graham.

So I slipped out his bed when dawn rose. I snuck out of his room, out to the living area, where I quietly packed everything I needed to take with me and placed it all near the front door. Once the coffee finished brewing, I set out two mugs at the corner of his island, and waited there, with his borrowed spare key sitting in the middle of the snowy granite.

I must have woken Graham, because he appeared much sooner than I expected. From my place at the counter, I watched him shuffle out of his room in a new pair of boxers.

He looked pretty beat. Dark circles hung under his eyes. His hair seemed more disheveled than usual. And his bearing was all wrong—complete devoid of his usual elegance or cockiness.

My stomach lurched while his midnight gaze ran over me warily, then fell to the keys on his countertop. He stood utterly still for the longest moment, staring at them. When he finally moved, he kept his eyes downcast and plucked the coffee mug off the counter before retreating all the way to the far side of the island.

Without looking up, he spoke down to his mug. "So you're going."

Why lie to him? What was the point?

"Yes," I murmured.

I heard him breathe out of his nose while he stared down at the granite expanse between us. His face remained as stony as his voice. "Alright, then. I assume from the keys that you won't be back?"

Tears pricked my eyes. "No. I'll shred your check."

A slight nod. "I should pay you for the work you did, at least. I plan to use it."

The thought of looking at his money in my bank account sent a wave of nausea spiraling through my core. "Please don't," I whispered. "I don't want it. Just use the contracts and research we did; they were a team effort, anyway."

Graham nodded again. "I'll have your clothes messengered to Abuelita's. Most were designer. Non-refundable. We can consider that an even trade."

Thrown, I watched him avoid my gaze. I didn't know what I expected when I told him I was leaving, but it wasn't this. I figured he'd fight me. Try to seduce me or charm me the way he always did.

Throughout our time together, I thought I'd seen every part of him. But this weary, detached man felt like a stranger.

"Look at me," I snapped, unable to bear it.

He kept his eyes down. His lips tightened. "I can't. If you're going, then just… leave, okay? I can't do this."

His coolness goaded me. "Do *what*?" I shouted. "All you've done is stare at the damned counter. I'm trying to have a serious conversation, here, Graham."

A bleak smile turned up the corners of his mouth. "No you're not. You've made up your mind. I don't need to hear all of your excuses. I know the truth. You're running scared. And nothing I say will change that. So, go."

My heart hammered into my ribs. "I'm not *scared*."

The lie finally spurred him into action. His head snapped up, pinning me with his dark, turbulent eyes.

"Don't fucking lie to me," he thundered. "I know you're terrified because I told you I love you. I'm sure you've convinced yourself there are other reasons to go; but you didn't care about any of those, yesterday. As far as you know, the only thing that's changed is what I said to you."

He had me so squarely pegged, it prickled my guts. But, still, I had to fight back. "*As far as I know*, huh? Whose fault is that? I asked you over and over what changed yesterday and you didn't tell me."

Rage twisted Graham's expression. "Would that help? You want to hear how I found out that the broker number on all the fraudulent accounts is Christian's? That my father pinned all this shit on him? So now I have to turn my dad in to save my brother? Does that fucking help somehow?"

My insides heaved. "Graham—"

"Spare me your goddamn pity, Juliet!" he yelled. "You were leaving, anyway. Because you're too scared to stay!"

Unable to bear the look on his face, I denied it. "That's not the reason," I started, "I really just—"

"Enough!" he roared. "I don't need the list. Just leave, Juliet. I was stupid for saying what I said to you last night. I shouldn't have thought you could handle it."

His lack of faith in me felt like an insult, even as I proved him completely correct. Outraged and without a single way to defend myself, I hurled out the first rationale I could think of.

"I'm not leaving because you think you love me," I yelled, jumping to my feet. "I'm leaving because you're about to lose everything and I don't want to get stuck in the middle while your life blows up!"

The horrible, selfish statement hung in the air between us, sucking all of the oxygen out of the room. I spat it out thinking it was another falsehood, but, as I stood there, with my chest throbbing, unable to call back the words, I wondered… were they really untrue? Now that I knew just how messed up his family situation was… would part of me feel relieved to extricate myself from it?

Graham went eerily silent, staring at me. His midnight gaze looped over my face as if seeing me for the first time. And hating what he saw.

"If that's really what you think," he finally said, his voice dead, "then you're not the person I thought you were. And I have nothing left to say to you."

See? The practical part of me sneered. *I'm smart for protecting myself. He doesn't love me. He's already doubting what he ever saw in me in the first place. I should just take what little dignity I have and get out.*

But my feet felt planted to the wood floor. Panic sliced through my center. I was so upset, my thoughts came out half in Spanish.

"I don't—*no quiero*—*tú*—you don't love me, Graham," I finally cried. "This is all just some insane… *something*. I don't even know *what*! I bet if I walked out right now, you would forget about me in a week."

He stared right at me for an endless second, weighing my words. I watched the moment a new wave of certainty took hold of him. "You're wrong," he said finally. "And so am I."

He waved a hand at me. "This isn't you. This is fear. Not the Juliet I know. And I *do* love her. *You*. I love you. I love you so goddamn much, I have no idea how I'm going to stand here and watch you leave me, but I'll do it if that's what you need."

It shamed me how much I needed to leave. Call it fear or stubbornness or pride. All I knew was that every cell in my body vibrated with the need to flee.

"It is."

I said the words—admitting it to myself as much as him—and suddenly felt nothing. A chasm opened inside of me. Everything fell in, leaving a cold, hollow place where my heart should've been. And, in its place, dread.

"Then go," he murmured. "And I'll watch."

True to his word, he stood there, ashen, as I took a step back. Then another. And one more. He didn't flinch or turn away, even when I wished he would.

I finally spun for the door, fearing he would catch the sheen of tears stinging my eyes. He said my name, so soft I barely heard it. But I was already at the door, with my bag in hand.

Graham

Grayson found me sometime later.

I didn't know where I was, but he suddenly appeared, wearing a navy tee shirt and sweatpants the same color, along with a formal coat and white sneakers.

Weird, my drunk brain decided. *Unless... this is what you're supposed to wear here?*

I looked down at my own clothes. Grey joggers and a black tee shirt under the Columbia hoodie that still smelled like jasmine. My stomach roiled at the scent. Gaping pain throbbed vaguely, somewhat numbed by the seven scotches sloshing on top of it.

"Jesus," he muttered, dropping into the barstool next to mine. "What the fuck happened to you? Did someone die?"

In a manner of speaking.

"Nope." My lips popped on the "P." "I'm just… drinkin'."

Grayson frowned at the bartender passing by and held two fingers up to him. "Water," he requested and then shook his head at me. "So you just thought you'd come here and get wasted all day?" he asked, eyeing me strangely. "You never even called Ava, Graham. She needs to talk to you."

The idea of any woman at all tightened my guts. I rode out the wave of nausea I'd just about gotten used to—it ran straight over me every time I so much as thought Juliet's name.

"Can't today," I told him, holding up my latest glass of scotch. "Drinkin' and whatnot."

Grayson pushed a glass of water toward me and rubbed at the back of his neck. "Stop saying 'drinking' like that. And where are your *clothes*? You're freaking me out. What happened?"

I smirked down at my casual outfit, but felt no trace of humor. "I have on clothes. Sheesh." Another slug of scotch burned a path down my throat. "So how was your week in Ella? I mean—*Aruba*. Fuck. I keep getting those two mixed up."

Pissed, Grayson snatched my drink away. "How many of these have you *had*, Graham? You're sitting here in the dark. You're not answering your phone. People are worried about you. Have you been here all day?"

I flinched. So far, the whiskey had done an admirable job of blocking out the first few hours after Juliet left. That morning would go down as the lowest point in my existence. At the moment, I would do anything to blot out the details.

"A few hours, I think. Eight scotches? Is that a few hours? I dunno." I shrugged and took my glass back. "Listen, we can hang or whatever, but I'm gonna need to keep this. Deal?"

Grayson's green gaze turned flinty as he stared me down. After a long moment, he exhaled loudly through his nose and turned to the waiter. "Gin and tonic," he ordered.

To me, he spread his hands. "Happy?"

The idea of ever feeling happiness again struck me as laughably impossible. I snorted. "Ec-fucking-static."

Fed up, my best friend turned toward the bar and sighed again. He let me drink in peace until his own beverage arrived. Then he took a long draught. His eyes dropped to the ice cubes clinking in his cup.

"Christian called me," he said quietly.

My scalp tingled. *Fuck me—I forgot about Chris.*

Goddamn it. I was a horrible brother and a hotheaded, dumbass businessman. A lying, scheming, shithead friend. Not to mention a clueless sap of a lover.

A failure in all categories.

Grayson looked back at me. "From a rehabilitation clinic in Chelsea," he went on. "Told me you were supposed to come visit today… with your *girlfriend.* But you never showed up. He got worried because he called you but your phone didn't ring."

I couldn't answer. All of my deceits were stacked too closely. Like Dominoes, if I touched one, the rest of the lies would fall.

Grayson drank again, the motion agitated. "Graham, what the fuck is going on, man? You come to me two weeks ago and want to start your own firm out of nowhere. Then I get pictures of you decking your old man in public. Now your brother's in *rehab*? Calling me and telling me you have a girlfriend named Juliet. Which *happens* to be the name of a woman I employ. A woman you've worked with very recently. Did I miss anything?"

The emptiness echoing though my chest was terribly ironic. This reckoning had been on my mind for weeks. I dreaded it with every fiber of my being, before. Now that I sat facing it, I found I didn't feel a thing. Couldn't.

I remembered, a couple weeks ago, entertaining the notion that Juliet could make me invincible to any other pain, because *she* would be my only weakness. Seemed I'd fulfilled my own prophecy.

I let myself love her. Now, having lost her, nothing else could touch me.

Without a flicker of feeling, I blinked at him. "Sounds like you have it all figured out. What do you need me for? You should go home to Ella."

Grayson finished his first round and slammed his glass down. "Damn it, Graham. I'm giving you *every* benefit of *every* doubt right now. But I'm going to kick your ass if you don't start talking to me."

Even emotionless, I knew he had a point. *Might as well tell him all of it, anyway.* It wasn't like I cared what happened to me anymore.

But… Juliet.

All the feelings so conspicuously absent before flooded back in. My chest ached fiercely. I rubbed my hand over it, wishing I could reach in, pluck the throbbing organ out, and pitch it behind the bar.

Even if I wanted to hate her… or forget her… I couldn't do either.

So I had to protect her.

"I'll tell you everything," I offered. "But you have to promise me you won't hold any of this against her. Because it was me. Always me, chasing her. And I won't tell you anything unless you swear not to ever mention me to her."

His stony eyes glared at me. "Did you guys fuck in my office?"

"No."

"Did she give you any private information about my business?"

"No."

"Does anyone at the office know about you two?"

"No."

His jaw worked for a long moment. "Fine," he gritted out. "I agree to your terms. But I'm fucking pissed, Graham. Juliet is a good employee. A *great* one. And Ella's friend. What the hell did you do to her?"

God. The *pain*. Maybe it only felt life-altering because I couldn't feel anything else.

I looked down into my glass, waiting for my throat to open up before I spoke. "I fell in love with her."

"Juliet?"

I winced. The sting in my eyes felt desperately close to actual tears. *Christ.*

My voice rasped. "Do you have to keep saying her *name*?"

I didn't look up, though Grayson sat silent for a long time. "Sorry," he finally said, subdued. "Go on."

Not daring to so much as blink, I fixed my gaze on the dregs of my liquor and spilled my guts. I told him everything I could think of, starting from the moment I got slapped in his elevator to the worst sound I'd ever heard—the quiet *snick* of my front door as Juliet left me.

I included all of the sordid details about my father, my brother, my doomed business. I figured there wasn't anything left for me to lose, since I planned to go to the feds Monday morning. It was the only way to protect Christian's good name.

When I finished, Grayson didn't reply. He plucked my empty glass out of my hand and carefully replaced it with water. "Drink this, okay?"

I nodded at the clear liquid, still not able to look up at him, and took a swig. My stomach seethed, protesting. I realized I never ate anything. The last time I had solid food was at lunch with Christian the day before.

Whatever my face did finally pushed Grayson over the edge. His hand fell on my shoulder. "Come on," he said, tugging me to my feet. "I'm taking you home."

Chapter Twenty-Two

February 12, 2017

Juliet

"Do you think she's awake?"

A hissed whisper answered, "Well she *will* be, if you don't stop shouting."

"I'm not shouting," the first person replied, shouting. Then quieter, "Okay, okay. I see your point. But what do we do? Make her coffee?"

I recognized the reluctant way she admitted to being wrong—Tris. Which could only mean the other person was her roommate, Alice. And I was on their futon.

It felt like a futon, anyway. A hard one that smelled like the inside of an Anthropologie. The fluffy knit blanket draped over me had the same bright, exotic scent. I wanted to pull it over my head and hide from the world, but I couldn't bring myself to move. I didn't want them to know I was awake.

The jagged pieces of my heart pulsed and bled as memories came trickling back. A tide of shame and regret surfeited my stomach.

That tide nearly eroded my dignity the day before. I almost gave in to it so many times after I left. I wandered around Lower Manhattan for hours, never letting myself stop moving for fear I would end up turning around.

Eventually, on one of the dozens of occasions where I unlocked my phone and hovered my thumb over Graham's name—wanting to call him more than I wanted my own honor—I realized I'd wind up losing the battle with myself if I didn't find some distraction. So I texted the only other people I knew in the city… and spent Saturday pretending to have a "girls' night in" with them.

Blessedly, my phone died sometime in the night. I managed to text Marco and Abuelita before it did, though. So at least no one would come looking for me.

"Or tea," Alice suggested, her sweet voice steeped in quiet concern. "I have a lovely lemon tea that might cheer her up… maybe with some banana bread. Do we have bananas?"

Silence swelled. "Tris," Alice tutted, sounding small. "You forgot the groceries *again*?"

An embarrassed cough. "Well you *know* I can't remember these things, Ali."

"Oh yes," Alice muttered. "*Things* like food to eat and toilet paper and detergent to clean clothes. Who needs them? Until you run out of underwear and have to use Kleenex to wipe. Or, God forbid, get hungry. Then *I'm* the one who gets to deal with your moods."

Tris paused. "So you agree," she finally said, "It's best if you get grocery duty from now on?"

I pictured the flash of her winning grin. Alice sighed.

"Sure, sure. Along with cleaning duty and cooking duty and laundry duty." She blew out another breath. "Juliet seemed really sad, right?"

Talking about me. Well, I guess I deserved it. I all-but invited myself to their apartment then spent the whole afternoon and evening drinking their wine and watching their television in as much silence as I could get away with.

I should have gone back to Queens, but I couldn't face Abuelita yet. I hadn't been home in three nights, and I knew she'd be furious. But I didn't have any fight in me at the moment.

Only… cold.

"I bet it was that douche bag, Everett," Tris grumbled. "You remember what happened that night we all went for drinks…"

A charge of distress zipped up my spine. *Dios mío. What did they see?*

"Um… nothing?" Alice squeaked. "We all hung out the whole time and *nothing* happened. Why do you keep insisting something did?"

Tris scoffed. "C'mon. You saw him. He's a shameless man-whore. He spent the entire night flirting with you and me and never once even *glanced* at her. Jules is sexy as hell! Why would he ignore her unless there was already something going on between them and he was trying to throw us off?"

A pregnant pause swelled between them. "Well…" Alice mumbled.

"Well nothing!" Tris harrumphed. "And then he disappeared while Jules was in the bathroom? Without saying goodbye to us? I bet he said goodbye to *her*… And then, two weeks later, she had a three-hundred-dollar bouquet delivered to her at work…"

"You're ridiculous," Alice chided. "She's our friend. Don't go starting rumors."

"I would never!" Tris exploded, indignant. "I *love* Jules. She's the best thing to happen to Stryker & Sons since *me*. I'm just *saying*, I bet that smarmy bastard has something to do with all of this. What else was she doing in Lower Manhattan? Alone? With an overnight bag and nowhere to go?"

Ugh. I wanted to shudder. *Busted*.

"Maybe it's a different man," Alice whispered, thoughtful. "Though, it is weird Graham didn't try to flirt with her. She's so pretty. And he *is*… friendly."

"You mean *slutty*?"

"Tris!" Alice's quiet giggle bubbled. "He's your boss's best friend!"

"Still a slut," she replied. "Although, come to think of it, he also didn't *actually* try to take either of us home that night. Maybe he really liked her."

He loved me.

And I almost let him.

Graham

"Do you think he's awake?"

Ella's whispered voice pulled me from my dream. A very pleasant one, where Juliet and I were back on the floor of my closet, but with much softer carpet.

Cracking my eyes open sent a jolt of pain through my skull. *Right.* My weak mind rasped. *I'm not in my closet. I'm on Grayson's couch. Because I'm the most miserable, sorry son-of-a-bitch in Manhattan.*

As if on cue, my insides seized up, clutching and roiling. I squeezed my eyes shut again, willing myself not to puke all over the white leather sofa. One unfortunate vomit incident per weekend was my absolute limit.

"Probably not, if he knows what's good for him," Grayson mumbled back. "I thought he sobered up a bit after you made him dinner, but that last fifth of scotch really knocked him out. I haven't seen him that fucked up since his whole spring-break-jellyfish thing."

Usually, when my friend brought up his favorite embarrassing memory of me, he laughed. But his voice was quiet. Troubled.

"I've *never* seen him like this," Ella murmured. "He's wearing a *hoodie*, Gray."

My best friend sighed heavily. "He lost the woman he loves. I remember that feeling. He thinks he's in hell right now. I wish I could say it gets better, but it seems like he's still pretty firmly planted in denial. Once that clears… and the anger burns itself out… and he's just alone, without her… *that's* hell."

Fucking great. Something to look forward to.

"Gray…" Ella *tsk*ed. I heard her kiss him. "I'm so sorry. I know you keep telling me to stop apologizing but I still—"

More kissing sounds. *Jesus.* Maybe it was a mistake to come to the love-nest while I was distinctly love-sick.

"I believe what I said was: next time you apologize, I'm going to punish you," he growled softly.

Teetering on the verge of laughter, Ella wondered out loud, "Hmm…how?"

I nearly groaned. Their little foreplay skit was the *last* thing I needed to hear at the moment.

Unaware of my eavesdropping, Grayson planted another loud kiss on his fiancée before shooting back, "Your punishment will be another afternoon of shopping. With my *mother*—you can't say no to *her* when she asks you to try things on."

Ella giggle-groaned. "Okay, okay! I surrender. I hereby rescind my apology." More kissing. Then Ella gave a quiet hum. "I'm so worried about him, Gray. I know you can't tell me what happened but maybe there's something I could do… Should I call Juliet?"

Grayson made a noncommittal sound. "She left him, Ellie. It wasn't like you and me… She made a choice and broke up with him to his face. And she doesn't know we know about their relationship at all. Graham said she would be upset if anyone found out."

"But still," Ella replied. "Can we really just… do nothing? *Look* at him."

A long, ominous pause proved I looked as shitty as I felt. Finally, Grayson spoke again. "It's tricky, you know? She works for me. Can

I really offer her unsolicited advice on her personal life? Or meddle by bringing Graham around the office? Where's the line?"

I heard a heavy sigh. "You know I'm bad with the lines," Ella admitted, sounding resigned.

A smile warmed Grayson's voice. "That's why I love you, Ellie."

"I love you, too."

I love you, too. I never got to hear Juliet say those words. Even if I didn't chase her off with my issues, she probably never would have said it, anyway. Because she didn't love me. I'd realized, somewhere around my fifth scotch—all that time I spent falling deeper and harder… to her, I was just a paycheck and hard dick.

The bitterness of that thought struck me, burning down through my haze like a hot coal melting gauze.

Huh. As Grayson predicted, I'd moved from denial to anger.

The flicker of outrage flared under the heap of ash where my heart used to be. I grabbed it eagerly, happy to move on from misery to fury. Using it as motivation, I drug myself upright with a loud grunt. The unfamiliar room spun on its side, blurring as my stomach lurched.

Right, my feeble brain murmured. *I've never been here before. This is their new townhouse.*

Honestly, what the fuck? How many things could I screw up in one month? Waking up hungover and heartbroken on their couch was not exactly the housewarming I had in mind for my best friends.

"Christ," I muttered, dropping my face to my hands.

Grayson settled onto the sofa beside me. He passed me a mug of coffee. "Keep your eyes closed and drink this fast."

Too weak to argue, I snapped my eyes shut and gulped. The contents of the mug were lukewarm, but they burned down my throat. *Whiskey.* I nearly gagged.

"I told him not to put liquor in there," Ella mumbled, coming to sit on my other side. Her hand brushed over my arm, the gesturing comforting. "He insisted it was the only way to help your hangover."

I felt Grayson shrug. "Unless he wants an IV."

My insides protested violently for a long second as the coffee burned its path to my stomach. There, the warmth flared out and settled. Languid numbness smothered my nausea.

Relieved not to blow chunks all over their brand new living room, I tilted my head back and chanced cracking my eyes back open. Blinding white, the stark, high ceiling reflected morning down at me. Cringing, I complained, "Damn it, Stryker, why is your house so *bright*?"

"I like natural light," Ella chirped. "The windows are my favorite thing about this room."

My retinas burned. "Remind me to look around when I'm no longer blind."

"You're not missing much," Grayson claimed. "We've only been back for thirty-six hours. The movers did what they could, but going from four rooms to twenty-four rooms makes for a whole lot of empty. Doesn't help that the lady of the house refuses to shop for furniture..."

Holding my breath, I forced myself to sit up and look around. The Upper West Side townhome was a magnificent find. Pre-war but fully renovated, the space combined classic charm with modern amenities; Ella's warmth and Grayson's trademark minimalism.

Her whimsy was evident in the gold bubble-cluster chandelier, the textured white wallpaper, antique molding, and pale herringbone floor. Grayson's penchant for simplicity seemed to dictate the gold-and-white color palette, though I suspected it wouldn't remain pristine for long if he intended to let Ella pick the décor. The girl had shit taste in shoes but she shared my love for bright colors.

Although unfurnished, we appeared to be in a living room or sitting room of some sort. After looking around at the high, wide windows at the front and back of the space, I spied a balcony out back and realized we weren't even on ground level. Off to the right,

I thought I spied an elevator, disguised as a set of gilded doors with mercury glass in-lay.

"How many floors do you guys have?"

Ella groaned, "Please don't remind me," at the same moment Grayson clipped, "Seven."

Obviously, this was a sore subject.

"One of them is a basement," she hastened to add, obviously chagrinned. "And the top is just an outdoor living area."

Grayson smiled into his own coffee while he pointed out, "A basement with a five-car garage, a theater room, a gym, and a security office for Marco. Kitchen, dining, drawing room, and formal living on the first floor. Master bedroom, bathroom, dressing rooms, and sunroom on the third. This is the second floor—informal living, Ella's library, and the solarium." He rolled his shoulders again. "The other floors are just my office, guest rooms, and a terrace each."

Jesus. No wonder he dropped twenty mil on the place.

I looked around, noting the sheer size of the one room we sat in. *They must have a quarter of the block.* "Where the fuck *are* we anyway?"

"West 75th and Amsterdam," he said. "Ish. We have a good chunk of the block so it's hard to determine which cross street is actually closest… some would argue Columbus."

Ella's cheeks pinked while she fidgeted with her homemade sweater. "I once told Gray I liked the view of the San Remo," she murmured, as if to explain.

I couldn't fault her for that. The San Remo was a famous New York co-op facing Central Park. The building itself was beautiful; views from inside and out were incredible. I'd always secretly liked it, despite growing up on the East Side.

And then something horrible happened.

For a few seconds, I backslid into denial. My stupid, sluggish mind forgot. And I found myself picturing what it would be like if I took a cue from my best friend, sold my bachelor pad, and bought a real family place. *Jules would like the San Remo*, I thought stupidly. *She could have her own office. All purples, if she wants…*

Like a bucket of frigid water, reality suddenly rushed over me.

I swallowed hard, hoping neither Elle or Grayson noticed my expression. My friend was watching his fiancée, but, unfortunately, she had her eyes on me. The hand resting on my arm slid down to grip my hand. She laid her blonde head against my shoulder.

"Oh, Graham," she said softly. "I'm sorry. We shouldn't be talking about all of this right now."

I wanted to laugh it off, stuff it down. I mean, was I seriously so fucked that I couldn't even be happy for them? But every time I tried to reassure her, I found I couldn't speak.

Grayson coughed. "Right. Sorry."

Ella reached up to pat my cheek. It reminded me of Abuelita. Another blade of pain sliced through me, followed by a staggering wave of guilt.

I all but promised to take care of her granddaughter. And I failed. Just like the other men that failed them before me. I need to call her. That was the right thing to do. I'd also have to deal with the Valentine's gift I'd already purchased…

While that stone sank down into my center, Ella stood. And—I swear—I was so fucking depressed I couldn't even enjoy the way her sweater rode up in back when she stretched.

"I'm going to go start breakfast. Do we want waffles or pancakes?" she asked no one in particular, then answered herself. "You know what? I'll make both. And eggs."

She paused, looking around the big room as if disoriented before shaking her head at herself, stomping over to the elevator, and muttering, "Ridiculous to have to use a damn elevator to make my fiancé breakfast…"

Grayson stared straight ahead, doing his best to keep his lips straight. Once Ella disappeared behind the mercury glass doors,

I drank another burning mouthful of cool coffee and sarcastically quipped, "So that's going well, then?"

His good humor got the best of him for a beat, turning his mouth up at the corners. "She'll get used to it. Yesterday, she wouldn't even *use* the elevator. Spent the entire day walking up and down the stairs. By dinnertime her legs were shaking."

That sounded like Ella. She would never complain about Grayson's largesse. She'd just stage a peaceful protest and inadvertently martyr herself in the process.

"Well she got in it today," I pointed out. "Wonder what changed her mind."

That time, he couldn't get a hold of his grin. "Something must have gotten into her..."

I knew that look. Smug, but trying to be a gentleman. It was the same one I had on just two days before, when Christian asked why my back hurt.

"You bastard," I mumbled. "Seducing that sweet girl to the dark side. You should be ashamed."

"Mind your own business, shithead."

My mind whirled, wondering what my business even *was* anymore. "Hard to do when you don't have any," I commented. "No job, no family, no woman. And, soon, no money."

Grayson and I had been friends for a long time. We didn't need a lot of words. Instead of speaking, he sat back and settled in, making it clear he wasn't going anywhere.

I drank another slug of coffee, staring ahead at the window with him. It was a nice view. Trees, other beautiful townhomes across the street, the San Remo's towers beyond.

I stared out at the windy day, watching the few intrepid spring leaves dance. My mind wandered, again, to the woman I lost. "Hey, Grayson?"

"Yeah?"

"What does *pinchao* mean?"

He gave a deep sigh, not enjoying my misery one bit. "Pretty boy."

A hopeless laugh scraped up my throat. Because, damn it all, she was *funny*. And brilliant and sharp and beautiful and all of the things I would never have again.

Bittersweet hit my heart like an arrow. "What a fucking bitch."

I missed her already.

Juliet

I came home just as twilight settled over the Heights.

The smell of *ajiaco* met me on the stairs. Tears flooded my eyes, part shame and part gratitude. How did she know what happened? Unless something else was wrong…

I pushed into the tiny apartment and paused on the threshold. There was Abuelita, tiny and stooped, at her cramped countertop, cooking. It all felt so much smaller than ever before, in that moment. And so did I.

She didn't even glance up at me. I could tell from the tight set of her shoulders how angry she was. But she still ladled soup into two bowls and pointed her chin at our table. "You sit."

All the fight I spent hours storing up drained right out of me. I slumped into my usual chair. "I should have called. *Lo siento*, Abuelita," I apologized. I stared down into my supper, wondering again how she knew I would need it. "Why did you make *ajiaco*?"

Abuelita slowly lowered herself across from me. She picked up her spoon without looking up. "*El pinchao* call todays. He say *tu necessita*."

A scratchy lump lodged itself in my throat. My voice trembled. "What else did *el pinchao* say?"

"Same you say," she muttered, then pinned me with a searching look. "'*Lo siento, Abuelita*.'"

Chapter Twenty-Three

February 13, 2017

Graham

Back in college, *The Deadliest Catch* was one of the few shows Grayson and I could agree on.

I usually got sucked in, while he claimed it was one of the least annoying programs to study through. Once, though, I caught him grimacing at a shiver of sharks on screen, all swimming circles around each another.

I asked what his problem was—they weren't even biting anything. And he shook his head at his textbook before muttering, "Their eyes. They're so… dead. Black and cold. Freaks me out."

I never understood why until I looked in the mirror Monday morning and saw shark eyes staring back at me. Flat and empty. They matched my insides.

I had to take two showers to wash away the scotch oozing from my pores—one before my workout and another after. I did my usual Sunday shave a day late and picked a boring ass suit without a flicker of feeling.

Ordinarily, the plain Navy set pained me. I reserved it for staid events like wakes or meetings with politicians. And I typically paired it some sort of colorful vest, shirt, or tie.

Not today. White shirt, no vest, a blue tweed tie.

Hell. I looked like my dad. Ironic, considering my destination.

It wasn't lost on me that I hadn't heard from him since Friday. He sent a few indignant texts asking me what the hell was wrong before cutting all contact completely. My concierge informed me that he tried to come by Saturday afternoon, while I was out. Per my instructions the day before, they sent him away.

I was fairly certain he knew that I knew. If he truly didn't understand my knock-out punch, I figured, he'd probably still be trying to get in touch with me.

In any case, I knew it'd probably become clear to him that I had no intention of speaking to him again when I didn't show up for work that morning.

Instead of calling a car on the Everett Alexander account, I hailed a taxi. "Federal Plaza," I told the driver. "And don't take Centre. It's a cluster-fuck at this hour."

The cabbie grunted and charted our course. Out the dirty window, I watched the Lower East Side smudge into downtown. My fingertips rapped against the briefcase full of evidence at my side.

After twenty excruciating minutes, I found myself in the charmless office of the Federal Bureau of Investigation. Specifically, the Department of Justice. The nearest agent caught sight of me and stopped in his tracks, his expression furrowing. "You lost?"

I searched inside myself one final time, looking for a shred of doubt or dread or *anything.* But resounding emptiness roared back at me. Even with everything on the line, I felt like I had nothing left to lose.

"No," I determined. "My name is Graham Everett. My father owns one of the wealthiest investment firms in Manhattan. And I'm here to turn him in for fraud."

I wound up in a small grey office without windows.

While I waited for whoever would interview me, I laid out all of my documents. When the assigned agent finally swept into the room, she found me sitting at the plastic table with my arms crossed, staring up at the ceiling.

"Mr. Everett?"

I noticed her hair first—a full head of long black braids, pulled into a textured bun. Her eyes were dark but her skin was darker; her black pantsuit even darker still. Though I could tell she had a good fifteen or twenty years on me, the woman had a sharp, striking way about her. I got the distinct notion she could kick my ass if necessary.

My spine straightened automatically. "Yes."

Her calculating gaze roamed over my face. "No attorney?"

A gasp of pain—there then gone—sailed through me. "No."

She jaunted to the other seat at the table and fell into it. "That's either extremely stupid," she told me. "Or very, very smart."

I wished, vaguely, that I had any of my usual wit or charm. I'd typically smile at a statement like that, make some sort of wry joke. Instead, I only nodded. "Yes."

Her eyes narrowed. "You're young. This all some sort of vendetta against your old man? A way to stick it to your daddy?"

"No," I said again. "This is me losing everything because it's the right thing to do."

Her lips pursed to the side, considering. Never breaking our staring stalemate, she reached out and slid one of the piles over to her side of the table. Her eyes finally left mine to skim over the pages.

After ten minutes of tense silence, she set the stack back down and met my gaze. "This broker number listed here… is it yours?"

I knew I had to tread carefully, for Christian's sake. Whatever else happened, I needed to be sure he was exonerated. Instead of answering, I asked, "Why would you assume that?"

She shrugged, her face straight. "As you said, you're risking a lot by coming here. Your company could have gone on defrauding people forever and we may never have caught you. But now you'll have to give up everything. I can't see why a person would do that unless they discovered that they'd been implicated and worried that they might have to take the fall, should anyone else blow the whistle before they did."

She spread her hands in a questioning gesture. "Or," she posited, "Maybe it's really your father's number. And you're the one who committed the fraud. And now that you've squirreled away all of the money you need in off-shore accounts, you're going to turn your dear old dad in to be indicted for a crime you committed."

Sharp, as I suspected.

"No," I replied. "It's not my number. Nor is it my father's. Or any other person our company has ever employed in an official capacity. I can give you time to go look them both up and corroborate that in your system, if you'd like. I also have copies of our employment records here, if you'd prefer to see those instead."

Without so much as blinking, she pulled the stack I indicated over. Another heavy silence descended as she perused. Finally, she sighed. "Say I believe you—and you really have done nothing illegal and you're not turning your own father in for personal reasons. Why are you here?"

Flashes streaked through my mind, filling it with memories. Juliet's fierce, earnest eyes. My little brother, dying in a gutter. Grayson meeting my gaze, telling me he knew I could make it on my own. All the reasons I cared, back when I still had the capacity to feel.

"Two weeks ago," I said, "when I discovered all of this, I wasn't sure I would be here. I had been planning to start my own company, anyway. With new clients, a different name. Not because I hated my father but because I wanted independence. So when I got my hands on the wrong set of books and saw what he'd been doing, my instinct was to leave it alone. As you said, I wasn't personally implicated… so why not cut and run while I could?"

She gave a single, hearty nod, as if I hadn't just admitted to plotting fraud evasion. "Right."

"But, then, I recognized the number."

Her black brows arched. "Who is it?"

"My little brother." For the first time, my eyes fell to the table. "And he's just a kid. He took the broker licensing exam the summer after he graduated high school because he helped me study for mine. No one knew he passed except for him, me… and our dad. But they aren't… close. So I guess my father took the assigned broker number and used it to commit millions in fraud, probably planning to turn the whole thing around on my brother if he ever got caught."

I folded my hands on the tabletop. "I'm here to make sure that never happens."

The woman took my measure one final time. Finally, she shuffled the papers in front of her and began to stack everything together. "Frankly, Mr. Everett, you seem too smart to be this stupid."

I swallowed a scoff. "Excuse me?"

She raised a brow at me. "The case you're handing me is a slam-dunk for this department. Your father is a big name. If you didn't hand me these papers today, and you came back with a lawyer, you would have an opportunity to make a few demands. Like protection for your brother. Or yourself. Or maybe even this new company you claim you started before you knew about the fraud.

"But," she continued. "If I were to put this conversation on the record and take these documents… or use your statement to obtain a warrant to tear Everett Alexander apart, there's a distinct possibility you or your brother could be left holding the bag. And any business you started for yourself would be seized, as well. I don't think that's what you want."

I thought of Grayson's investments, all the money I'd made so far. Fifteen-percent of seven-percent of five million. *$52,500*, my mind automatically informed me. Not bad for two weeks. If I did that sort of business every two weeks for a year… *one-point-three million*. For one client. If I had five… or ten…

"No," I said carefully. "That wouldn't be ideal."

The woman stood. I finally caught a glimpse at her FBI ID, clipped to her belt. *Shondra Adams.*

"So, we agree, then," Shondra said. "Someone as smart as you would come back... say, Wednesday? Maybe around ten A.M.? With a list of demands and a lawyer."

A lawyer. Ha. I had no idea who to call.

As if she read my thoughts, Shondra paused with her hand on the door handle. Not turning back, she sighed again. "I would also hope that that lawyer is *not* Rachel Black, the best defense attorney on Wall Street. Because she would be a *pain in my ass.*"

Shondra exited without another word, leaving me blinking at the closed door.

Rachel Black.

What the hell? I figured. *Couldn't turn out much worse than the last time I hired a lawyer.*

Juliet

Valentine's Day.

It came as a surprise to no one that I'd always hated the holiday the same way I loathed fairy tales and singing princesses. For the most part, I did my best to avoid it. Even before I broke up with the only boyfriend I ever had.

At least there was no threat of Dominic being overcome with lust on such an amorous day; I seemed to get frumpier by the hour, lately.

Monday morning, my stubborn sense of dignity took over and I actually tried. I put on some makeup, brushed my hair out, chose a blue dress. But, all day, this crazy thing happened where I found tears dripping down my face every few minutes. Sitting on the subway… passing the meeting pods on my way to lunch… riding in the elevator…

By midday, my makeup was ruined. My hair kept getting wet from brushing my chest and chin. The blue dress left me feeling vulnerable and chilly.

So, Tuesday, I didn't wear any eye makeup at all. I also gave up on styling my hair. Everything—my arms, my hands, the sinking weight on top of my lungs—felt so heavy that so much as scraping the locks into a ponytail left me winded.

In case there was any doubt, Abuelita told me I looked weak and spent the morning pushing food under my nose. By lunch, Tris also noticed. She pointed out my pale complexion and red eyes, asking if I felt sick.

I did.

I felt sick to my very core. Like a horrible flu, all the time. My brain buzzed. Constant nausea turned and churned in my middle. I couldn't seem to get warm.

That day, I tried layers. Tights under my grey dress, black boots over my tights, a matching onyx sweater *and* one of Abuelita's mourning shawls.

"Oh God," Tris blurted, her gaze jumping from my bare eyes to the black wrap. "Did someone *die*?"

If I didn't feel like I was about to retch on her Louboutins, I may have laughed. "Do I look that bad?" I asked, smiling as best I could. "I didn't sleep much last night."

In fact, I'd discovered I no longer slept at all.

Night time was the worst time. During the day, I could distract myself with work and chores and errands and more work. But after giving in and climbing into bed, all I could do was stare up at the shadows and feel all of the pain I spent the day denying.

After passing Saturday and Sunday night in agony, I decided Monday night to steer into the skid and simply dozed while watching documentaries on my laptop. Apparently, I didn't look any better for it.

Tris furiously tapped at her cell phone, frowning without looking up. "Work stuff?"

"Yeah," I lied. "How about you? Any big plans today?"

She flashed her winning grin. "Karaoke. I go every year on Valentine's Day. People get soooo much drunker than usual. It's *gold.* Do you want to come? I'm inviting some other friends from other offices, too!"

I considered it for a minute. "I should probably go home," I decided. "My Abuelita is alone, so…"

Tris gave an exaggerated sigh. "I get it. Us single ladies have to stick together, today of all days. Next time?"

A brief image of Tris belting out karaoke almost made me chuckle for the first time in days. "Count me in for next time for sure."

Observing the men in the legal department also proved mildly entertaining. Nothing could completely distract me from the crater in my center; but watching grown men either sulk in their cubicles or scurry around placing last-minute orders and begging for restaurant reservations helped a bit.

See? I told myself, *You did the right thing. You could be one of these pitiful girls simpering over a sixteen-dollar box of chocolates right now.*

Though, a small voice in my head argued back, *Graham would never have gotten me a box of chocolates. He would have gotten something flashy and inappropriately expensive. Maybe custom lingerie… or an exotic floral arrangement, or a bottle of wine so expensive I'd feel sick about drinking it…*

All stupid, vain gifts. Things that would make him feel masculine and smug. *Not really a gift for me at all, then,* I decided. *He would have made it about* him.

After days of endless guilt, it felt good to trash talk him, even in my own mind. *El pinchao wouldn't know a selfless gift if it smacked him in his perfect ass….*

But then, it arrived.

Not a fuck-you note or a giant flashy arrangement he accidently forgot cancel. Not anything at all, really—just a FedEx envelope I had to sign for.

If not for the signature request, it may have gotten mixed in with my other mail. It looked just as innocuous as any other letter. A flat white sleeve, with my name typed on an equally blank label. I only ripped it open right away because I had to take it from the delivery guy directly.

Three slips of paper floated out, landing on my desk. The first two were nearly identical. I held them under my nose for an endless moment, reading and re-reading until their contents sank in.

Airline tickets.

To Colombia.

For me. And Abuelita.

With shaking fingers, I picked up the third slip. My lungs shriveled into dust at the sight of the familiar, slashing cursive.

Juliet, it read. *I purchased these for you Friday, intending to give them to you today. It would mean a lot to me if you would still accept them, as my parting gift. I hope you will consider using them to visit your mother, though they are fully refundable or exchangeable, if you prefer. No need to inform me of your choice. I'm sure you'll do whatever is best for you and your family, as you always have.*

Sincerely (for once), Graham Everett

I sat blinking at the note, my thoughts scattered. The strange thing happened again—my eyes filled and spilled over, just from the sight of a notecard. Tears dripped down onto the high neckline of my sweater-dress.

"Miss Rivera?"

A wall of mortification slammed into me as soon as I recognized the voice. I swiped at my cheeks and slid the notecard under my keyboard before slowly turning my chair around.

Mr. Stryker stood just beyond my desk, his hands in the pockets of his navy suit. The light pink color of his shirt—just like Graham's infamous blush ensemble—made my heart pinch all over again. The second he caught my gaze lingering on it, he smirked slightly.

"Not my color, right? I told Ella that, but she had this whole idea about festive clothes. She sewed heart-shaped patches all over one of her sweaters, so I think I got off easy."

With a head shake somewhere between exasperation and amusement, he paused for a moment. His bright green eyes flickered around my department, settling on Dominic's dark office. "Is Carter out today?"

I tried to swallow the lump in my throat. My voice still came out hushed. "Lunch, I think. He left around noon."

Grayson glanced down at his watch. His mouth tightened. "Well, seeing as it's two-thirty, I guess I'll email him and let him know I need to see him when he returns."

He looked back at me for just a beat too long. And that's when I saw it in his eyes. The one thing I dreaded more than anything else.

Pity.

Ayúdame Dios. He knows everything.

"I came to tell him that I need to meet with you," Mr. Stryker went on. "I didn't want any confusion about it on his end, but since he's not here… are you available now? We can meet in my office or the conference room..."

Because he's too decent to fire me in front of my colleagues.

My fists tensed at my sides as fear flooded my throat with bile, pushing against the knot I couldn't force down. Tears pricked my swollen eyelids, sending a fresh round of shame rolling over me.

"Yes, sir," I murmured, smoothing my charcoal skirt. "I'll just gather my things and be in your office momentarily."

Obvious discomfort pulled at his features. He nearly grimaced while he nodded. "Very good, Miss Rivera. Thank you."

Turning on his heel, he stalked out of our pod with his head slightly ducked. I sat motionless, my mind and body oddly detached from one another. Phones rang and keyboards clacked. The sounds echoed in my ears but did not hit my brain.

Without another thought, I swiveled to my desk. Neat piles of work, organized by due date and priority, sat beside my one personal item—the coffee maker. With numb fingers, I unplugged the machine and wrapped the cord around it. Then I took my purse, lunchbox, and tote bag out of my drawer, leaving one single item sitting in the bottom.

My little silver frame, with the picture of Mami in it. I originally brought it in to work so I could look at it if my resolve ever wavered. I wanted a reminder of all the things I spent so long fighting for.

Now, it's all slipping away.

I held the picture in both of my hands, peering down at it. My father took the photo on their honeymoon. In it, Mami stood in the lush jungle along the sand with one arm raised up over her head and her other hand holding a hibiscus flower under her nose. Behind the bloom, the camera just barely managed to catch her laughing lips.

Perhaps it was the perspective that came with having lost someone recently, but, for some reason, I saw the picture through a different lens than ever before. I used to see a happy woman headed for a cliff—one too caught up in her own romantic notions to realize the man holding the camera didn't care about her at all.

Now, I saw, that wasn't true at all. Couldn't be.

Because it was the sort of candid photo a man in love took. The kind that almost said more about his feelings for her than her grin could ever say about her feelings for him. He clearly looked up at some point and found himself so overcome by her beauty that he had to capture it for posterity.

Because he loved her.

Until he threw it away.

The image swam while my eyes refilled. Blinking the wetness back, I pressed the frame into my chest for one moment before slipping it into my purse.

Leaving my personal effects there on the desk, I decided to go get fired and then come back for them. Better to do it that way, lest everyone on the entire executive floor witness me schlepping my stuff around.

As I approached Mr. Stryker's office, I wished I'd also had the forethought to choose the conference room over his personal space. Now, I had to face Beth.

Her lined features were every bit as solicitous as I feared. "Miss Rivera," she said, standing to greet me. She glanced at my empty hands. "Did you forget your tablet?"

I didn't have the heart to tell her I wouldn't be needing it. "Oh, yes. It seems I did."

She frowned softly. "Here," she said, offering hers. "It has all the same access as yours. Just use the Notes app to keep track of whatever Mr. Stryker requires and then forward the note to yourself."

I pictured a note that read "Get out" and nearly smirked at the hopelessness of it all.

"Yes, ma'am," I replied instead. After taking the pad, I paused, figuring it may be the last time I would ever speak to her. Though my eyes still burned, I forced myself to meet her grey gaze. "Thank you, Beth. For everything. Truly."

Suspicion seemed to pinch her brow. "You're welcome, Juliet."

I strode past her before I started crying again. With one final deep breath, I pushed into Mr. Stryker's office.

Off to the right side of the room, just beyond the place where the back wall of glass and its panoramic view curved halfway into the space, I noted a new addition. An antique wood drafting table, completely out of place among all of the modern furnishings and monochromatic colors.

Further off to the side, where the window ended, I also noticed a new arrangement of framed sketches. Nine of them, each in a black frame, matted with bright colors.

Graham would like those, I thought, wincing as a fresh torrent of pain whipped through me. *He's always so colorful…*

"Ella," Grayson's voice explained, interrupting my reverie.

I snapped to, realizing I'd frozen just inside the door. "The table? Or the pictures?"

Mr. Stryker smiled warmly at the arrangement adorning his wall. "Both. She and Beth were in cahoots. They snuck it all in here last night while I was at a function. As a surprise, for Valentine's Day."

"That's so sweet," I murmured. "They look nice in here. Who drew them?"

A rueful air filled the space around his grin. "I did, actually." He rubbed his hand over the back of his neck. "Years ago. I thought I threw them away but Ella saved them for me. And she found the drafting table in my storage unit when we moved, apparently. It used to be a favorite of mine, in college. She had it restored for me."

A thoughtful, selfless gesture. Just like Graham buying those tickets. My heart pulsed painfully.

"She's a keeper," I mumbled weakly, not daring to attempt more than a few words. God forbid my voice should wobble.

"Yes," he agreed heartily. He waved at one of the leather Eames chairs facing his desk. "Ready to get going?"

Dread smothered the sorrow trembling in my stomach. "Yes, sir." I sat down and made a show of opening the Notes app, though I knew I wouldn't need it. I stared down at the screen, waiting.

Mr. Stryker sounded much quieter than before. "Juliet?"

But I couldn't look up. My eyes had flooded once again. I knew he would see. And then I'd be labeled an unprofessional, overly-emotional *girl,* along with whatever other terms he'd use anytime a prospective employer called for a reference.

He was too kind to call me "easy." I wondered… would he say "promiscuous?" "Inappropriate?" Or perhaps he'd show some mercy and use a bland, non-descript term like "unfocused."

"Yes, sir?"

His long pause told me saw the tears even though I didn't lift my face. "We can do this tomorrow," he muttered. "I only meant to… I just thought you'd like something new to focus on is all. A new project."

Air whooshed into my lungs and stayed there, trapped. *New project?* Was I seriously so pitiful that he changed his mind about firing me today? Or had he really just planned to assign me a new project all along?

Either way, I snapped my head up, shocked. "You did?"

Grayson's solemn green eyes regarded me steadily, seeing the tears and not so much as blinking. "Yes. I need your guidance on some things pertaining to the pre-nuptial agreement, as well as one other project. You'll have to work with Miss Dunn on that one. I'm looking into a property in the Village."

It was the first time I'd ever felt stupid at work; but my brain couldn't seem to get around the fact that he didn't appear to be firing me at all…

"The Village?" I repeated.

"Yes." His gaze dropped to his desk. Chagrin filled his handsome features. "I can explain but I'm afraid I'll have to ask you not to share any of the details with Ella. As much as I hate it… I need to keep this from her until the right time." His eyes slid back to mine. "Understood?"

I agreed without compunction. After all, I was his attorney. It wasn't as though I could share any information with anyone at all—even his fiancée—without his permission.

Grayson nodded. "I'm purchasing a building in the Village. Not the company. Me. It won't be an investment, per se… though, I will be renovating it and renting out many of the units. I'd like to use the contractors and vendors Stryker & Sons usually employs at our properties, but you'll have to walk me through the legality of using those company contacts for a personal project."

I tapped notes while he spoke. "May I ask why you'd like to keep it as a personal holding? From what I gathered when I met with Milton about the taxes on your other properties, the company gets significant breaks on rental units like this."

Mr. Stryker blew out a breath. "Because I can't in good conscience claim I'm buying this place for any sort of financial return. The truth is, Ella's little sister is applying to NYU. When she gets in, she'll need affordable housing. Ella had to live halfway to Brighten Beach just to afford a place when she went there and I don't want Darcy to deal with that mess. Plus, it's safer for her to be close by."

I'd "met" Darcy in Ella's wedding group chat. She seemed like a sweet, odd girl with an off-beat sense of humor and absolutely atrocious fashion sense. Neither sister ever mentioned NYU to me, though. One possible pitfall seemed obvious.

"What if she doesn't get in?"

Mr. Stryker visibly cringed. His voice went flat. "She'll get in."

Carajo. "Because you've already made a donation?" I guessed. "And didn't tell Ella?"

His grimace grew. "An annual donation, actually. I suppose she'll find out soon, considering they're going to call it the Stryker-Callahan Endowment. I have to remember to have Ava keep it out of the papers…"

I almost giggled at him. Most men plotted behind their fiancée's backs to hire strippers in Vegas or hide their financial assets in separate bank accounts. Grayson seemed more concerned with how much he could *give* to Ella without her knowledge.

"Alright," I agreed, working to keep my face straight. I leaned into my seat, thinking. "Well, what if the building in the Village *was* a Stryker & Sons project, but not one for *profit*?"

He stilled as he thought through my meaning. "I'm not sure I follow."

"How many units are there?"

"Twenty-four."

"Well," I went on, piecing the idea together as I spoke. "What if the company bought the building, renovated it, and then used the other twenty-three units as company housing? For interns or lower-level employees. Anyone whose income could use supplementation. Giving priority to those with student loans, maybe. Instead of generally increasing pay levels, we could go in on a case-by-case basis and subsidize their housing costs. Charge them very little—or no—rent. This way, they get affordable housing in the city; we get happy, loyal employees; and you get your building. Ella's sister could even work here as an intern for us—if only for a couple hours a week—to make herself eligible to live there rent-free."

Silence.

Mr. Stryker fell into his chair. His eyes widened. "Damn it, Juliet. That is *brilliant*."

I bent over my tablet, warming to the idea while I typed. "If we plan to give the housing away on the basis of need, I may be able to work with Milton on some tax refunds or write-offs," I muttered.

Another thought occurred to me. "Oh, what about doing a special security and technology plan for the whole building? I can draft a contract between us and the tenants-slash-employees, but, assuming they agree, that could be a great way to ensure none of our people are engaged in illegal activities. Like a morality clause, only less Victorian and more safety-oriented. An extra layer of protection for us. It will also attract candidates of a higher caliber, I would think. And more women, generally. Women work and live where they feel secure and valued."

After so many days in a miserable fog, it felt amazing to *work*. My fingers, flew, trying to keep up with my brain. "Is there a ground level or a basement? We could add a gym or in-house minute-clinic as another benefit for our people. Cuts down on reimbursement programs for us to manage, helps verify if people are *actually* sick when they call out… and it's a nice perk for them. Lower healthcare costs, no gym membership fees. Good for community-building, too. I'll make a note to research our potential liability in case of personal gym injuries..."

More silence.

When I finally glanced back over the desk, I found Grayson staring at me strangely. Almost… regretful. It didn't make any sense to me, but, a second later, he refocused.

His eyes blazed. "I love this idea. It's exactly the sort of thing I want to implement for talent retention. And it's just plain *good*. I have a few other buildings I've been on the fence about because I'm unsure about the potential profit margins on them. One in the Bronx, another in Hell's Kitchen. I'd like to do this with those as well. Get with Milton on the tax issues and then consult Miss Dunn for specific addresses. She has the list."

I smiled to myself. I felt relieved to still have a job; but even more relieved to have something productive to devote my thoughts to, other than endlessly mourning the loss of Graham Everett.

"Yes, sir."

"You're going to run this," he told me, his tone turning stern. "I will tell Dominic you're not to be disturbed. He has three other junior attorneys who seem to sit around with their hands in their pants all day while he runs back and forth to your desk for every minor thing. I intend to inform him that those days are behind him. I'd appreciate it if you'd let me know if he bothers you or gives you a hard time about this project."

Gracias a Dios. I agreed eagerly.

When we finished up our other work, I stood and started for the door. The sincere gratitude on his face stopped me in my tracks. "Thank you, Juliet."

I wasn't sure what he felt so grateful for—all of my work, or my honest respect for him. Either way, I nodded once. "Of course, sir."

"And Juliet?"

"Yes, sir."

His rueful grin made him impossibly good-looking, even in the pink shirt that he could not pull off. My heart gave a now-familiar pang of longing when I remembered Graham in his all-blush suit. I bit the side of my lower lip, trying to stave off a fresh round of grief and focus on my boss.

"Please stop calling me sir," Mr. Stryker said. "We're peers. Hell, *you're* advising *me*. And Ella wants to be your friend. Plus, every time someone calls me sir or Mr. Stryker, I think my father somehow snuck up behind me. So, it's Grayson, okay?"

For the first time in days, I didn't feel chilled to the bone. "Okay, Grayson."

Graham

I could not think of a single place I wanted to be *less* than I wanted to be in the fucking King Cole Bar on Valentine's Day.

I didn't choose the venue, though. And the woman who did—the bane of my existence—was about to walk in. I threw a wad of twenties onto the counter, halting the bartender in her tracks.

"I want a triple scotch on the rocks. The thirty year. And anytime you see my glass is less than half-full, I want a new one," I muttered, then thought better of it and pulled out another stack of bills. "Actually, just bring me two at a time."

The waitress scurried off, wide-eyed. I didn't give a fuck. I'd hated the place with a passion ever since I found out that Daniel—my former friend and Grayson's scum-sucking excuse for a cousin—had roofied countless girls there, right before my very eyes.

Now, every tray of drinks that sailed past made my stomach cramp.

Or maybe that was the fact that I hadn't eaten since I had breakfast at Grayson's. Or because I had to hire another attorney just hours before. Or the notion of sitting next to Ava Goddamn Morgan for Lord-knew-how-long. And then *paying* the poisonous bitch.

My first cocktail arrived and I slammed it. The bartender blinked, deer-in-headlights, then turned to make me another.

That's right, sweetheart. I've been drunk since Saturday. Can't slow down now or I'll probably die. So keep up.

"Well, well, well."

A burst of crimson fabric filled my peripheral vision. A flip of long, dark tresses. Then a flash of slender, porcelain thighs. The sort of thing that would have dried my mouth, just a month ago. Now, I only felt the same sick misery that clawed at me all day long.

In the barstool beside mine, Ava caught the bartender's attention. "Oh, lovely," she commented, her prim, cultured voice pricking my ears. "You've decided to do your job. How advantageous for the both of us."

Oh *God*. I was going to hit a woman. In a bar. In *that* bar.

Appalled, I snapped my head to the side to glare at her. Ava took no notice. Her milky green eyes pinned our poor waitress in place. Painted red lips tipped up in a smirk, filling her fine, aristocratic features with venom.

"Tell me, pet, how much do you make in a night?" she asked, then scoffed at her own question. "On second thought, it's of no consequence. I know your worth. I'll give you one-thousand dollars if you bring me a glass of mineral water and then leave us alone for the rest of the evening. My… *companion*, here, doesn't need another drop. In fact…"

Her manicured hand reached over and snatched my second scotch up. Before I could speak, she swallowed the entire thing and handed the glass back to the bartender. "Run along, now, pet."

My mouth gaped when the server immediately followed her instructions and rushed off. My hands fisted as I spun back to Ava. "What the *fuck* is wrong with you?" I bellowed.

Her mineral water appeared as if by magic. She took a slow sip before smiling at me. Dagger-sharp, and full of acid, her beatific grin chilled me to my core. Traipsing one slim finger around the rim of her glass, she regarded me intently, like a cat eying a mouse trapped under its paw.

"Oh I'd say you're the one with the problem, Graham. After all…" She reached behind her and extracted two photos from her Birkin bag. "I didn't cause a scene last week."

I glanced at the images of me decking my father in the middle of Butter. A second later, another photo fell on top of the first two. It looked entirely different. My scalp tingled.

"…or lose my lunch on Park Avenue."

Damn this horrible woman to hell. She had *pictures* of me puking in the gutter? How? *Why*?

She pushed back and crossed her long legs, regarding me with amusement. "You looked great in that emerald suit, by the way. However unpleasant our personal history may be, I must admit, you carry off certain ensembles in a way few others can." Her jade gaze flicked over my current outfit—another navy suit. "This one is a bit of a letdown, though. Perhaps you're trying to keep a low profile?"

She wanted us to play, but I couldn't. Not anymore. The idea of touching her disgusted me. The thought of any sort of intimacy with anyone tore at all the wounds I'd spent three days super-gluing together with scotch.

The truth was, sex would never just be sex for me ever again. Not after Jules.

Each night since she left, I laid in my bed, yearning so intensely that my body physically ached for hers. I fell asleep, hard, remembering all of the times I had her. How every time—no matter how rough or fast or spontaneous—I felt an indescribable reverence between us. Even after she ripped my heart out, I still treasured those precious moments of connection when our eyes met and she gave herself over to me.

I still loved her.

Fuck this.

I had no patience for Ava's little game. Without the possibility of sex, it held no charm for me. I didn't know what Grayson was thinking when he hired her, but I couldn't do it.

"Keep the pictures," I told her, moving to stand up. "I know Grayson already paid you not to release them. And I'm sure you don't want to disappoint him, seeing as he and Ella are the toast of the town and you're a vicious social-climbing narcissist."

I straightened my sleeves and tie, turning to go. But she gripped my forearm, her French nails digging in. "Sit back down, Graham."

"There's no point," I spat, yanking myself free. "I'm no longer interested in you in any capacity, so I don't need to sit here and take your shit. Go con someone else."

This time, she rearranged the cross of her legs, kicking her heel out to keep me boxed between our barstools. She tilted her head, sending a haze of mahogany hair over her shoulder. "Won't you stay and hear the plan, *mon amour*? It's a good one. Didn't Grayson tell you as much?"

My control snapped. I leaned into her beautiful face, snarling, "Hate-sex does *not* make me your lover. You were nothing but a diversion for me. And—now more than ever—I'm revolted by the fact that I ever wanted you."

All traces of coyness fled her features, leaving them cold. "I forgot what a gentleman you are," she sneered. "But never fear. I thought we may have one of our little spats, so I came prepared."

She whipped out another photo. My blood ran cold. It was the scene at Butter from another angle. This camera caught the whole scene… including Juliet sitting at our table, watching the whole thing.

Ava dropped one more picture onto her growing pile. An image that sucked the air right out of me—because it pierced the place where my heart used to be. *Jules and I.*

We were at Dirty French, our heads bent together over our small, candle-lit table. She spoke while I laughed. Anyone who looked at it would see how much I adored her. It was all over my stupid face.

"She surprised me," Ava sniffed. "I didn't realize you liked girls that chunky."

I had to grip the polished wooden bar with both hands to keep from wrapping them around her throat. The creamy column beckoned to me as she swallowed hard, reading my expression. "Oh my," she said lightly, "Have I offended you? I do apologize."

"Ava," I gritted, fearing for her safety and my sanity. "Let. Me. Go."

"See, here's what I think happened," she went on, ignoring me. "I think you and Thunder Thighs here were an item. Only, you've obviously shot that to hell, since you're here with me on Valentine's Day. And I'm willing to bet the reason has a lot to do with why you made a spectacle of yourself in front of half of polite society by smashing your daddy's face in. If memory serves, you work for him? Or *worked* for him?"

I bit the inside of my cheek hard enough to draw blood. When I opened my mouth to cut her off, she rushed on. "Grayson mentioned you were starting your own venture. And, then, my trusty private investigator told me that your little companion is none other than Juliet Rivera—a *lawyer*. So I put all of this information in my pretty head and rolled it around for a while. And do you know what I think?"

"Ava, I've never hit a woman in my life, but, by God—"

"I think," she continued, undeterred, "that you hired this slutty, chubby little lawyer to help you start your company. Only something went wrong, which would explain your fight with your father. And I bet Miss Rivera knows *everything*."

One last picture appeared in her hand. A snap of me, going into the Federal Plaza offices.

"I wonder what would happen if the feds found out just *how* much she knew and didn't report," Ava mused. "Can you be disbarred for colluding in a crime? I thought I read that somewhere…"

Forget hitting her. I would murder her. In cold blood. In that godforsaken bar. I met her venomous gaze, torn between spitting in her face and throwing her out of her chair to get past her.

But then I saw it, laced throughout her expression…

"You're jealous," I determined. "Because I fucked you fifteen times and never even wanted to look at you afterward. You thought I was like that with everyone. Now you've seen these pictures of me with Jules and you realize I just hate *you* in particular."

Her eyes hardened.

"You got that part right. I do hate you. But here's where you're wrong," I murmured, leaning my face closer to hers. "I treated every woman the way I treated you, more or less. Although, I admit, our hook-ups had a bit more… *venom* than others. Because of the whole hating-you thing."

With a flash of shame, I recalled just how depraved the whole thing had gotten. "I regret that," I admitted, picking a speck off of my sleeve. "You have my apologies. Whatever else you may be, you are still a lady. I probably shouldn't have left you in a closet with your dress destroyed." *Twice.* "Or left you with that hotel bill." *And stolen your wallet so you wouldn't be able to pay it…*

Ava drew back, considering me for a long moment. The malicious glee in her gaze dimmed. "Yes, well, perhaps I could have avoided my run-ins with your little brother… and your father. That was rather ill-mannered of me."

I still loathed her for going after my baby brother when he was barely out of high school, but the night she attempted to make me jealous by seducing Hugh simply disgusted me. "You really got the short end of that stick."

She lifted one shoulder in an elegant show of impudence. "They served my purposes at the time. Besides, you're not the only Everett with… *an inheritance*, if you catch my drift."

Blech. Another flash of loathing moved through me before I realized—there was a time when I would have done the same to her, if she had any sisters.

With a reluctant huff, I fell back into my barstool. "We've been at this a long time," I mused. "Fucking with each other. Spreading rumors. Publicly humiliating each other. The hate-sex." My hand fell on top of the photos. "Blackmail."

Ava's eyes narrowed. "You don't remember, do you?"

I looked over the bar longingly, wishing our bartender wasn't too afraid of my companion to come back with another scotch. "Remember what?"

She bleated a laugh. "What *started* all of this! In prep school."

"Prep school?" I couldn't remember her in prep school. Only later, the summer before I began Columbia. We ran into each other at a Hamptons house party and ended up fighting over who got the last available bedroom.

"I only recall you stealing a bed from me in Bridgehampton and then running into you some months later when our fraternity hosted your sorority." I shrugged. "You didn't *want* your own bed that time."

She rolled her eyes. "No, you oaf. Back when I was at Dalton and you went to Chapin, we were in the same Cotillion course for debutante season. I asked you to be my escort."

My mind drew a complete blank. "No, you didn't."

"Yes," she hissed. "I did."

"No," I insisted. "I only got asked by two girls. One was my date, Michelle or Mandy or something. Blonde chick. And then there was one other girl, but she was a *disaster*. Squat and flabby with pimples and frizzy hair and…"

Green eyes.

…

Oh dear God.

"That was *you*?" I exploded. In disbelief, my eyes moved from one of her lovely features to another, looking for any resemblance to the pitiful creature who asked me to the deb ball a decade ago. It simply did not compute. "*How?* What did you do, sell your soul to the devil or something?"

She laughed again, this time with a touch less bitterness. "No. Puberty was… a transitional period for me. But I grew up. That's all."

Still confounded, I leaned on the bar and stared, remembering. "So you're doing all of this because I turned you down for Cotillion?"

She held my gaze. "No. I'm doing all of this because of the ongoing war we've started since then. But, just out of curiosity, do you happen to remember what you *said* when you 'turned me down' back then?"

I didn't want to remember. I was a little shit as a teenager. A thousand times worse than the man I was before Juliet. Christ, just thinking about some of the things I used to Google withered my insides.

"If you're going to tell me, I think I need another drink first."

With a sigh, Ava signaled to the terrified bartender, who promptly brought her another mineral water and me another scotch. I took a slug, waiting.

Ava didn't waste any time. "You told me that my hair was the same color as dog-shit and then suggested I get plastic surgery. You told me I might 'look less like a fat little piglet who dunked its head in manure' if I got a nose job."

Ah fuck.

Defeated, appalled with myself, I heaved out a deep breath. "Shit."

"Yes, quite," she agreed. "Though, I did feel a bit better when my brother kicked your ass outside the Ninety-second Street Y the following day."

I remembered her twin, Lucien Morgan, kicking my ass. At the time, I didn't know why he sucker punched me outside the gym. Later, once I knew Ava, I just assumed psychotic tendencies were a family trait. Now it all made sense.

I'd been a shithead my whole life and it seemed the universe deemed it time for me to pay up. In guilt and gold.

"Okay, okay. I'm a dick. And an idiot. Because you are obviously gorgeous now and I didn't foresee that possibility. So how much do you want for the pictures? And the insult? Hell, I'll spring for the dresses I ruined, too. Wasn't one an Elie Saab? If so, I really am an asshole of the highest order."

Ava regarded me steadily, as if trying to un-riddle something she could only figure out by watching my face. When she finally reached her conclusion, a small smile stirred on her red lips.

"You're different."

Lucky for me, I'd consumed just enough liquor to enter my new favorite phase of intoxication—numbly bitter with a dark sense of humor. "Yes, well, I fell in love and had my heart shredded just last weekend, so."

Ava chuckled, delighted. "That. Is. *Marvelous.* Best Valentine's Day ever. Seriously, I'm in such a good mood, I may not even extort you for the rest of the photos."

I glowered at her. "Yeah, right. You're going to screw me."

She lifted her shoulder again, unbothered. "Of course I am. I just thought it might be fun to get your hopes up before dashing them. I see you're too smart to fall for that again, though."

Ava sipped her water and ran her intent gaze over my face one last time. "It will be five-grand for all the photos to stay buried. Ten, if you want me to continue to bury any that may pop up as the week goes on. You know how these things are now—everyone always with their phones in their hands, recording things. But you could take your chances. I'm sure Juliet won't *actually* be disbarred…"

If I didn't hate her so much, I might admire her technique. And the sheer *audacity* of her, in general.

"Fine," I said, catching myself almost smiling. "Ten." Raising my brows, I stared back at her. "Knowing you, I assume there's more you want?"

She extracted one last thing from her bag—a chart. Color-coded and meticulously labeled, with a business card clipped to the top left corner. "This is my PR strategy for G&C Capital. Assuming whatever is going on with your father is about to become public knowledge, and since you seem determined to turn him in; this is a plan to mitigate fall-out for you personally and professionally. As I'm sure you know by now, I'm *very* expensive."

With a flip of her hair, she canted her head and continued, "You can shop around for other plans, but they won't be as good as mine.

And no other PR pro in Manhattan has the connections I have. Plus, I thought you might get a kick out of working with a woman your father slept with to bring him down." Mischief gleamed in her eyes. "Just a thought."

Goddamn it.

I had to hire her. And she knew it.

Even worse, I didn't entirely dread working with her.

Ava stood suddenly, fishing her wallet out of her bag and extracting ten hundred-dollar bills to leave for the bartender. She shook out her hair and adjusted her fitted red dress before turning to me, her face somewhere between expectant and bored.

"Shall we get our room? I'd like to be home in time to make a trans-Atlantic phone call."

I couldn't blame her for assuming we would sleep together. We'd done it a dozen or so times, all over the city, over a span of eight years. The push-pull dynamic between us always resulted in sexual tension that we banged out whenever and wherever we could.

Her offer hung in the air. For a moment, I thought I might grasp it. After all, eventually, I would have to be sober enough to function. And that meant finding other ways to deaden the pain of living without the one woman I truly wanted.

I tried to imagine touching Ava… taking her clothes off… talking dirty to her…. We typically didn't kiss, so I wouldn't have to worry about *that*… But, then it hit me.

I felt *nothing*. No heart pounding, no dry mouth, no thrill for the hunt. Not even the faintest twinge of arousal.

I didn't want to fight with or fuck anyone but my *bijou*.

The realization that I'd be a monk for the foreseeable future—possibly forever?—stung. But I didn't know how I'd ever be with anyone else.

Yet another depressing question for Stryker. "Hey, so, after Ella left you and before she came back, when you were still a broken man, how did you manage to start fucking other women again? Were there blindfolds involved? Viagra? A sheet with a hole in it?"

Depressed, I dropped my gaze to my shoes as I shook my head. "I can't. Sorry."

Ava froze, her eyes wide with disbelief. "You can't? *You*?"

The agony filtered back, filling my insides with more hurt than I ever knew one person could hold. "Yeah. I can't. Trust me, I want to. Or, *I want* to want to. But I just…"

Love Juliet.

Miraculously, Ava's icy, perfect features thawed… ever-so-slightly. "I see," she mumbled, still staring. "Well, in that case…"

She rearranged herself in her seat and flicked the bartender a look. As soon as the waitress appeared, she demanded, "Two steaks, medium rare, with fries and side salads."

Then to me, she sighed. "You look like you haven't eaten in a week. We'll have a working meal. Maybe then this evening won't be a *complete* waste of my time."

I flinched. The truth was, she reminded me of Jules, in some ways. Not enough to where I could pretend I was with the woman I loved, but just enough to hurt.

Still, I owed her a shot to pitch her ideas; after calling her pig, ruining two designer gowns… and then there was that time I hung her underwear out my fraternity house's third-story window for a week, along with a name tag…

Giving in, I slumped over the bar I hated. "Fine. I'll eat. But I'm having another scotch."

I arrived home, alone, just after nine.

My head swam with stresses and strategies, all of it buzzing in the background of my general grief. Still, I tried to focus while I slid my key-card into the elevator panel and rode up to my floor. As much as I hated to admit it, Ava Morgan made a lot of good points.

She proposed a bold PR plan—instead of burying the conflict with my father, she suggested creating a narrative around it. If we held on to the photos until after I struck my deal with the feds, then we could release them along with a carefully-crafted story.

"It's… *mythological*," Ava described. "Zeus versus Cronos. A dark knight spearing a corrupt king. A tale as old as time. This way, when we release the news of your father's—and Everett Alexander's—demise, instead of wondering if you're as crooked as Hugh, they'll all assume you had nothing to do with it and immediately smashed his face in as soon as you found out.

"Then, we push the pictures of you going into the FBI building, offering your full cooperation. After that, we'll leak the articles of incorporation for your new company to a choice financial paper. *The Journal*. Or *Time Magazine*. Along with an interview. 'Golden Boy Gives It All Up to Go His Own Way.' Or something. I'll basically write it. The bottom line is: you'll be a hero instead of an accomplice."

The idea had merit. And—while I still didn't know if I'd even be able to launch G&C… or if a few choice articles would be enough to reverse the damage my reputation would sustain by virtue of my very *name*—I liked it. In the end, I wound up paying her exorbitant client fee while she paid for our dinner.

Resounding silence greeted me as I paused on the threshold of my great room. I stood there, remembering. Juliet's feet in my lap. Making love to her against the wall. The wide-eyed surprise on her face whenever I did anything thoughtful like making her breakfast or adjusting her necklaces for her. Drinking wine on the floor and having debates. Tying her to my pot rack. Eating *ajiaco* together.

I wondered if Abuelita made her that soup after I called on Sunday. I hoped so. I also hoped the elder Ms. Rivera would eventually forgive me, even though I'd never see her again.

The sad, stark truth of that sank in as I stood there, all alone. I'd never sit in that warm little kitchen, at the worn wood table. I'd never watch the two of them bicker back and forth in Spanish. I'd never hear another story about Jules as a bright, brave little girl.

I'd never have that… family.

Or any family at all, soon.

With a thick throat and stinging eyes, I collapsed into my barstool and put my head in my hands. In all my misery, I'd managed not to cry after the morning she left. But I felt it all come up, now.

I didn't care anymore. *Why should I?* I could cry, alone, in my empty apartment, on Valentine's Day, like a little bitch, if I wanted to.

No one ever had to know.

Juliet

The phone rang four times before he picked up.

"Graham?"

For a long moment, he didn't make a sound. I heard quiet swell behind him and assumed he must be home alone, like me. A bolt of instant relief hit me straight in the chest.

"Are you there?" I asked.

He made an odd coughing sound. "Yes."

My chest cramped at the sound of his voice. Clogged and rough. Almost as if he were… crying? *Dios mío.*

Instantly, my own tears returned. They never seemed more than a breath away, these days. "Oh Graham," I whispered, not wanting him to hear. Knowing he didn't want me to hear him, either. "I'm going to hang up, okay? You don't have to talk now."

And he didn't. He stayed silent, though I swore I heard him snuffle.

"I only called to thank you for the tickets," I rushed on, hurrying to get my point out before my eyes spilled and water washed over my words. "I will use them. Mami will be so happy. What you did—"

My voice broke and I had to pause. *Damn it.*

"This gift," I tried again, "means everything to me. I just wanted you to know that I'm really grateful." For so many things. So much more than the tickets or the clothes or any of the other things his wealth afforded me.

I was grateful to have had a man touch me with such reverence. To have been held through the night. To have had someone believe in my abilities and appreciate my mind. To have been looked at like I was the whole world, right there in his hands.

Even if I couldn't love him back… I was grateful to have *been* loved. By him.

"I'm sorry I didn't get you anything. And… I'm sorry this is the way things have to be. I'm so sorry, Grah—" The apology cracked. Ironic, since I meant it more than I'd ever meant any other in my life.

He still didn't speak. I knew, in my soul, that he couldn't. I also knew listening to me weep would only upset him. He'd worry about me, instead of taking care of himself the way he needed to. I couldn't bear that guilt on top of all the shame already seething inside of me.

So, before I dissolved into hysterics, I hung up.

Chapter Twenty-Four

February 15, 2017

Graham

Wednesday, I woke up sober for the first time in four days.

Weak winter sunlight filtered in through my bedroom's picture window, casting the space in a pallid yellow. I blinked at the ceiling, breathing through my nose to fight the grief-stricken nausea pressing into my center. My eyes burned, irritated after my dark night of the soul.

Rolling onto my side, I cast my arm over into the empty place next to me. My fingers clutched the sheets.

She called me, I thought, trying for the hundredth time to understand the gesture.

Why did she do that?

I *knew* Jules. She was the clean-break type, to a fault. And, sure, maybe Valentine's Day got the best of her… I couldn't *picture* that, but it was *possible…*

Or maybe she really was just… grateful?

Part of me hated that she called. Because the second her name appeared on my phone, I felt the one thing more deadly than any anguish or regret or loneliness could ever be for a man in my position.

Hope.

If I thought Ava Morgan was a terrifying sociopath, I was in for a rude awakening. Because Rachel Black turned out to be the scariest person I ever met.

Holy. Shit.

A bulldog of a woman, she stood a full two heads shorter than me. With a thick, muscled frame, short-cropped brown hair, and a positively *vicious* frown. When she barreled right at me in the lobby of the Federal Plaza, it was all I could do not to shrink back.

She came to halt about a foot away. Sharp intelligence shifted in her blue eyes.

"Graham Everett," she said. "They told me and I didn't believe them. You have my retainer?"

I extracted her check from the breast pocket of my tan jacket. It was the same one I wore the day I had dumplings with Juliet. Another of my most serious, least favorite outfits.

Today, I disliked it even more than usual due to the conspicuous lack-of the red handkerchief. Every time I looked down at the empty pocket, wind whistled through the void inside of me.

Rachel took her payment and scowled at me. "You're lucky you dressed like an upstanding gentleman, or I'd send you home."

She turned and started to trudge to the elevators. I jogged to catch her. "Don't you work for me?"

Spitting a laugh, she replied, "Yeah, sure, kid. Listen, before we get in this elevator and they start recording us, let me ask you: why didn't you fax over the documents I asked for?"

Because I don't know you or trust you. I hedged by reaching for one of Juliet's oft-used buzz words. "If I did that, they would become part of discovery, right?"

Rachel *hmmm*ed. "The pretty ones are usually stupid," she finally replied, facing the elevator doors as they slid open. "But there may be hope for you yet."

Thanks to my bijou.

Pride swelled in my chest. Even now, after letting her break me and then pining for her for four days, I had to swallow the silly urge to brag about her.

"Wait," I blurted, my brain catching up to my mouth. "Did you say *record—*"

"Shut up," Rachel bleated. Then cast a meaningful look at the elevator as it opened. Chastened, I followed her into the vestibule and hit the button. As soon as we stepped onto the proper floor, she snapped at the nearest agent.

"Shondra Adams. Now."

The young guy took one look at her and ran off to do her bidding. Rachel adjusted the wrist of her black pantsuit, rolling her eyes at his retreating back. "Like I said—pretty and stupid."

We were escorted back into the same office I sat in Monday. Once inside, Rachel helped herself to my briefcase, unpacking it and flipping through the papers rapidly. She began plucking certain pages out, stacking them directly on my lap.

"What are you—" She shot me a severe look. *Oh. Right. Recording.*

Once she finished her sorting, she swept the pages in my lap back into my bag and snapped it shut. She stacked the rest into their original piles, acting as if she'd never removed a single piece. Outside, I heard someone approach the door.

"You remember what else I said to you before we got in the elevator?" Rachel asked.

"Um…" I thought back. "Shut up?"

"Yes. Good."

I opened my mouth to protest, but Shondra appeared that same second, stepping into the room and casting me a sideways glance. "Mr. Everett." Her dark eyes flickered to Rachel. "I see you did *not* honor my request."

Again I tried to speak. Rachel held up a hand. "Shut. Up."

Shondra sent me a bleak smile as she sank into her seat. "When I told you she'd be a pain in my ass, I may have neglected to mention that she'll also be a pain in yours."

The next two hours were like sitting courtside at Wimbledon. They lobbed volleys back and forth—questions, answers, the occasional snide comment—while my head spun. Every few minutes, Shondra would ask me a direct query. I quickly learned that I was not to answer unless Rachel looked at me. And by "looked at me," I really mean, "pinned me with a glare that seemed to threaten my very life if I said too much."

For the most part, I stuck to "yes" or "no."

Finally, we wound back to the one topic I actually cared about. Shondra held up the articles of incorporation for G&C Capital, sighing.

"Mr. Everett, I appreciate that you came here in good faith. And I appreciate your willingness to cooperate in our impending investigation of your father's company. However, I must say, regardless of my person feelings on the matter, most others in my department are going to see the date on these articles and assume you created G&C Capital as your life raft."

Rachel's hand flicked up, halting me before I breathed a word. "My client and I aren't interested in your colleagues' assumptions. They have no bearing on the law or the legality of Mr. Everett's personal business holdings."

Shondra glowered at her. "They will be considered fruit of the poison tree, particularly if we're granted a warrant for Graham Everett's personal financials and find that any money obtained from his CFO position went into funding his start-up."

Fuck. Fuck. Fuck.

Rachel kept her hand up; I kept my mouth shut. "Why would you attempt to obtain a warrant for the personal financials of a whistleblower? My client is upstanding employee and citizen. That's why he's here."

Shondra rolled her eyes. "Don't bullshit me, Black. He's a playboy trust-fund baby in a four-thousand-dollar jacket who's trying to send his daddy to jail so he can give his baby brother a job."

"Are you criminalizing my client due to his personal life? That seems discriminatory," Rachel returned. "And counter-productive, considering his testimony and these documents are currently the only case you've got."

With a slight shrug, Shondra folded her hands in her lap. "I agree. I can't speak for my superiors, though."

A sharp laugh burst out of my attorney. "You *agree*?"

Shondra slid her eyes to me. "I happen to believe him. Don't you?"

"Immaterial," Rachel judged, giving nothing away. "Though, one would assume, since *you* believe him, that you'll have no issue agreeing to our terms. Otherwise, my client and I are taking our case and walking out of here."

With another exasperated scowl, Shondra picked up the list of demands and stood. "I'll see what I can do, Rachel. Mr. Everett."

Juliet

I still had no idea what Mr. Stryker said to Dominic, but it worked.

For the rest of the week, he more or less left me alone... apart from a handful of frigid glances and one out-right gawk. The latter came Friday, when I finally ran out of clothing and had to don a dress I previously wore around Graham.

I couldn't bring myself to touch any of the new outfits he had messengered to me, nor could I stomach putting on anything he'd ever taken off of me… But, still, every time I looked down at the teal tulip skirt, fresh pain pinched my heart.

Dominic, on the other hand… He stopped by my desk for the first time since my Valentine's Day meeting with my boss, his stony eyes trailing over the fall of the asymmetrical hem on my thighs.

"Miss Rivera," he said, brusque. "I haven't heard much from you this week. I assume your assignments are going well?"

They were. *Very* well. In fact, Tris and I had just finalized purchase agreements for the apartments in the Village.

"Yes, sir," I replied, discreetly re-crossing my legs and tugging my skirt down my lap. "I believe Mr. Stryker will be pleased."

His lip curled in an insincere smile. "Well, that's all that matters, I suppose." He slipped his leer from my legs to my chest. "Any plans this weekend?"

Aside from missing my ex-boyfriend and wallowing? The truth was, whatever else I might do, I'd be missing Graham while I did it. Although, hopefully, my weekend would provide a little distraction. Marco and I planned to shuttle our very-sullen Abuelita and his equally-displeased mother around to potential properties.

Secretly, I hoped we could persuade them to choose one on the spot, so I could start looking for my own place. Though, these days, the idea of independence held less appeal than the notion of distracting myself with house-hunting, furnishing, painting, and moving my stuff.

I'd take any project I could get, truly. Anything to occupy my mind, even if it only worked for a few precious moments.

I actually intended to raise the issue with Dominic when I had a chance. I knew I might need to take a few personal days for Abuelita's move or my own. I also needed to rearrange my schedule to meet with a couple prospective landlords during their business hours.

I hoped he'd be more lenient if he didn't feel blindsided. So I shared, "My weekend will be filled with apartment showings and packing; I'm in the process of moving."

His sneer widened. “Finally moving into the city, eh?”

I demurred, not wanting to give him any specific location. “Hopefully! I have viewings all over, though.”

He finally looked me in the eye. “It will be good to have you nearby,” he said evenly, nodding once. “I’ll see you Monday, then?”

For a second, I blinked, thrown. Why was he suddenly acting so… normal? Did he finally realize he couldn’t bully me into submission? Did it have something to do with my upward mobility? Maybe he only respected women who weren’t broke? That didn’t even make sense, but I figured it might be some twisted superiority complex…?

“Yes, sir,” I agreed again.

He rapped on my desk and then headed toward the exit. “Alright, well, it’s quarter-till-five. I’ve told the others they can head out a little early today. Feel free to do the same.” With that, he took his leave. I stared after him, not quite believing the pleasant turn of our conversation.

Huh…

Before I could ponder it further, Beth appeared in the archway Dominic had just vacated. “Juliet, dear?”

It was unusual for her to come get me so late in the day; Mr. Stryker usually tried to get out of the office on time to make it home to Ella, particularly on Fridays. I felt my brows knit. “Yes?”

“There’s someone waiting for you down at reception,” she reported. “They’ve been there for over an hour, apparently, but asked Raul not to ring me until the end of the day. They said they would wait for you finish with work and didn’t want to disturb anyone.”

My heart clenched. *Could it be…?*

I knew my father wouldn’t have waited or showed any sort of courtesy, so it wouldn’t be him. But, while Graham always respected my job, I couldn’t exactly picture him twiddling his thumbs in the lobby all afternoon, either. More likely, he’d come up under some false pretense… right?

Either way, I thanked Beth, rushed to pack up, and spent the entire ride down to the lobby holding my breath. The doors slid open and I stepped onto the onyx expanse bisecting the floor. Due to the hour—not yet time for most people to leave, but too late for anyone to arrive—the enormous space felt oddly empty. I saw my visitor immediately, standing all the way off to the side.

Lucia.

I recognized the hunched, dejected set of her shoulders. She swayed from one foot to the other with her arms wrapped over her huge belly. When I got close enough, I heard her humming.

To the baby, I realized. A bittersweet blend of sympathy and chagrin whirled through me.

"Lucia?"

Her head snapped up, revealing puffy brown eyes and sallow skin. Her limp brown hair and squeaky voice reminded me a mouse. "Juliet. I'm sorry to come here again… I tried to get your grandmother's address from Julio but he would not tell me. I hope I didn't interrupt something important… I asked the guard not to call until you were finished for the day…"

She shifted again, then winced, her hand going to her lower back.

"You must be uncomfortable on your feet," I noted, leading her to one of the benches rimming the oval lobby. "Let's sit down."

She huffed, dropping down beside me. "I'm sorry," she said again. "I am supposed to have the baby any day now. It's getting harder for me to move around."

I nodded. "It's fine. Thank you for waiting until I finished for the day. Why didn't Julio give you Abuelita's address, though?"

Her dull eyes watered. "I think he knew I was planning to come to you for help. He's angry that you would give me money but not him. I think he planned to ask you for more than we really needed, so he could keep the extra."

I suspected as much. Fifty-thousand-dollars seemed excessive. "How much do you think you need? Just for yourself and the baby?"

Lucia looked down at her belly. "I have insurance. My mother's. I know Julio told you we needed money for medicine, but that isn't true. He just wanted you to feel guilty."

"I do," I told her, hating the truth as I said it. "I know I shouldn't, but..." Dismayed, I shook my head. "He's very good at manipulating people, Lucia. I hope you realize that."

Tears sprinkled over her swollen center. "I see it, now. I feel stupid for not seeing it sooner." She hugged her stomach again. "The truth is, though, I love this baby boy. I want to do everything I can for him. I have a job lined up, once I can work again. The doctors say six weeks at the most. But if I leave Julio before he is born, I won't have any money to support us until I get paid..."

Her plan sounded terrible. Where would she go if she left? Did she have a place? And six *weeks*? Six months sounded more appropriate, in terms of healing and having time to bond with her son.

With a deep sigh, I realized I was about to do something extremely stupid.

"I have twenty-thousand saved," I told her. "The fifty Julio was after didn't happen. And, I agree, it was too much. Do you have a place to go if you leave his apartment?"

Lucia bit her lip. "My mother's... she wants to help me, but I have four little sisters, all teenagers. They live in a two-bedroom apartment. There is no room for me... and a baby. But they would take me in if they had to."

It sounded chaotic. And possibly unsafe. I had another idea, but it was absolutely *loco*.

And stupid. So, so stupid. But I just kept picturing the photo of Mami up in my desk... and the way she cried over the phone.

Hermanito, she kept saying. *Little brother*.

"I'm getting my own place, soon," I sighed. "What if you and the baby stayed with me? I'm not home very much, because of work. You would have the place to yourself. I'd pay our rent and buy all of our groceries. The only thing is… Julio could never know where you live, because I don't want him to know where *I* live. Could you do that?"

Lucia's eyes were wide. "I don't… I'm not sure."

Well, at least she was honest.

"Think about it. Maybe over the weekend." I turned and fished a receipt out of my purse along with a pen. "Here's my phone number," I told her, jotting it down. "Please don't mention that you spoke with me. Call me when you decide where you want to live. Once you move out of his place, we can talk about the money for the baby."

Her chin trembled as she accepted the note. "Thank you, Juliet."

Graham

"So," Chris said, biting into his pizza. "Are you going to tell me why you're here?"

Over the week, our meals moved from bedside picnics to seated affairs at the small table in the corner of his room. Beside it, the dark window offered a view of Chelsea nightlife. Not that either of us could partake in it. According to his doctors, Christian wouldn't be going out anytime soon. And, once he did, bars and clubs would be low on the list.

I watched a taxi drop off a gaggle of girls just up the block and shoved my own slice into my mouth. "The fuck do you mean?" I grumbled. "I'm here every day."

It was true. Ever since blowing him off the previous weekend, I made a point to show every single day with some of his favorite food. Most days, I swore talking to him about everything was all that kept me sane.

He knew about Juliet leaving me, my meeting with Ava, and—finally—all about the fraud situation. That one was tricky; I actually wound up asking one of his therapists to be present when I told him. He took it all surprisingly well, though I suspected he may still have been in denial.

"Yeah," he said, chewing. "You're here every *day*. But it's night time. On a Friday. Shouldn't you be out? Moving on or something?"

Probably.

But my traitorous dick wanted nothing to do with even the *idea* of another woman. I'd discovered that unrequited love did strange things to my libido. The rest of me might be in agony, but my stupid cock didn't get the memo. He still thoroughly approved of anything to do with her… and had no reaction to anyone or anything else.

"Can't," I reported succinctly. "Not up for it."

He shrugged, unmoved. "So call Ava again, then. Have her do whatever she did Tuesday."

With a sigh, I shook my head. "We didn't fuck on Tuesday. Where did you get that idea? I told you we had dinner and talked about the PR strategy."

Christian frowned at me. "You had a meal with Ava Morgan and *didn't* have sex with her?"

Ugh. The idea of touching the woman still made me queasy. "I *told* you that's what happened. Why is that so hard to believe?"

He glowered at me. "Seriously?"

"Alright, alright." It was a stupid question, anyway.

My brother stared at me for a moment too long. "So Juliet hasn't called again?"

A bolt of pain stuck itself in my gullet. I had to swallow hard to get around it. "No. We haven't spoken. I don't expect we will anytime soon. I sent the clothes to her Wednesday and—"I caught myself just in time. I was about to say *"—and the ring I moronically purchased is locked in the offices of Everett Alexander I no longer have access to…"*

I tried not to think about how much money I spent on something Juliet would never even see. I also didn't enjoy the fact that my office keys no longer worked. I went downtown and tried them out the previous night, after everyone had left. Seemed our father caught the hint when my fist caught his jaw.

If I hadn't already suspected as much, I got confirmation early Friday morning when Rachel called me cackling. Apparently, our dad tried to retain her for a "sensitive matter."

"This is fun," Rachel crowed, "I usually have to *defend* idiots like him. This time I got to tell him to shove his case up his ass."

When I told Christian about it, he pushed his dinner away, disgusted. "Did she say anything else?" he asked, ever-serious. "I'm worried about your new company. I don't want you to lose your venture because you're trying to protect me, Graham."

I kicked my heels out and shrugged. *Too late.*

"It's done. The feds have the case. They've promised not to prosecute you or me for fraud or embezzlement in return for my testimony. That's all they can guarantee without doing a forensic deep-dive into all of our accounts."

A dark smirk twisted his mouth. "Well there isn't jack-shit in my account. I made damn sure of *that*…"

I still couldn't believe he blew through his entire savings on drugs. Sure, his trust was *significantly smaller* than mine… But, still. Unless I figured out a way to keep myself solvent, he wouldn't have any money to pay for school. Or his rehab.

I clapped a reassuring hand on his shoulder. "Exactly. They'll look at the accounts, see we haven't benefitted from what Dad did in any way, and let us go on our merry way."

I put on all the bravado I could muster; but, inside, I wasn't so certain. The money I earned for Stryker and myself grew every day. If the FBI took the stance that I only made that money after starting my own company as a safety-net to escape my father's fraud, it made me partially complicit. They would take every cent from G&C, effectively shutting us down before we even got started.

Not to mention, I had contracts on hold. McAllister's, as well as few others. I didn't want to sign them until I knew I'd be able to fulfill them. With the added scrutiny on our family created by a federal investigation, I couldn't afford to do anything even remotely shady. And, eventually, I'd have to come clean to my clients before they caught wind of Everett Alexander's demise in the news…

"Ava is on it," I went on, bolstering myself as much as him. "She's launched her plan of attack. She's standing by with the pictures. It's all going to be fine."

It had to be. I was all Christian had, now. I needed to step up for him.

The wheels of my mind spun. "And," I added, recalling his living situation, "As soon as you're ready, I'll get you out of here and you can come stay with me. We might have to get adult bunk-beds but at least it won't cost you anything. I can pay your tuition with the money I'm currently using on this place…"

My thought trailed off when I saw the look on his face. Christian was always a grim motherfucker, but I'd honestly never seen him look *so* solemn. Or doubtful.

"Graham," he finally said, blowing out a breath. "I need to stay here."

"Yeah," I agreed, not following. "Of course you need to be here right now, but soon, when you're better, we'll—"

He shook his head again. "I'm not going to *get better*, Graham."

His blue eyes met mine, icy seas of regret. His meaning sank in bit by bit.

"But," I started, wanting to believe, "you *will*, Chris. Before you know it. You'll see—"

For the first time in as long as I could remember, he interrupted. And he sounded… *angry*. "Do you remember last week when I asked you about your back hurting?"

Because of Jules. I repressed a wince. "Yeah…"

His features stretched into a bleak facsimile of a smile. "Do you know why I asked you that?"

"…because I was acting weird?"

"Because I wanted to know if you had a back problem, in order to figure out whether or not you might have pain killers at your place," he exploded. "My own *brother*, *who is paying for my rehab*, came to visit me and bring me lunch. I saw you were in *pain*; and the *first thing* to come into my brain was how to get my hands on whatever you might be taking so I could *steal it* from you."

He sat back, glaring, and demanded, "Do you get it now? Do you understand? It will never be safe for me to be around normal people. I'm practically deranged."

I had no idea what to say to him.

Because, well, he sort of had a point. His admission *did* make him sound like a heartless fiend hell-bent on his own destruction.

"You're sick, Chris, but that's why you're here," I argued. "To get better. I'm going to help you."

He folded his arms, his face turning to stone. "And what if you can't help me? What if you just gave up your inheritance, your company, our family name, Dad…? And—fuck, Graham—*Juliet*. You should have seen the way you looked when you talked about her and now she's gone. Because of *me*. Your whole *life* is fucked up because of me. What if you gave all of that up to pursue this case and preserve my good name, and I turn out to be a useless junkie for the rest of my life?"

I sat completely still, unsure what I could say or do. Tension gripped the air between us. The horrible silence expanded, swelling with all of the dismal possibilities that haunted us both.

How could I reassure him? Was reassurance even the right course? Would it be better for him to constantly fear relapse? Or should I try to get him to believe in himself? Some combination of encouragement and accountability seemed like the safest course, but how the fuck was I supposed to accomplish *that*?

His voice cracked in the quiet. "I—I think I need to be alone."

In the end, I only left because I honestly couldn't think of a single goddamn thing to say. I told him I'd be back the next day with breakfast or lunch and suggested we venture down to the exercise facilities together, but he barely met my gaze as I walked out of his room.

All the way across town, I fought the impulse to call Juliet with herculean effort. And I almost made it. Until we hit the Lower East Side and I realized the car had stopped right next to the alleyway where I almost ripped her dress off because she wouldn't buckle her damned coat.

I stared down the dark passage for a long second, remembering how she clung to me. How hot and wet she got… the way she gripped my cock when she slid her hand into my pants. And then, just moments later, how she sprang into action and helped me find my brother.

Before I could finish forming my decision, I found myself holding my phone to my ear, listening to it ring.

It's nine on a Friday, I jeered at myself. *There's no way in hell she'll pick up. She's probably out finding a new guy to spend "just one night" with…*

Unless she figured she didn't have to uphold her old rule now that I smashed it to bits. *Oh God.* I hadn't even thought of that. Would I be the reason some other jackass got to have her over and over and over and…

"Hello?"

I didn't realize I was holding my breath until I heard her voice. "Juliet."

"Yes," she replied. In the background, something heavy hit the floor. "It's me. Are you okay?"

Say yes. Say, "Sorry, wrong number." Make a joke or a smirk or something. Anything but—

"No," I admitted, because even though she ruined me, I still couldn't lie to her. "I just left Christian and…" *There's a chance I lost you for nothing.* "No, I'm not okay."

Alarm pierced her voice. "Is he alright? He's still in the treatment center in Chelsea, right? He didn't check himself out or get lost or anything?"

Somehow, her concern hurt worse than apathy. More proof she was exactly who I believed her to be—the person I adored.

"He's physically fine," I sighed, leaning my head into the glass. "Just depressed and hopeless. He doesn't think he can get better. I think he feels a lot of pressure, because I gave up so much to clear his name… now he thinks he has to prove he was worth it or something."

Juliet sounded outraged on my behalf. "You would never think that way! Did you tell him that's crazy?"

My fire-filled *bijou*. Always ready to fight. For me.

Ah God.

Was it possible to have a heart attack from longing? The pain in my chest seemed unbearable. Everything in me throbbed, begging me to throw what little pride I had left aside and crawl back to her, begging for any scrap she might deign to give me.

"I tried," I croaked before I lost the thread of the conversation and wound up pleading with her. "I told him he could still recover and have all the things he's always wanted, but he didn't seem to believe me. He thinks I don't understand how sick he is."

Her voice softened to the tone I loved most. "Do *you* think you understand it?"

I closed my eyes. "I thought I did, but tonight he told me something… fucked up. And I realized he likely has dozens of similar stories I'd find equally chilling. Or worse. So now I'm really just thinking that I don't know shit."

About anything, I wanted to add. *Like why I called* you, *for example.*

Juliet sighed. And—I swear to God—the innocuous sound travelled right to my disloyal dick, stirring it for the first time all day. "You're second-guessing your decisions," she murmured.

Yes. All of them. Especially letting you walk out of my apartment.

"It's complicated," I hedged.

My cab stopped. Wordlessly, I paid the man and got out just as Juliet graced me with a husky chuckle. "I can usually keep up, you know."

Her teasing voice gutted me. I froze mid-stride, unable to move another step. "Jules…"

I stood there, fighting to breathe, craning my neck back and staring up at my own building, dreading the quiet, sanitary solitude I'd find once I got home. Words just tore out of me; ripped from the place where the desperation welled.

"I miss you so goddamned much, *bijou*."

There wasn't anything I could do to take it back. So I lingered on the blustery street, looking upward, hating her and myself and everything that happened in the past week. Hating the lonely cold and the stupid hope hidden in my heart. But hating the silence on the other end of the line most of all.

After a moment, I couldn't take it anymore. I opened my mouth to do damage control… only to have the words die my throat when I heard her sniffle. Twice.

Shit. Was she *crying*? Because I missed her?

When she called during my Valentine's Day break-down, she had the decency not to make me talk through it. She respected my pride. I felt the same for hers.

"You don't have to talk now," I mumbled, repeating the words she said to me. "I only called to…" *What? Why did I call her?* I still didn't really even know. The only thing I felt completely sure of was that moronic splinter of optimism embedded in my soul.

Maybe one day.

But I turned out to be a coward. "Never mind."

Her breath stuttered. I had to press my palm into my chest to cover the pain. If I listened to one more second, I knew I'd fling myself back into the nearest cab and drive straight to Queens.

So I pulled the phone away from my face and whispered, "I'm sorry, baby," before hanging up.

Chapter Twenty-Five

February 18, 2017

Juliet

"Juuuuules," Marco groaned, dropping his forehead against the steering wheel of our borrowed Mercedes. "What are they doing *now*?"

In truth, I was as exasperated as him. But something about watching my calm, cool, collected big cousin pout at his mother amused me. And it felt so good to laugh a little bit, after crying myself to sleep the night before.

I'm sorry, baby.

Why was he sorry? For changing his mind about turning his father in? For calling me in the first place? Because I started crying? That seemed to be all I did, lately.

"Juliet?" Marco snapped me back to reality.

I glanced over at the two women, bent on the front walk. "I think they're measuring the walkway," I giggled.

"As in, the *sidewalk*?" He leaned over me, peering out the passenger window. "They are. *Carajo*. Jules, I swear, I can't do another one."

"This was *your* idea," I pointed out. "*I told you* they'd be impossible together."

We saw three apartments and two townhomes before noon. My aunt and grandmother bickered and tutted in Spanish—arguing, critiquing, sniping at one another—while I translated. For his part, Marco stood off to the side, arms crossed over his chest, and watched each exchange with the long-suffering mien of a true martyr.

Sitting back into the driver's seat, he scowled and scrubbed a hand over his face. "Who knew Abuelita *needed* an eastern-facing window."

I scoffed. "Who knew your mom *needed* a cabinet trash can."

Marco heaved out a deep breath. "I thought we had them when I showed them the back porch. Then Abuelita went off about the pantry and Mom started in on the carpet in the hallway…"

I had to agree—of all the places we saw, that one seemed the most promising. The two-story home had a lot going for it. Located in the southern, more residential portion of the Heights, it was still close to Tía Esme's job and Abuelita's church. It also had a decent-sized kitchen with a gas range and a deck out back that the ladies could use for entertaining. It all appeared to be going well… until Tía pointed out the train tracks three blocks down and Abuelita realized she'd have to take a new bus route to the meat market…

I felt Marco's eyes glance over my profile. His voice got gravelly. "How are you doing?"

Clearly, despite my best efforts at distraction, I looked as terrible as I felt. That morning, I only spent two minutes in front of the mirror—long enough to brush my teeth, throw my hair back, and confirm that, yes, the swollen circles under my eyes *could* in fact get darker.

I watched as Abuelita swatted Tía's hand. "I'm fine," I told Marco.

His steady stare didn't let up one bit. "That's a lie, but I think I'm too exhausted to call you out."

I turned and met his gaze, noting the half-moon shadows under his eyes for the first time. They almost matched mine. "I've been so wrapped up in all my *mierda*, I haven't even asked about you," I realized. "*Lo siento, primo. Que pasa?*"

Marco's stoic expression tightened. "Just work stuff. Grayson and Ella hired a PR person to manage their image in the media, but now they're in even *more* tabloids and there are whole Instagram and Twitter accounts dedicated posting and re-posting photos of them… People are getting *insane.*"

I saw some of the magazine features when I passed newspaper stands in the city. They heralded the Strykers' nuptials as the Wedding of the Century. Many publications called Grayson "American royalty" and compared Ella to figures like Grace Kelly and Kate Middleton. Others labeled her a gold-digger and speculated that Grayson may be using her as a way to escape his playboy-CEO reputation.

"I almost had to tackle some *puta loca* outside Nobu last night," Marco went on, shaking his head. "And last week there was a guy with a knife skulking around Ella's yoga class. When we brought him in, we found like fifty pictures of her saved on his phone.

"The press hasn't gotten wind of their new address yet, but I'm sure it's only a matter of time, now that Ella's ordering furniture and they have a spread in *Architectural Digest* next month; so I'm working on security plans for the place but it's *huge.* Not to mention I'm still looking for whoever broke into Stryker's penthouse.... Things aren't adding up, ever since I determined that I have a leak in my security team…"

He suddenly went completely still. Our eyes met.

"Leak?" I asked.

Marco blew air out of his nose and clenched his jaw. "Damn it. I didn't mean to mention that. Forget it, Jules."

"You have a *leak*?" I asked again, ignoring him. "Like someone telling the press where the Strykers live and their schedules and stuff?"

"I can't talk about it," he bit back. "You know that. I'm sorry I said anything. I'm not thinking clearly, today. I think I need more coffee."

"Or maybe some *sleep.*"

"Says *la prima* with purple bags under her eyes."

"Those are from crying, not working all night," I snapped before I could think better of it.

Regret hit me instantly when Marco's expression darkened. "Juliet—"

"No," I clipped. "If you won't talk about your thing, I'm not talking about mine." Besides, he already knew the whole story. Or, at least, the broad strokes. I knew Tía Esme relayed the basic gist after Abuelita told her.

Marco decided not to push me. His dark gaze drifted back over to the window behind me. He changed the subject. "So, when are you using the tickets for Colombia?"

Whenever my heart stops aching at the thought of them.

"Mami's birthday is in September," I mumbled. "The weather is nice then, too. Plus, waiting a bit will give us all time to move, and plenty of notice at work so Dominic doesn't bitch."

Before my cousin could comment, I heard voices approaching. Still sniping at each other, Tía and Abuelita made their way back to the Mercedes. Marco automatically hopped out to open their doors for them. Their argument never broke stride. Something about garden gnomes?

Once they both strapped themselves in, Marco huffed back into the driver's seat and pulled up the next listing on his phone, grousing as he did so. His mother kept complaining, too, using Spanglish to point out the house's mismatched shingles.

"*At-tat-tat*," Abuelita barked, silencing her daughter and grandson. "*Suficiente!*"

Enough.

Chastened silence engulfed the car for a long moment before our grandmother sat up, lifted her chin, and pronounced, "Éste."

My eyes widened. Marco turned to me.

"She says, 'this one,'" I reported, halting him. Then, to Abuelita, "*A ti te gusta este? Estas segura*?"

She gave one stern nod, holding her purse tightly in her lap. "*Sí, éste.*"

"Mami?" Marco asked, looking at his mother through the rearview mirror. "Is this one okay with you?"

I could tell Esmeralda would have preferred a different place. But she looked at her mother's profile for a long moment, then at the hopeful gleam in her son's eye. With a sigh, she nodded. "It is good, *mijo*. Thank you."

Before I could comprehend her gratitude, Marco had his phone in his hand. Calling Tris, I realized. "Hey, it's Amir," he said, brusque as ever. "Yeah. The one on 92nd. Full price. That's fine. Can you do it now? Great."

To the rest of us, he announced. "This one. Done."

By the time we got Tía back to her place, another argument—this time over the appropriate height for a curtain rod—broke out.

Dios, I thought, watching Marco walk his mother to her door. *Will this be me and Mami one day?*

Of course, that was a silly thought, since my mother couldn't even come *visit* me…

"Last stop," Marco announced a few minutes later, pulling alongside the curb outside the tailor shop. Just as Abuelita got out, Marco's phone buzzed. He frowned down at it, stopping me.

"Someone is requesting access to the executive floor through office security," he muttered, "but security has to go through me on weekends. The guy says he's in the legal department."

A quick chill ran through me. *Dominic? Why would he work on the weekend alone? Unless he has some other woman there…?*

"What's the guy's name?" I asked.

Marco's frown deepened. "Chad?"

"Oh." I must have looked as relieved as I felt, because Marco stopped scowling. "Just Chad? He's harmless. He knows I've worked late there, alone. Maybe he wants to get some extra stuff done. I wonder why he didn't just use the stairs and text me for the keypad code. He knows I have it."

I slipped my phone out of my jeans. Sure enough, a text from Chad asking for the key code, along with another, more panicked message about forgetting an assignment Dominic gave him and rushing in to finish it before he got caught.

"Damn it," I sighed, reading his pleas. "I should go down there and help him."

"I can drive you," Marco offered. "But let's hurry. I have to be at Stryker's in an hour and he's on the Upper West Side now."

I ran upstairs to grab work stuff and we took off. The drive wasn't as bad without weekday traffic, but I still felt grateful to be finished with the commute. The sun started to set as we pulled up in front of Stryker & Sons. I leapt out. Marco saluted me and took off, speeding toward the park.

I didn't recognize the guard on weekend duty at the front desk, but Marco must have told him to expect me, because he waved me into the elevator before picking up his phone to send a text—presumably confirming my safe arrival.

Up on the top floor, the city still seemed sunny. I paused in the center of the executive floor, admiring the stunning effect sunset had on the panoramic windows and walls of glass. Golden bursts slanted over the white marble floor, forming puddles of light I splashed through on my way to the legal department.

My footsteps echoed in the quiet. Foreboding pricked me. It had been dark the only other time I came to the office after hours. For some reason, the silence seemed eerier in the daylight.

"Chad?" I called, almost to our pod. "I swear if you made me haul my ass over here and you're already done, I'm going to—"

The rest of my threat dissipated as I rounded the opaque archway and caught sight of a male figure, standing at Chad's desk with his back to the door. Only, it wasn't Chad. This person was too tall, too broad, too dark-haired…

Ay Dios mío.

"Oh!" My hand flew up to cover my racing heart. I suddenly struggled to breathe, my throat sucking closed on every draw. "Dominic?"

"Miss Rivera." He turned, impaling me with his frigid grey gaze. "I had a feeling you'd be here."

I hovered near the entrance, debating the wisdom of taking another step. After all, I couldn't exactly turn and run. I'd clearly come to the office for a reason…

"Where is Chad?" I asked, attempting to glance around without being obvious. "He texted me and asked me to help him…"

"Ah, yes," Dominic replied, spinning around to face me. "He was supposed to finish a worker's comp issue for one of our building sites, but forgot to take the case file home with him. He texted you hoping you'd help him catch up on the project."

My boss's features pulled into a predatory grin. "He didn't realize I have a standing arrangement with the front desk. They alert me any time one of my people comes in over the weekend."

I started to take a step back. "Oh," I said again. "Well, as long as you're here, then I'm sure he doesn't need *my* help. I'll just head home…"

Every instinct told me to flee as quickly as possible. I hitched my bag up my shoulder, preparing to hurry back to the lift.

But Dominic's answering laugh cracked like a whip. "Don't be silly, Miss Rivera. I just fired Chad. Now you and I are going to have to play catch-up with his work."

My thoughts whirled, trying to keep up. Just a moment ago I thought I was meeting a co-worker to do him a favor. Now, he was… gone?

I fell back another step. "You *fired* Chad? He only forgot a file, Dominic."

"He forgot a file and then tried to cover up his mistake by sneaking in here without permission. Sort of like *you're* sneaking in here without permission." He raised his brows, his expression a taunt. "I'd hate to have to take disciplinary action against you, too."

I started to protest, but he cut me off. "I know you think you have Mr. Stryker wrapped around your finger," Dominic went on. "But I think you may have a hard time explaining why you were willing to come in and work on an urgent case for one of your peers, but not for your supervisor. Maybe he'll assume you and Chad had some sort of personal relationship. Which, as you know, would be against company policy."

The last thing I needed was another reason to dread impromptu meetings with Grayson. Besides, now that I was *there*, I couldn't think of a single believable excuse why I couldn't stay. My eyes flashed up overhead, where the department's security camera had a bird's eye view of all the junior attorneys' desks. Before I lost my nerve, I marched to my own space and started unpacking my bag.

"Give me whatever needs to be done," I muttered, not bothering to look at him. "I need to get out of here as soon as possible."

He dropped a copy of the lawsuit on my desk and stood across from me, his eyes trailing down my front. Fortunately, there wasn't much for him to see. A red V-neck sweater over dark jeans, with a pair of faux-fur-trimmed boots. And I knew for certain that my face wasn't at its best, either; with all the crying, lack-of sleep, and no makeup.

Perversely pleased by my plain appearance, I set to work reading the suit. Dominic plodded into his office, leaving the glass door hanging open behind him.

After about thirty minutes, I started to feel overly dramatic. There we were, working on a weekend… without incident. After all the weeks I'd done everything in my power to avoid being alone in the office in with him, it turned out to be just as innocuous as any other work day.

Chad's case notes were pitiful, so I supplemented them, using my tablet to send each page to our portal as I completed them. Next, I tackled the research and found it predictably lacking. Another half hour of pulling past cases and recent court rulings remedied that as well.

By eight, Dominic poked his head out of his office to tell me he was ordering pizza and ask if I wanted any dinner. I would have turned him down, but my stomach kept rumbling and I still had at least two more hours of work to do.

Again, my reluctance proved unnecessary. He took my order and disappeared back into his office, where he presumably placed the order and paid. Thirty minutes later, he didn't even bother me to go downstairs and get the food; he went himself, walking past me without even a grunt.

Did I honestly think that my boss—a married, big-shot Manhattan attorney—would lure me into our offices so he could sexually harass me? Carajo.

Clearly, my ego had gotten the best of me. Sure, he may check me out when I wore attractive clothing… and he obviously resented any success that didn't benefit him… but he wasn't a *monster*…

I shook my head at myself as I watched him jaunt to the break room and grab us paper plates. When he returned to the department, he simply nodded toward his office. "Want to eat in there? More room on the bigger desk."

Still feeling like a ridiculous egomaniac, I agreed and followed him in. Though, I did slip my cell phone into my back pocket, just in case I needed to make or receive a fake phone call as an excuse to bail.

Outside his window-wall, the lights of midtown Manhattan winked. He caught me staring as I took my usual seat across from his and sent me a slight smile. "Nice view, right?"

I nodded. "Very. I've never been up this high in the city at night. It always seemed like a touristy thing to do, but now I think I was just being stuck-up."

He chuckled, "Maybe so, Miss Rivera."

After we finished I cleaned up the box and the plates, figuring it was only fair since he set everything up. *See? I can be a good, normal employee. We can have a good, normal working relationship.*

As I stepped back into the pod, Dominic called my name. "Juliet? Can you come look at this for me? I have two sets of notes here in the portal and I don't know which are the current ones."

Such a normal, salient request. *What was I thinking when I got so worked up about this?*

Once I got into his office, I had to walk around his desk to look at his screen. The space was nowhere near as airy as Mr. Stryker's—the area between the desk and the wide window only consisted of a few square feet. I squeezed in beside Dominic's chair as best I could, bending forward to squint at the two documents open side-by-side onscreen.

"Oh." I moved to point. "It's this—"

Dominic's hand brushed my lower back and slid down to cup the curve of my ass.

After talking myself down for the better part of three hours, I was so shocked, it took a second for the action to register in my mind. When it did, I jerked upright.

A gasp tore out of my mouth. "Dominic!"

The computer cast his crooked grin in a cold, blue glare. I only caught a glimpse of the perverse expression before he bolted to his feet. In one more motion, he had his arms around me, pinning my backside to the edge of the desk.

"Dominic!" I protested again, louder. I tried to squirm away from him, but he pressed his legs into my hips to hold me still. "What are you *doing*?"

One of his hands reached up and pulled on my hair, dragging my head back to bring us face-to-face. "I'm giving us both what we want," he told me.

I tried to go limp and fall backward onto the desk, but only managed to trap my hands behind myself. They whacked into his phone, knocking the mouthpiece loose and mashing a few of the buttons before he wrestled me back into his clutches.

His arms came around my elbows, squeezing like bands of steel, but his hand skimmed down again, grabbing me roughly. "You've been waving this sexy ass in my face for over a month," he growled. "And now I want what you've been advertising."

I tried bucking my hips to throw him off of me, but it didn't work. His weight wouldn't budge. "Dominic, stop!" I screamed, "I don't know what messages you think I've been sending, but you're wrong, okay? I don't want this. Get *off* of me!"

His hold tightened to the point of pain. "You'll put out for that faggot, Everett, but not for me?" he spat. "I saw that note he sent you. You must be one talented fuck to get flowers like those from a queer like him. Or maybe they were from Grayson, not Graham. That would explain why he gives you all the work that should be mine."

Desperate, I tried snapping my teeth at his face to get him to balk. Instead, he smiled again. "You want to play rough, Juliet? Is that what you like?"

I thought of all the times Graham and I shoved each other, bit each other. The way I clawed into him when he told me he loved me. The time he tied me up and fucked me over the island to prove his point.

"Not with you," I snarled, thrashing again. "*Let me go!*"

He tugged my hair so hard that my eyes stung, filling. "Not until you show me whatever you did to Stryker to make you his go-to girl," he retorted. "What was it? Did you blow him in that big office he has? Or maybe you let him fuck you on the conference table? I'm your boss, too, you know. It's only fair I get the same treatment you give that over-privileged piece of shit."

I'd been harassed and manhandled enough times in my life to keep my wits about me and try to fight him back. But the vicious bitterness in his voice sent a prickle of panic up my spine.

This wasn't just some random asshole at a club who'd had one-too-many; this was my *boss*. And the taunts he hurled at me felt disturbingly rehearsed. As though he thought them often. As if he truly had, as I always suspected, planned to force himself on me all along.

"*What is wrong with you?*" I yelled, clawing at him. "Mr. Stryker's never *touched* me."

"So, what did you do, then? Did you send him some pictures? Or maybe he sent *you* some?"

Dominic's hand drifted alarmingly close to my waistband. I tried to bite him again, but he flinched out of the way.

Seething, I shouted, "I would never come on to Mr. Stryker! He's a good man who loves his fiancée! And Ella is my *friend*!"

"Don't act like you're not a home-wrecking little tease," Dominic jeered, pulling my head back further. "I've spent so many nights jacking off next to my wife while she's sleeping, thinking about your hot little outfits and this sexy ass."

Ugh. Sick fucking creep.

His hand slid between my jeans and my panties. For a moment, I felt so violated that I froze. With a victorious sneer, he leaned his face closer to mine. "See?" he purred. "You want my hands on you. Just like any other dirty little slut—you fight and scratch but you like it once it's in."

My brain caught up to the adrenaline streaking through my body. I realized I'd never best him physically in a fight. I'd only be able to escape if he thought he was about to get what he wanted.

Sure enough, as soon as I stopped struggling, he ducked his head to plant his mouth on mine. For a long moment, I held my breath and let him.

Then I sank my teeth into his lip. *Hard.*

As I predicted, he reared back in pain. The distance created just enough space for me to draw my bent leg straight up into his package. I kneed him in the balls and shoved his shoulders at the same second, sending him careening backward into the window.

I heard a thud and muffled bellow as I spun blindly, already running.

Graham

"Motherfucking asshole," I muttered, pacing. "That son-of-a-bitch. Scum-sucking piece of dog shit."

No one was there to witness me cursing my father's existence. My voice echoed off the high ceiling, reverberating in the emptiness. For once, it didn't bother me. After the phone call I'd just had with my lawyer, I didn't have the capacity to care about much else.

First, Rachel told me the good news: that after completing their forensic accounting measures, Shondra and the FBI would honor our deal and had no plans to prosecute me or Christian.

After that, she told me the bad news: they would, however, conduct a "raid" of Everett Alexander on Tuesday. And, because I knew the office, they required my presence to help them with their search and seizure. Then—in a fitting end to what I assumed would be a *lovely* family reunion—they'd walk my dad out in handcuffs.

Ava would *love* that shit.

Finally, Rachel got to the *really* bad news: unless I could produce some sort of proof that G&C Capital existed—at least, conceptually—before I discovered my father's fraud, the FBI would shut me down. Indefinitely.

Of course, no such proof existed. Video footage from the office would show me taking those godforsaken account books home the afternoon I met Juliet… and I didn't approach anyone with the idea for G&C until five days later, when I burst into Grayson's office and started talking crazy.

I had no one to vouch for the idea before then because there *wasn't* any idea before then. And no way to prove that my basic mathematical abilities utterly deserted me the moment I saw Juliet Rivera in that damned red dress… only to be magically recovered a week later, after I finally had enough of her to think straight.

In short, I couldn't prove what I knew and when I knew it. In their book, that made G&C illegitimate.

As soon as I hung up, I started pacing and cursing. I'd been at it for almost ten minutes before the intercom buzzed, interrupting my tirade. When I picked up, the girl at the concierge desk downstairs sounded flustered.

"Um… Mr. Everett, sir? There's a visitor here… her name is on your list but she seems…disturbed. Do you want me to call the authorities or…?"

I only had three women on that list—my housekeeper, Ella, and Juliet.

Why would Ella be here? Did she have a fight with Grayson? Or maybe she wants advice on some gift for him?

"I'm sure that isn't necessary," I replied. "You said she's on the list? Who is it?"

"Juliet Rivera?"

…

Holy fucking shit.

"Send her up," I practically barked. "You *always* send her up, you understand? Immediately."

"Yes, sir. So sorry, sir. She's on her way now."

I hung up and spun around, panicking. What the fuck was she doing at my place? Why didn't she call first?

I looked for any incriminating evidence—anything that might give away how miserable I was since our break-up. But the apartment was as vacant and staged as ever. The half-bottle of wine on the island didn't exactly seem like a smoking gun.

Thank God it's not scotch.

My hands smoothed over the front of my shirt. One of my black ones, half un-tucked from my grey slacks. *Maybe I should put on—*

It didn't matter; it was too late for me change. A knock sounded from my front door and I threw it open gracelessly.

All of the air sloughed out of my lungs.

I'd never seen the look on her face before. Helpless, hopeless *terror*. Her eyes were wide as saucers, her hair hung sideways in a snarled, lopsided ponytail. She had her arms wrapped around herself and tear tracks on her cheeks. As soon as our gazes met, every last ounce of color drained from her face.

"Juliet! What the fuck happened to you?" I demanded, rushing forward just in time to catch her as she fainted dead away.

Chapter Twenty-six

February 19, 2017

Juliet

"So help me God," I warned, glaring at Graham from my nest on his couch. "If you say the word 'hospital' again, I'm going to scream."

He stood leaning against his island with his ankles crossed, just… staring. He'd been that way ever since he finished settling me into a small mountain of blankets with a glass of wine. He tried to cajole me into tea and attempted to convince me to lie down in his bed, but I refused both.

Because I was *fine*.

Graham disagreed. He seemed prepared to call in the National Guard when I woke up in his arms just a few moments after passing out. Luckily he couldn't get that far. He only had time to carry me to the sofa before I started stirring.

Now, I felt like a spectacle. Or some zoo animal in a cage. He watched me warily, as if I'd disappear or take a swing at him the second he looked away.

As soon as his mouth re-opened, I snapped, "And if you say 'police' I will throw this pinot noir on your white leather chair."

He pressed his lips into a tight line, but kept watching me. I didn't realize how much I missed those midnight eyes until I woke up on his sofa, with his face hovering over mine. It was the first thought to enter my consciousness—I saw his dark, turbulent irises and wanted to sag with relief.

Only, I couldn't. Because I was already limp.

Once more, he moved to speak. I lowered my eyebrows at him. "Don't even *think* about mentioning Marco again, because I will get up and walk out of here."

I was somewhat kidding, but my threat hit home. Graham ducked his head, hiding his face as he blew out a breath. Before I could read into why, he turned away and refilled his drink. With a full wine glass, he ventured a bit closer, but still hugged the periphery of the room, standing near his dining table instead of coming over to the couch.

I hated it. More than that, I hated how ridiculously *beautiful* he looked. Only one week had passed… but I felt like it may as well have been a year. I kept running my eyes down his entire body, drinking in every detail. His thick, combed-back hair. The slash of his stubbled jaw. His full, perfect mouth.

I missed the intangible things, too. How he could somehow smirk without moving his lips. How his brows arched to question my sanity. The loose, leonine way he moved.

I wanted to moan. *Dios mío, Juliet, why did you come* here*?*

At the time, I only knew I didn't have my wallet or my keys. I couldn't pay for the subway or a taxi. I didn't have any way to get into my apartment if Abuelita was out, and I didn't want to call her and tell her what happened. I knew she would forbid me from ever going to work again if she knew.

Mostly, though, I think I just wanted to feel *safe*. And Graham was honestly the only person who ever made me feel that way.

Irritated, embarrassed, and—much to my dismay—still shaken up, I blew up on him. Again.

"And *what* are you doing hovering around the edges of the room?" I demanded. "Why won't you just *sit down*?"

Graham regarded me steadily, more achingly handsome by the second. "Can't."

"*Why?*"

He took a sip of wine, his gaze intent, his expression impassive. "I don't trust myself."

I understood; he didn't know what would happen if he came close to me. Neither did I. It was one thing when he had to keep me from falling to the floor and make sure I was still breathing… but now that I was *sentient*…

Our attraction was still as potent as ever. It pulsed in the air between us, swirling like a vortex. A physical force, tugging at my middle. The same inevitable, insistent attraction that started this whole mess in the first place.

"Oh." I sniffed, tossing my hair back. "I see your point."

A spark of amusement settled in his black eyes. "I thought you might."

Gradually, the ember smoldered into a blaze. Then a raging inferno. It went from lust to fury in a flash. Graham bared his teeth. "You know," he started for the tenth time. "If you'd just *tell me what happened…*"

But I knew if I told him, he'd feel obligated to tell his best friend. And I wasn't sure I wanted that, yet. I needed time to consider all of my options, once I felt steady.

I pulled the blanket around my shoulders and took a sip of wine. "I already told you, it's a conflict of interest."

He gave one of his signature shrugs. "Isn't that sort of the theme of our relationship?"

When I fled the office in a panic, I never expected to find myself laughing just a couple hours later. But there I was, giggling at his wry expression.

Graham's eyes ran over my face, watching me. His smile was forlorn. "See?" His hand gestured at the space between us. "This is too easy."

Any good humor between us evaporated as our gazes meshed. Poignant stillness filled the room, underscoring everything we couldn't put into words. *I miss you,* I wanted to cry. *I'm sorry I can't do this. I wish I could stay here forever. With you.*

I didn't say any of it. Somehow, though, I knew he heard all of it. I knew he *understood* all of it, because I saw all the same broken dreams shifting in his eyes.

Our hearts are the same.

My mind whispered the words weakly, recalling Marco's description for his parent's unspoken bond. His rationale for their long and successful love.

"We're probably meant for each other," I finally admitted, staring across the expanse between us.

Graham held his breath, his black gaze gleaming. "Yes."

For one precious moment, I allowed myself to imagine what our lives could be like if the circumstances were different. I envisioned us sharing wine and trading work issues. We'd debate solutions and drive each other crazy with our over-protective suggestions.

His outfits would make me laugh; mine would make him growl. We could cook for each other… or even try cooking *with* one another. Though, that would probably end with me bent back over the island.

That would happen a lot, I figured. Even if we settled down together… we were still combustible. The dynamite and the match, like he said.

It felt more complex than that, though. We weren't just chemical agents, foaming and bubbling over because we *had* to. I found, even now, when sex was the furthest thing from my mind, that I simply longed to be close to him. He always gave me what I needed.

"We'd be happy," I realized out loud. "If everything wasn't so…"

Impossible.

An unfathomable emotion roiled in his eyes. Yearning creased every line on his face. "Yes."

I couldn't stand knowing that I caused him such pain. It drew me to my feet and flung me across the room, where Graham caught me as though he expected me all along.

With a jagged groan, he hauled my body up into his and sealed his mouth over mine. The feel of his lips—so warm and full of reverence—erased the memory of Dominic's bruising force.

I moaned, opening for him to brush his tongue over mine in a slow, soothing glide that curled my toes and sent a sluice of heat through my core. He adjusted our positions, slinging my arms around his neck as he held my face in one hand and my body with the other.

We kissed feverishly until another desperate sound scraped up his throat. His hands softened as they cradled me closer.

"Nothing scares me the way you do," he murmured, pulling back just far enough to meet my eyes. Both of his palms smoothed the hair off of my face as he examined my features. "When you passed out… I've never been so panicked. Are you sure you're alright?"

"I am now." My arms tightened around him. He was all I wanted. "Just… hold me?"

Graham fell into the nearest chair and pulled me onto his lap. He tucked my head between his shoulder and his neck. The familiar scent of his cologne sent a quiver down my spine, tightening my nipples.

I nearly laughed again as my lips found his neck. "I can honestly say that you are the only man on earth who could turn me on right now."

The hand wrapped around my waist tightened. I felt his chest expand and contract on quick breaths when my tongue touched the shell of his ear. "Juliet," he rasped, then cleared his throat as he shifted his legs. "You're upset, *bijou*. Let me take care of you."

I felt the ridge of his erection pressing up into his slacks. I ached to touch him, but worried I might have some sort of panic attack if he made any sudden moves. Sighing, I pulled back just far enough to frown at him. "I'm sort of a mess, huh?"

The roguish grin that stole my breath made its first appearance all night. "A gorgeous mess. Always." Something solemn settled in his eyes. "I *missed* it. And you."

A sudden rush of sadness overwhelmed me as I wondered what in the world was *wrong* with me? Why couldn't I just let this beautiful man love me? Why couldn't I find the strength to fight for us the way he clearly wanted to?

"Juliet?" he breathed. "I mean it. I'm so glad you came back."

Is that what I was doing? Going back to him? I didn't mean to. I didn't even know if I *could*. All the reasons I originally left still stood.

Nausea cramped my stomach. I slid off of his body in a rush, worried I might be sick, and spun away. "I can't do this," I muttered, frantic. "I don't even know what I'm doing here. I—I freaked, and I just… I need to go."

Jesucristo. The look on his face would haunt me forever. The absolute picture of anguish, with a heartrending streak of honest surprise.

"Juliet," he started, lurching to his feet. "Please don't do this—"

My lungs shriveled as anxiety closed off my airway. "I shouldn't have come," I said again, rambling. "I need to go. I promise I won't come back this time. I swear I'll never do this to you again. I'm sorry. I'm so, *so* sorry."

I dropped my eyes, ashamed of all my weakness—my feelings for him, my inability to love him back the way he deserved, the entitled way I showed up on his doorstep, needing someone who had every right to tell me to get lost.

"I'll call Marco," I mumbled. "I can't stay here."

I couldn't bring myself to look up at him. But I heard another swallow. His footsteps came next, a soft padding sound heading for his bedroom.

I finally chanced a glance just in time to catch him pausing on the threshold, facing away from me, his shoulders drawn tight. "Go, Juliet," he murmured, hoarse. "But don't come back."

Graham

Everything changed after Juliet left.

I laid in my bed, still dressed, listening while she called her cousin. I heard her wash the wine glasses and put her shoes on. The entire time, I held my breath, thinking she might wander into my room to say a final goodbye. Or, even, *maybe*, lie down beside me.

But the front door opened and clicked closed.

And the last flicker of hope sheltered in my heart snuffed out.

I couldn't believe the pain. I thought I'd already felt every variation of misery a person could wade through.

I was so pathetically *wrong*.

Grayson's muttered words returned to me at some point. "*He lost a woman he loves. I remember that feeling. He thinks he's in hell in right now. I wish I could say it gets better…but it seems like he's still pretty firmly planted in denial. Once that clears… and the anger burns itself out… and he's just alone, without her…* that's *hell.*"

It truly was.

Night stretched into dawn. I laid in the shadows, staring at a wall, lost in my loss.

The sun rose. How? Why? What was the point in the world continuing to turn, now?

I still didn't move. Quite simply, I didn't have the will to. Every time I even thought about getting up, my entire chest clenched. I didn't want to take a step in any direction—because none of them would have Juliet.

The shadows shifted, growing longer. When they stretched all the way across the room, I heard the front door. Without hope, though, the sound meant nothing. I knew it wasn't Juliet. So I didn't care who else it might be.

A few moments passed. Grayson appeared in my bedroom, standing just at the edge of my peripheral vision. "Graham?"

I didn't have anything to say. What was the point in speaking? Nothing I said would bring her back.

With a quiet sigh, my best friend kicked his loafers off and rounded the bed, coming to lie in the spot that used to be Juliet's. He folded his hands on his chest and stared up at the ceiling for a long time.

A while later, one question occurred to me.

"Is this as bad as it gets?"

I needed him to say yes. If there was a bottom beneath this one, I didn't think I'd survive it.

"Yeah," he said quietly. "It lasts a long time, though."

Jesus. I was white-knuckling my way through an amputation without anesthetic. My teeth gritted at the thought of going on indefinitely.

"How long?"

Grayson thought for a moment. "It isn't linear, I guess. It gets better for a few weeks, then worse again. You'll find things that help, stuff that makes it hurt again. It's a process…"

I didn't like the ominous way he trailed off at the end. "…but?"

"But, if I'm being honest with you, it never really went away," he confessed. "I never stopped loving Ellie or missing her. *Longing* for her, as stupid and dramatic as that sounds."

It felt neither stupid nor dramatic, in that moment. I knew that longing intimately.

I felt him look over at me. "Are you sure you and Juliet won't ever—"

A shudder clapped through me. "No. She's gone. She won't come back again. So just… tell me what you would have done if Ellie hadn't come back."

"Shit." He blew out another breath. "I don't know. I guess I was fine? Living, at least. I probably would have wound up with someone like Ava Morgan, for convenience's sake. Gotten married so I could have some kids to pass the business down to. Spent more time at work to avoid the home-life I didn't want."

I didn't have to ask him if he wanted all of that stuff, now. I could picture him and Ellie, happily married in their new home. Having babies.

I never even got to ask Juliet how she felt about kids. Did she hate them? Want ten? Would she be a single workaholic forever… or would some other man eventually put his baby inside of her?

Oh dear *God*. Agony.

"You said you found things that helped?" I asked, clenching my teeth through the wave of misery. "Like what?"

"Well, gin, for a while," he muttered sardonically. "Then exercise. I used to work out three times a day. That probably had something to do with not being able to have sex for a long time, too. Other women didn't do it for me for a while… about a year. Eventually, I just got so fucking cross-faded I couldn't even see straight. Took some party drugs and shit. Met a random woman I don't remember…"

I remembered that night. "New Year's, 2015. You were a fucking mess."

"My point is," he cut in. "None of it really worked. And I hurt Ella, sleeping around like I did. When she found out just *how hard* I tried to get over her, it was devastating. I regret all of it, now, because I didn't even enjoy it at the time. I was just lying to myself." He went on, rushing to finish before I could stop him. "I don't want you to end up like I did, okay? If this girl is the one, then you can't give up. Giving up on Ellie was the biggest mistake I ever made."

Grayson always blamed himself for everything. "You didn't give up. She left you."

Just like Juliet left me. Twice.

"And I didn't ask enough questions or fight to get her back, because I believed in the worst in her," Grayson retorted, vehement. "I *knew*, deep down, that she loved me. I should have trusted that."

Was I doing the same thing with Juliet? I couldn't tell. On one hand, I felt that she would be happy with me if she'd just *let* herself... but, on the other...

"She doesn't love me."

At least, she all but *said* as much... Though, there was the one moment, the night she came to me on the couch... when I *swore* she loved me back. For a few minutes, it felt so real that it almost didn't matter whether she admitted it out loud.

Or was that just... amazing sex? Because it was *amazing*. Could I really trust anything I thought with that gorgeous woman naked on top of me?

"How did you know?"

"What?"

"That she loved you. How did you know for sure?"

Grayson's eyes roamed the ceiling overhead. "It wasn't any one thing... but when my dad got sick and all of my plans changed, she supported me. I tried to give up my interest in architecture and design to focus on learning how to run the company, but she thought I could do both. She believed in me, even when I didn't. I found out that she kept one of my sketches and went to my dad herself, to show him that I had potential. I think that's when it really sank in."

That raised another good point. Even if Juliet *told* me she loved me at some point... would I believe it, now that I knew she didn't want to hang in with me through the tough times?

No, said the bleak voice of reason. *Because she never loved you at all.*

Juliet

Marco spent most of Sunday afternoon frowning at me across Abuelita's kitchen table.

Honestly? I was grateful. Downright *thankful* for anything that could keep me from calling Graham… or racing to the subway and running right back to his apartment.

I never should have gone there. Even cracked-out on adrenaline, I should have known better than to allow myself that one small taste of everything I'd already sworn off.

Instead of remembering the horrible look on his beautiful face as he turned to walk away, I forced myself to focus on my family. Tía Esme and Abuelita spent the better part of the morning fighting as they took turns packing the apartment and stuffing empanadas for their church potluck.

Finally, after cooking three courses of food and having fifteen different arguments in the space of four hours, they went off to Mass, leaving us to clean up. While I scrubbed dishes, Marco dried them.

Halfway through, he turned his head toward me, but didn't move his eyes off of his task. "Want a ride to work tomorrow? I have to pick up Mr. Stryker, too, but he specifically told me to offer you a lift. He has to be in by eight-forty-five."

I nodded, though the thought of returning to the office made me queasy. "Sure."

Marco heard the panic pinching my voice. "Are you ever going to tell me what happened last night?"

I gripped the sponge harder, scraping it against a pan. "No."

"Jules, c'mon. I had to pick you up at your ex-boyfriend's house… and then I had to go to Stryker & Sons to get all of your work… which was all *open*, by the way. None of it saved or filed or anything... and you *refused* to go up yourself, which was weird…"

A shiver moved through me. "You're sure there wasn't anyone else there?"

"No. Your desk lamp was the only light on whole floor."

I nodded, my mind racing. What would Dominic *do*? Would he honestly show up for work the next morning like nothing ever happened? Did he expect me to stay quiet? If I told someone, what would that entail? HR? A lawsuit?

I knew I'd be out-gunned on any legal matter. He had more money and more connections than I ever would. He'd even clerked for a federal judge, at one point…

If I sued him directly, he'd burn through my savings with counter-suits and defamation claims within a month. If I went directly to Mr. Stryker, it might seem like I was using my personal relationship with Ella to sway him to my side. Not to mention, if he knew anything about my relationship with Graham, he'd probably start to wonder if I made a habit of seducing men I worked with…

All men would assume that. Just like Dominic did when he saw those flowers and Graham's note. I ruined my credibility the minute I let Graham Everett lure me into the corner of Meeting Pod C.

Marco reached for the next clean pan and I flinched. His scowl deepened. "Are you sure you're okay? You're even jumpier today than you were last night."

He had a point. I expected my mind to dull the memories as time went on; but the further I got from the incident, the clearer it became.

When I was with Graham, I felt safe. Now, though, every passing hour took me further away from him and further away from any sense of security. Even Marco's hulking frame and watchful eyes couldn't banish the residual nerves.

"I'm fine." I tried to internalize the words as I said them, willing them into truth. "Just a work thing."

Marco's gaze narrowed. "You know I review all the footage from the office right? When I look at the videos from this weekend… I won't see anything?"

Carajo.

"What are you implying?" I asked, waving my sponge at him.

He crossed his arms over his chest and looked down his nose at me, every inch the intimidating detective. "I'm saying that if Everett showed up at the office while you were there and *something* went down—*something* that would cause you to leave your work un-saved and adjourn back to his apartment with him in a hurry—you'd better tell me now before I accidentally watch the video and have no choice but to tell Stryker whatever I see."

My stomach cramped, as much from the thought of Graham holding me again as the notion of getting caught with my pants down at work. "*Que carajo, primo*?" I snapped, "How stupid do you think I am, anyway? There's a camera right above my desk!"

…

A camera that probably caught me running out of Dominic's office like a bat out of hell….

And Lord knew what he looked like when he limped out of there, after…

Or if he tried to chase me down…

Marco read the alarm all over my face. "*What?*" he asked, grabbing both of my arms. "Jules, you're white as a ghost. What *happened* last night?"

I couldn't open my mouth without the whole story leaping past my lips. After a moment, he shook me lightly. "Jules?"

Pity already prodded the edges of his expression. And I didn't want it. From anyone. Standing there, looking up at his sympathetic face, I felt more like a victim than I did during the actual assault.

I made up my mind on the spot—if reporting Dominic and filing a complaint against him would make me "that girl," I wouldn't do it. I refused to be reduced to a subject of pity in front of my peers. I needed their respect.

My eyes fell to the floor, feigning embarrassment as I thought up a lie. "I got my period early, okay? A really… bad one. And I had to run out of Dominic's office and leave all of my stuff because I didn't… have what I needed. And then, when I got on the street, I realized I left my wallet and key card inside so I couldn't get back in or go buy the supplies I required. I was mortified and I didn't want to call upstairs and explain it all to Dominic… so I went to Graham's to clean up, okay?"

Marco immediately let go of me. His features filled with chagrin while he winced. "Oh. Shit. Sorry. Never mind."

Men. Honestly. They made it too easy.

We went back to washing and drying in stilted silence. A few moments later, I caught him peeking over at me sheepishly. "So, I, uh, got the house for Mami and Abuelita," he offered.

A pot clattered out of my hand. "*Already?* Don't you have to get pre-approved and get a mortgage and all that?"

He shrugged, playing it off. "I paid cash. It seemed easier that way. No monthly payments for us to worry about."

My mind reeled. "*Cash?* You had four-hundred-thousand-dollars *cash* lying around? You still drink coffee from the gas station!" I threw my hands up, beyond exasperated. "Marco, I can't even pay one-twentieth of what that place cost! How am I supposed to reimburse you for Abuelita's half?"

My cousin kept drying the glass in his hand, holding it up to the light to squint at the water spots he missed. "Oh I never intended to let you pay for half. I just didn't want to tell you that because I knew you'd be *una puta loca* about it."

I whipped him with the nearest dish rag. "Marco! I wanted to help!"

He chuckled. "Too late now. It's all done. I'm closing tomorrow afternoon for their place and closed last week for my own." When he saw my incredulous face, he flashed a quick smile. "It's just an apartment. West Fifty-Seventh."

My jaw dropped open. "That's practically the Upper West Side! The rent must be a *fortune*!"

"Mortgage," he corrected, grinning. "And yes, it is. But the place has a gym… and a doorman… and valet… plus, I needed my own parking space."

I bounced in place, vicariously ecstatic. "*Ay Dios mío, primo*! That's incredible!"

He was too humble to brag, but couldn't seem to swallow his smile. He went back to the dishes, shrugging again. "Turns out living with your mother gives you plenty of time to save up. And Mr. Stryker gave me a very generous salary when he promoted me. Honestly, though, I wasn't looking for anything quite so nice… But then he bought the place up on West Seventy-Fifth… so I just thought somewhere between his house and the office would make the most sense."

"I cannot *wait* to see it," I pronounced. "When will you move?"

His grin morphed into a half-grimace. "I already have, mostly. I just want my mom settled with Abuelita before I call it official."

Sighing, I looked around the cramped little kitchen I'd cooked in for as long as I could remember. "Wow. It's hard to believe. You and I have been hustling for so long. I feel like we finally made it somewhere."

He bumped my shoulder with his elbow. "Now we just need to find you a place, and all of us will be on to bigger and better things."

I wanted to tell him the truth: that every apartment I looked at felt wrong to me, because none of them were Graham's. Or maybe just because none of them *had* Graham.

"Yeah," I mumbled, agreeing even though I couldn't quite shake the feeling that my "bigger, better thing" had already passed.

Chapter Twenty-Seven

February 20, 2017

Juliet

I took care to choose another ultra-drab ensemble on Monday morning.

Because I still didn't know what Dominic might say or do, I figured appearing completely sexless would be the safest move.

While I pulled on the boring black skirt and one of Abuelita's baggiest blouses, I muttered to myself. "Fucking ridiculous to have to worry about this *mierda*. Men don't get accused of 'asking for it' when *they* wear nice clothes. And men don't have to worry that their careers will be ruined if someone *attacks* them…"

Marco seemed beat when he picked me up. I could tell he had a long night of some sort, but decided not to press the issue.

When I noticed he deviated from our usual route, it took me a moment to remember why—the Strykers' new townhome was on the other side of Central Park. I expected something stark and modern like Graham's place, but instead Marco pulled into a concealed alley running behind a row of pre-war facades and made a sharp turn into a basement driveway.

"*Dios*," I whispered, thrown. "It's *huge*."

"It's a five-car garage," Marco murmured back. He sent a text message, then pointed out the windshield. "There's a security office in there that I'm supposed to use." His voice dropped. "I still feel kind of creepy, watching them at home. But, honestly, the amount of attention they're getting is just insane. They need constant active surveillance."

Before I could ask any questions, a steel door to my right slid open, revealing an elevator. Mr. Stryker stepped right out of the vestibule and into the backseat of the car. "Good morning, Marco. Miss Rivera."

He seemed uncharacteristically reserved. I tried not to feel paranoid about it, but couldn't help myself. I wondered if Dominic sent an email or memo mentioning me....

"Marco," Grayson clipped, swiping at his phone. "I need you to get me the system specs on that new building in SoHo before noon. I want the same camera set-up that we used on the Gold Street property. And Ava Morgan assures me there will be more press than usual this weekend, because she's doing a post of some sort Friday—get the new men you need in my office at some point this week after you've vetted them. I want to meet anyone you select before we put them on payroll.

"Also, Maggie Danvers should be in contact with you at some point regarding security for the bachelorette party she has in the works—if she doesn't contact you before five, I'd like you to work with the wedding planner directly and she can coordinate with Maggie. I want *full* security measures taken at *every* venue they visit; and you will attend as Ella's personal body guard. She knows you're going to be there and she's not happy about it, so... I apologize if she gives you attitude. Speaking of which—Ella's appointment this afternoon? Saks Fifth Avenue. It's non-negotiable."

I caught my cousin's very slight wince. "Yes, sir."

Was I completely losing my mind or did Mr. Stryker's eyes flash to the back of my head every few seconds? And why did he seem so put out?

"I mean it, Marco," he added. "*Absolutely* non-negotiable."

We slid smoothly onto the street. "And if Miss Callahan objects?"

"God," Grayson muttered, "I said 'non-negotiable,' did I not? Do *you* understand that term? I know my fiancée doesn't."

I felt my eyes go wide. In over a month at Stryker & Sons, I'd never heard our boss speak to anyone in a demeaning manner. Even when he put Dominic in his place… he always did so respectfully.

Marco's mouth tightened. "Yes, sir."

A tense second passed. "Marco?"

"Yes, sir?"

I caught Mr. Stryker meeting my cousin's gaze in the rearview mirror. "I'm an asshole."

Marco grinned broadly. "Yes, sir."

They both nodded, content with the exchange. It seemed almost commonplace for them, which actually made sense. I supposed, if someone followed me around all day, every day… I might occasionally lash out at them, too.

"Miss Rivera, I apologize," Grayson added.

Again, his tone seemed frosty to me. Instead of dwelling, I just nodded.

He muttered to himself some more. "Beth keeps calling me. She usually just sends an email or a text…" He shook his head. "How far out are we?"

"Eight minutes."

I tried to breathe through my paranoia. *It's not about me,* I coached myself. *Beth has better things to worry about than me. And Dominic would never tell* her *anything, anyway. She hates him.*

"You'd better drop me off at the entrance," Mr. Stryker replied, yanking at his navy tie. "If Beth has a stroke while she waits for us to park and go through garage security, Ella will never forgive me."

Marco released our boss on the curb in front of Stryker & Sons seven-and-a-half minutes later. We watched him stride toward the building and Marco shrugged, casting me a baffled look.

"Don't ask me," he grumbled. "You want to ride down to the garage with me? You're early."

Eight-thirty-six. Less than twenty-five minutes until I had to face Dominic. My stomach seethed. "Yeah, sure." *Anything to prolong the inevitable…*

Marco's phone started blowing up before we even reached his parking spot, though. He furrowed his brows at the screen, but said nothing as he popped open his door and leapt out of the car. "Let's go. Now."

Some sort of security breach, I reasoned, following him to the service elevator and holding my silence up all fifty levels. My cousin barely waved goodbye when it spat us out on the executive floor.

I stuffed down a series of deep breaths while I lingered near the entrance, preparing myself. I didn't notice Tris barreling toward me until her heels screeched on the marble. "Jules!"

I blinked at her stupidly. "Oh. Hello."

She gripped my arm and spun us toward her pod, lowering her voice to a hushed murmur. "Do you know what the fuck is going on?" she asked. "I came in way early because I had a couple things I forgot to do Friday and Dominic was here. At like, seven A.M. He had some sort of early meeting with HR? I saw him go into their pod, anyway. And now Beth is *crying*. I, like, didn't even know that was *possible…*"

Her face froze as she stared at mine. "Oh no," she gasped. "Oh shit. Is it you? Did you do something?"

I concentrated on not vomiting. My lips felt numb as I lied. "Not that I'm aware of."

My eyes roamed out over the floor, trying to get a feel for what might happen next. I spotted Beth, dabbing at her eyes while she lingered outside Mr. Stryker's office. Marco's large, black-clad figure stood out beyond the office's see-through door. From my vantage point, it looked as if he was bent with his hands on the desk, reading something written there… or maybe listening to something coming out of a speaker?

Maybe someone died. And Dominic's meeting this morning was pure coincidence…

But then, I saw him, standing just behind the legal department's partition. Staring directly at me with a shit-eating smirk on his face.

"You're, like, really white," Tris reported. "Do you want to sit down or something?"

The door to Grayson's office burst open and he appeared on the threshold, visibly fuming. His eyes snapped across the floor, capturing mine. "Miss Rivera."

A bolt of panic ran through me.

"My office," he said. "Now."

I stayed completely still until Tris pushed me lightly. "Everyone's watching. You have to go," she urged. "Go, Jules."

Thankfully, my feet obeyed her. I shuffled forward, almost stumbling. Desperate, I searched inside for something—*anything*—that could help keep me calm while I, presumably, got fired. The memory of Graham holding me was enough to at least allow me to breathe. I clutched the image close as I ducked into the appropriate pod and whispered good morning to Beth. Her grave grey eyes speared me with pity, but her mouth pinched instead of replying.

I followed Mr. Stryker into his office without looking up at him or Marco. I stood just inside the room, beside the sketches Ella had framed. With my gaze on the floor, I waited.

"Juliet."

Grayson's voice sounded… wrong. Soft. Almost solicitous. "Would you have a seat, please?"

Still not able to look at him or Marco, I fumbled for my usual chair. Sitting seemed to help. Having something solid under me allowed reality to sink in. Once I settled myself, I finally forced my eyes up, raising my head. *If I'm going to get canned, I'm going to do it with dignity.*

But the picture was all wrong. I expected Mr. Stryker to sit at his desk, looking down at me, while my cousin stood off in the corner with his arms folded in his bodyguard pose….

Not *this.*

Grayson eschewed his own seat and took the second Eames chair, beside mine. Marco stood with his back to me, bent forward, hands pressed into the desk. His eyes were closed, his nostrils flaring on exaggerated breaths.

Maybe he's sick, and that's why I got called in here…? That didn't explain Dominic's sneer, though…

"Is Marco… okay?" I whispered, thrown.

"He's taking a moment," Grayson murmured, eying my cousin's broad back before turning his sympathetic gaze on me. "He just heard something very upsetting."

I pressed my hands to my sinking stomach. "Mr. Stryker," I started, "I don't know what Dominic told you, but I swear I can explain."

His thick brows knit. "He didn't *tell me* anything," he reported. "I have an HR memo here for a claim he filed this morning, alleging that you committed some very disturbing acts of harassment. Particularly while you were both working here over the weekend…"

Ayúdame Dios. I was going to throw up. On the CEO. I didn't even trust myself to open my mouth.

Marco suddenly burst into motion. He ripped a paper off of Grayson's desk and thrust it at me, his expression murderous. "You want to tell me what the fuck actually happened on Saturday, *prima*?"

I took the page he offered and skimmed my eyes over it, confirming all my worst fears.

"Mr. Stryker." My voice didn't even sound like my own. "Grayson. I can explain—"

He held up one hand, silencing me. "Ordinarily, I'd let you. But, while Dominic was in with HR this morning, Beth went around and collected voicemails from the various communal phones in the office. Apparently some people call in looking for a specific person and accidently route themselves to the conference room or one of the phones in the meeting pods. As a result, she routinely retrieves stray messages. And she gathered a disturbing one from the conference line this morning. A call that came from inside the legal department."

My mind reeled, trying to understand what he implied. "I—I'm sorry, but I don't remember leaving any messages."

With a regretful frown, he nodded at Marco and cast his green gaze down at his shoes. "Play it."

Marco stabbed the desktop phone with his finger and then spun away, pacing like a caged panther while the audio recording began with a spurt of static and a thud. Then a rough, menacing voice spat, "*You've been waving this sexy ass in my face for over a month. And now I want what you've been advertising.*"

I gasped, rearing back.

Grayson shot to his feet, moving to pause the clip just as my own words played, *"Dominic, stop! I don't know what messages you think I've been sending, but you're wrong, okay? I don't want this—"*

In a flash, I recalled the way my trapped hands knocked Dominic's phone out of its cradle and swiped at some of the buttons in the process. I felt the color drain from my face.

Ay Dios mío. Get it together, Juliet. Don't puke on your boss.

"Jesus," Grayson cursed at himself. "I shouldn't have had you listen to that. You look sick. It makes *me* sick and I wasn't even there. I'm sorry, Juliet. Truly. I—there isn't any protocol for how to handle something like this..."

The existence of a recording somehow made the entire incident more real than a thousand memories ever could. I found I had to focus to draw breath. An embarrassingly loud one, at that.

Grayson spoke very gently. "Juliet, I know you understand what I have to do, now. I'm assuming, since you decided not to report him or tell Marco what happened, that you'd like to keep this as private as possible. So I'm going to clear the executive floor for the day and deal with Dominic. He'll be gone by lunch. I'll need you to stay, though, to get your official statement for HR. If you want to press formal charges against him, we can help coordinate that with the police, too. This tape is obviously evidence. But before we do any of that… is there someone I can call to come be with you?"

There was only one person I wanted, but the thought was so horribly selfish, I dismissed it instantly. Recalling Graham's pain-filled expression Saturday night, I shook my head. "No. No one."

Graham

"Where is she?"

I was *fuming*. I'd never been so fucking pissed in my entire life. Which was truly saying something, considering recent events.

Grayson caught me by the shoulder as I charged out of his elevator, holding me in place. "Easy," he muttered. "I told you; she doesn't know you're here." He frowned as he considered my face. "I also told you to try to use the car ride to calm down—remember?"

Another jolt of fury moved through me. I pushed against his hold. "Calm down? I'm gonna fucking kill him. Where is he? I will *fucking kill him*, Grayson."

My best friend gripped both shoulders of my topcoat and the royal blue suit jacket underneath, shaking me. "Hey. *Hey!* Look at me." He jostled me again. "Graham, *look at me*."

It took every modicum of control I possessed to stop searching the empty executive floor for the miserable piece of shit who tried to violate Jules. Another spiral of regret whipped through me. *I should have known the second I saw her.*

Saturday night replayed in my mind. I figured she got mugged or chased or possibly had a near-death run-in with a cab. The fact that I never suspected her sleaze-ball boss shamed me, now.

I should have known, *goddamn it.*

"Hey," he said again, locking eyes with me. "Listen. I know, okay? I know the feeling. Trust me. But she's freaked out and embarrassed. I'm not letting you go in there until you get a grip."

He thought she was some broken, traumatized victim who needed coddling. I knew better. Not my *bijou.*

Incensed by his presumption, I shoved at him. "She's not Ella," I bellowed. "*I* know what she needs! Now, *where is she?*"

Grayson dropped back. His eyes flashed as they ran over my expression, examining me as if I were suddenly a different person. "Pod C," he mumbled. "Someone once pointed out that there's a decent amount of privacy in there..."

I stalked off, not even bothering to shuck my coat before I flew into Pod C and threw myself at Juliet's figure, yanking her out of her seat. With her forearm firmly in my grip, I spun us both into the corner where our entire affair started.

"Graham?! What are you—?"

"Doing here?" I finished, raging right into her painfully beautiful face. "*I'm* here because Grayson called me and filled in all of the blanks *you* left empty on Saturday!"

Grayson rushed into the room. "Graham, good God. *What* are you doing?"

I stared down into Juliet's beloved face, basking in her outrage. She was mad as hell. Full of fire, with wounded pride snapping in her ocher eyes.

My brilliant *bijou*.

I spread my hands on either side of her head, boxing her between my body and the wall. "We need a minute," I growled.

Grayson hesitated. "Juliet, are you alright with that?"

Her gaze traced my face, seeing my fury. Adoring it. "Yes," she replied, quiet but steady. "I'll be fine."

I waited until I heard the door close behind him. Then I snapped, slapping my palm into the wall next to her face. Glaring down, I demanded, "Woman, what the *hell* is the matter with you? How could you *not tell me*?"

Hot color filled her high cheeks. "I don't have to tell you *shit*," she hissed back. "We broke up!"

"Bullshit," I called. "You came to me for a goddamned reason. Because you know that you can *always* come to me. You can *always* tell me when someone hurts you. I don't give a fuck what our relationship status is—*you come to me*."

A sheen of tears glossed her golden eyes, but did not diminish her spirit. "Fine," she spat. Her stubborn little chin rose. "But you don't get to be pissed at me right now."

My brows arched. "You have some fucking nerve. The love of my life leaves me and then shows up on my doorstep after her scumbag boss assaults her and she *doesn't even tell me what he did* before deserting me, again. Leaving me to find out from *someone else*. Why, pray tell, don't I get to be pissed right now?"

She was so angry, her nose twitched. Seething, she bored her eyes into mine and yelled, "Because this is our spot!"

I jerked back slightly. My eyes narrowed. "Our *spot*?"

She sniffed, embarrassed but unwilling to back down. "Yes. This is where we had our first… whatever. It's our spot," she replied with a queenly nod. "You're not allowed to be mad at me in our spot. You have to forgive me."

Christ. I loved her so damn much. And she was there, in my reach.

I thought I'd never see her again when she left Saturday… Now that I knew the truth, I wondered how much of her panic that night was actually related to Dominic and how much was truly about me. About *us*.

The stupid spark of hope reignited in my heart. And I didn't even try to stop it. It mingled with the rage burning there, kicking up into wildfire.

I cupped her jaw in one hand. "You know what?" I whispered, moving to press my lips to hers. "Make me."

"You should take your coat off," Juliet mumbled into my neck. She snuggled closer, though, making the task even less likely.

I ran my hand over her hair and looked down at her, curled into my lap. "Eh. It's probably the one thing keeping this suit from getting wrinkled to hell."

We *were* on the floor, after all. Sitting in our spot.

"I like this one," she murmured next, fingering the paisley purple-and-blue vest. "Although, it was a bad day not to bring the red handkerchief."

My arms tweaked tighter at the thought of her crying. "I will never go anywhere without the red handkerchief again."

She smirked. "Even if it doesn't match your outfit, *pinchao*?"

My joy at holding her easily smothered the frisson of pain caused by her special nickname. I knew I couldn't keep her. I knew I'd end up having to pay for this, just like I did after Saturday night's visit. But I was just so damn *happy*; I convinced myself it was a fair trade.

"Don't be ridiculous," I retorted, keeping my voice airy. "I'll tuck it into the inside pocket if it doesn't match the suit. I'm not an *animal*."

Her giggle tickled my throat. I practically heard her roll her eyes. "*Que gonorrea.*"

Everything precious about her hit me all at once. I ducked my face to hide it in her hair, breathing her jasmine scent and reassuring myself. *Safe. She's safe. She's okay.*

Out loud, I muttered, "I don't think I've ever been this close to murdering someone before."

"You can't—"

"Do anything," I finished for her, scowling. "I know, I know. I can't *say* anything. I can't *do* anything. Story of my fucking life." I ground my molars for a moment, stewing. "What would hurt more—being decapitated by a trash compactor, or having a thousand shallow stab wounds and then getting drowned in a bathtub full of wine?"

A startled laugh blurted out of her. "*What?*"

"When I kill him," I went on, my tone utterly serious. "I want it to *hurt.* My building has a trash compactor. That would be quick, I suppose. Cleaner, too. But I *love* the idea of stabbing him…"

"Graham!" she snickered, flicking her hand at my chest. "Don't even joke about that."

Lord, how I loved to make her laugh. I covered her fingers with my palm, holding them against me. "I'm not joking. I honestly think the bathtub is the way to go. I'll even let *you* do the stabbing, if you'd prefer."

She shrugged one shoulder, deciding to play along. "Eh, I don't think I'd have the restraint to make shallow cuts. You better do the stabbing."

"Suppose I'd need a new tub, after," I mused, tilting my head back to look up at the ceiling. "And probably some more wine."

"There are much better uses for your tub," she pointed out, brushing her lips over my earlobe. "And your wine."

Overeager, my dumb dick stirred beneath her. Poor bastard didn't know any better... Unlike me, he didn't have the foresight to see this fleeting moment for what it was.

"Stop trying to seduce me," I told her, mostly to keep from getting ahead of myself. "You're still in trouble. This is a temporary, location-based *détente*."

Her thin brows furrowed while she skimmed her fingers down my purple tie. I could tell it was hard for her to admit, "I don't know that word."

"It's French," I murmured. "It means 'truce.'"

She made a content sound and settled her head back into my shoulder. "We've been in here a while... What do you think they're doing out there?"

"Firing that ass-clown," I grumbled, repressing the urge to bolt to my feet and rush out to beat him to death. "Giving the police the evidence. I'm sure Marco and security will help escort him out..."

Juliet shrank down slightly, her eyes squeezing closed. "Let's talk about something else. Tell me about what's going on with your case."

With bone-deep weariness, I relayed the latest information. Juliet listened, tipping her head back occasionally to give me certain looks. When I finished, I found her chewing on the sides of her lips, thinking hard.

"So unless Grayson or I submitted testimony saying you came up with the idea for G&C Capital a week before you actually did... and we both claimed that you mentioned it to us on... oh, say, that first Friday? The morning we met? Unless there's some sort of evidence to support that claim, you will lose the company?"

I nodded, numb to the situation. "Yep."

Juliet searched my face, her gaze wary. "Then... why didn't you ask either of us to testify?"

I held her eyes with mine, needing her to see my earnestness. "Because that would involve you—an officer of the court—lying under oath. And my best friend—a soon-to-be-married CEO—committing perjury. You both could be charged. You could be disbarred. It's not an option. I would never even consider it."

Something bright and bold flared in her gaze. If I wasn't so certain—for so many reasons—that it was impossible, I may have thought it was love.

"I'm sorry you had to come down here," she said, still staring at me. "I didn't want them to call you because I couldn't stand hurting you again. I hope you know… I never, ever *meant* to."

It wasn't a confession of love—or even a commitment to end my suffering—but I appreciated it.

"I believe in the best in you," I told her, borrowing Grayson's words. "I never think that you intend to hurt me."

"But I *do* hurt you," she moaned quietly.

I couldn't deny that. It was all over my face. So, instead, I pressed my forehead into hers. "Yes, you do," I admitted. "But I let you. I don't think I'm going to do that anymore."

The epiphany didn't dawn on me all at once. It crept, bit by bit, into my consciousness. Until I found myself wondering if, somehow, I already knew it before I even tore into the room.

"I'm not going to let you," I said again, seeing the beauty of the words.

Drawing back, I grinned at her. Her frown deepened, becoming suspicious once more. "Graham… why are you looking at me like that?"

Because I finally solved the only problem that matters.

"Because it just hit me; you keep running and I keep letting you leave, believing you won't come back, believing you don't want this. But you *do*. Of course you do." I gestured to the way our bodies were arranged, then moved to frame her gorgeous face with my hands.

"I love you, Juliet. And I may not be able to control whether that scares you and whether you run from it, but I can damn sure be waiting here every time you come back."

Her split reaction betrayed mixed emotions. Indignance flashed in her eyes while her lips softened and her chin trembled. "And if I don't come back?" she asked, her voice thick.

I felt strangely peaceful. "You will. Because we belong together. And you know that."

She had so much fight in her and nowhere to put it. Her brows snapped together over a ferocious frown. "You can't just—I don't—you—we—" She huffed out an exasperated breath. "It doesn't *work* like that."

I shrugged. "I think our relationship works however we want it to work. I love you. I'll wait however long it takes to prove that to you." She opened her mouth to protest, but I arched my brows, halting her. "And I'm not asking you for your permission, *bijou*."

She started muttering a string of Spanish obscenities. But she tucked herself back against my body all the same. And I swore I caught a glimmer of a smile darting across her face.

Juliet

Ridiculous, spoiled, pompous, high-handed...

I continued my throng of insults internally, but nuzzled my face into Graham's solid warmth. On the floor next to us, my cell phone displayed an unknown number and I ignored it.

Graham turned and brushed his lips over the crown of my head, chuckling quietly. "This is going to be fun, baby."

I couldn't tell whether I should feel outraged by his cockiness... or beyond flattered by his determination. Either way, I launched a taunt of my own back at him. "Remember what I said before about not wanting to hurt you? I think I changed my mind."

"Well," he chipped, delighted, "If you want to slap me, you know where to find me."

His obvious amusement riled me... but it also sent a burst of sparks twinkling throughout my chest. Clutching his jacket in my hands, I pulled myself closer to him.

"Graham?"

He dropped another kiss on my forehead. "Hmm?"

"I'm really glad you're here," I confessed. It was a relief to admit it, even if I had no idea what the words meant for me.

He knew what they meant for him, though. Adoration shone in his dark eyes as he pinned my gaze and vowed, "I will always be here, Juliet."

Heat suffused my center, trickling down to gather low in my belly. I shifted in his lap, wanting to feel his body grind up into mine. As soon as I settled the curve of my backside against his erection, his eyes flickered to my lips.

"Careful, *bijou*. It's been eight days. I can't be held responsible for what I'll do if you start teasing me."

I wanted to laugh... or maybe just reach for his fly... but Dominic's vicious jeer chose that moment to intrude. His bitter words echoed in my mind. *"Don't act like you're not a home-wrecking little tease."*

Leaning my head back, I searched Graham's features. "Do you think I'm a tease? I've always liked bright colors and fitted clothing... and I've always thought that if a man couldn't control himself because of what I chose to wear or how I walked or *whatever* then that was *his* problem. But now I—"

His lips came down hard on mine, his kiss fierce. "No," he said against my mouth. "Stop it. *Nothing* that fucking creep did was your fault. You are beautiful and professional and brilliant. He only saw a piece of ass because that's all he wanted to see.

"Take it from a man who couldn't keep his eyes off of you the first time he saw you—the second you opened your mouth, I knew there was so much more to you than a tight dress and sexy body. And, even so, you were right to smack me that day. I deserved it, objectifying you that way. I wish you could smack him, too."

I nearly groaned. How did he always say exactly what I needed to hear? Like he had a special viewfinder to peer into my soul. As I moved to kiss him again—properly, this time—my phone went off for the third time in two minutes, displaying the same unsaved phone number.

"Get it," Graham murmured against my cheek. "Like I said, I'll be here."

Scowling, I swiped at the screen. "Hello?"

"*Julieta*." My father's panicked voice filled my ear. "You must come now, *mija*. Lucia, she's is in labor and I have to leave."

My mind struggled to shift gears from Graham to my dad. Once it finally processed, I balked—surely he wasn't *serious*?

"She's in labor and you have to *leave*?" I repeated, not understanding.

Graham gaped at me, mouthing, "*What?*"

I froze, listening as Julio attempted to explain. "She is at Mount Sinai. I dropped her off there."

"You *dropped her off?!*" I shrieked, automatically struggling to my feet. "Papi, no! You have to go back for her. She can't be *alone* at the hospital! Have you lost your mind?"

Deafening quiet came as my reply. Graham reached up to touch my arm—probably to remind me that everyone on the floor could likely hear me screaming at my deadbeat dad—but I threw his hand back at him.

"Papi," I repeated, furious. "You go back *right now*, or I am calling Abuelita."

My father sounded suitably ashamed, for once. "I could not stay, Julieta. I need you to go meet her there and stay with her."

I, on the other hand, felt apoplectic. "You *couldn't stay*? What does that even *mean*? Unlike you, Papi, I have a *job*. I can't just go to the hospital and be your girlfriend's birthing partner. She needs *you*. Your *baby* needs you."

I was vaguely aware of Graham rising from our spot on the floor. I knew, somewhere in my mind, that I should be embarrassed, but I wasn't. He would understand.

"You were going to take her in, anyway," my father argued. "Well… take her now."

"Papi! You have to be there. Even if she leaves you… don't you want to be a part of this baby's life? This is your *son*! *Tu hijo! El te necesita, Papi.*"

Julio heaved out a sigh that stopped me cold. His bravado slipped away entirely, turning his next words into a dark, defeated confession. "You know better than anyone, *mija*. It's not me that baby needs. I am no one's father."

All of my indignation stuck in my throat, leaving me hoarse. "Papi, *por favor*—"

"I am sorry, *mija*. Will you tell your baby brother that I am sorry?"

The line went dead. I pulled the phone away from my face and stared at it like it had bitten me. Graham's fingers landed on my wrist, bringing me back to reality.

"Where is she?" he murmured, already dialing his phone.

"Mount Sinai."

Belatedly, it occurred to me that my father purposefully drove his girlfriend into the city, to the hospital closest to my office… so I would be forced to go stand in for him. That particular bit of betrayal hit me especially hard. My stomach pricked at the same second my eyes did.

"I'll call Abuelita," Graham mumbled, pulling me to the door. "I hired a new car service yesterday—I'll send that car for her to come meet us there. You and I will hail a cab."

I spun around in a half circle, panicked. "I can't just *leave*!"

His hands cupped either side of my jaw while his dark eyes melted into mine, calming me. "You have to. I'll deal with Grayson. He probably planned on sending you home today, anyway, given the rest of the floor was dismissed."

How could I simply walk out of the office… and *today* of all days? But what other choice did I have? Could I really just leave Lucia there?

"No, Graham, I can't—I don't want to—" How did I explain the horrible feeling crushing my chest? Guilt and panic and absolute *shock*.

Abuelita picked up before I could finish. His halting, sloppy Spanish floundered through an explanation until I held out my hand and took over the call. While we talked, Graham rushed me out to the elevators and then across the first floor lobby.

He hailed a taxi and explained the situation as I hung up and handed his phone back to him. He immediately dialed for his car service while our cabbie attempted to break every traffic law in existence simultaneously.

On one hand, it was good the rest of the ride passed quickly, because Lucia obviously needed help. On the other, I had *no clue* what to do once I actually got there. Twice, Graham had to reach across the seat and smooth his fingers over mine to still their nervous tapping.

It alarmed me how badly I wanted to bring him into the hospital with me. I debated how I could possibly explain his presence to Lucia… and Abuelita. In the end, I realized the poor girl giving birth with strangers probably wouldn't appreciate if one of them was a man. An attractive, young man at that.

When we pulled up to the ER, I turned to tell him I had to leave him behind, only to find him smiling wistfully at me. "I know," he said, then nodded at the building. "Go. I told you; you know where to find me."

You can do this, I told myself. *Game face. You've got this.*

Though, as I walked through the automatic doors, I couldn't help but recall… the last time I gave myself the same pep talk was the same day I met Graham Everett. And the man had unexpectedly stolen past every last one of my defenses.

Chapter Twenty-eight

February 21, 2017

Juliet

It was well after midnight when Abuelita shook me awake.

I snapped to, jerking upright in the plastic waiting room chair, ready for some sort of emergency. Instead, Abuelita smiled. A twinkle lit her dark eyes.

"Julieta," she murmured, almost sounding… soft. "*Vamos. Tu tienes un hermano.*"

Blinking sleep from my eyes, I followed her down the familiar stretch of hallway I spent the better part of twenty-four hours pacing. In the third room on the left, I found Lucia.

Gone was the petrified, stammering girl I spent the day consoling and advocating for. In her place, a small-but-radiant woman held a white-swathed bundle to her bare chest. Her cheeks glowed deep rose when she spotted me on the threshold.

"Juliet," she whispered, and then smiled at me for the very first time. "Do you want to see?"

It absolutely floored me how much I wanted to see. My gaze locked on the little bundle as some unknown force pulled me across the room. "*Sí.*"

I felt Abuelita hovering behind me, watching as I came to stand at Lucia's shoulder and peer down at the tiny face pressed to her breast.

My heart swelled as my eyes stung. "*Qué… perfecto.*"

Perfect. It was the only word for him. My baby brother—with his head of velvety black hair, his rumpled, rounded features, and the tiny rosebud lips that quivered while he dreamed.

"You want to hold him?" Lucia offered, beaming. "Here."

Without warning, she handed me the baby. He didn't so much as stir while his solid warmth settled into my bosom. I shifted his weight, finding that I knew exactly how to cradle him.

My body seemed to have a mind of its own. While warmth sluiced through my center, I found myself tracing his tiny, sweet cheek with the back of one finger. The motion tickled him—his little lips reflexively pulled up in the world's smallest half-smile.

And I was done for.

Finished. Utterly enchanted.

"*Ay Dios mío,*" I whispered. *I love him.*

The instant devotion left me dazed, staring down at his little face in wonder. Abuelita set her hand on my shoulder and ran the other over my baby brother's hair. "He look likes you did, *Julieta.*"

Instinctively, my arms held him closer. "He's my brother," I announced to the room, sniffing back tears and lifting my chin. "*Of course* he looks like me."

He nuzzled into my chest with an adorable snorting sound. I felt like my heart may burst out to touch him. And I realized, all at once, that I would do *anything* for him.

"*Es un amor imposible, no?*" Abuelita said.

It is an impossible love.

And, yet, so very real. Tears slipped down my face. Still holding my baby brother, I felt behind me for the nearest chair and lowered myself into it. I stared down at our little miracle, with love bursting through my entire being. The impossible love—so deep and real and sure and *true*… it made every other truth obvious.

Because, in all honesty, I'd felt that way before. Not *exactly* the same—less warmth, more heat; less sudden, more surprising—but an equally unparalleled sensation. For one other man. For *my* man.

It sprang out of me, like a tight coil someone finally released. "I love him."

A hundred memories flooded my mind. Graham's intense black eyes staring down at me the first time we kissed, imploring me to stop him. His consternation as he offered me the red handkerchief in the stairwell. The ludicrous slippers he pulled off effortlessly.

The night I came to his apartment and he asked me to dance with him, just so he could hold me for a moment before we took our clothes off. His possessive, attentive love-making—always about me, even when it was for him. All the times he seemed to know just what I needed, when I didn't.

His generous heart. His hands massaging my feet, scrubbing my dishes, holding my head between his palms as if my mind contained some mysterious treasure only he could see. Those quick, feral grins. The way he tried to leap to action the second anyone he cared for needed help.

So many moments when, deep inside, I *knew*.

I *loved* him.

I'd loved him so much, for so long, that it was mortifying to realize how utterly clueless I was not to recognize it. How could I have ever tried to leave him? Why? *Because he decided to blow up his life to protect…*

His baby brother.

I stared down into my baby brother's sweet face and realized I'd do the same thing for him. Today. That very moment. In half a heartbeat. Of course Graham had to give up all of his family's wealth, if it meant saving Christian from going to prison one day.

As understanding trickled through me, I had a brief moment where I loved Graham even *more* for what he chose to do… and then a swift jolt of shame kicked me in the gut.

He told me he loved me and I left him the very next day… because he sacrificed himself to save his brother? That's what I told myself, all of the times I doubted my decision—that his choices made things too complicated for me…

How on earth did I convince myself to believe that *mierda*?

I was Juliet Isabelle Rivera. I did *not* run from a fight.

So… what did I run from?

Abuelita began clucking in Spanish, muttering about my father, lamenting how her son turned out to be such a "gutless pig". The shame pulsing in my center doubled as Lucia caught my eye and shot me a questioning glance—she clearly didn't speak our language as fluently as I originally thought.

"She is…" I started, searching for the right words while my eyes traced the baby's sweet features again. "She wonders how my dad could ever miss this."

Lucia's gaze snagged on her son. Her expression remained tranquil while sadness filled her gaze. "He is afraid of us," she said simply.

…

"What?"

Lucia shrugged one shoulder, the sluggish gesture betraying her exhaustion. "When I heard the stories about your father and your mother," she started. "I was worried. I thought, maybe, that I'd fallen for a man who couldn't love. But, then, he *could*. He loved me very much. Easily, actually. I was surprised by that…"

It hurt to listen to her. My heart ached for Mami. But I was also intrigued. I'd always assumed, like Lucia did, that my father just couldn't love anyone because he was too selfish…

What if that wasn't quite right?

Lucia continued. "He didn't start acting distant and strange until I got closer to our due date. Finally, one day, I realized: he was *terrified.* He drank too much one night and came to bed, talking nonsense. But one thing he kept saying, over and over, was, 'I love you too much.'"

The hairs at the back of my neck stood upright. My arms automatically tightened around my precious *hermanito*. "Too much?"

"He said he loved me too much," she confirmed, with a sound nod. "And when he wouldn't stop saying it, I realized he meant he loved me too much to stay with me. That's when I knew he would leave me, the same way he left you and your mom. It was my own fault—I knew the stories but I thought I'd be different."

My mother's abiding adoration for the man never made sense to me—why would anyone love someone incapable of loving them back? I always wondered… until the day I unearthed the photo from their honeymoon and viewed it through new eyes, finally recognizing a snapshot taken by a man in love.

So, if he originally loved my mother as much as she loved him, why did he abandon her? If he loved me, why did he drift in and out of the fringes of my life instead of remaining a central fixture? If he loved Lucia, why did he drop her off at the hospital and run for the hills?

Was it really because loving *any* of us paralyzed him with *fear*?

A horrifying thought occurred to me. After spending my entire life working to make sure I didn't end up like my mother… did I somehow wind up being like my *father* instead? Running from someone who loved me… *because* I loved him, too?

Because I loved him… *too much*… and that petrified me.

Abuelita caught my eye. Her solemn expression told me she understood every word Lucia said. And, moreover, she *agreed.*

Her dark brown eyes bored into mine. "Is normal. Beings afraid. But the courage is rare."

A hot rush of fresh tears flooded my face. Lucia shook her head slowly, her own eyes watering. "I only regret that Julio won't be here for Hugo."

I turned back to my brother's perfect face and tested his name out. "Hugo?"

Another tired half-shrug. "It's not the name we originally chose, but I like it better. It's as close to *Julieta* as I could get without naming him *Julio*."

Abuelita squeezed my shoulders. My vision swam as I lost the battle with my emotions. I tossed my hair back and sniffed. "Well it's *perfect*. Obviously."

I offered Hugo my finger, marveling when he instinctively wrapped his own around it. "We will be great friends, won't we?" I whispered. "I think you're going to come live at—"

Carajo. I didn't even have a place for Lucia to bring him home.

My head snapped up just in time to catch Lucia casting Abuelita a guilty glance. "Actually…" she mumbled. "Abuelita offered me the spare bedroom at their house…"

I turned to my grandmother, who suddenly wore her sternest game face. It made me want to smile for some reason. "This is why you picked the house with the third bedroom, isn't it?" I asked.

Abuelita waved a dismissive hand. "*No comprendo ingles, muñeca.*"

At seven A.M., a delivery arrived.

Just as I started to panic about showing up for work in the same clothes as the day before—and whether I should show up for work at all, actually—Marco knocked on the door.

Lucia had just finished nursing Hugo. They both slept under Abuelita's watchful eye while my cousin swept into the room with his arms completely full of flowers and bags.

He laid out four floral arrangements on the table in the corner, along with two shopping bags. When I raised my eyebrows at him, he raised his right back.

"Everett," he reported, nodding at the bags. "Had it all waiting for me this morning at Grayson's. Clothes for you to wear to work, he said. And shoes."

I sighed. *El pinchao* did like to dress me. It might irritate me if it didn't turn me on. "And the flowers?"

Marco pointed to the happiest arrangement—a collection of yellow roses and sprigs of green. "That's from Grayson and Ella, for Lucia. The rest are from Everett. The blue ones for Lucia and the baby, the white ones for Abuelita, and those"—he gestured to a lovely collection of red ranunculus and fuchsia orchids—"are yours."

Of course they are. The flashiest of the group, all elegance and bold, sensual color. How very Graham.

I loved them.

Without an ounce of grace, I ripped into the first bag I touched and pulled out a gorgeous crimson bustier, trimmed in handmade black lace. Marco's expression darkened. A second later, I unearthed a completely professional red dress—intended to go over the lingerie, of course.

"I truly cannot decide whether I need to kick that guy's ass or not," my cousin muttered.

I smirked, recalling our first meeting in the elevator. "Join the club."

"At least you got a good swing in," he grumbled, crossing his arms over his black tee shirt. He jerked his chin at the bed. "The baby's… good?"

Dios mío. Men.

"He's perfect," I reported. "Did Abuelita tell you he's going to be your new tenant?"

Marco nodded, unbothered. "My mom is in heaven. She went baby shopping yesterday for, like, six hours."

That sounded like Tía Esme. I chuckled. "I think it will be good for her to have a new baby boy to dote on. Since you're, you know, *thirty*."

He rolled his eyes, but cracked a reluctant smile. "So you are going in today? I know Grayson texted you to tell you that you didn't have to, but he asked me to reiterate the offer."

Honestly, I was dying to get back to work. I felt unsettled without it. Plus, I needed to get the lay of the land now that my boss was gone. Would they hire someone with more experience than Dominic? Or—dare I hope—perhaps even a woman?

"I want to go in," I told him. "Can you drive me?"

He shrugged. "Sure. But, I mean, it's like four blocks away."

I pulled out the Christian Louboutin box with a grimace. "Yeah, but these are four-hundred-dollar shoes."

His expression twisted. "*No joda?* Damn. '*El pinchao*' is right."

My heart gave a pang. He may not be *el pinchao* much longer, if he couldn't figure out a way to keep G&C Capital and all of the profits he'd earned thus far…

I bolted upright in my chair. "We need to go."

Marco looked at his Apple Watch. "Not until, like, eight-thirty…"

"No," I snapped, snatching my new outfit out of its bag. "We need to go to Grayson's. Now. I have to talk to him. Right away."

I knew exactly what to do. To save Graham. To show him how much I cared. But I only had a few hours to get it done. Sensing my urgency, Marco stood and started toward the door without hesitation. "I'll make the call."

Graham

I decided, if I ever wrote a memoir, I'd use the word "surreal."

There really was no other way to describe standing at the end of Everett Alexander's hated hallway, watching FBI agents and forensic techs rip through every room of my family's company with the same sort of methodical determination they'd use to disarm a terrorist cell.

Off to the left, near the elevators, Rachel and Ava hovered with their phones in their hands, each typing a million miles a second. Rachel wore another of her boxy pantsuits, while Ava was dressed to kill in an emerald jumpsuit and black spiked heels. Being polar opposites, I worried they might clash—turned out they got along swimmingly.

"You know," Ava commented, not looking up from her iPhone. "If you wore tapered suit jackets, you wouldn't look so butch."

"I am butch," Rachel replied easily, still typing.

Ava's fingers didn't even pause. "Ah."

I repressed a snort and went back to observing. The team already cleared my old office, the file room, seven traders' offices. My father's was next.

Inside the pocket of my navy suit, my hand clenched into a fist. Ironic—the last time I wore the same outfit—complete with the white vest, tie, and red handkerchief—I had to fist my hands in my pockets for an entirely different reason.

I knew Dad was in there, with his lawyer, waiting. A captain going down with his ship. At least, Ava claimed, that's how she would spin it if she were doing *his* PR.

As it stood, though, she had every news network in the city outside, awaiting his perp walk. I'd already spent the better half of the morning at a press conference, delivering the statement she wrote for me.

I originally thought I'd make my speech *after* I watched my legacy go through the shredder. But Ava and Rachel explained the importance of setting the narrative before anyone else could create one. That meant speaking to the press before a single photo of my father in handcuffs hit the internet.

I wondered if Jules had turned on the news yet, wherever she was. I tried not to let it bother me that I never heard from her after sending her the clothes and flowers. My watch informed me that it wasn't even midday, though.

I need to relax. She just spent a day and night helping her dad's girlfriend give birth. She probably raced right to office this morning, running on fumes.

Still, it stung that she couldn't reach out to me. Today of all days. As much as I hated it… I needed her.

I resisted the urge to rock on my heels. No matter how anxious I felt, I had to stay still. Rachel said any body language observed by a federal agent was admissible as evidence.

I'd already caught Shondra glancing at me multiple times. Waiting for me to fuck up, most likely. The fist in my pocket tightened as I met her gaze from across the hall.

She stood at the opposite end, interviewing my dad's watering-pot of an assistant. Her attention snapped from me to my father's office the second her colleagues approached it. I read her lips as she excused herself and strode forward, joining her fellow agents while one rapped on my father's door.

"Mr. Everett?" she called, pounding the slab again. "FBI. We have a warrant for your arrest and we're coming in!"

The team burst into his office, where I heard a small scuffle and then nothing but the sound of handcuffs. One of the larger men on the team held my dad's bound hands behind his back as he shoved him out into the hallway, glibly stating his Miranda rights en route to the elevators beside me.

The herd of agents accompanying Hugh huddled at his back as he faced me, teeth bared.

"How could you do this?" he demanded, yelling over his attorney's warnings to stay silent. "How could you do this to your own *father*?"

I wanted to tell him I hadn't planned on it—that I wouldn't have, if he hadn't positioned Christian as his patsy. But, of course, I couldn't say any of that.

I held his irate gaze as long as I could, knowing it might be the last time I ever got to see him up close. "I feel sorry for you," I told him, giving as much honesty as I was allowed. "It didn't have to be like this."

He lunged at me, but barely managed to squirm before three agents steered him onto the elevators. He screamed and fought while the door slid closed, his jeers incoherent when mixed with the agents' threats and his attorney's objections.

I expected the scene, almost exactly as it played out. So why did I still feel gutted? My fist tightened more, finally ripping the pocket's seam.

Goddamn it. I just want Juliet.

At my back, Ava clapped with glee. "He's *furious*," she exulted, hailing another elevator. "It's going to be *perfect* for pictures. I'll go down now and make sure the paps have the correct story to go along with the images. Then I'll shoo everyone off. Wait twenty minutes before you come down."

With that, she disappeared. Rachel stepped up and shook her head appreciatively. "Absolutely *vicious*. I like her. She's straight, though, right?"

I blew a deep breath out of my nose, exasperated. "Afraid so."

She shrugged and went back to her phone. Shondra finished murmuring to her colleagues and sent the rest of them down the next available lift before rounding on us.

"Mr. Everett," she said, clipping over to our spot. "Ms. Black. I think we're done here. I'll be in contact with you about your testimony for the trial, though these cases typically take a few months to reach the judge's desk. Oh, and, Mr. Everett, my people back at the office informed me that they received two notarized affidavits shortly after our raid began. I asked that they be forwarded to me here."

I started to open my stupid mouth and ask what the fuck she was talking about, but Rachel held up her hand, halting me and stepping forward, eyebrows furrowed. "Give me those."

She ripped the copies from Shondra's hand and read them, turning each over twice before pushing them into my chest and casting me a *shut-the-hell-up* look.

"Yes," she told Shondra, "We were expecting those to come through. I assume that…"

Their conversation faded into the background while I read the documents as quickly as I could, my eyes flying from the sworn statements to the signatures beneath them. *Grayson Stryker*, one said.

And the other, clear as day—*Juliet Rivera.*

Their names, each signed under *lies.*

They both testified that I approached them about my new venture, G&C Capital, the morning before I took home the tainted Everett Alexander books. Grayson claimed I told him between our two meetings. Juliet stated that she was informed while we rode the elevator together…

None of it was true. They knew the potential consequences should anyone prove them liars. But they signed their names to false facts. For me.

My eyes scanned the date on each affidavit. *Today.* That's *where she's been all morning…*

Getting to Stryker, explaining what they needed to do, convincing him to commit perjury, crafting the statements, finding a notary to sign them… All of it must have taken every available second she had to get them sent out in time.

I'd never worked harder to keep a smile off of my lips. Dazed by nerves and gratitude, I barely managed a poker face as I tuned back in to the women's discussion.

"...able to keep G&C Capital running in the future?"

Shondra met my gaze instead of looking at Rachel. A knowing gleam shone there, telling me she knew as well as I did that the sworn statements in my hand were *bullshit.*

But she *smiled.*

"With those affidavits," she said, "our agency will have no choice but to drop the pending investigation into G&C Capital and Mr. Everett's personal holdings. They can no longer qualify as fruit of the poison tree. So, yes, Mr. Everett will be able to keep G&C Capital. And its profits. Past and future."

Fuck. Yes.

Rachel's grip dug into my forearm, warning me to stay calm. Next to impossible, when I wanted to pump my fist into the air and shout.

I couldn't quite help myself. I grinned as I nodded. "Excellent. Thank you for taking them into evidence."

Shondra shrugged. "An officer of the court and one of the most influential CEO's in the country? We'd *never* assume two upstanding professionals were spinning lies."

Jesus. I owed Stryker. And Juliet. *Everything.*

Why would she do this for me? I wondered, watching while Rachel and Shondra exchanged a handful of barbs. *Does she...*

I couldn't think straight. I'd never been through such a wide array of emotions in such a short span of time. Shock, dread, fear, joy, gratitude.

And then, right before my eyes, my attorney and Shondra exchanged phone numbers. For the first time since I met her, Rachel actually *blushed.* Then she squared her shoulders and marched off, mumbling something about interviewing the secretary for herself.

Shondra snagged my wide eyes and—I swear—she *winked.* "You had to wonder why I'd tip you off about the best attorney in Manhattan. I've been wanting to ask her out forever. So thanks for that." She put both her hands into her pockets. "Oh," she added, "By the way…"

From her pants, she extracted a small blue Tiffany box. The one I'd stashed in the safe…

"I found this," she went on, frowning down at the case. "It was in your dad's safe but it had a receipt with your name on it folded inside. I'd take that out of there before you pop the question. I almost passed out when I saw the dollar figure."

Unceremoniously, she tossed me the box. My numb fingers caught it. "Isn't this part of your search or whatever?" I asked, not quite believing my luck.

Shondra shook her head. "We aren't investigating *you* or seizing *your* assets." Her eyes fell on the papers still pressed between my arm and my jacket. "Especially now. And the ring is clearly yours, not Hugh's. So take it. Better for you to use it for its intended purpose than for it to molder in some evidence bin for all eternity."

I snapped the case open, peering down at the emerald-cut diamond and its shimmering frame of matching stones. *Maybe one day…* I caught myself thinking, fishing the receipt out. *If I wear her down. If she falls in love with me.*

The small ember of hope was a thing of the past. Now, a roaring blaze of determination took its place, warming my insides. I *would* get my ring on that gorgeous woman. As soon as possible.

"Thanks," I said, meaning it.

Shondra glanced at her wristwatch and hit the elevator button. "I'd say it's been about twenty minutes," she commented, and then walked off.

I slipped the golden affidavits into my breast pocket and wrapped my handkerchief around the ring case, hoping to keep it from getting scratched in my one remaining pocket. With a final glance at the past I thought would become my future, I stepped into the lift.

I'd seen enough.

Juliet

Marco kept looking at me.

"Stop it," I snapped, but the words lost their heat when they passed through my smiling lips.

He raised his hands innocently against the steering wheel. "I didn't say anything."

He didn't need to. He saw the whole thing. Watched me run out of the hospital without shoes on, witnessed me turning up unannounced at the Stryker's townhome and interrupting their breakfast. Stood outside Grayson's study while we crafted our absurdly false statements. Dashed us both across town to Stryker & Sons so Beth could notarize them.

After our work was done, before I even considered how to approach the subject of leaving to go be with Graham, Mr. Stryker frantically waved me out of his office.

"Well, *go*," he urged. "He'll want you there, not me."

Now, half an hour later, Marco sped around the final corner to get me to my destination. The Mercedes slid to a stop and I jumped out.

"Should I wait?" he called.

"No!" Because I wasn't going to wait anymore, either. I needed to tell Graham everything.

I rushed in from the throng of off-duty cameramen and reporters, all packing up their news vans. My head swiveled as I looked around the plaza in front of the sky-rise, hoping I hadn't missed him.

I pulled out my phone to call him just as the revolving door swung open, revealing a sinfully handsome man in a dark blue suit. He jaunted out, hands in his pockets, moving in a way I found all-too familiar and all-too appealing.

A slow grin spread over my face.

"Hey, *pinchao*!"

Graham's steps faltered. He halted, standing two dozen feet away from me.

For a long moment, he simply stared, drinking me in as pedestrians milled between us. He didn't seem to mind that I hadn't refreshed my makeup or touched my hair in thirty-some hours. Our electric current snapped to life, crackling across the distance. He pivoted, turning to face me head-on without moving any closer.

I held my ground, refusing to run to him. "You were wrong!" I called.

The slightest hint of a smirk made him impossibly more handsome. "Oh, yeah? Why this time?"

Blood rushed through my ears, drowning out the traffic behind me, the people around us. Everything but him.

Courage, I reminded myself, stepping closer.

"When I left; you said I was afraid because you told me that you loved me," I went on. "And yesterday, you said it again. That I ran from you because you love me. But you were wrong."

I wasn't sure how we crept closer together. How many steps were his, how many were mine… I didn't know. But we drifted toward one another, drawn like planets creating their own orbit. He came close enough for me to touch, but I didn't. I wanted to get everything out first.

Staring into his dark, heated gaze gave me the words I needed. "I didn't get scared because you said you loved me," I explained, raising my chin. "I was afraid because I loved you, too. More than I ever loved anyone else before."

A spark ignited in his midnight depths. He reached over, carefully tracing his fingertips along the slant of my jaw before he touched my chin, his expression unfathomable. "You love me or you love*d* me?"

This was it. The moment I had to be brave. Only, now that it had arrived, I wasn't scared anymore. We'd gone through so much, already—this was our other side. And it felt right.

I took his face between my hands, holding him steady while I looked right into him. "I *love* you, Graham Fucking Everett."

Electric determination swirled in his eyes. "You love me?"

"Yes," I confirmed, holding my head higher. "I do."

"And you want us to be together? For real? No matter what happens?"

Of course he had to ask me that. I'd made every excuse to hide from my feelings for him. "Yes. None of the rest of it matters. It never really mattered. I was just… afraid. But now I'm not. Now I know. *I love you.*"

I expected him to kiss me. Instead, he held my gaze with his for a long beat, searching my depths. Finally, he moved, slipping out of my hands and stepping back.

"Well," he said, "in that case…"

Graham suddenly dropped, going to one knee right there on the pavement. From his pocket, he extracted a red ball of fabric.

The handkerchief. Wrapped around a small, bright blue box.

A ring box.

As he extended both, offering me everything, his eyes burned into mine. "Marry me."

"How did you—" Graham's mouth landed on mine, occupying my tongue for a moment before moving back to my neck. "—have a ring?"

He bit the place below my ear that always made my knees wobble, then gave a satisfied hum when I quivered. "I bought it before Valentine's Day," he said against my clavicle. "The second I saw it, I knew it was yours. Ours."

"You're crazy." I moaned as he ran his tongue over the pulse fluttering in my throat. My fingers dug into his back. "*Graham.*"

"I know, *bijou*, I know," he rumbled, trailing his lips along my jaw next. "I will have you the second this elevator opens and we get into the apartment. Promise."

I didn't even know if I'd make it *that* far. But I still felt compelled to ask, "Don't we have a lot of things we need to talk about?"

He held himself over me with his forearm pressed into the padded elevator wall, then pulled back just far enough to cock an eyebrow. "You mean *fight* about?"

Knowing us, probably.

"We just got engaged," I pointed out instead of agreeing. "We have about a thousand things to figure out."

An ecstatic grin broke across his dark features. He swooped down and kissed me full on the lips again. "God, I love that. Say that again."

"We're engaged," I whispered, unable to keep myself from mirroring his expression.

With a grunt, he hauled me up into his arms, pushing my dress up my thighs and slinging my legs around his waist. Cradling my head as he sealed his mouth over mine, he kissed me like a wild man, devouring every last bit of my self-control.

"Jules, baby," he hummed between glides of his tongue. "I love you so damn much."

Brushing my hands through his hair, I pulled myself closer. "I love you, too."

The doors slid open. Graham made short work of the distance to his apartment, spinning us inside within seconds. As the electronic lock clicked at our backs, he started undressing me without skipping a beat.

"Graham," I moaned again, tilting my head back when he pulled my dress down my arms and bit my shoulder blade. "We have to *talk*."

"Hmmm." He rubbed his stubbled jaw along the lace lining my cleavage. "How about you keep talking and I keep doing this and we see who gives in first?"

He sucked the swell of my breast into his mouth and I gasped, tightening my legs around his torso. Inside the frilled cups, my nipples hardened instantly.

"Seriously," I argued, short of breath. "I'm technically homeless right now."

Graham gave an unimpressed snort. "Gonna have to try harder than that," he mumbled to my skin, then moved to unhook the bustier altogether. "You'll live here. Obviously."

I secretly hoped he'd say that. I loved his place. I loved *us* in his place. Though, I had some conditions…

"I want to pay rent."

That managed to trip him up for all of two seconds. "No way. I own the place. You're not paying me rent," he insisted before drawing my pebbled nipple into his mouth.

Ay, Dios.

A broken sound tore out of me. My entire body arched, pushing myself as close to him as I could get. "Fight about it later?" I offered weakly, unable to think straight.

He seemed distracted as well. His free hand palmed my other breast, weighing it, as his hungry eyes roamed down to where my panties rubbed against his fly. "…yeah, fine."

With my nipple out of his mouth, I could finally recall what else I wanted to say. "I don't want a big wedding," I panted.

"Is 500 people big?" he asked, toeing off his shoes and flicking my heels from my feet.

I went for his vest, starved for the sight of his bare body. "Fight about it later?"

"Yep."

He set me down just long enough to discard my dress and his pants, then picked me right back up. While we both worked on his shirt and tie, I added, "And I don't want any babies for *at least* three years."

He nodded that time. "Agreed. Two or three?"

"Years?"

"Babies."

"*Babies?!*" I guffawed, recalling the scene of Lucia in labor. "Um, *one*."

He wagged his head back and forth, considering as he watched my fingers free his last button from its slip. Just before I shucked the shirt, he said, "Fine. Deal."

Our mouths met, tongues gliding together. He reached for my panties, feeling the outline of my wetness while I traced his waistband. His rock-hard cock pressed into the soft spot between my sex and my hip, sending an ache through my core.

I was ready to give in, admit defeat… when he made a statement of his own. "We'll need a bigger place," he huffed, leaning back just far enough to glance into my eyes. "For family. I like the San Remo."

"I like this one," I returned.

His chest heaved as he looked down at my soaked underwear, his raging erection. "Fight about it later?"

"Okay."

I went for his cock, stroking him through his silk boxers until he groaned my name. Which reminded me… "I'm not changing my name."

Graham spun us, walked a few steps across the hall, and pushed me back into the opposite wall, balancing me there while he removed both our pairs of underwear.

"So I get to call you 'Miss Rivera' forever? Done."

"And we're going to need a pre-nup," I pointed out, watching him sink to his knees and open my legs around his shoulders.

"Another contract negotiation," he muttered, eyeing my sex like priceless jewel. "…that will be fun. Think we can borrow Pod C?" Before I replied, he stopped me. "Hold on a second for me, will you?"

Without wasting another breath, his tongue found the trembling opening of my pussy, licking in a circle. He gave a snarl so salacious I thought I'd come then and there, then he kissed and sucked and devoured me as if I was his first meal in weeks.

Raw, urgent need spiraled through me. I squeezed my legs around him and ground myself into his working mouth.

His hums of approval and praise vibrated over my slick, sensitive flesh. I cried his name again, sifting my fingers through his thick hair and pulling at the roots. "I missed you so much," I sobbed, beyond thought.

Pulling back to gaze up, Graham pushed two fingers into me. He used his other hand to press into the hollow beneath my belly. The combination of pressure and penetration made me writhe against him, moaning once more.

When he pulled the swollen bud of my clit between his lips and lashed it with his tongue, I let go, unable to stem the stream of Spanish praises that flowed out of me without any translation.

With a satisfied groan of his own, he held me into the wall and rose back to his feet. One of his hands shackled my wrists, then, holding them above my head the way he liked. With the other, he lifted and angled me, thrusting upward to finally bring our bodies together.

The second he pushed all the way in, I felt how close he hovered to the edge. His cock throbbed so hard, I felt it pulsating. A serrated sound ripped from his chest. His hands clutched at me restlessly as he squeezed his eyes shut, doing his best to prolong our moment.

I brushed his hair back and nuzzled my cheek into his, gentling him. "I love you," I whispered again, knowing he would need to hear me say it, over and over, to make up for all the time I lost being afraid.

His eyes flickered open; two dark, swirling pools of wounded longing. "I love you more."

He would think that until I convinced him otherwise. But I wasn't worried; I would make sure he knew how much I adored him. "No," I argued softly. "You don't."

Graham held my face between his hands, pinning me with a loving gaze so fierce, it pierced my soul. "Fight about it later?"

I pressed my forehead into his and offered him a small smile, tightening my legs to pull myself closer, making us one. "Fight about it forever."

One Month Later

March 24, 2017

Graham

My fiancée stepped out of the elevator right on cue, smiling to herself until she saw me lingering outside our door.

I took a moment to drink her in. A month of living together had done nothing to diminish her appeal. It seemed to grow, day by day… hour by hour, sometimes. When she left for work that morning, with her hair half-back, wearing her silky emerald dress, I thought she couldn't possibly look any sexier. Yet, there she stood, proving me wrong.

Her black eyebrows folded together while she glided over, coming close enough for me to kiss her cheek before she frowned up at me. "What are you doing out here, *amor*? Isn't everyone inside?"

I pressed my nose into the jasmine-scented place behind her ear and inhaled. The moment we reunited each evening had come to be my very favorite part of every day. "I wanted a minute alone with you," I told her, plucking her tote bag and purse out of her arms so I could wrap her up in mine.

Without giving too much away, I surreptitiously read her features, searching for any trace of pride or elation or anxiety. My *bijou* had a one-track mind, though. She slid her arms around my neck and pressed the length of her body into mine.

"A minute alone?" she hummed, her golden eyes shimmering like champagne. "Whatever for, Mr. Everett?"

God. Would the day ever come when she couldn't make my blood roar with a single look? I hoped not.

On a quiet growl, I sealed my lips over hers. Pouring all of my adoration in our kiss, I moved her back into the wall, bending my knee between her legs and suspending myself over her with my bent arms.

"I missed you," I confessed. It still bewildered me, how I could long for someone I saw all the time, even when I knew I'd see her again in hours.

Her fingers combed into my hair while her gaze flickered down over my outfit—the notorious pink suit. A glimmer of amusement touched the sensual curves of her mouth. "Me, too, *pinchao*."

Our gazes locked. I probed her depths, searching for some indication that she might have news for me… But damn if the woman didn't have a world-class poker face.

Finally, I broke. "So….?" I asked, raising my brows. "Anything to tell me…?"

A slow grin stretched over her face. "What are you talking about?" she asked, a touch too shrill. "I didn't say I had any news, did I?"

No, she didn't. But I *knew*.

"Come on, tell me," I begged, bending to brush my lips over the sensitive spot at the base of her throat. "I've known for weeks and I can't fucking take it. I'm horrible at keeping secrets."

Another new discovery I'd made about myself since acquiring a sexy, all-too-observant fiancée.

"I thought something weird might be going on when you started giving me the third-degree every day after work." She shook her head, still smiling at me. "Why didn't you just *ask* him when it was happening?"

I read between the lines. "So he did it?" I demanded, holding my breath. "He told you?"

Juliet's lustrous laughter filled the hallway. "Yes!" she finally burst, gripping my shoulders. "He told me today. You are looking at the new director of Stryker & Sons' legal department."

I scooped her into my arms and spun her in a circle. I'd never felt such pride. My gorgeous, brilliant future wife. She never ceased to amaze me.

"Actually," I corrected, bringing my face back to hers. "I'm kissing her."

Jules let me have my way with her for a few minutes before pulling back to give me my favorite scolding expression. "You knew and you didn't tell me?!"

Yes. And I *hated* it.

"When Stryker told me he was going to promote you, I figured he'd do it right away," I groused. "I never thought he'd wait *three weeks*. Asshole. I ought to punch him. It's been a few years since we beat the shit out of each other, anyway. We're probably due."

Juliet giggled, rolling her eyes. "You're absurd. Besides, he's been a little… busy." Some of the joy drained from her face as she looked down at her nude heels, scuffing one over the floor. "Ella still isn't doing any better."

My chest seized up every time I thought about my best friend's fiancée and everything she'd been through. A familiar, helpless sort of rage burned through me. I grit my teeth, pushing it down; this was Juliet's special night. I couldn't let anything detract from all of her hard work.

"Well, tonight is all about you," I told her, hoping to distract us both. "And we better go in soon. Abuelita is here, ordering Christian around the kitchen. I don't know what terrifies him more—being out of rehab for the night or the possibility that he might misunderstand one of her orders."

Most patients couldn't wait for someone to break them out of the rehabilitation center, but my little brother clung to it the way someone lost at sea would cleave to a dinghy. I'd only coaxed him out twice, and both times he spent the entire excursion twitching.

Jules mouth curved into a thoughtful scowl. "Poor guy. You hid all the wine right?"

"I put the bottles in your boots," I reported, smirking at the memory. "I think Hugo is successfully distracting him, though. Kid loves babies."

My fiancée pursed her lips, attempting to hold back a smug grin. "And you don't?"

I held up my hands, relenting. "He's pretty damn cute, I admit."

"You *love* him!" Juliet accused, bending to retrieve her things. "You can't deny it after last weekend. I caught you *singing* to him."

I snatched both bags from her, pouting. "It was *one* good song. Van Morrison. You *have* to sing to Van Morrison."

But *bijou* knew better. She gave a knowing chuckle. "Sure. And, if I remember correctly, didn't you *volunteer* to change his diaper?"

Jesus. I'd never get away with anything ever again.

Why did I *love* it?

"Lucia's hands were full!"

"Uh-huh," she bleated, nodding at the apartment. "I'm sure they were."

"Look," I joked, pushing the door open, "I'm sleeping with Hugo's hot sister. It's literally his job to give me shit."

"Hmm." Juliet brushed a sweet kiss over my lips. "Don't worry, *pinchao*," she murmured, sauntering past me. "I won't tell."

Where I used to dread returning to my empty apartment, now, coming home was my very favorite thing to do. Well, that… and pushing into Juliet. Both types of home-coming, I suppose.

We found Christian sitting at the island, diligently peeling potatoes with the same somber devotion to detail he displayed in most things. On the red couch, Juliet's aunt cooed to little Hugo.

The baby looked zonked. He didn't even flinch when Juliet sailed straight over to him, bubbling a stream of Spanish endearments before dropping kisses on his downy black hair.

Slipping out of my jacket, I leaned into the counter to watch until I caught my own brother smirking at me. When I met his eyes, he grunted, "*Whipped*."

Oh completely.

"Fuck you," I muttered on principle, rolling my sleeves. I took his peeled potatoes and reached for a knife. "Abuelita," I called, "*Como quiere las papas?*"

"*Cuarteadas*."

I started to cut them into quarters. Juliet slipped up behind me and pressed her face against my shoulder. "*Muy bien, pinchao*. Have you been practicing?"

I nodded. "I don't want your mother to think I'm a bumbling idiot when we visit next month," I stage-whispered. "And I can't stand it when you talk over my head. You know how nosy I am."

It was more than that, though. Juliet and her family had become my own in a way I never experienced with my father or mother. I wanted to fully participate when we all got together.

Christian already fit right in, thanks to multiple years of AP Spanish. Abuelita took a shine to him immediately. She fussed over his pitiful ass, doting on him each week by sending Marco or Jules running to Chelsea with baskets of Colombian pastries or Tupperware full of *empanadas* and *arepas*.

Occasionally, I got special deliveries, too. They arrived at the temporary workspace I rented in the Flatiron District, often without so much as a note. But, usually, Abuelita just invited herself over. More than once, I came home to discover her alone in my kitchen, cooking up a storm.

Juliet seemed mortified by her tendency to help herself. I secretly loved it. It reminded me of the night I found Jules making *ajiaco* in my sweats. It also touched that long-withered piece of me where only maternal affection could reach.

Plus, I mean, the *food*…

Juliet's eyes filled with love and appreciation, beaming up at me. "I know. And your trainwreck of an accent has finally sorted itself out."

Chris chortled again. "God, that was funny."

The first time I took Juliet to meet him, a couple days after our engagement, the two of them sank into Spanish almost immediately… then spent the rest of the morning gleefully mocking my attempts to keep up. I might have been put-out if Jules didn't distract me with a blow job the second we got in our car.

"How was the market today?" she asked, reaching down to remove her heels.

Before I could reply, Chris went back to scowling at the half-peeled potatoes. "It dropped twelve points," he reported.

Concern filled Juliet's eyes. She definitely didn't have the stomach for investing—any small dip in the market sent her scrambling for "solutions." I flashed a reassuring grin at her. "All good baby. Your *pinchao* knows what he's doing."

In fact, I made about four-hundred-grand that week, all told. Secretly, my own success still surprised me.

So did Ava's. But her PR plan worked like a charm—my story seemed to resonate with others.

Turned out, there were a lot of young executives in Manhattan who understood my animosity toward my old man. With the twenty-some different clients I'd on-boarded since my feature in Time Magazine went viral, I was set to clear about three million in my first quarter.

I owed a lot of it to Christian—now that he was clean, his strategies were more coherent and inspired than ever. The work helped keep his mind occupied, too.

He wasn't an official employee or owner at G&C yet, but I felt more certain every day that he would be, eventually. If he could stop being scared of his own damn shadow every time he stepped out of the clinic…

That reminded me. "Are you sure you don't want to come tomorrow night?" I asked Chris, wrapping my arms around Jules and tucking her head under my chin. "You could just do the dinner and then take my car back to the clinic."

At the mention of Grayson's bachelor party, both Christian and Juliet stiffened. My brother looked as though I suggested he walk a tightrope over a tank of piranhas. "Absolutely *not*."

Juliet leaned back, her face torn between wifely suspicion and genuine worry. "Are we sure that whole thing is still a good idea?" she put in. "After everything Ella's been through… it seems inappropriate."

I vacillated on the issue daily. Grayson was a shell of his former self… so, on the one hand, I saw her point. Sometimes, the epic bachelor party I planned sounded like a horrible idea. Who would want to go out partying after what he'd been through?

But, then, I remembered that almost a month had passed, and they had to start trying to move on eventually. Especially if they honestly expected to make it down the aisle in just a handful of weeks….

In the end, I always came back to the same thought: what could possibly happen to make the situation any *worse*?

Not a whole lot. Things between Ella and Grayson were already muddled. What harm could a fun night out do? Besides, my best friend probably needed to blow off *a lot* of steam, considering…

I shrugged. "It's tradition. And you girls will be out having your own party, anyways. What are we supposed to do, sit home and watch *Bridget Jones* with a pint of ice cream?"

My *bijou's* golden eyes snapped at me. We'd already had this argument. Several times. I always won, but that didn't mean she liked it.

"No one said *that*. I just think it's…" She sighed, shaking her head before folding herself back into my embrace. "Just watch out for him, okay? And I'll try my best to be a chill fiancée."

I gave her a squeeze, making a mental note to spend the next morning blowing her mind. Literally. She'd be the most chilled-out woman in the group when I was through with her.

She read the way my body responded to the idea, tightening around her, and cast me one of her sexy scolding glances. "This is serious, Graham. The wedding may not even happen, at this rate…"

I hated that thought. Picking at my tie, I muttered, "It *better* happen. That tux he made me buy is an affront to my sensibilities. Boring-ass motherfucker. And let's not even get *started* on those dresses Ella picked."

Juliet's laugh brightened everything. "How is it possible that *you're* the diva in this relationship?"

"I am not."

Beside us, Christian snorted some more. "Um, yeah, you are. Have you already forgotten the Mariah-Carey-level hissy fit you threw over your own wedding plans just two weeks ago?"

I regarded each of them steadily, not the least bit ashamed. "*What* wedding plans? This woman refuses to *make* any wedding plans."

Juliet's bright gaze flickered to Chris's, sharing mutual amusement. "He's pouting again."

Christian rolled his eyes. "Graham, c'mon man, I thought this was all decided. The elopement? June? That famous court house in San Francisco?"

Followed by almost a month-long honeymoon in Greece.

That was the arrangement—after fighting and fucking over it non-stop for weeks, Jules and I finally agreed that she would plan the wedding and I would plan the honeymoon.

Turned out, there would be no wedding arrangements to plan, though. We would simply hop a jet to California for a simple ceremony at the country's most ornate court house. Just the two of us.

Even if it meant no one would be there to witness the whole affair, I had to admit; I was honored that she felt content only sharing our wedding day with me.

While I liked to complain about the elopement's lack-of pomp, I had to bite back my excitement at the thought of having my girl all to myself for four weeks. Our villa in Santorini boasted the best views on the whole island. Not to mention a private Infinity pool on the balcony, an indoor/outdoor hot tub, our own personal grotto, and *multiple* beds.

Juliet would be lucky if I ever let her get dressed. Though, just in case, I'd already pre-ordered some of the summer pieces from a few designer lines…

"And he gets to pick my dress, too!" Juliet added. "I don't even get to see it until the day of. He says he's going to have Abuelita blindfold me for the fittings."

She pretended to hate my love of dressing her, but I knew better. Every time I came home with a new hand-picked purchase, she melted. And I figured I knew her body better than anyone. Who better to help design the most important dress she'd ever wear?

"Do you get to pick his suit?" Chris asked.

"No!" we both blurted.

Jules smirked and scoffed simultaneously. "Please. *El pinchao esta loco por esa mierda.* Do you honestly think I'd take *that* bullet?" She lifted her arm to eye my latest gift—the elegant gold Ferragamo timepiece gracing her wrist. "Speaking of bullets, where is Marco? Isn't he supposed to be here? It's almost seven."

Abuelita interjected, shooting off a stream of less-than flattering opinions about Marco's recent odd behavior. I didn't catch most of it, but Juliet cringed. "*Sí*, Abuelita."

Then to me, she translated, "He's late. Again. Abuelita says he better not flake on us or she's going to drive up to Hell's Kitchen and wait for him in his lobby with a plate of food. Last time, she got in a fight with his doorman."

I didn't dare comment. Marco and I had a strange, begrudging relationship—he didn't like me fucking his cousin and I didn't like his general air of moral superiority. But, nevertheless, I tended to think his whole family expected way too much of the guy. After all, he was only human. And I knew how much shit the Strykers put him through. Why couldn't his mother and grandmother cut him some slack?

"He's bringing a girl," Juliet went on, pitching her voice low for privacy. "*The* girl. The reason he's been so off-the-grid lately.... I can't believe he's just going to waltz her in here after keeping her a secret for so long."

Poor thing. I wondered if the chick knew that she was walking right into a den of fierce lionesses. With a pork chop strapped around her neck.

"So long? It's been, like, one month, *bijou*."

"Which is about how long we knew each other before you bought this," she shot back, flashing her ring.

I gazed at her, unable to keep the stupid grin off of my face. "Did you have a point?"

Christian shook his head, interjecting with a mumble. "I think you're all fucking nuts."

Juliet worried the inside of her cheek as she touched his shoulder. "You're not upset about missing our wedding, are you?"

Christian grimaced. "Honestly? I'm relieved. No wedding, no open bar, no excuse for me to wind up in an alley somewhere..." He blew out a breath. "And the Strykers are going to throw a big party when you guys get home, right? Kind of like a reception?"

Jules nodded heartily. "Yes. Against all my protests. Ella can't do much these days, but she *is* quite insistent about that."

It reminded me of the other piece of news we needed to celebrate. Sweeping Jules into another embrace, I settled my arms around her waist and murmured quietly, "Should we tell everyone about your promotion now? Or after dinner?"

My fiancée's glowing grins never stopped stealing my breath. She smiled as she peered around my shoulder and then turned her golden gaze back to me.

"Abuelita made a *merengón*," she replied, nodding at the beautiful pavlova-like stack of meringue and strawberries sitting in the center of our dining table. "Let's announce it during dessert." Her beaming smile took on a mischievous shade. "I'm sure we'll be busy interrogating Marco's girl during dinner."

Her sly expression reminded me of my favorite photograph—the one from our first date, at Make Believe. I'd since taken dozens of other pictures of her, but I suspected that one would always be special to me.

Framing her gorgeous face with my hands, I bent to kiss her as thoroughly as I could get away with in mixed company.

…or so I thought.

A spatula speared the space between our bodies, flicking back and forth to separate us. Abuelita's stern face suddenly loomed just beyond Juliet's. "No married yet," she huffed, frowning at each of us in turn. "No Pees-Dees-A."

Juliet's eyes filled with love as she stared up at me, sharing a conspiratorial smirk.

"PDA," we corrected in unison.

Abuelita swatted the backs of our necks before shuffling past. "Is what I said!"

Juliet

An hour after everyone finally left, I found Graham standing at our kitchen sink, washing the last of the dishes.

I leaned my hip into the island, absently running my fingers along the hem of my favorite purple robe while I watched him for a long moment. In his blush shirtsleeves and matching suit pants, he was as dark and delicious as ever. More so, maybe, because he was doing housework.

Familiar gratitude rushed up over me. How did I ever find my one-of-a-kind man? My own good fortune still staggered me. Often.

I waited until he turned off the tap and started to dry his hands before sneaking up behind him and slipping my arms around his waist. It was a bit thicker, thankfully. Eating regular meals and keeping up with my voracious appetite for him had his body more solid and sexier than ever.

He plucked one of my hands up and pressed a reverent kiss into my knuckles. "*Bijou,*" he murmured, gruff. "I was just thinking how proud I am of all your hard work and your promotion. I can't wait to brag about you to everyone I see tomorrow."

I let him turn and back me into the island, moving my arms up to wind around his neck. "Funny, I was just thinking how lucky I am that you stalked me into that elevator."

He flashed one of his feral grins before leaning down and trailing a series of kisses from my collarbone to my ear. *Dios*. My knees trembled every time he did that.

"Wouldn't have mattered," he told me, brushing his lips over my temple until I quivered again. "Even if I missed you in the lobby, I would have gone after you the second I saw you in that meeting."

I turned to catch his mouth with mine, kissing him deeply until he lifted me onto the counter and stepped between my bare legs. Leaning back, I captured his eyes and whispered, "I love you more."

A boyish smile filled his handsome features. "Starting this fight again, are you? I won last time, if I recall."

I giggled, remembering. "Pretending you're going through a tunnel and hanging up on me before I can argue my point is *not* winning, *pinchao*."

"Mmm." He nuzzled his face into my throat. "Fair enough, *bijou*. Luckily, I have a new strategy for this round."

And then Graham Everett, my future everything, picked me up and carried me to our bed… where we happily spent the rest of the night, proving our points.

A NOTE TO READERS

THANK YOU SO MUCH FOR JOINING ME ON THIS JOURNEY.
GRAHAM EVERETT MAY BE MY ALL-TIME FAVORITE LEADING MAN…

ASIDE FROM MY NEXT ONE!

FOR YOU—COMING SOON

THE NEXT INSTANT ALWAYS STAND-ALONE NOVEL
FEATURING ONE OF OUR FAVORITE MANHATTAN GENTLEMEN
WHO WILL IT BE?

I KNOW I LEFT YOU HANGING ABOUT GRAY AND ELLA'S
SITUATION AT THE END OF THIS STORY!
I'LL BE RELEASING SNEAK PEAKS OF THEIR UPCOMING SEQUEL,
ALMOST ALWAYS, SO SOON!
PLEASE SUBSCRIBE TO MY MAILING LIST FOR ACCESS.
(ALSO, I MEAN, GRAYSON STRYKER IN A TUX?
YES, PLEASE.)

Acknowledgments

As always, a very special note of gratitude to Kelly, who might love Graham Everett more than Juliet. Thank you for gassing me up throughout this whole story and being my go-to "Everett Advisor." You continue to be the very best editor, beta-reader, social media advisor, Basic Bitch music consultant, and kick-in-the-ass I could ever hope for! I love you forever. We're the dream team, baby.

A special note of thanks to my grandmothers—Kathleen, Margaret, and Rebecca. Writing a fabulous grandmother like the one in this story was so very easy because I am blessed with three. Thank you for always feeding me, even when I thought I wasn't hungry (literally and metaphorically).

And to my mom, Jean, who will hate this compliment, but nevertheless—Mom, you taught me what a true "bad bitch" looks like. As I stepped into the mind of my heroine for this story, I kept finding myself in your shoes… and I think you are incredible. Thank you for always teaching me what hard work, perseverance, and *faith* look like.

To my Aunt Mary, who imbued me with an abiding love for all things pink and fabulous—you are the most fabulous of all. And her husband, John, who taught me a life lesson that proved invaluable for this book: real men wear pink.

Always saving the best for last: thank you to Matthew. I appreciate you always answering my ridiculous questions about how men think.

I also thank you for welcoming me into your family. They inspired so much of this book and I am blessed to say I know what it was like for Graham to be welcomed by the Riveras. Matthew, you are the very best partner, best friend, and father I know. Thank you for choosing me and our dreams every day.

About Ari

Ari Wright resides in a sun-soaked corner of the United States, where she spends her days raising littles, cooking, reading, consuming massive amounts of music, and doing entirely too much daydreaming.

Ari began writing novels at the age of twelve. A passionate book-lover all her life, her mother once joked that she had to start writing her own stories because she had read everyone else's. After fifteen years of writing, Ari finally set out to author her debut contemporary romance novel. It has been her lifelong dream to share the worlds inhabiting her mind with others. Welcome to her dream come true!